The Ghost Pirates
and Others:

THE BEST OF

WILLIAM HOPE HODGSON

Other books edited by Jeremy Lassen

After Shocks: An Anthology of So-Cal Horror
The Collected Fiction of William Hope Hodgson
Z: Zombie Stories (as J. M. Lassen)

The Ghost Pirates
and Others:

THE BEST OF
WILLIAM HOPE HODGSON

EDITED BY JEREMY LASSEN

NIGHT SHADE BOOKS
SAN FRANCISCO

The Ghost Pirates and Others: The Best of William Hope Hodgson
© 2012 by Night Shade Books

Cover art by Matthew Jaffe
Interior layout and design by Amy Popovich

Edited by Jeremy Lassen

The Ghost Pirates is based on the 1909 Stanley Paul & Company edition, where it was originally published.

"A Tropical Horror" is based on its publication in *Out of the Storm*: (Grant, 1975). It was originally published in *Grand Magazine* (April 1905).

"Sea Horses" is based on its appearance in *Men of the Deep Waters* (Eveleigh Nash, 1914). It originally appeared in *London Magazine*, March 1913.

"The Searcher of the End House" is based on its publication in *Carnacki The Ghost-Finder* (Eveleigh Nash, 1913). It was originally published in *The Idler No. 92* (May 1910).

"The Stone Ship" (AKA "The Mystery of the Ship in the Night") is based on its publication in *The Luck of the Strong* (Eveleigh Nash, 1916). It was originally published as "The Mystery of the Ship in the Night" in *Red Magazine No. 126* (July 1, 1914).

"The Voice in the Night" is based on its publication in *Men Of Deep Waters* (Eveleigh Nash, 1914). It was originally published in *Blue Book Magazine 6, No. 1* (November 1907).

"Eloi Eloi Lama Sabachthani" (aka "Baumoff's Explosive") is based on its appearance in *Out of the Storm* (Donald M. Grant, 1975). It originally appeared in *Nash's Illustrated Weekly*, Sep. 20, 1919.

"The Mystery of the Derelict" is based on its publication in *Men Of Deep Waters* (Eveleigh Nash, 1914). It was originally published in *Story-teller No. 4* (July 1907).

"We Two and Bully Dunkan" (AKA "The Trimming of Captain Dunkan") is based on its publication in *The Luck of the Strong* (Eveleigh Nash, 1916). It was originally published as "The Trimming of Captain Dunkan" in *Red Magazine No. 128* (August 1, 1914).

"The Shamraken Homeward-Bounder" (AKA "Homeward Bound") is based on its publication in *Men Of Deep Waters* (Eveleigh Nash, 1914). It was originally published in *Putnam's Monthly 4, No. 1* (April 1908).

"Demons of the Sea" (AKA The Crew of the Lancing) is based on its publication in *Terrors of the Sea* (Grant, 1996). It was initially published in *Sea Stories Magazine 6, No. 5* (October 5, 1923).

"Out of the Storm" is based on its publication in *Out of the Storm* (Grant, 1975). It was originally published in *Putnam's Monthly 5, No. 5* (February 1909).

First Edition

ISBN: 978-1-59780-441-7

Night Shade Books
www.nightshadebooks.com

The editor would like to dedicate this volume to all the dreamers of the dark seas… the authors, editors, scholars and fans who have helped ensure that the works of William Hope Hodgson continue to find their way into the imaginations of new readers.

CONTENTS

Haunted Ships and Broken Men...
The Life and Work of
William Hope Hodgson

◆+◆ ◆ +◆

William Hope Hodgson was one of the most influential fantasists of the 20th Century. Weird fiction masters such as H. P. Lovecraft and Clark Ashton Smith were very vocal in their appreciations of him. Later generations of fantasists, ranging from Fritz Leiber to C. S. Lewis also heaped praise upon his work, and that influence has continued to this day; writers as diverse as Greg Bear and China Miéville both point to Hodgson as an influence and as one of the important founding voices of fantastic fiction.

Hodgson's life was almost as unique as his fictional output. He served aboard merchant sailing ships for 8 years... he was of the last generation to serve aboard the merchant sailing fleets that populated so much of his fiction. He was also an amateur photographer of significant note, and took many photos chronicling life aboard ship. During his time at sea, which began when he was 13 years old, he became an accomplished pugilist and weight lifter.

The abuse he received aboard ship, combined with the general poor quality of life afforded to merchant sailors of the era led Hodgson to leave the sea, and speak out often, and vehemently against the institutions that perpetuated and profited from brutal conditions sailors faced. In 1889, at the age of 22, Hodgson opened "W. H. Hodgson's School of Physical Culture" in Blackburn, England. Hodgson was a body builder before there were body builders. Though short in stature, he was an incredible physical specimen. He took numerous photographs of his incredibly developed musculature and used them to promote his gym, and his lectures on the subject of personal fitness.

It was the subject of personal fitness that led to Hodgson's first (non-fiction) publications, and his successes in this realm lead him to pursue fiction writing as an vocation. His first success came in 1904, with a story entitled "The Goddess of Death." But his second published story, "A Tropical Horror," (included herein) was published in one of the more prestigious fiction magazines of the time; this story brought Hodgson to the attention of some very influential editors, and his fiction writing career took off.

Hodgson had a unique voice that combined a haunting cosmic sensibility with an ability to depict the common place, and the common man. During his lifetime, it was his ability to depict life at sea that garnered most of his commercial successes. His straight adventure narratives always sold to prestigious markets, but it was his body of weird sea fiction that really made him stand out from his peers. In particular, the strange haunted dead space in the Atlantic where currents didn't flow and ships floundered for days waiting for breeze proved to be fertile ground for Hodgson's fantastic imagination... The Sargasso Sea cycle of stories formed a significant subset of his weird sea fiction. Stories of haunted ships and broken men rolled off of Hodgson's typewriter and into the imaginations of a generation.

Hodgson dabbled in many different commercial subgenres and the "psychic detective" genre was a rather significant one during his lifetime. Carnacki the Ghost-Finder is the protagonist of a series of stories that found success and significant readership both during his lifetime and after his death. With this character alone, Hodgson would become a significant foot note in the literary history of ghost fiction.

After his death, it was the weird cosmic narratives of *The House on the Borderland* and *The Night Land* that would be pointed to as his great achievements. These novels were a commercial failure during his lifetime but a new generation of editors reprinted his work, not in the context of popular "mainstream" fiction, but in the "ghetto" of weird fiction. What was too strange for turn-of-the-century mainstream readers was exactly what sf/fantasy readers in the 30's and 40's were looking for. Hodgson continued to find an audience amongst genre readers, being reprinted in mass market paperback form numerous times, most notably in the Ballantine Adult Fantasy series in the early 70s.

This book gathers together a sampling of Hodgson's styles and works. Alongside his novel-length weird sea adventure *The Ghost Pirates* are several other weird and supernatural tales of the sea—one of his Sargasso Sea stories, "The Mystery of the Derelict" is included amongst these. Hodgson's seminal occult detective is represented herein with the story "The Searcher of the End House." While it is only hinted at, the weird cosmic wonder and melancholy that is found in abundance in *The Night Land* and *The House on the Borderland* can be found in several short stories within, including one of his most atypical stories, "Eloi Eloi Lama Sabachthani." No summation of Hodgson's work could be complete without a story that featured an abusive first mate or captain, and a lowly cabin boy or deck hand who manages to serve them their just deserts. This plot device is one that occurs so frequently in Hodgson's work that one can't help but speculate as to the horrific abuses Hodgson must have suffered aboard ship as a thirteen-year-old cabin boy. "We Two and Bully Dunkan" is a quality example of this type of revenge narrative.

This volume is only a primer that scratches the surface of the dark seas of William Hope Hodgson's fiction. While his stories may have been written for the commercial fiction markets of his day, they still resonate with a power that transcends the ephemeral tastes of those markets. A hundred years later new readers are still discovering the joy of Hodgson for the first time. And these new readers, along with those of us who have been reading Hodgson for a lifetime, continue to be transported to the cosmically weird and thrillingly wondrous places that only Hodgson can take us.

Jeremy Lassen
San Francisco,
August 2012

The Ghost Pirates

❖▸◆◂❖

To Mary Whalley

"Olden Memories that shine against death's Night —
quiet stars of sweet Enchantments, that are seen
In Life's lost distances..."
The World of Dreams

❖▸◆◂❖

Author's Preface

THIS BOOK FORMS THE last of three. The first published was "THE BOATS OF THE 'GLEN CARRIG'"; the second "THE HOUSE ON THE BORDERLAND"; this, the third, completes what, perhaps, may be termed a trilogy; for, though very different in scope, each of the three books deals with certain conceptions that have an elemental kinship. With this book, the author believes that he closes the door, so far as he is concerned, on a particular phase of constructive thought.

The Hell O! O! Chaunty

Chaunty Man.	Man the capstan, bullies!
Men	Ha!-o-o! Ha!-o-o!
Chaunty Man.	Capstan-bars, you tarry souls!
Men	Ha!-o-o! Ha!-o-o!
Chaunty Man.	Take a turn!
Men	Ha!-o-o!
Chaunty Man	Stand by to fleet!
Men	Ha!-o-o!
Chaunty Man.	Stand by to surge!
Men	Ha!-o-o!
Chaunty Man.	Ha!—o-o-o-o!
Men	TRAMP! And away we go!
Chaunty Man.	Hark to the tramp of the bearded shellbacks!
Men	Hush! O hear 'em tramp!
Chaunty Man.	Tramping, stamping—treading, vamping,
. . . .	While the cable comes in ramping.
Men	Hark! O hear 'em stamp!
Chaunty Man.	Surge when it rides!
. . . .	Surge when it rides!
. . . .	Round-o-o-o handsome as it slacks!
Men	Ha!-o-o-o-o! hear 'em ramp!
. . . .	Ha!-o-o-o-o! hear 'em stamp!
. . . .	Ha!-o-o-o-o-o! Ha!-o-o-o-o-o!
Chorus	They're shouting now; oh! hear 'em
. . . .	A-bellow as they stamp:—
. . . .	Ha!-o-o-o! Ha!-o-o-o! Ha!-o-o-o!
. . . .	A-shouting as they tramp!
Chaunty Man	O hark to the haunting chorus of the
. . . .	capstan and the bars!
. . . .	Chaunty-o-o-o and rattle crash—
. . . .	Bash against the stars!
Men	Ha-a!-o-o-o! Tramp and go!
. . . .	Ha-a!-o-o-o! Ha-a!-o-o-o!
Chaunty Man.	Hear the pawls a-ranting: with
. . . .	the bearded men a-chaunting;
. . . .	While the brazen dome above 'em
. . . .	Bellows back the 'bars.'
Men	Hear and hark! O hear 'em!

. . . . Ha-a!-o-o! Ha-a!-o-o!

Chaunty Man. . . . . . . Hurling songs towards the heavens—!

Men . . . . Ha-a!-o-o! Ha-a!-o-o!

Chaunty Man. . . . . . . Hush! O hear 'em! Hark! O hear 'em!

. . . . Hurling oaths among their spars!

Men . . . . Hark! O hear 'em!

. . . . Hush! O hear 'em!

Chaunty Man. . . . . . . Tramping round between the bars!

Chorus . . . . They're shouting now; oh! hear 'em

. . . . A-bellow as they stamp:—

. . . . Ha-a !-o-o-o! Ha-a !-o-o-o! Ha-a !-o-o-o!

. . . . A-shouting as they tramp!

Chaunty Man. . . . . . . O do you hear the capstan-chaunty!

. . . . Thunder round the pawls!

Men . . . . Click a-clack, a-clatter

. . . . Surge! And scatter bawls!

Chaunty Man. . . . . . . Click-a-clack, my bonny boys, while

. . . . it comes in handsome!

Men . . . . Ha-a!-o-o! Hear 'em clack!

Chaunty Man. . . . . . . Ha-a!-o-o! Click-a-clack!

Men . . . . Hush! O hear 'em pant!

. . . . Hark! O hear 'em rant!

Chaunty Man. . . . . . . Click, a-clitter, clicker-clack.

Men . . . . Ha-a!-o-o! Tramp and go!

Chaunty Man. . . . . . . Surge! And keep away the slack!

Men . . . . Ha-a!-o-o! Away the slack:

. . . . Ha-a!-o-o! Click-a-clack

Chaunty Man. . . . . . . Bustle now each jolly Jack.

. . . . Surging easy! Surging e-a-s-y!!

Men . . . . Ha-a!-o-o! Surging easy

Chaunty Man. . . . . . . Click-a-clatter — Surge; and steady!

. . . . Man the stopper there! All ready?

Men . . . . Ha-a!-o-o! Ha-a!-o-o!

Chaunty Man. . . . . . . Click-a-clack, my bouncing boys:

Men . . . . Ha-a!-o-o! Tramp and go!

Chaunty Man . . . . . Lift the pawls, and come back easy.

Men . . . . Ha-a!-o-o! Steady-o-o-o-o!

Chaunty Man . . . . . Vast the chaunty! Vast the capstan!

. . . . Drop the pawls!

. . . . Be-l-a-y!

Chorus . . . . Ha-a!-o-o! Unship the bars!

. . . . Ha-a!-o-o! Tramp and go!

. . . . Ha-a!-o-o! Shoulder bars!

. . . . Ha-a!-o-o! And away we blow!

. . . . Ha-a!-o-o-o! Ha-a!-o-o-o-o! Ha-a!-o-o-o-o-o!

✦✦✦

I

The Figure Out of the Sea

HE BEGAN WITHOUT ANY circumlocution.

"I joined the *Mortzestus* in 'Frisco. I heard before I signed on, that there were some funny yarns floating round about her; but I was pretty nearly on the beach, and too jolly anxious to get away, to worry about trifles. Besides, by all accounts, she was right enough so far as grub and treatment went. When I asked fellows to give it a name, they generally could not. All they could tell me, was that she was unlucky, and made thundering long passages, and had more than a fair share of dirty weather. Also, that she had twice had the sticks blown out of her, and her cargo shifted. Besides all these, a heap of other things that might happen to any packet, and would not be comfortable to run into. Still, they were the ordinary things, and I was willing enough to risk them, to get home. All the same, if I had been given the chance, I should have shipped in some other vessel as a matter of preference.

"When I took my bag down, I found that they had signed on the rest of the crowd. You see, the 'home lot' cleared out when they got into 'Frisco, that is, all except one young fellow, a cockney, who had stuck by the ship in port. He told me afterwards, when I got to know him, that he intended to draw a payday out of her, whether any one else did, or not.

"The first night I was in her, I found that it was common talk among the other fellows, that there was something queer about the ship. They spoke of her as if it were an accepted fact that she was haunted; yet they all treated the matter as a joke; all, that is, except the young cockney—Williams—who, instead of laughing at their jests on the subject, seemed to take the whole matter seriously.

"This made me rather curious. I began to wonder whether there was, after all, some truth underlying the vague stories I had heard; and I took the first opportunity to ask him whether he had any reasons for believing that there was anything in the yarns about the ship.

"At first he was inclined to be a bit offish; but, presently, he came round, and told me that he did not know of any particular incident which could be called unusual in the sense in which I meant. Yet that, at the same time, there were lots of little things which, if you put them together, made you think a bit. For instance, she always made such long passages and had so much dirty weather—nothing but that and calms and head winds. Then, other things happened; sails that he knew, himself, had been properly stowed, were always blowing adrift *at night*. And then he said a thing that surprised me.

" 'There's too many bloomin' shadders about this 'ere packet; they gets onter yer nerves like nothin' as ever I seen before in me nat'ral.'

"He blurted it all out in a heap, and I turned round and looked at him.

" 'Too many shadows!' I said. 'What on earth do you mean?' But he refused to explain himself or tell me anything further—just shook his head, stupidly, when I questioned him. He seemed to have taken a sudden, sulky fit. "I felt certain that he was acting dense, purposely. I believe the truth of the matter is that he was, in a way, ashamed of having let himself go like he had, in speaking out his thoughts about 'shadders.' That type of man may think things at times; but he doesn't often put them into words. Anyhow, I saw it was no use asking any further questions; so I let the matter drop there. Yet, for several days afterwards, I caught myself wondering, at times, what the fellow had meant by 'shadders.'

"We left 'Frisco next day, with a fine, fair wind, that seemed a bit like putting the stopper on the yarns I had heard about the ship's ill luck. And yet—"

He hesitated a moment, and then went on again.

"For the first couple of weeks out, nothing unusual happened, and the wind still held fair. I began to feel that I had been rather lucky, after all, in the packet into which I had been shunted. Most of the other fellows gave her a good name, and there was a pretty general opinion growing among the crowd, that it was all a silly yarn about her being haunted. And then, just when I was settling down to things, something happened that opened my eyes no end.

"It was in the eight to twelve watch, and I was sitting on the steps, on the starboard side, leading up to the fo'cas'le head. The night was fine and there was a splendid moon. Away aft, I heard the timekeeper strike four bells, and the lookout, an old fellow named Jaskett, answered him. As he let go the bell lanyard, he caught sight of me, where I sat quietly, smoking. He leant over the rail, and looked down at me.

" 'That you, Jessop?' he asked.

" 'I believe it is,' I replied.

" 'We'd 'ave our gran'mothers an' all the rest of our petticoated relash'ns comin' to sea, if 'twere always like this,' he remarked, reflectively—indicating, with a sweep of his pipe and hand, the calmness of the sea and sky.

"I saw no reason for denying that, and he continued:—

" 'If this ole packet is 'aunted, as some on 'em seems to think, well all as I can say is, let me 'ave the luck to tumble across another of the same sort. Good grub, an' duff fer Sundays, an' a decent crowd of 'em aft, an' everythin' comfortable like, so as yer can feel yer knows where yer are. As fer 'er bein' 'aunted, that's all 'ellish nonsense. I've comed 'cross lots of 'em before as was said to be 'aunted, an' so some on 'em was; but 'twasn't with ghostesses. One packet I was in, they was that bad yer couldn't sleep a wink in yer watch below, until yer'd 'ad every stitch out yer bunk an' 'ad a reg'lar 'unt. Sometimes—' At that moment, the relief, one of the ordinary seamen, went up the other ladder on to the fo'cas'le head, and the old chap turned to ask him 'Why the 'ell' he'd not relieved him a bit smarter. The ordinary made some reply; but what it was, I did not catch; for, abruptly, away aft, my rather sleepy gaze had lighted on something altogether extraordinary and outrageous. It was nothing less than the form of a man stepping inboard over the starboard rail, a little abaft the main rigging. I stood up, and caught at the handrail, and stared.

"Behind me, someone spoke. It was the lookout, who had come down off the fo'cas'le head, on his way aft to report the name of his relief to the Second Mate.

" 'What is it, mate?' he asked, curiously, seeing my intent attitude.

"The thing, whatever it was, had disappeared into the shadows on the lee side of the deck.

" 'Nothing!' I replied, shortly; for I was too bewildered then, at what my eyes had just shown me, to say any more. I wanted to think.

"The old shellback glanced at me; but only muttered something, and went on his way aft.

"For a minute, perhaps, I stood there, watching; but could see nothing. Then I walked slowly aft, as far as the after end of the deck house. From there, I could see most of the main deck; but nothing showed, except, of course, the moving shadows of the ropes and spars and sails, as they swung to and fro in the moonlight.

"The old chap who had just come off the look-out, had returned forrard again, and I was alone on that part of the deck. And then, all at once, as I stood peering into the shadows to leeward, I remembered what Williams had said about there being too many 'shadders.' I had been puzzled to understand his real meaning, then. I had no difficulty *now*. There *were* too many shadows. Yet, shadows or no shadows, I realised that for my own peace of mind, I must settle, once and for all, whether the thing I had seemed to see stepping aboard out of the ocean, had been a reality, or simply a phantom, as you might say, of my imagination. My reason said it was nothing more than imagination, a rapid dream—I must have dozed; but something deeper than reason told me that this was not so. I put it to the test, and went straight in amongst the shadows There was nothing.

"I grew bolder. My common sense told me I must have fancied it all. I walked over to the mainmast, and looked behind the pinrail that partly surrounded it, and down into the shadow of the pumps; but here again was nothing. Then I went in under the break of the poop. It was darker under there than out on deck. I looked up both sides of the deck, and saw that they were bare of anything such as I looked for. The assurance was comforting. I glanced at the poop ladders, and remembered that nothing could have gone up there, without the Second Mate or the Time-keeper seeing it. Then I leant my back up against the bulkshead, and thought the whole matter over, rapidly, sucking at my pipe, and keeping my glance about the deck. I concluded my think, and said 'No!' out loud. Then something occurred to me, and I said 'Unless—' and went over to the starboard bulwarks, and looked over and down into the sea; but there was nothing but sea; and so I turned and made my way forrard. My common sense had triumphed, and I was convinced that my imagination had been playing tricks with me.

"I reached the door on the port side, leading into the fo'cas'le, and was about to enter, when something made me look behind. As I did so, I had a shaker. Away aft, a dim, shadowy form stood in the wake of a swaying belt of moonlight, that swept the deck a bit abaft the mainmast.

"It was the same figure that I had just been attributing to my fancy. I will admit that I felt more than startled; I was quite a bit frightened. I was convinced now that it was no mere imaginary thing. It was a human figure. And yet, with the flicker of the moonlight and the shadows chasing over it, I was unable to say more than that. Then, as I stood there, irresolute and funky, I got the thought that someone was acting the goat; though for what reason or purpose, I never stopped to consider. I was glad of any suggestion that my common sense assured me was not impossible; and, for the moment, I felt quite relieved. That side to the question had not presented itself to me before. I began to pluck up courage. I accused myself of getting fanciful; otherwise I should have tumbled to it earlier. And then, funnily enough, in spite of all my reasoning, I was still afraid of going aft to discover who that was, standing on the lee side of the maindeck. Yet I felt that if I shirked it, I was only fit to be dumped overboard; and so I went, though not with any great speed, as you can imagine.

"I had gone half the distance, and still the figure remained there, motionless and silent—the moonlight and the shadows playing over it with each roll of the ship. I think I tried to be surprised. If it were one of the fellows playing the fool, he must have heard me coming, and why didn't he scoot while he had the chance? And where could he have hidden himself, before? All these things, I asked myself, in a rush, with a queer mixture of doubt and belief; and, you know, in the meantime, I was drawing nearer. I had passed the house, and was not twelve paces distant; when, abruptly, the silent figure made three quick strides to the port rail, and *climbed over it into the sea.*

"I rushed to the side, and stared over; but nothing met my gaze, except the shadow of the ship, sweeping over the moonlit sea.

"How long I stared down blankly into the water, it would be impossible to say; certainly for a good minute. I felt blank—just horribly blank. It was such a beastly confirmation of the *unnaturalness* of the thing I had concluded to be only a sort of brain fancy. I seemed, for that little time, deprived, you know, of the power of coherent thought. I suppose I was dazed—mentally stunned, in a way.

"As I have said, a minute or so must have gone, while I had been staring into the dark of the water under the ship's side. Then, I came suddenly to my ordinary self. The Second Mate was singing out:— 'Lee fore brace.'

"I went to the braces, like a chap in a dream.

II

What Tammy the 'Prentice Saw

THE NEXT MORNING, IN my watch below, I had a look at the places where that strange thing had come aboard, and left the ship; but I found nothing unusual, and no clue to help me to understand the mystery of the strange man.

"For several days after that, all went quietly; though I prowled about the decks at night, trying to discover anything fresh that might tend to throw some light on to the matter. I was careful to say nothing to any one about the thing I had seen. In any case, I felt sure I should only have been laughed at.

"Several nights passed away in this manner, and I was no nearer to an understanding of the affair. And then, in the middle watch, something happened.

"It was my wheel. Tammy, one of the first voyage 'prentices, was keeping time—walking up and down the lee side of the poop. The Second Mate was forrard, leaning over the break of the poop, smoking. The weather still continued fine, and the moon, though declining, was sufficiently powerful to make every detail about the poop, stand out distinctly. Three bells had gone, and I'll admit I was feeling sleepy. Indeed, I believe I must have dozed, for the old packet steered very easily, and there was precious little to do, beyond giving her an odd spoke now and again. And then, all at once, it seemed to me that I heard some one calling my name, softly. I could not be certain; and first I glanced forrard to where the Second stood, smoking, and from him, I looked into the binnacle. The ship's head was right on her course, and I felt easier. Then, suddenly, I heard it again. There was no doubt about it this time, and I glanced to leeward. There I saw Tammy reaching over the steering gear, his hand out, in the act of trying to touch my arm. I was about to ask him what the devil he wanted, when he held up his finger for silence, and pointed forrard along the lee side of the poop. In the dim light, his face showed palely, and he seemed much agitated. For a few seconds, I stared in the direction he indicated, but could see nothing.

" 'What is it?' I asked in an undertone, after a couple of moments' further ineffectual peering. 'I can't see anything.'

" 'H'sh!' he muttered, hoarsely, without looking in my direction. Then, all at once, with a quick little gasp, he sprang across the wheel-box, and stood beside me, trembling. His gaze appeared to follow the movements of something I could not see.

"I must say that I was startled. His movement had shown such terror; and the way he stared to leeward made me think he saw something uncanny.

" 'What the deuce is up with you?' I asked, sharply. And then I remembered the Second Mate. I glanced forrard to where he lounged. His back was still towards us, and he had not seen Tammy. Then I turned to the boy.

" 'For goodness sake, get to looard before the Second sees you!' I said. 'If you want to say anything, say it across the wheel-box. You've been dreaming.'

"Even as I spoke, the little beggar caught at my sleeve with one hand; and, pointing across to the log-reel with the other, screamed:— 'He's coming! He's coming—' At this instant, the Second Mate came running aft, singing out to know what was the matter. Then, suddenly, crouching under the rail near the log-reel, I saw something that looked like a man; but so hazy and unreal, that I could scarcely say I saw anything. Yet, like a flash, my thoughts ripped back to the silent figure I had seen in the flicker of the moonlight, a week earlier.

"The Second Mate reached me, and I pointed, dumbly; and yet, as I did so, it was with the knowledge that *he* would not be able to see what I saw. (Queer, wasn't it?) And then, almost in a breath, I lost sight of the thing, and became aware that Tammy was hugging my knees.

"The Second continued to stare at the log-reel for a brief instant; then he turned to me, with a sneer.

" 'Been asleep, the pair of you, I suppose!' Then, without waiting for my denial, he told Tammy, to get to hell out of it and stop his noise, or he'd boot him off the poop.

"After that, he walked forrard to the break of the poop, and lit his pipe, again— walking forrard and aft every few minutes, and eyeing me, at times, I thought, with a strange, half-doubtful, half-puzzled look.

"Later, as soon as I was relieved, I hurried down to the 'prentice's berth. I was anxious to speak to Tammy. There were a dozen questions that worried me, and I was in doubt what I ought to do. I found him crouched on a sea-chest, his knees up to his chin, and his gaze fixed on the doorway, with a frightened stare. I put my head into the berth, and he gave a gasp; then he saw who it was, and his face relaxed something of its strained expression.

"He said: 'Come in,' in a low voice, which he tried to steady; and I stepped over the washboard, and sat down on a chest, facing him.

" 'What was *it*?' he asked; putting his feet down on to the deck, and leaning forward. 'For God's sake, tell me what it was!'

"His voice had risen, and I put up my hand to warn him.

" 'H'sh!' I said. 'You'll wake the other fellows.'

"He repeated his question, but in a lower tone. I hesitated, before answering him. I felt, all at once, that it might be better to deny all knowledge—to say I hadn't seen anything unusual. I thought quickly, and made answer on the turn of the moment.

" 'What was *what*?' I said. 'That's just the thing I've come to ask you. A pretty pair of fools you made of the two of us up on the poop just now, with your hysterical tomfoolery.'

"I concluded my remark in a tone of anger.

" 'I didn't!' he answered, in a passionate whisper. 'You know I didn't. You know *you* saw it yourself. You pointed it out to the Second Mate. I saw you.'

"The little beggar was nearly crying between fear, and vexation at my assumed unbelief.

" 'Rot!' I replied. 'You know jolly well you were sleeping in your time-keeping. You dreamed something and woke up suddenly. You were off your chump.'

"I was determined to reassure him, if possible; though, goodness! I wanted assurance myself. If he had known of that other thing, I had seen down on the maindeck, what then!

" 'I wasn't asleep, any more than you were,' he said, bitterly. 'And you know it. You're just fooling me. The ship's haunted.'

" 'What!' I said, sharply.

" 'She's haunted,' he said, again. 'She's haunted.'

" 'Who says so?' I inquired, in a tone of unbelief.

" 'I do ! And you *know* it. Everybody knows it; but they don't more than half believe it… I didn't, until tonight.'

" 'Damned rot!' I answered. 'That's all a blooming old shellback's yarn. She's no more haunted than I am.'

" 'It's not damned rot,' he replied, totally unconvinced. 'And it's not an old shellback's yarn…. Why won't you say you saw it?' he cried, growing almost tearfully excited, and raising his voice again.

"I warned him not to wake the sleepers.

" 'Why won't you say you saw it?' he repeated.

"I got up from the chest, and went towards the door.

" 'You're a young idiot!' I said. 'And I should advise you not to go gassing about like this, round the decks. Take my tip, and turn-in and get a sleep. You're talking dotty. Tomorrow you'll perhaps feel what an unholy ass you've made of yourself.'

"I stepped over the washboard, and left him. I believe he followed me to the door to say something further; but I was half-way forrard by then.

"For the next couple of days, I avoided him as much as possible, taking care never to let him catch me alone. I was determined, if possible, to convince him that he had been mistaken in supposing that he had seen anything that night. Yet, after all, it was little enough use, as you will soon see. For, on the night of the second day, there was a further extraordinary development, that made denial on my part useless.

◆◆◆

III

The Man Up the Main

It OCCURRED IN THE first watch, just after six bells. I was forrard, sitting on the forehatch. No one was about the main-deck. The night was exceedingly fine; and the wind had dropped away almost to nothing, so that the ship was very quiet.

"Suddenly, I heard the Second Mate's voice—

" 'In the main-rigging, there! Who's that going aloft?'

"I sat up on the hatch, and listened. There succeeded an intense silence. Then the Second's voice came again. He was evidently getting wild.

" 'Do you damn well hear me? What the hell are you doing up there? Come down!'

"I rose to my feet, and walked up to wind'ard. From there, I could see the break of the poop. The Second Mate was standing by the starboard ladder. He appeared to be looking up at something that was hidden from me by the topsails. As I stared, he broke out again:—

" 'Hell and damnation, you blasted sojer, come down when I tell you!'

"He stamped on the poop, and repeated his order, savagely. But there was no answer. I started to walk aft. What had happened? Who had gone aloft? Who would be fool enough to go, without being told? And then, all at once, a thought came to me. The figure Tammy and I had seen. Had the Second Mate seen something—someone? I hurried on, and then stopped, suddenly. In the same moment there came the shrill blast of the Second's whistle; he was whistling for the watch, and I turned and ran to the fo'cas'le to rouse them out. Another minute, and I was hurrying aft with them to see what was wanted.

"His voice met us half-way:—

" 'Up the main some of you, smartly now, and find out who that damned fool is up there. See what mischief he's up to.'

" 'i, i, Sir,' several of the men sung out, and a couple jumped into the weather rigging. I joined them, and the rest were proceeding to follow; but the Second shouted for some to go up to leeward—in case the fellow tried to get down that side.

"As I followed the other two aloft, I heard the Second Mate tell Tammy, whose time-keeping it was, to get down on to the maindeck with the other 'prentice, and keep an eye on the fore and aft stays.

" 'He may try down one of them if he's cornered,' I heard him explain. 'If you see anything, just sing out for me, right away.'

"Tammy hesitated.

" 'Well?' said the Second Mate, sharply.

" 'Nothing, Sir,' said Tammy, and went down on to the main-deck.

"The first man to wind'ard had reached the futtock shrouds; his head was above the top, and he was taking a preliminary look, before venturing higher.

" 'See anythin', Jock?' asked Plummer, the man next above me.

" 'Na'!' said Jock, tersely, and climbed over the top, and so disappeared from my sight.

"The fellow ahead of me, followed. He reached the futtock rigging, and stopped to expectorate. I was close at his heels, and he looked down to me.

" 'What's up, anyway?' he said. 'What's 'e seen? 'oo're we chasin' after?'

"I said I didn't know, and he swung up into the topmast rigging. I followed on. The chaps on the lee side were about level with us. Under the foot of the topsail, I could see Tammy and the other 'prentice down on the maindeck, looking upwards.

"The fellows were a bit excited in a sort of subdued way; though I am inclined to think there was far more curiosity and, perhaps, a certain consciousness of the strangeness of it all. I know that, looking to leeward, there was a tendency to keep well together, in which I sympathised.

" 'Must be a bloomin' stowaway,' one of the men suggested.

"I grabbed at the idea, instantly. Perhaps— And then, in a moment, I dismissed it. I remembered how that first thing had stepped over the rail *into the sea. That* matter could not be explained in such a manner. With regard to this, I was curious and anxious. *I* had seen nothing this time. What could the Second Mate have seen? I wondered. Were we chasing fancies, or was there really someone—something real, among the shadows above us? My thoughts returned to that thing, Tammy and I had seen near the log-reel. I remembered how incapable the Second Mate had been of seeing anything then. I remembered how natural it had seemed that he should not be able to see. I caught the word 'stowaway' again. After all, that might explain away *this* affair. It would—

"My train of thought was broken suddenly. One of the men was shouting and gesticulating.

" 'I sees 'im! I sees 'im!' He was pointing upwards over our heads.

" 'Where?' said the man above me. 'Where?'

"I was looking up, for all that I was worth. I was conscious of a certain sense of relief. 'It is *real*, then,' I said to myself. I screwed my head round, and looked along the yards above us. Yet, still I could see nothing; nothing except shadows and patches of light.

"Down on deck, I caught the Second Mate's voice.

" 'Have you got him?' he was shouting.

" 'Not yet, Zur,' sung out the lowest man on the leeside.

" 'We sees 'im, Sir,' added Quoin.

" 'I don't!' I said.

" 'There 'e is agen,' he said.

"We had reached the t'gallant rigging, and he was pointing up to the royal yard.

" 'Ye're a fule, Quoin. That's what ye are.'

"The voice came from above. It was Jock's, and there was a burst of laughter at Quoin's expense.

"I could see Jock now. He was standing in the rigging, just below the yard. He had gone straight away up, while the rest of us were mooning over the top.

" 'Ye're a fule, Quoin,' he said, again. 'And I'm thinking the Second's juist as saft.'

"He began to descend.

" 'Then there's no one?' I asked.

" 'Na',' he said, briefly.

"As we reached the deck, the Second Mate ran down off the poop. He came towards us, with an expectant air.

" 'You've got him?' he asked, confidently.

" 'There wasn't anyone,' I said.

" 'What!' he nearly shouted. 'You're hiding something!' he continued, angrily, and glancing from one to another. 'Out with it. Who was it?'

" 'We're hiding nothing,' I replied, speaking for the lot. 'There's no one up there.'

"The Second looked round upon us.

" 'Am I a fool?' he asked, contemptuously.

"There was an assenting silence.

" 'I saw him myself,' he continued. 'Tammy, here, saw him. He wasn't over the top when I first spotted him. There's no mistake about it. It's all damned rot saying he's not there.'

" 'Well, he's not, Sir,' I answered. 'Jock went right up to the royal yard.'

"The Second Mate said nothing, in immediate reply; but went aft a few steps and looked up the main. Then he turned to the two 'prentices.

" 'Sure you two boys didn't see any one coming down from the main?' he inquired, suspiciously.

" 'Yes, Sir,' they answered together.

" 'Anyway,' I heard him mutter to himself, 'I'd have spotted him myself, if he had.

" 'Have you any idea, Sir, who it was you saw?' I asked, at this juncture.

"He looked at me, keenly.

" 'No!' he said.

"He thought for a few moments, while we all stood about in silence, waiting for him to let us go.

" 'By the holy poker!' he exclaimed, suddenly. 'But I ought to have thought of that before.'

"He turned, and eyed us individually.

" 'You're all here?' he asked.

" 'Yes, Sir,' we said in a chorus. I could see that he was counting us. Then he spoke again.

" 'All of you men stay here where you are. Tammy, you go into *your* place and see if the other fellows are in their bunks. Then come and tell me. Smartly now!'

"The boy went, and he turned to the other 'prentice.

" 'You get along forrard to the fo'cas'le,' he said. 'Count the other watch; then come aft and report to me.'

"As the youngster disappeared along the deck to the fo'cas'le, Tammy returned from his visit to the Glory Hole, to tell the Second Mate that the other two 'prentices were sound asleep in their bunks. Whereupon, the Second bundled him off to the Carpenter's and Sailmaker's berth, to see whether they were turned-in.

"While he was gone, the other boy came aft, and reported that all the men were in their bunks, and asleep.

" 'Sure?" the Second asked him.

" 'Quite, Sir,' he answered.

"The Second Mate made a quick gesture.

" 'Go and see if the Steward is in his berth,' he said, abruptly. It was plain to me that he was tremendously puzzled.

" 'You've something to learn yet, Mr. Second Mate,' I thought to myself. Then I fell to wondering to what conclusions he would come.

"A few seconds later, Tammy returned to say that the Carpenter, Sailmaker and 'Doctor' were all turned-in.

"The Second Mate muttered something, and told him to go down into the saloon to see whether the First and Third Mates, by any chance, were not in their berths.

"Tammy started off; then halted.

" 'Shall I have a look into the Old Man's place, Sir, while I'm down there?' he inquired.

" 'No!' said the Second Mate. 'Do what I told you, and then come and tell me. If any one's to go into the Captain's cabin, it's got to be me.'

"Tammy said 'i, i, Sir,' and skipped away, up on to the poop.

"While he was gone, the other 'prentice came up to say that the Steward was in his berth, and that he wanted to know what the hell he was fooling round his part of the ship for.

"The Second Mate said nothing, for nearly a minute. Then he turned to us, and told us we might go forrard.

"As we moved off in a body, and talking in undertones, Tammy came down from the poop, and went up to the Second Mate. I heard him say that the two Mates were in their berths, asleep. Then he added, as if it were an afterthought—

" 'So's the Old Man.'

" 'I thought I told you—' the Second Mate began.

" 'I didn't, Sir,' Tammy said. 'His cabin door was open.'

"The Second Mate started to go aft. I caught a fragment of a remark he was making to Tammy.

" '—accounted for the whole crew. I'm—'

"He went up on to the poop. I did not catch the rest.

"I had loitered a moment; now, however, I hurried after the others. As we neared fo'cas'le, one bell went, and we roused out the other watch, and told them what jinks we had been up to.

" 'I rec'on 'e must be rocky,' one of the men remarked.

" 'Not 'im,' said another. ' 'e's bin 'avin' forty winks on the break, an' dreemed 'is mother-en-lore 'ad come on 'er visit, friendly like.'

"There was some laughter at this suggestion, and I caught myself smiling along with the rest; though I had no reason for sharing their belief, that there was nothing in it all.

" 'Might 'ave been a stowaway, yer know,' I heard Quoin, the one who had suggested it before, remark to one of the A.B.'s, named Stubbins—a short, rather surly-looking chap.

" 'Might have been hell!' returned Stubbins. 'Stowaways hain't such fools as all that.'

" 'I dunno,' said the first. 'I wish I 'ad arsked the Second what 'e thought about it.'

" 'I don't think it was a stowaway, somehow,' I said, chipping in. 'What would a stowaway want aloft? I guess he'd be trying more for the Steward's pantry.'

" 'You bet he would, hevry time,' said Stubbins. He lit his pipe, and sucked at it, slowly.

" 'I don't hunderstand it, all ther same,' he remarked, after a moment's silence.

" 'Neither do I,' I said. And after that I was quiet for a while, listening to the run of conversation on the subject.

"Presently, my glance fell upon Williams, the man who had spoken to me about 'shadders.' He was sitting in his bunk, smoking, and making no effort to join in the talk.

"I went across to him.

" 'What do you think of it, Williams?' I asked. 'Do *you* think the Second Mate really saw anything?'

"He looked at me, with a sort of gloomy suspicion; but said nothing.

"I felt a trifle annoyed by his silence; but took care not to show it. After a few moments, I went on.

" 'Do you know, Williams, I'm beginning to understand what you meant that night, when you said there were too many shadows.'

" 'Wot yer mean?' he said, pulling his pipe from out of his mouth, and fairly surprised into answering.

" 'What I say, of course,' I said. 'There *are* too many shadows.'

"He sat up, and leant forward out from his bunk, extending his hand and pipe. His eyes plainly showed his excitement.

" ' 'ave yer seen—' he hesitated, and looked at me, struggling inwardly to express himself.

" 'Well?' I prompted.

"For perhaps a minute he tried to say something. Then his expression altered suddenly from doubt, and something else more indefinite, to a pretty grim look of determination.

"He spoke.

" 'I'm blimed,' he said, 'ef I don't tike er piy-diy out of 'er, shadders er no shadders.'

"I looked at him, with astonishment.

" 'What's it got to do with your getting a pay-day out of her?' I asked.

"He nodded his head, with a sort of stolid resolution.

" 'Look 'ere,' he said.

"I waited.

" 'Ther crowd cleared'; he indicated with his hand and pipe towards the stern.

" 'You mean in 'Frisco?' I said.

" 'Yus,' he replied; ' 'an withart er cent of ther piy. I styied.'

"I comprehended him suddenly.

" 'You think they saw,' I hesitated; then I said 'shadows?'

"He nodded; but said nothing.

" 'And so they all bunked?'

"He nodded again, and began tapping out his pipe on the edge of his bunk-board.

" 'And the officers and the Skipper?' I asked.

" 'Fresh uns,' he said, and got out of his bunk; for eight bells was striking.

+>+ • +<

IV

The Fooling with the Sail

IT WAS ON THE Friday night, that the Second Mate had the watch aloft looking for the man up the main; and for the next five days little else was talked about; though, with the exception of Williams, Tammy and myself, no one seemed to think of treating the matter seriously. Perhaps I should not exclude Quoin, who still persisted, on every occasion, that there was a stowaway aboard. As for the Second Mate, I have very little doubt *now*, but that he was beginning to realise there was something deeper and less understandable than he had at first dreamed of. Yet, all the same, I know he had to keep his guesses and half-formed opinions pretty well to himself; for the Old Man and the First Mate chaffed him unmercifully about his 'bogy.' This, I got from Tammy, who had heard them both ragging him during the second dog-watch the following day. There was another thing Tammy told me, that showed how the Second Mate bothered about his inability to understand the mysterious appearance and disappearance of the man he had seen go aloft. He had made Tammy give him every detail he could remember about the figure we had seen by the log-reel. What is more, the Second had not even affected to treat the matter lightly, nor as a thing to be sneered at; but had listened seriously, and asked a great many questions. It is very evident to me that he was reaching out towards the only possible conclusion. Though, goodness knows, it was one that was impossible and improbable enough.

"It was on the Wednesday night, after the five days of talk I have mentioned, that there came, to me and to those who *knew*, another element of fear. And yet, I can quite understand that, at *that* time, those who had seen nothing, would find little to be afraid of, in all that I am going to tell you. Still, even they were much puzzled and astonished, and perhaps, after all, a little awed. There was so much in the affair that was inexplicable, and yet again such a lot that was natural and commonplace. For, when all is said and done, it was nothing more than the blowing adrift of one of the sails; yet accompanied by what were really significant details—significant, that is, in the light of that which Tammy and I and the Second Mate knew.

"Seven bells, and then one, had gone in the first watch, and our side was being roused out to relieve the Mate's. Most of the men were already out of their bunks, and sitting about on their sea-chests, getting into their togs.

"Suddenly, one of the 'prentices in the other watch, put his head in through the doorway on the port side.

" 'The Mate wants to know,' he said, 'which of you chaps made fast the fore royal, last watch.'

" 'Wot's 'e want to know that for?' inquired one of the men.

" 'The lee side's blowing adrift,' said the 'prentice. 'And he says that the chap who made it fast is to go up and see to it as soon as the watch is relieved.'

" 'Oh! does 'e ? Well 'twasn't me, any'ow,' replied the man. 'You'd better arsk sum of t'others.'

" 'Ask what?' inquired Plummer, getting out of his bunk, sleepily.

"The 'prentice repeated his message.

"The man yawned and stretched himself.

" 'Let me see,' he muttered, and scratched his head with one hand, while he fumbled for his trousers with the other. ' 'oo made ther fore r'yal fast?' He got into his trousers, and stood up. 'Why, ther Or'nary, er course; 'oo else do yer suppose?'

" 'That's all I wanted to know!' said the 'prentice, and went away.

" 'Hi! Tom!' Stubbins sung out to the Ordinary. 'Wake up, you lazy young devil. Ther Mate's just sent to hinquire who it was made the fore royal fast. It's all blowin' adrift, and he says you're to get along up as soon as eight bells goes, and make it fast again.'

"Tom jumped out of his bunk, and began to dress, quickly.

" 'Blowin' adrift!' he said. 'There ain't all that much wind; and I tucked the ends of the gaskets well in under the other turns.'

" 'P'raps one of ther gaskets is rotten, and given way,' suggested Stubbins. 'Anyway, you'd better hurry up, it's just on eight bells.'

"A minute later, eight bells went, and we trooped away aft for roll-call. As soon as the names were called over, I saw the Mate lean towards the Second and say something. Then the Second Mate sung out:—

" 'Tom!'

" 'Sir!' answered Tom.

" 'Was it you made fast that fore royal, last watch?'

" 'Yes, Sir.'

" 'How's that it's broken adrift?'

" 'Carn't say, Sir.'

" 'Well, it has, and you'd better jump aloft and shove the gasket round it again. And mind you make a better job of it this time.'

" 'i, i, Sir,' said Tom, and followed the rest of us forrard. Reaching the fore rigging, he climbed into it, and began to make his way leisurely aloft. I could see him with a fair amount of distinctness, as the moon was very clear and bright, though getting old.

"I went over to the weather pinrail, and leaned up against it, watching him, while I filled my pipe. The other men, both the watch on deck and the watch below, had gone into the fo'cas'le, so that I imagined I was the only one about the maindeck. Yet, a minute later, I discovered that I was mistaken; for, as I proceeded to light up, I saw Williams, the young cockney, come out from under the lee of the house, and turn and look up at the Ordinary as he went steadily upwards. I was a little surprised, as I knew he and three of the others had a 'poker fight' on, and he'd won over sixty pounds of tobacco. I believe I opened my mouth to sing out to him to know why he wasn't playing; and then, all at once, there came into my mind the memory of my first conversation with him. I remembered that he had said sails were always blowing adrift *at night*. I remembered the, then, unaccountable emphasis he had laid on those two words; and remembering that, I felt suddenly afraid. For, all at once, the absurdity had struck me of a sail—even a badly stowed one—blowing adrift in such fine and calm weather as we were then having. I wondered I had not seen before that there was something queer and unlikely about the affair. Sails don't blow adrift in fine weather, with the sea calm and the ship as steady as a rock. I moved away from the rail and went towards Williams. He knew something, or, at least, he guessed at something that was very much a blankness to me at that time. Up above, the boy was climbing up, to what? That was the thing that made me feel so frightened. Ought I to tell all I knew and guessed? And then, who should I tell? I should only be laughed at—I—

"Williams turned towards me, and spoke.

" 'Gawd!' he said, 'it's started agen!'

" 'What?' I said. Though I knew what he meant.

" 'Them syles,' he answered, and made a gesture towards the fore royal.

"I glanced up, briefly. All the lee side of the sail was adrift, from the bunt gasket outwards. Lower, I saw Tom; he was just hoisting himself into the t'gallant rigging.

"Williams spoke again.

" 'We lost two on 'em just sime way, comin' art.'

" 'Two of the men!' I exclaimed.

" 'Yus!' he said tersely.

" 'I can't understand,' I went on. 'I never heard anything about it.'

" 'Who'd yer got ter tell yer abart it?' he asked.

"I made no reply to his question; indeed, I had scarcely comprehended it, for the problem of what I ought to do in the matter had risen again in my mind.

" 'I've a good mind to go aft and tell the Second Mate all I know,' I said. 'He's seen something himself that he can't explain away, and—anyway I can't stand this state of things. If the Second Mate knew all—'

" 'Garn!' he cut in, interrupting me. 'An' be told yer're a blastid hidiot. Not yer. Yer sty were yer are.'

"I stood irresolute. What he had said, was perfectly correct, and I was positively stumped what to do for the best. That there was danger aloft, I was convinced; though if I had been asked my reasons for supposing this, they would have been hard to find. Yet of its existence, I was as certain as though my eyes already saw it. I wondered whether, being so ignorant of the form it would assume, I could stop it by joining Tom on the yard? This thought came as I stared up at the royal. Tom had reached the sail, and was standing on the foot-rope, close in to the bunt. He was bending over the yard, and reaching down for the slack of the sail. And then, as I looked, I saw the belly of the royal tossed up and down abruptly, as though a sudden heavy gust of wind had caught it.

" 'I'm blimed—!' Williams began, with a sort of excited expectation. And then he stopped as abruptly as he had begun. For, in a moment, the sail had thrashed right over the after side of the yard, apparently knocking Tom clean from off the foot-rope.

" 'My God!' I shouted out loud. 'He's gone!'

"For an instant there was a blur over my eyes, and Williams was singing out something that I could not catch. Then, just as quickly, it went, and I could see again, clearly.

"Williams was pointing, and I saw something black, swinging below the yard. Williams called out something fresh, and made a run for the fore rigging. I caught the last part—

" ' —ther garskit.'

"Straightway, I knew that Tom had managed to grab the gasket as he fell, and I bolted after Williams to give him a hand in getting the youngster into safety.

"Down on deck, I caught the sound of running feet, and then the Second Mate's voice. He was asking what the devil was up; but I did not trouble to answer him then. I wanted all my breath to help me aloft. I knew very well that some of the gaskets were little better than old shakins; and, unless Tom got hold of something on the t'gallant yard below him, he might come down with a run any moment. I reached the top, and lifted myself over it in quick time. Williams was some distance above me. In less than half a minute, I reached the t'gallant yard. Williams had gone up on to the royal. I slid out on to the t'gallant foot-rope until I was just below Tom; then I sung out to him to let himself down to me, and I would catch him. He made no answer, and I saw that he was hanging in a curiously limp fashion, and by one hand.

"Williams's voice came down to me from the royal yard. He was singing out to me to go up and give him a hand to pull Tom up on to the yard. When I reached him, he told me that the gasket had hitched itself round the lad's wrist. I bent beside the yard, and peered down. It was as Williams had said, and I realised how near a thing it had been. Strangely enough, even at that moment, the thought came to me how little wind there was. I remembered the wild way in which the sail had lashed at the boy.

"All this time, I was busily working, unreeving the port buntline. I took the end, made a running bowline with it round the gasket, and let the loop slide down over the boy's head and shoulders. Then I took a strain on it and tightened it under his arms. A minute later we had him safely on the yard between us. In the uncertain moonlight, I could just make out the mark of a great lump on his forehead, where the foot of the sail must have caught him when it knocked him over.

"As we stood there a moment, taking our breath, I caught the sound of the Second Mate's voice close beneath us. Williams glanced down; then he looked up at me and gave a short, grunting laugh.

" 'Crikey!' he said.

" 'What's up?' I asked, quickly.

"He jerked his head backwards and downwards. I screwed round a bit, holding the jackstay with one hand, and steadying the insensible Ordinary with the other. In this way I could look below. At first, I could see nothing. Then the Second Mate's voice came up to me again.

" 'Who the hell are you? What are you doing?'

"I saw him now. He was standing at the foot of the weather t'gallant rigging, his face was turned upwards, peering round the after side of the mast. It showed to me only as a blurred, pale-coloured oval in the moonlight.

"He repeated his question.

" 'It's Williams and I, Sir,' I said. 'Tom, here, has had an accident.'

"I stopped. He began to come up higher towards us. From the rigging to leeward there came suddenly a buzz of men talking.

"The Second Mate reached us.

" 'Well, what's up, anyway?' he inquired, suspiciously. 'What's happened?'

"He had bent forward, and was peering at Tom. I started to explain; but he cut me short with:—

" 'Is he dead?'

" 'No, Sir,' I said. 'I don't think so; but the poor beggar's had a bad fall. He was hanging by the gasket when we got to him. The sail knocked him off the yard.'

" 'What?' he said, sharply.

" 'The wind caught the sail, and it lashed back over the yard—'

" 'What wind?' he interrupted. 'There's no wind, scarcely.' He shifted his weight on to the other foot. 'What do you mean?'

" 'I mean what I say, Sir. The wind brought the foot of the sail over the top of the yard and knocked Tom clean off the foot-rope. Williams and I both saw it happen.'

" 'But there's no wind to do such a thing; you're talking nonsense!'

"It seemed to me that there was as much of bewilderment as anything else in his voice; yet I could tell that he was suspicious—though, of what, I doubted whether he himself could have told.

"He glanced at Williams, and seemed about to say something. Then, seeming to change his mind, he turned, and sung out to one of the men who had followed him aloft, to go down and pass out a coil of new, three-inch manila, and a tail-block.

" 'Smartly now!' he concluded.

" 'i, i, Sir,' said the man, and went down swiftly.

"The Second Mate turned to me.

" 'When you've got Tom below, I shall want a better explanation of all this, than the one you've given me. It won't wash.'

" 'Very well, Sir,' I answered. 'But you won't get any other.'

" 'What do you mean?' he shouted at me. 'I'll let you know I'll have no impertinence from you or any one else.'

" 'I don't mean any impertinence, Sir—I mean that it's the only explanation there is to give.'

" 'I tell you it won't wash!' he repeated. 'There's something too damned funny about it all. I shall have to report the matter to the Captain. I can't tell him that yarn—' He broke off abruptly.

" 'It's not the only damned funny thing that's happened aboard this old hooker,' I answered. '*You* ought to know that, Sir.'

" 'What do you mean?' he asked, quickly.

" 'Well, Sir,' I said, 'to be straight, what about that chap you sent us hunting after up the main the other night? That was a funny enough affair, wasn't it? This one isn't half so funny.'

" 'That will do, Jessop!' he said, angrily. 'I won't have any back talk.' Yet there was something about his tone that told me I had got one in on my own. He seemed all at once less able to appear confident that I was telling him a fairy tale.

"After that, for perhaps half a minute, he said nothing. I guessed he was doing some hard thinking. When he spoke again it was on the matter of getting the Ordinary down on deck.

" 'One of you'll have to go down the lee side and steady him down,' he concluded.

"He turned and looked downwards.

" 'Are you bringing that gantline?' he sung out.

" 'Yes, Sir,' I heard one of the men answer.

"A moment later, I saw the man's head appear over the top. He had the tail-block slung round his neck, and the end of the gantline over his shoulder.

"Very soon we had the gantline rigged, and Tom down on deck. Then we took him into the fo'cas'le and put him in his bunk. The Second Mate had sent for some brandy, and now he started to dose him well with it. At the same time a couple of the men chafed his hands and feet. In a little, he began to show signs of coming round. Presently, after a sudden fit of coughing, he opened his eyes, with a surprised, bewildered stare. Then he caught at the edge of his bunk-board, and sat up, giddily. One of the men steadied him, while the Second Mate stood back, and eyed him, critically. The boy rocked as he sat, and put up his hand to his head.

" 'Here,' said the Second Mate, 'take another drink.'

"Tom caught his breath and choked a little; then he spoke.

" 'By gum!' he said, 'my head does ache.'

"He put up his hand, again, and felt at the lump on his forehead. Then he bent forward and stared round at the men grouped about his bunk.

" 'What's up?' he inquired, in a confused sort of way, and seeming as if he could not see us clearly.

" 'What's up?' he asked again.

" 'That's just what I want to know!' said the Second Mate, speaking for the first time with some sternness.

'I ain't been snoozin' while there's been a job on?' Tom inquired, anxiously.

"He looked round at the men appealingly.

" 'It's knocked 'im dotty, strikes me,' said one of the men, audibly.

" 'No,' I said, answering Tom's question, 'you've had—'

" 'Shut that, Jessop!' said the Second Mate quickly, interrupting me. 'I want to hear what the boy's got to say for himself.'

"He turned again to Tom.

" 'You were up at the fore royal,' he prompted.

" 'I carn't say I was, Sir,' said Tom, doubtfully. I could see that he had not gripped the Second Mate's meaning.

" 'But you were!' said the Second, with some impatience. 'It was blowing adrift, and I sent you up to shove a gasket round it.'

" 'Blowin' adrift, Sir?' said Tom, dully.

" 'Yes! blowing adrift. Don't I speak plainly?'

"The dullness went from Tom's face, suddenly.

" 'So it was, Sir!' he said, his memory returning. 'The bloomin' sail got chock full of wind. It caught me bang in the face.'

"He paused a moment.

" 'I believe—' he began, and then stopped once more.

" 'Go on!' said the Second Mate. 'Spit it out!'

" 'I don't know, Sir,' Tom said. 'I don't understand—'

"He hesitated again.

" 'That's all I can remember,' he muttered, and put his hand up to the bruise on his forehead, as though trying to remember something.

"In the momentary silence that succeeded, I caught the voice of Stubbins.

" 'There hain't hardly no wind,' he was saying, in a puzzled tone.

"There was a low murmur of assent from the surrounding men.

"The Second Mate said nothing, and I glanced at him, curiously. Was he beginning to see, I wondered, how useless it was to try to find any sensible explanation of the affair? Had he begun at last to couple it with that peculiar business of the man up the main? I am inclined *now* to think that this was so; for, after staring a few moments at Tom, in a doubtful sort of way, he went out of the fo'cas'le, saying that he would inquire further into the matter in the morning. Yet, when the morning came, he did no such thing. As for his reporting the affair to the Skipper, I much doubt it. Even did he, it must have been in a very casual way; for we heard nothing more about it; though, of course we talked it over pretty thoroughly among ourselves.

"With regard to the Second Mate, even now I am rather puzzled by his attitude to us aloft. Sometimes I have thought that he must have suspected us of trying to play off some trick on him—perhaps, at the time, he still half suspected one of us of being in some way connected with the other business. Or, again, he may have been trying to fight against the conviction that was being forced upon him, that there was really something impossible and beastly about the old packet. Of course, these are only suppositions.

"And then, close upon this, there were further developments.

✦ ✦ ✦

V

The End of Williams

As I HAVE SAID, there was a lot of talk, among the crowd of us forrard, about Tom's strange accident. None of the men knew that Williams and I had seen it *happen*. Stubbins gave it as his opinion that Tom had been sleepy, and missed the foot-rope. Tom, of course, would not have this by any means. Yet, he had no one to appeal to; for, at that time, he was just as ignorant as the rest, that we had seen the sail flap up over the yard.

"Stubbins insisted that it stood to reason it couldn't be the wind. There wasn't any, he said; and the rest of the men agreed with him.

" 'Well,' I said, 'I don't know about all that. I'm a bit inclined to think Tom's yarn is the truth.'

" 'How do you make that hout?' Stubbins asked, unbelievingly. 'There haint nothin' like enough wind.'

" 'What about the place on his forehead?' I inquired, in turn. 'How are you going to explain that?'

" 'I 'spect he knocked himself there when he slipped,' he answered.

" 'Likely 'nuff,' agreed old Jaskett, who was sitting smoking on a chest near by.

" 'Well, you're both a damn long way out of it!' Tom chipped in, pretty warm. 'I wasn't asleep; an' the sail did bloomin' well hit me.'

" 'Don't you be imperent, young feller,' said Jaskett.

"I joined in again.

" 'There's another thing, Stubbins,' I said. 'The gasket Tom was hanging by, was on the after side of the yard. That looks as if the sail might have flapped it over? If there were wind enough to do the one, it seems to me that it might have done the other.'

" 'Do you mean that it was hunder ther yard, or hover ther top?' he asked.

" 'Over the top, of course. What's more, the foot of the sail was hanging over the after part of the yard, in a bight.'

"Stubbins was plainly surprised at that, and before he was ready with his next objection, Plummer spoke.

" ' 'oo saw it?' he asked.

" 'I saw it!' I said, a bit sharply. 'So did Williams; so—for that matter—did the Second Mate.'

"Plummer relapsed into silence, and smoked; and Stubbins broke out afresh.

" 'I reckon Tom must have had a hold of the foot and the gasket, and pulled 'em hover the yard when he tumbled.'

" 'No!' interrupted Tom. 'The gasket was under the sail. I couldn't even see it. An' I hadn't time to get hold of the foot of the sail, before it up and caught me smack in the face.'

" ' 'ow did yer get 'old er ther gasket, when yer fell, then?' asked Plummer.

" 'He didn't get hold of it,' I answered for Tom. 'It had taken a turn round his wrist, and that's how we found him hanging.'

" 'Do yer mean to say as 'e 'adn't got 'old of ther garsket?' Quoin inquired, pausing in the lighting of his pipe.

" 'Of course, I do,' I said. 'A chap doesn't go hanging on to a rope when he's jolly well been knocked senseless.'

" 'Ye're richt,' assented Jock, 'Ye're quite richt there, Jessop.'

"Quoin concluded the lighting of his pipe.

" 'I dunno,' he said.

"I went on, without noticing him.

" 'Anyway, when Williams and I found him, he was hanging by the gasket, and it had a couple of turns round his wrist. And besides that, as I said before, the foot of the sail was hanging over the after side of the yard, and Tom's weight on the gasket was holding it there.'

" 'It's damned queer,' said Stubbins, in a puzzled voice. 'There don't seem to be no way of gettin' a proper hexplanation to it.'

"I glanced at Williams, to suggest that I should tell all that we had seen; but he shook his head, and, after a moment's thought, it seemed to me that there was nothing to be gained by so doing. We had no very clear idea of the thing that had happened, and our half facts and guesses would only have tended to make the matter appear more grotesque and unlikely. The only thing to be done was to wait and watch. If we could only get hold of something tangible, then we might hope to tell all that we knew, without being made into laughing-stocks.

"I came out from my think, abruptly.

"Stubbins was speaking again. He was arguing the matter with one of the other men.

" 'You see, with there bein' no wind, scarcely, ther thing's himpossible, an' yet—'

"The other man interrupted with some remark I did not catch.

" 'No,' I heard Stubbins say. 'I'm hout of my reckonin'. I don't savvy it one bit. It's too much like a damned fairy tale.'

" 'Look at his wrist!' I said.

"Tom held out his right hand and arm for inspection. It was considerably swollen where the rope had been round it.

" 'Yes,' admitted Stubbins. 'That's right enough; but it don't tell you nothin'.'

"I made no reply. As Stubbins said, it told you 'nothin'.' And there I let it drop. Yet, I have told you this, as showing how the matter was regarded in the fo'cas'le. Still, it did not occupy our minds very long; for, as I have said, there were further developments.

"The three following nights passed quietly; and then, on the fourth, all those curious signs and hints culminated suddenly in something extraordinarily grim. Yet, everything had been so subtle and intangible, and, indeed, so was the affair itself, that only those who had actually come in touch with the invading fear, seemed really capable of comprehending the terror of the thing. The men, for the most part, began to say the ship was unlucky, and, of course, as usual! there was some talk of there being a Jonah in the ship. Still, I cannot say that none of the men realised there was anything horrible and frightening in it all; for I am sure that some did, a little; and I think Stubbins was certainly one of them; though I feel certain that he did not, at that time, you know, grasp a quarter of the real significance that underlay the several queer matters that had disturbed our nights. He seemed to fail, somehow, to grasp the element of personal danger that, to me, was already plain. He lacked sufficient imagination, I suppose, to piece the things together—to trace the natural sequence of the events, and their development. Yet I must not forget, of course, that he had no knowledge of those two first incidents. If he had, perhaps he might have stood where I did. As it was, he had not seemed to reach out at all, you know, not even in the matter of Tom and the fore royal. Now, however, after the thing I am about to tell you, he seemed to see a little way into the darkness, and realise possibilities.

"I remember the fourth night, well. It was a clear, star-lit, moonless sort of night: at least, I think there was no moon; or, at any rate, the moon could have been little more than a thin crescent, for it was near the dark time.

"The wind had breezed up a bit; but still remained steady. We were slipping along at about six or seven knots an hour. It was our middle watch on deck, and the ship was full of the blow and hum of the wind aloft. Williams and I were the only ones about the maindeck. He was leaning over the weather pinrail, smoking; while I was pacing up and down, between him and the fore hatch. Stubbins was on the look-out.

"Two bells had gone some minutes, and I was wishing to goodness that it was eight, and time to turn-in. Suddenly, overhead, there sounded a sharp crack, like the report of a rifle shot. It was followed instantly by the rattle and crash of sailcloth thrashing in the wind.

"Williams jumped away from the rail, and ran aft a few steps. I followed him, and, together, we stared upwards to see what had gone. Indistinctly, I made out that the weather sheet of the fore t'gallant had carried away, and the clew of the sail was whirling and banging about in the air, and, every few moments, hitting the steel yard a blow, like the thump of a great sledge hammer.

" 'It's the shackle, or one of the links that's gone, I think,' I shouted to Williams, above the noise of the sail. 'That's the spectacle that's hitting the yard.'

" 'Yus!' he shouted back, and went to get hold of the clewline. I ran to give him a hand. At the same moment, I caught the Second Mate's voice away aft, shouting. Then came the noise of running feet, and the rest of the watch, and the Second Mate, were with us almost at the same moment. In a few minutes we had the yard lowered and the sail clewed up. Then Williams and I went aloft to see where the sheet had gone. It was much as I had supposed; the spectacle was all right, but the pin had gone out of the shackle, and the shackle itself was jammed into the sheavehole in the yard arm.

"Williams sent me down for another pin, while he unbent the clewline, and overhauled it down to the sheet. When I returned with the fresh pin, I screwed it into the shackle, clipped on the clewline, and sung out to the men to take a pull on the rope. This they did, and at the second heave the shackle came away. When it was high enough, I went up on to the t'gallant yard, and held the chain, while Williams shackled it into the spectacle. Then he bent on the clewline afresh, and sung out to the Second Mate that we were ready to hoist away.

" 'Yer'd better go down an' give 'em a 'aul,' he said. 'I'll sty an' light up ther syle.'

" 'Right ho, Williams,' I said, getting into the rigging. 'Don't let the ship's bogy run away with you.'

"This remark I made in a moment of lightheartedness, such as will come to any one aloft, at times. I was exhilarated for the time being, and quite free from the sense of fear that had been with me so much of late. I suppose this was due to the freshness of the wind.

" 'There's more'n one!' he said, in that curiously short way of his.

" 'What?' I asked.

"He repeated his remark. I was suddenly serious. The *reality* of all the impossible details of the past weeks came back to me, vivid, and beastly.

" 'What do you mean, Williams?' I asked him.

"But he had shut up, and would say nothing.

" 'What do you know—how much do you know?' I went on, quickly. 'Why did you never tell me that you—'

"The Second Mate's voice interrupted me, abruptly:—

" 'Now then, up there! Are you going to keep us waiting all night? One of you come down and give us a pull with the ha'lyards. The other stay up and light up the gear.'

" 'i, i, Sir,' I shouted back.

"Then I turned to Williams, hurriedly.

" 'Look here, Williams,' I said. 'If you think there is *really* a danger in your being alone up here—' I hesitated for words to express what I meant. Then I went on. 'Well, I'll jolly well stay up with you.'

"The Second Mate's voice came again.

" 'Come on now, one of you! Make a move! What the hell are you doing?'

" 'Coming, Sir!' I sung out.

" 'Shall I stay?' I asked definitely.

" 'Garn!' he said. 'Don't yer fret yerself. I'll tike er bloomin' piy-diy out of 'er. Blarst 'em. I ain't funky of 'em.'

"I went. That was the last word Williams spoke to anyone living.

"I reached the decks, and tailed on to the haulyards.

"We had nearly mast-headed the yard, and the Second Mate was looking up at the dark outline of the sail, ready to sing out 'Belay'; when, all at once, there came a queer sort of muffled shout from Williams.

" 'Vast hauling, you men,' shouted the Second Mate.

"We stood silent, and listened.

" 'What's that, Williams?' he sung out. 'Are you all clear?'

"For nearly half a minute we stood, listening; but there came no reply. Some of the men said afterwards that they noticed a curious rattling and vibrating noise aloft, that sounded faintly above the hum and swirl of the wind. Like the sound of loose ropes being shaken and slatted together, you know. Whether this noise was really heard, or whether it was something that had no existence outside of their imaginations, I cannot say. I heard nothing of it; but then I was at the tail end of the rope, and furthest from the fore rigging; while those who heard it were on the fore part of the haulyards, and close up to the shrouds.

"The Second Mate put his hands to his mouth.

" 'Are you all clear there?' he shouted again.

"The answer came, unintelligible and unexpected. It ran like this:—

" 'Blarst yer… I've styed…. Did yer think… drive… bly—dy piy-diy.' And then there was a sudden silence.

"I stared up at the dim sail, astonished.

" 'He's dotty!' said Stubbins, who had been told to come off the look-out and give us a pull.

" ' 'e's as mad as a bloomin' 'atter,' said Quoin, who was standing foreside of me. ' 'e's been queer all along.'

" 'Silence there!' shouted the Second Mate. Then:—

" 'Williams!'

"No answer.

" 'Williams!' more loudly.

"Still no answer.

"Then:—

" 'Damn you, you jumped-up cockney crocodile! Can't you hear? Are you blooming-well deaf?'

"There was no answer, and the Second Mate turned to me.

" 'Jump aloft, smartly now, Jessop, and see what's wrong!'

" 'i, i, Sir,' I said, and made a run for the rigging. I felt a bit queer. Had Williams gone mad? He certainly always had been a bit funny. Or—and the thought came with a jump—had he seen— I did not finish. Suddenly, up aloft, there sounded a frightful scream. I stopped, with my hand on the sheer-pole. The next instant, something fell out of the darkness—a heavy body, that struck the deck near the waiting men, with a tremendous crash and a loud, ringing, wheezy sound that sickened me. Several of the men shouted out loud in their fright, and let go of the haulyards; but luckily the stopper held it, and the yard did not come down. Then, for the space of several seconds, there was a dead silence among the crowd; and it seemed to me that the wind had in it a strange moaning note.

"The Second Mate was the first to speak. His voice came so abruptly that it startled me.

" 'Get a light, one of you, quick now!'

"There was a moment's hesitation.

" 'Fetch one of the binnacle lamps, you, Tammy.'

" 'i, i, Sir,' the youngster said, in a quavering voice, and ran aft.

"In less than a minute, I saw the light coming towards us along the deck. The boy was running. He reached us, and handed the lamp to the Second Mate, who took it and went towards the dark, huddled heap on the deck. He held the light out before him, and peered at the thing.

" 'My God!' he said. 'It's Williams!'

"He stooped lower with the light, and I saw details. It was Williams right enough. The Second Mate told a couple of the men to lift him and straighten him out on the hatch. Then he went aft to call the Skipper. He returned in a couple of minutes with an old Ensign which he spread over the poor beggar. Almost directly, the Captain came hurrying forrard along the decks. He pulled back one end of the Ensign, and looked; then he put it back quietly, and the Second Mate explained all that we knew, in a few words.

" 'Would you leave him where he is, Sir?' he asked, after he had told everything.

" 'The night's fine,' said the Captain. 'You may as well leave the poor devil there.'

"He turned, and went aft, slowly. The man who was holding the light, swept it round so that it showed the place where Williams had struck the deck.

"The Second Mate spoke abruptly.

" 'Get a broom and a couple of buckets, some of you.'

"He turned sharply, and ordered Tammy on to the poop.

"As soon as he had seen the yard mast-headed, and the ropes cleared up, he followed Tammy. He knew well enough that it would not do for the youngster to let his mind dwell too much on the poor chap on the hatch, and I found out, a little later, that he gave the boy something to occupy his thoughts.

"After they had gone aft, we went into the fo'cas'le. Every one was moody and frightened. For a little while, we sat about in our bunks and the chests, and no one said a word. The watch below were all asleep, and not one of them knew what had happened.

"All at once, Plummer, whose wheel it was, stepped over the starboard washboard, into the fo'cas'le.

" 'What's up, anyway?' he asked. 'Is Williams much 'urt?'

" ' 'Sh!' I said. 'You'll wake the others. Who's taken your wheel?'

" 'Tammy—ther Second sent 'im. 'e said I could go forrard an' 'ave er smoke. 'e said Williams 'ad 'ad er fall.'

"He broke off, and looked across the fo'cas'le.

" 'Where is 'e?' he inquired, in a puzzled voice.

"I glanced at the others; but no one seemed inclined to start yarning about it.

" 'He fell from the t'gallant rigging!' I said.

" 'Where is 'e?' he repeated.

" 'Smashed up,' I said. 'He's lying on the hatch.'

" 'Dead?' he asked.

"I nodded.

" 'I guessed 'twere somethin' pretty bad, when I saw the Old Man come forrard.

'ow did it 'appen?'

"He looked round at the lot of us sitting there silent and smoking.

" 'No one knows,' I said, and glanced at Stubbins. I caught him eyeing me, doubtfully.

"After a moment's silence, Plummer spoke again.

" 'I 'eard 'im screech, when I was at ther wheel. 'e must 'ave got 'urt up aloft.'

"Stubbins struck a match and proceeded to relight his pipe.

" 'How d'yer mean?' he asked, speaking for the first time.

" ' 'ow do I mean? Well, I can't say. Maybe 'e jammed 'is fingers between ther parrel an' ther mast.'

" 'What about 'is swearin' at ther Second Mate? Was that 'cause 'e'd jammed 'is fingers?' put in Quoin.

" 'I never 'eard about that,' said Plummer. ' 'oo 'eard 'im?'

" 'I should think heverybody in ther bloomin' ship heard him,' Stubbins answered. 'All ther same, I hain't sure he *was* swearin' at ther Second Mate. I thought at first he'd gone dotty an' was cussin' him; but somehow it don't seem likely, now I come to think. It don't stand to reason he should go to cuss ther man. There was nothin' to go cussin' about. What's more, he didn't seem ter be talkin' down to us on deck—-what I could make hout. 'sides, what would he want ter go talkin' to ther Second about his pay-day?'

"He looked across to where I was sitting. Jock, who was smoking, quietly, on the chest next to me, took his pipe slowly out from between his teeth.

" 'Ye're no far oot, Stubbins, I'm thinkin'. Ye're no far oot,' he said, nodding his head.

"Stubbins still continued to gaze at me.

" 'What's your idee?' he said, abruptly.

"It may have been my fancy; but it seemed to me that there was something deeper than the mere sense the question conveyed.

"I glanced at him. I couldn't have said, myself, just what my idea was.

" 'I don't know!' I answered, a little adrift. 'He didn't strike me as cursing at the Second Mate. That is, I should say, after the first minute.'

" 'Just what I say,' he replied. 'Another thing—don't it strike you as bein' bloomin' queer about Tom nearly comin' down by ther run, an' then *this*?'

"I nodded.

" 'It would have been all hup with Tom, if it hadn't been for ther gasket.'

"He paused. After a moment, he went on again.

"'That was honly three or four nights ago!'

" 'Well,' said Plummer. 'What are yer drivin' at?'

" 'Nothin',' answered Stubbins. 'Honly it's damned queer. Looks as though ther ship might be unlucky, after all.'

" 'Well,' agreed Plummer. 'Things 'as been a bit funny lately; and then there's what's 'appened ter-night. I shall 'ang on pretty tight ther next time I go aloft.'

"Old Jaskett took his pipe from his mouth, and sighed.

" 'Things is going wrong 'most every night,' he said, almost pathetically. 'It's as diff'rent as chalk 'n' cheese ter what it were w'en we started this 'ere trip. I thought it were all 'ellish rot about 'er bein' 'aunted; but it's not, seem'ly.'

"He stopped and expectorated.

" 'She hain't haunted,' said Stubbins. 'Leastways, not like you mean—'

"He paused, as though trying to grasp some elusive thought.

" 'Eh?' said Jaskett, in the interval.

"Stubbins continued, without noticing the query. He appeared to be answering some half-formed thought in his own brain, rather than Jaskett:—

" 'Things is queer—an' it's been a bad job tonight. I don't savvy one bit what Williams was sayin' of hup aloft. I've thought sometimes he'd somethin' on 'is mind—'

"Then, after a pause of about half a minute, he said this:—

" '*Who* was he sayin' that to?'

" 'Eh?' said Jaskett, again, with a puzzled expression.

" 'I was thinkin',' said Stubbins, knocking out his pipe on the edge of the chest. 'P'raps you're right, hafter all.'

VI

Another Man to the Wheel

THE CONVERSATION HAD SLACKED off. We were all moody and shaken, and I know I, for one, was thinking some rather troublesome thoughts.

"Suddenly, I heard the sound of the Second's whistle. Then his voice came along the deck:—

" 'Another man to the wheel!'

" ''e's singin' out for someone to go aft an' relieve ther wheel,' said Quoin, who had gone to the door to listen. 'Yer'd better 'urry up, Plummer.'

" 'What's ther time?' asked Plummer, standing up and knocking out his pipe. 'Must be close on ter four bells, 'oo's next wheel is it?'

" 'It's all right, Plummer,' I said, getting up from the chest on which I had been sitting. 'I'll go along. It's my wheel, and it only wants a couple of minutes to four bells.'

"Plummer sat down again, and I went out of the fo'cas'le. Reaching the poop, I met Tammy on the lee side, pacing up and down.

" 'Who's at the wheel?' I asked him, in astonishment.

" 'The Second Mate,' he said, in a shaky sort of voice. 'He's waiting to be relieved. I'll tell you all about it as soon as I get a chance.'

"I went on aft to the wheel.

" 'Who's that?' the Second inquired.

" 'It's Jessop, Sir,' I answered.

"He gave me the course, and then, without another word, went forrard along the poop. On the break, I heard him call Tammy's name, and then for some minutes he was talking to him; though what he was saying, I could not possibly hear. For my part, I was tremendously curious to know why the Second Mate had taken the wheel. I knew that if it were just a matter of bad steering on Tammy's part, he would not have dreamt of doing such a thing. There had been something queer happening, about which I had yet to learn; of this, I felt sure.

"Presently, the Second Mate left Tammy, and commenced to walk the weather side of the deck. Once he came right aft, and, stooping, peered under the wheel-box; but never addressed a word to me. Sometime later, he went down the weather ladder on to the maindeck. Directly afterwards, Tammy came running up to the lee side of the wheel-box.

" 'I've seen it again!' he said, gasping with sheer nervousness.

" 'What?' I said.

" 'That *thing*,' he answered. Then he leant across the wheel-box, and lowered his voice.

" 'It came over the lee rail—*up out of the sea*,' he added, with an air of telling something unbelievable.

"I turned more towards him; but it was too dark to see his face with any distinctness. I felt suddenly husky. 'My God!' I thought. And then I made a silly effort to protest; but he cut me short with a certain impatient hopelessness.

" 'For God's sake, Jessop,' he said, 'do stow all that! It's no good. I must have some one to talk to, or I shall go dotty.'

"I saw how useless it was to pretend any sort of ignorance. Indeed, really, I had known it all along, and avoided the youngster on that very account, as you know.

" 'Go on,' I said. 'I'll listen; but you'd better keep an eye for the Second Mate; he may pop up any minute.'

"For a moment, he said nothing, and I saw him peering stealthily about the poop.

" 'Go on,' I said. 'You'd better make haste, or he'll be up before you're half-way through. What was he doing at the wheel when I came up to relieve it? Why did he send you away from it?'

" 'He didn't,' Tammy replied, turning his face towards me. 'I bunked away from it.'

" 'What for?' I asked.

" 'Wait a minute,' he answered, 'and I'll tell you the whole business. You know the Second Mate sent me to the wheel, after *that*—' He nodded his head forrard.

" 'Yes,' I said.

" 'Well, I'd been here about ten minutes, or a quarter of an hour, and I was feeling rotten about Williams, and trying to forget it all and keep the ship on her course, and all that; when, all at once, I happened to glance to loo'ard, and there I saw it climbing over the rail. My God! I didn't know what to do. The Second Mate was standing forrard on the break of the poop, and I was here all by myself. I felt as if I were frozen stiff. When it came towards me, I let go of the wheel, and yelled and bunked forrard to the Second Mate. He caught hold of me and shook me; but I was so jolly frightened, I couldn't say a word. I could only keep on pointing. The Second kept asking me "Where?" And then, all at once, I found I couldn't see the thing. I don't know whether he saw it. I'm not at all certain he did. He just told me to damn well get back to the wheel, and stop making a damned fool of myself. I said out straight I wouldn't go. So he blew his whistle, and sung out for some one to come aft and take it. Then he ran and got hold of the wheel himself. You know the rest.'

" 'You're quite sure it wasn't thinking about Williams made you imagine you saw something?' I said, more to gain a moment to think, than because I believed that it was the case.

" 'I thought you were going to listen to me, seriously!' he said, bitterly. 'If you won't believe me; what about the chap the Second Mate saw? What about Tom? What about Williams? For goodness sake! don't try to put me off like you did last time. I nearly went cracked with wanting to tell some one who would listen to me, and wouldn't laugh. I could stand anything, but this being alone. There's a good chap, don't pretend you don't understand. Tell me what it all means. What is this horrible man that I've twice seen? You know you know something, and I believe you're afraid to tell anyone, for fear of being laughed at. Why don't you tell me? You needn't be afraid of my laughing.'

"He stopped, suddenly. For the moment, I said nothing in reply.

" 'Don't treat me like a kid, Jessop!' he exclaimed, quite passionately.

" 'I won't,' I said, with a sudden resolve to tell him everything. 'I need someone to talk to, just as badly as you do.'

" 'What does it all mean, then?' he burst out. 'Are they real? I always used to think it was all a yarn about such things.'

" 'I'm sure I don't know what it all means, Tammy,' I answered. 'I'm just as much in the dark, there, as you are. And I don't know whether they're real—that is, not as we consider things real. You don't know that I saw a queer figure down on the maindeck, several nights before you saw that thing up here.'

" 'Didn't you see this one?' he cut in, quickly.

" 'Yes,' I answered.

" 'Then, why did you pretend not to have?' he said, in a reproachful voice. 'You don't know what a state you put me into, what with my being certain that I had seen it, and then you being so jolly positive that there had been nothing. At one time I thought

I was going clean off my dot—until the Second Mate saw that man go up the main. Then, I knew that there must be something in the thing I was certain I'd seen.'

" 'I thought, perhaps, that if I told you I hadn't seen it, you would think you'd been mistaken,' I said. 'I wanted you to think it was imagination, or a dream, or something of that sort.'

" 'And all the time, you knew about that other thing you'd seen?' he asked.

" 'Yes,' I replied.

" 'It was thundering decent of you,' he said. 'But it wasn't any good.'

"He paused a moment. Then he went on:—

" 'It's terrible about Williams. Do you think he saw something, up aloft?'

" 'I don't know, Tammy,' I said. 'It's impossible to say. It *may* have been only an accident.' I hesitated to tell him what I really thought.

" 'What was he saying about his pay-day? Who was he saying it to?'

" 'I don't know,' I said, again. 'He was always cracked about taking a pay-day out of her. You know, he stayed in her, on purpose, when all the others left. He told me that he wasn't going to be done out of it, for any one.'

" 'What did the other lot leave for?' he asked. Then, as the idea seemed to strike him— 'Jove! do you think they saw something, and got scared? It's quite possible. You know, we only joined her in 'Frisco. She had no 'prentices on the passage out. Our ship was sold; so they sent us aboard here to come home.'

" 'They may have,' I said. 'Indeed, from things I've heard Williams say, I'm pretty certain, he for one, guessed or knew a jolly sight more than we've any idea of.'

" 'And now he's dead!' said Tammy, solemnly. 'We'll never be able to find out from him now.'

"For a few moments, he was silent. Then he went off on another track.

" 'Doesn't anything ever happen in the Mate's watch?'

" 'Yes,' I answered. 'There's several things happened lately, that seem pretty queer. Some of his side have been talking about them. But he's too jolly pig-headed to see anything. He just curses his chaps, and puts it all down to them.'

" 'Still,' he persisted; 'things seem to happen more in our watch than in his—I mean, bigger things. Look at tonight.'

" 'We've no proof, you know,' I said.

"He shook his head, doubtfully.

" 'I shall always funk going aloft, now.'

" 'Nonsense!' I told him. 'It may only have been an accident.'

" 'Don't!' he said. 'You know you don't think so, really.'

"I answered nothing, just then; for I knew very well that he was right. We were silent for a couple of moments.

"Then he spoke again:—

" 'Is the ship haunted?'

"For an instant I hesitated.

" 'No,' I said, at length. 'I don't think she is. I mean, not in that way.'

" 'What way, then?'

" 'Well, I've formed a bit of a theory, that seems wise one minute, and cracked the next. Of course, it's as likely to be all wrong; but it's the only thing that seems to me to fit in with all the beastly things we've had lately.'

" 'Go on!' he said, with an impatient, nervous movement.

" 'Well, I've an idea that it's nothing *in* the ship that's likely to hurt us. I scarcely know how to put it; but, if I'm right in what I think, it's the ship herself that's the cause of everything.'

" 'What do you mean?' he asked, in a puzzled voice. 'Do you mean that the ship *is* haunted, after all?'

" 'No!' I answered. 'I've just told you I didn't. Wait until I've finished what I was going to say.'

" 'All right!' he said.

" 'About that thing you saw tonight,' I went on. 'You say it came over the lee rail, up on to the poop?'

" 'Yes,' he answered.

" 'Well the thing I saw, *came up out of the sea, and went back into the sea.*'

" 'Jove!' he said; and then:— 'Yes, go on.'

" 'My idea is, that this ship is open to be boarded by those things,' I explained. 'What they are, of course I don't know. They look like men—in lots of ways. But—well, the Lord knows what's in the sea. Though we don't want to go imagining silly things, of course. And then, again, you know, it seems fat-headed, calling anything silly. That's how I keep going, in a sort of blessed circle. I don't know a bit whether they're flesh and blood, or whether they're what we should call ghosts or spirits ⸺'

" 'They can't be flesh and blood,' Tammy interrupted. 'Where would they live? Besides, that first one I saw, I thought I could see through it. And this last one—the Second Mate would have seen it. And they would drown—'

" 'Not necessarily,' I said.

" 'Oh, but I'm sure they're not,' he insisted. It's impossible—'

" 'So are ghosts—when you're feeling sensible,' I answered. 'But I'm not saying they *are* flesh and blood; though, at the same time, I'm not going to say straight out they're ghosts—not yet, at any rate.'

" 'Where do they come from?' he asked, stupidly enough.

" 'Out of the sea,' I told him. 'You saw for yourself!'

" 'Then why don't other vessels have them coming aboard?' he said. 'How do you account for that?'

" 'In a way—though sometimes it seems cracky—I think I can, according to my idea,' I answered.

" 'How?' he inquired, again.

" 'Why, I believe that this ship is open, as I've told you—exposed, unprotected, or whatever you like to call it. I should say it's reasonable to think that all the things of the material world are barred, as it were, from the immaterial; but that in some cases the barrier may be broken down. That's what may have happened to this ship. And if it has, she may be naked to the attacks of beings belonging to some other state of existence.'

" 'What's made her like that?' he asked, in a really awed sort of tone.

" 'The Lord knows!' I answered. 'Perhaps something to do with magnetic stresses; but you'd not understand, and I don't, really. And, I suppose, inside of me, I don't believe it's anything of the kind, for a minute. I'm not built that way. And yet I don't know! Perhaps, there may have been some rotten thing done aboard of her. Or, again, it's a heap more likely to be something quite outside of anything I know.'

" 'If they're immaterial then, they're spirits?' he questioned.

" 'I don't know,' I said. 'It's so hard to say what I really think, you know. I've got a queer idea, that my head-piece likes to think good; but I don't believe my tummy believes it.'

" 'Go on!' he said.

" 'Well,' I said. 'Suppose the earth were inhabited by two kinds of life. We're one, and *they're* the other.'

" 'Go on!' he said.

" 'Well,' I said. 'Don't you see, in a normal state we may not be capable of appreciating the *realness* of the other? But they may be just as *real* and material to *them*, as *we* are to *us*. Do you see?'

" 'Yes,' he said. 'Go on!'

" 'Well,' I said. 'The earth may be just as *real* to them, as to us. I mean that it may have qualities as material to them, as it has to us; but neither of us could appreciate the other's realness, or the quality of realness in the earth, which was real to the other. It's so difficult to explain. Don't you understand?'

" 'Yes,' he said. 'Go on!'

" 'Well, if we were in what I might call a healthy atmosphere, they would be quite beyond our power to see or feel, or anything. And the same with them; but the more we're like *this*, the more *real* and actual they could grow *to us*. See? That is, the more we should become able to appreciate their form of materialness. That's all. I can't make it any clearer.'

" 'Then, after all, you *really* think they're ghosts, or something of that sort?' Tammy said.

" 'I suppose it does come to that,' I answered. 'I mean that, anyway, I don't think they're our ideas of flesh and blood. But, of course, it's silly to say much; and, after all, you must remember that I may be all wrong.'

" 'I think you ought to tell the Second Mate all this,' he said. 'If it's really as you say, the ship ought to be put into the nearest port, and jolly well burnt.'

" 'The Second Mate couldn't do anything,' I replied. 'Even if he believed it all; which we're not certain he would.'

" 'Perhaps not,' Tammy answered. 'But if you could get him to believe it, he might explain the whole business to the Skipper, and then something might be done. It's not safe as it is.'

" 'He'd only get jeered at again,' I said, rather hopelessly.

" 'No,' said Tammy. 'Not after what's happened tonight.'

" 'Perhaps not,' I replied, doubtfully. And just then the Second Mate came back on to the poop, and Tammy cleared away from the wheel-box, leaving me with a worrying feeling that I ought to do something.

✦ ✦ ✦

VII

The Coming of the Mist, and That Which It Ushered

WE BURIED WILLIAMS AT midday. Poor beggar! It had been so sudden. All day the men were awed and gloomy, and there was a lot of talk about there being a Jonah aboard. If they'd only known what Tammy and I, and perhaps the Second Mate, knew!

"And then the next thing came—the mist. I cannot remember now, whether it was on the day we buried Williams that we first saw it, or the day after.

"When first I noticed it, like everybody else aboard, I took it to be some form of haze, due to the heat of the sun; for it was broad daylight when the thing came.

"The wind had died away to a light breeze, and I was working at the main rigging, along with Plummer, putting on seizings.

" 'Looks as if 'twere middlin' 'ot,' he remarked.

" 'Yes,' I said; and, for the time, took no further notice.

"Presently he spoke again:—

" 'It's gettin' quite 'azy!' and his tone showed he was surprised.

" I glanced up, quickly. At first, I could see nothing. Then, I saw what he meant. The air had a wavy, strange, unnatural appearance; something like the heated air over the top of an engine's funnel, that you can often see when no smoke is coming out.

" 'Must be the heat,' I said. 'Though I don't remember ever seeing anything just like it before.'

" 'Nor me,' Plummer agreed.

"It could not have been a minute later when I looked up again, and was astonished to find that the whole ship was surrounded by a thinnish haze that quite hid the horizon.

" 'By Jove! Plummer,' I said. 'How queer!'

" 'Yes,' he said, looking round. 'I never seen anythin' like it before—not in these parts.'

" 'Heat wouldn't do that!' I said.

" 'N—no,' he said, doubtfully.

"We went on with our work again—occasionally exchanging an odd word or two. Presently, after a little time of silence, I bent forward and asked him to pass me up the spike. He stooped and picked it up from the deck, where it had tumbled. As he held it out to me, I saw the stolid expression on his face, change suddenly to a look of complete surprise. He opened his mouth.

" 'By gum!' he said. 'It's gone.'

"I turned quickly, and looked. And so it had—the whole sea showing clear and bright, right away to the horizon.

"I stared at Plummer, and he stared at me.

" 'Well, I'm blowed!' he exclaimed.

"I do not think I made any reply; for I had a sudden, queer feeling that the thing was not right. And then, in a minute, I called myself an ass; but I could not really shake off the feeling. I had another good look at the sea. I had a vague idea that something was different. The sea looked brighter, somehow, and the air clearer, I thought, and I missed something; but not much, you know. And it was not until a couple of days later, that I knew that it was several vessels on the horizon, which had been quite in sight before the mist, and now were gone.

"During the rest of the watch, and indeed all day, there was no further sign of anything unusual. Only, when the evening came (in the second dog-watch it was) I saw the mist rise faintly—the setting sun shining through it, dim and unreal.

"I knew then, as a certainty, that it was not caused by heat.

"And that was the beginning of it.

"The next day, I kept a pretty close watch, during all my time on deck; but the atmosphere remained clear. Yet, I heard from one of the chaps in the Mate's watch, that it had been hazy during part of the time he was at the wheel.

" 'Comin' an' goin', like,' he described it to me, when I questioned him about it. He thought it might be heat.

"But though I knew otherwise, I did not contradict him. At that time, no one, not even Plummer, seemed to think very much of the matter. And when I mentioned it to Tammy, and asked him whether he'd noticed it, he only remarked that it must have been heat, or else the sun drawing up water. I let it stay at that; for there was nothing to be gained by suggesting that the thing had more to it.

"Then, on the following day, something happened that set me wondering more than ever, and showed me how right I had been in feeling the mist to be something unnatural. It was in this way.

"Five bells, in the eight to twelve morning watch, had gone. I was at the wheel. The sky was perfectly clear—not a cloud to be seen, even on the horizon. It was hot, standing at the wheel; for there was scarcely any wind, and I was feeling drowsy. The Second Mate was down on the maindeck with the men, seeing about some job he wanted done; so that I was on the poop alone.

"Presently, with the heat, and the sun beating right down on to me, I grew thirsty; and, for want of something better, I pulled out a bit of plug I had on me, and bit off a chew; though, as a rule, it is not a habit of mine. After a little, naturally enough, I glanced round for the spittoon; but discovered that it was not there. Probably it had been taken forrard when the decks were washed, to give it a scrub. So, as there was no one on the poop, I left the wheel, and stepped aft to the taffrail. It was thus that I came to see something altogether unthought of—a full-rigged ship, close-hauled on the port tack, a few hundred yards on our starboard quarter. Her sails were scarcely filled by the light breeze, and flapped as she lifted to the swell of the sea. She appeared to have very little way through the water, certainly not more than a knot an hour. Away aft, hanging from the gaff-end, was a string of flags. Evidently, she was signalling to us. All this, I saw in a flash, and I just stood and stared, astonished. I was astonished because I had not seen her earlier. In that light breeze, I knew that she must have been in sight for at least a couple of hours. Yet I could think of nothing rational to satisfy my wonder. There she was—of that much, I was certain. And yet, how had she come there without my seeing her, before?

"All at once, as I stood, staring, I heard the wheel behind me, spin rapidly. Instinctively, I jumped to get hold of the spokes; for I did not want the steering gear jammed. Then I turned again to have another look at the other ship; but, to my utter bewilderment, *there was no sign of her*—nothing but the calm ocean, spreading away to the distant horizon. I blinked my eyelids a bit, and pushed the hair off my forehead. Then, I stared again; but there was no vestige of her—nothing, you know; and absolutely nothing unusual, except a faint, tremulous quiver in the air. And the blank surface of the sea, reaching everywhere to the empty horizon.

"Had she foundered? I asked myself, naturally enough; and, for the moment, I really wondered. I searched round the sea for wreckage; but there was nothing, not even an odd hencoop, or a piece of deck furniture; and so I threw away that idea, as impossible.

"Then, as I stood, I got another thought, or, perhaps, an intuition, and I asked myself, seriously, whether this disappearing ship might not be in some way connected with the other queer things. It occurred to me then, that the vessel I had seen was nothing real, and, perhaps, did not exist outside of my own brain. I considered the idea, gravely. It helped to explain the thing, and I could think of nothing else that would. Had she been real, I felt sure that others aboard us would have been bound to have seen her long before I had—I got a bit muddled there, with trying to think it out; and then, abruptly, the reality of the other ship, came back to me—every rope and sail and spar, you know. And I remembered how she had lifted to the heave of the sea, and how the sails had flapped in the light breeze. And the string of flags! She had been signalling. At that last, I found it just as impossible to believe that she had not been real.

"I had reached to this point of irresolution, and was standing with my back, partly turned to the wheel. I was holding it steady with my left hand, while I looked over the sea, to try to find something to help me to understand.

"All at once, as I stared, I seemed to see the ship again. She was more on the beam now, than on the quarter; but I thought little of that, in the astonishment of seeing her once more. It was only a glimpse I caught of her—dim and wavering, as though I looked at her through the convolutions of heated air. Then she grew indistinct, and vanished again; but I was convinced now that she was real, and had been in sight all the time, if I could have seen her. That curious, dim, wavering appearance had suggested something to me. I remembered the strange, wavy look of the air, a few days previously, just before the mist had surrounded the ship. And in my mind, I connected the two. It was nothing about the other packet that was strange. The strangeness was with us. It was something that was about (or invested) our ship that prevented me—or indeed, any one else aboard—from seeing that other. It was evident that she had been able to see us, as was proved by her signalling. In an irrelevant sort of way, I wondered what the people aboard of her thought of our apparently intentional disregard of their signals.

"After that, I thought of the strangeness of it all. Even at that minute, they could see us, plainly; and yet, so far as we were concerned, the whole ocean seemed empty. It appeared to me, at that time, to be the weirdest thing that could happen to us.

"And then a fresh thought came to me. How long had we been like that? I puzzled for a few moments. It was now that I recollected that we had sighted several vessels on the morning of the day when the mist appeared; and since then, we had seen nothing. This, to say the least, should have struck me as queer; for some of the other packets were homeward bound along with us, and steering the same course. Consequently, with the weather being fine, and the wind next to nothing, they should have been in sight all the time. This reasoning seemed to me to show, unmistakably, some connection between the coming of the mist, and our inability to *see*. So that it is possible we had been in that extraordinary state of blindness for nearly three days.

"In my mind, the last glimpse of that ship on the quarter, came back to me. And, I remember, a curious thought got me, that I had looked at her from out of some other dimension. For a while, you know, I really believe the mystery of the idea, and that it might be the actual truth, took me; instead of my realising just all that it might mean. It seemed so exactly to express all the half-defined thoughts that had come, since seeing that other packet on the quarter.

"Suddenly, behind me, there came a rustle and rattle of the sails; and, in the same instant, I heard the Skipper saying:—

" 'Where the devil have you got her to, Jessop?'

"I whirled round to the wheel.

" 'I don't know—Sir,' I faltered.

"I had forgotten even that I was at the wheel.

" 'Don't know!' he shouted. 'I should damned well think you don't. Starboard your helm, you fool. You'll have us all aback!'

" 'i, i, Sir,' I answered, and hove the wheel over. I did it almost mechanically; for I was still dazed, and had not yet had time to collect my senses.

"During the following half-minute, I was only conscious, in a confused sort of way, that the Old Man was ranting at me. This feeling of bewilderment passed off, and I found that I was peering blankly into the binnacle, at the compass-card; yet, until then, entirely without being aware of the fact. Now, however, I saw that the ship was coming back on to her course. Goodness knows how much she had been off!

"With the realisation that I had let the ship get almost aback, there came a sudden memory of the alteration in the position of the other vessel. She had appeared last on the beam, instead of on the quarter. Now, however, as my brain began to work, I saw the cause of this apparent and, until then, inexplicable change. It was due, of course, to our having come up, until we had brought the other packet on to the beam.

"It is curious how all this flashed through my mind, and held my attention—although only momentarily—in the face of the Skipper's storming. I think I had hardly realised he was still singing out at me. Anyhow, the next thing I remember, he was shaking my arm.

" 'What's the matter with you, man?' he was shouting. And I just stared into his face, like an ass, without saying a word. I seemed still incapable, you know, of actual, reasoning speech.

" 'Are you damned well off your head?' he went on shouting. 'Are you a lunatic? Have you had sunstroke? Speak, you gaping idiot!'

"I tried to say something; but the words would not come clearly.

" 'I—I—I—' I said, and stopped, stupidly. I was all right, really; but I was so bewildered with the thing I had found out; and, in a way, I seemed almost to have come back out of a distance, you know.

" 'You're a lunatic!' he said, again. He repeated the statement several times, as if it were the only thing that sufficiently expressed his opinion of me. Then he let go of my arm, and stepped back a couple of paces.

" 'I'm not a lunatic!' I said, with a sudden gasp. 'I'm not a lunatic, Sir, any more than you are.'

" 'Why the devil don't you answer my questions then?' he shouted, angrily. 'What's the matter with you? What have you been doing with the ship? Answer me now!'

" 'I was looking at that ship away on the starboard quarter, Sir,' I blurted out. 'She's been signalling—'

" 'What!' he cut me short with disbelief. 'What ship?'

"He turned, quickly, and looked over the quarter. Then he wheeled round to me again.

" 'There's no ship! What do you mean by trying to spin up a cuffer like that?'

" 'There is, Sir,' I answered. 'It's out there—' I pointed.

" 'Hold your tongue!' he said. 'Don't talk rubbish to me. Do you think I'm blind?'

" 'I saw it, Sir,' I persisted.

" 'Don't you talk back to me!' he snapped, with a quick burst of temper. 'I won't have it!'

"Then, just as suddenly, he was silent. He came a step towards me, and stared into my face. I believe the old ass thought I was a bit mad; anyway, without another word, he went to the break of the poop.

" 'Mr. Tulipson,' he sung out.

" 'Yes, Sir,' I heard the Second Mate reply.

" 'Send another man to the wheel.'

" 'Very good, Sir,' the Second answered.

"A couple of minutes later, old Jaskett came up to relieve me. I gave him the course, and he repeated it.

" 'What's up, mate?' he asked me, as I stepped off the grating.

" 'Nothing much,' I said, and went forrard to where the Skipper was standing on the break of the poop. I gave him the course; but the crabby old devil took no notice of me, whatever. When I got down on to the maindeck, I went up to the Second, and gave it to him. He answered me civilly enough, and then asked me what I had been doing to put the Old Man's back up.

" 'I told him there's a ship on the starboard quarter, signalling us,' I said.

" 'There's no ship out there, Jessop,' the Second Mate replied, looking at me with a queer, inscrutable expression.

" 'There is, Sir,' I began. 'I—'

" 'That will do, Jessop!' he said. 'Go forrard and have a smoke. I shall want you then to give a hand with these foot-ropes. You'd better bring a serving-mallet aft with you, when you come.'

"I hesitated a moment, partly in anger; but more, I think, in doubt.

" 'i, i, Sir,' I muttered, at length, and went forrard.

VIII

After the Coming of the Mist

AFTER THE COMING OF the mist, things seemed to develop pretty quickly. In the following two or three days a good deal happened.

"On the night of the day on which the Skipper had sent me away from the wheel, it was our watch on deck from eight o'clock to twelve, and my look-out from ten to twelve.

"As I paced slowly to and fro across the fo'cas'le head, I was thinking about the affair of the morning. At first, my thoughts were about the Old Man. I cursed him thoroughly to myself, for being a pig-headed old fool, until it occurred to me that if I had been in his place, and come on deck to find the ship almost aback, and the fellow at the wheel staring out across the sea, instead of attending to his business, I should most certainly have kicked up a thundering row. And then, I had been an ass to tell him about the ship. I should never have done such a thing, if I had not been a bit adrift. Most likely the old chap thought I was cracked.

"I ceased to bother my head about him, and fell to wondering why the Second Mate had looked at me so queerly in the morning. Did he guess more of the truth than I supposed? And if that were the case, why had he refused to listen to me?

"After that, I went to puzzling about the mist. I had thought a great deal about it, during the day. One idea appealed to me, very strongly. It was that the actual, visible mist was a materialised expression of an extraordinarily subtle atmosphere, in which we were moving.

"Abruptly, as I walked backwards and forwards, taking occasional glances over the sea (which was almost calm), my eye caught the glow of a light out in the darkness. I stood still, and stared. I wondered whether it was the light of a vessel. In that case we were no longer enveloped in that extraordinary atmosphere. I bent forward, and gave the thing my more immediate attention. I saw then that it was undoubtedly the green light of a vessel on our port bow. It was plain that she was bent on crossing our bows. What was more, she was dangerously near—the size and brightness of her light showed that. She would be close-hauled, while we were going free, so that, of course, it was our place to get out of her way. Instantly, I turned and, putting my hands up to my mouth, hailed the Second Mate:—

" 'Light on the port bow, Sir.'

"The next moment his hail came back:—

" 'Whereabouts?'

" 'He must be blind,' I said to myself.

" 'About two points on the bow, Sir,' I sung out.

"Then I turned to see whether she had shifted her position at all. Yet, when I came to look, there was no light visible. I ran forrard to the bows, and leant over the rail, and stared; but there was nothing—absolutely nothing except the darkness all about us. For perhaps a few seconds I stood thus, and a suspicion swept across me, that the whole business was practically a repetition of the affair of the morning. Evidently, the impalpable something that invested the ship, had thinned for an instant, thus allowing me to see the light ahead. Now, it had closed again. Yet, whether I could see, or not, I did not doubt the fact that there was a vessel ahead, and very close ahead, too. We might run on top of her any minute. My only hope was that, seeing we were not getting out of her way, she had put her helm up, so as to let us pass, with the intention of then crossing under our stern. I waited, pretty anxiously, watching and listening. Then, all at once, I heard steps coming along the deck, forrard, and the 'prentice, whose time-keeping it was, came up on to the fo'cas'le head.

" 'The Second Mate says he can't see any light, Jessop,' he said, coming over to where I stood. 'Whereabouts is it?'

" 'I don't know,' I answered. 'I've lost sight of it myself. It was a green light, about a couple of points on the port bow. It seemed fairly close.'

" 'Perhaps their lamp's gone out,' he suggested, after peering out pretty hard into the night for a minute or so.

" 'Perhaps,' I said.

"I did not tell him that the light had been so close that, even in the darkness, we should *now* have been able to see the ship herself.

" 'You're quite sure it was a light, and not a star?' he asked, doubtfully, after another long stare.

" 'Oh! no,' I said. 'It may have been the moon, now I come to think about it.'

" 'Don't rot,' he replied. 'It's easy enough to make a mistake. What shall I say to the Second Mate?'

" 'Tell him it's disappeared, of course!'

" 'Where to?' he asked.

" 'How the devil should I know?' I told him. 'Don't ask silly questions!'

" 'All right, keep your rag in,' he said, and went aft to report to the Second Mate.

"Five minutes later, it might have been, I saw the light again. It was broad on the bow, and told me plainly enough that she had up with her helm to escape being run down. I did not wait a moment; but sung out to the Second Mate that there was a green light about four points on the port bow. By Jove! it must have been a close shave. The light did not *seem* to be more than about a hundred yards away. It was fortunate that we had not much way through the water.

" 'Now,' I thought to myself, 'the Second will see the thing. And perhaps Mr. Blooming 'prentice will be able to give the star its proper name.'

"Even as the thought came into my head, the light faded and vanished; and I caught the Second Mate's voice.

" 'Whereaway?' he was singing out.

" 'It's gone again, Sir,' I answered.

"A minute later, I heard him coming along the deck.

"He reached the foot of the starboard ladder.

" 'Where are you, Jessop?' he inquired.

" 'Here, Sir,' I said, and went to the top of the weather ladder.

"He came up slowly on to the fo'cas'le head.

" 'What's this you've been singing out about a light?' he asked. 'Just point out exactly where it was you last saw it.'

"This, I did, and he went over to the port rail, and stared away into the night; but without seeing anything.

" 'It's gone, Sir,' I ventured to remind him. 'Though I've seen it twice now— once, about a couple of points on the bow, and this last time, broad away on the bow; but it disappeared both times, almost at once.'

" 'I don't understand it at all, Jessop,' he said, in a puzzled voice. 'Are you sure it was a ship's light?'

" 'Yes, Sir. A green light. It was quite close.'

" 'I don't understand,' he said, again. 'Run aft and ask the 'prentice to pass you down my night glasses. Be as smart as you can.'

" 'i, i, Sir,' I replied, and ran aft.

"In less than a minute, I was back with his binoculars; and, with them, he stared for some time at the sea to leeward.

"All at once, he dropped them to his side, and faced round on me with a sudden question:—

" 'Where's she gone to? If she's shifted her bearing as quickly as all that, she must be precious close. We should be able to see her spars and sails, or her cabin lights, or her binnacle light, or something!'

" 'It's queer, Sir,' I assented.

" 'Damned queer,' he said. 'So damned queer that I'm inclined to think you've made a mistake.'

" 'No, Sir. I'm certain it was a light.'

" 'Where's the ship, then?' he asked.

" 'I can't say, Sir. That's just what's been puzzling me.'

"The Second said nothing in reply; but took a couple of quick turns across the fo'cas'le head—stopping at the port rail, and taking another look to leeward through his night glasses. Perhaps a minute he stood there. Then, without a word, he went down the lee ladder, and away aft along the maindeck to the poop.

" 'He's jolly well puzzled,' I thought to myself. 'Or else he thinks I've been imagining things.' Either way, I guessed he'd think that.

"In a little, I began to wonder whether, after all, he had any idea of what might be the truth. One minute, I would feel certain he had; and the next, I was just as sure that he guessed nothing. I got one of my fits of asking myself whether it would not have been better to have told him everything. It seemed to me that he must have seen sufficient to make him inclined to listen to me. And yet, I could not by any means be certain. I might only have been making an ass of myself, in his eyes. Or set him thinking I was dotty.

"I was walking about the fo'cas'le head, feeling like this, when I saw the light for the third time. It was very bright and big, and I could see it move, as I watched. This again showed me that it must be very close.

" 'Surely,' I thought, 'the Second Mate must see it now, for himself.'

"I did not sing out this time, right away. I thought I would let the Second see for himself that I had not been mistaken. Besides, I was not going to risk its vanishing again, the instant I had spoken. For quite half a minute, I watched it, and there was no sign of its disappearing. Every moment, I expected to hear the Second Mate's hail, showing that he had spotted it at last; but none came.

"I could stand it no longer, and I ran to the rail, on the after part of the fo'cas'le head.

" 'Green light a little abaft the beam, Sir!' I sung out, at the top of my voice.

"But I had waited too long. Even as I shouted, the light blurred and vanished.

"I stamped my foot and swore. The thing was making a fool of me. Yet, I had a faint hope that those aft had seen it just before it disappeared; but this I knew was vain, directly I heard the Second's voice.

" 'Light be damned!' he shouted.

"Then he blew his whistle, and one of the men ran aft, out of the fo'cas'le, to see what it was he wanted.

" 'Whose next look-out is it?' I heard him ask.

" 'Jaskett's, Sir.'

" 'Then tell Jaskett to relieve Jessop at once. Do you hear?'

" 'Yes, Sir,' said the man, and came forrard.

"In a minute, Jaskett stumbled up on to the fo'cas'le head.

" 'What's up, mate?' he asked, sleepily.

" 'It's that fool of a Second Mate!' I said, savagely. 'I've reported a light to him three times, and, because the blind fool can't see it, he's sent you up to relieve me!'

" 'Where is it, mate?' he inquired.

"He looked round at the dark sea.

" 'I don't see no light,' he remarked, after a few moments.

" 'No,' I said. 'It's gone.'

" 'Eh?' he inquired.

" 'It's gone!' I repeated, irritably.

"He turned and regarded me silently, through the dark.

"' I'd go an' 'ave a sleep, mate,' he said, at length. 'I've been that way meself. Ther's nothin' like a snooze w'en yer gets like that.'

" 'What!' I said. 'Like what?'

" 'It's all right, mate. Yer'll be all right in ther mornin'. Don't yer worry 'bout me.' His tone was sympathetic.

" 'Hell!' was all I said, and walked down off the fo'cas'le head. I wondered whether the old fellow thought I was going silly.

" 'Have a sleep, by Jove!' I muttered to myself. 'I wonder who'd feel like having a sleep after what I've seen and stood today!'

"I felt rotten, with no one understanding what was really the matter. I seemed to be all alone, through the things I had learnt. Then the thought came to me to go aft and talk the matter over with Tammy. I knew he would be able to understand, of course; and it would be such a relief.

"On the impulse, I turned and went aft, along the deck to the 'prentices' berth. As I neared the break of the poop, I looked up and saw the dark shape of the Second Mate, leaning over the rail above me.

" 'Who's that?' he asked.

" 'It's Jessop, Sir,' I said.

" 'What do you want in this part of the ship?' he inquired.

" 'I'd come aft to speak to Tammy, Sir,' I replied.

" 'You go along forrard and turn-in,' he said, not altogether unkindly. 'A sleep will do you more good than yarning about. You know, you're getting to fancy things too much!'

" 'I'm sure I'm not, Sir! I'm perfectly well. I—'

" 'That will do!' he interrupted, sharply. 'You go and have a sleep.'

"I gave a short curse, under my breath, and went slowly forrard. I was getting maddened with being treated as if I were not quite sane.

" 'By God!' I said to myself. 'Wait till the fools know what I know—just wait!'

"I entered the fo'cas'le, through the port doorway, and went across to my chest, and sat down. I felt angry and tired, and miserable.

"Quoin and Plummer were sitting close by, playing cards, and smoking. Stubbins lay in his bunk, watching them, and also smoking. As I sat down, he put his head forward over the bunk-board, and regarded me in a curious, meditative way.

" 'What's hup with ther Second hofficer?' he asked, after a short stare.

"I looked at him, and the other two men looked up at me. I felt I should go off with a bang, if I did not say something, and I let out pretty stiffly, telling them the whole business. Yet, I had seen enough to know that it was no good trying to explain things; so I just told them the plain, bald facts, and left explanations as much alone as possible.

" 'Three times, you say?' said Stubbins when I had finished.

" 'Yes,' I assented.

" 'An' ther Old Man sent yer from ther wheel this mornin', 'cause yer 'appened ter see a ship 'e couldn't,' Plummer added in a reflective tone.

" 'Yes,' I said, again.

"I thought I saw him look at Quoin, significantly; but Stubbins, I noticed, looked only at me.

" 'I reckon ther Second thinks you're a bit hoff colour,' he remarked, after a short pause.

" 'The Second Mate's a fool!' I said, with some bitterness. 'A confounded fool!'

" 'I hain't so sure about that,' he replied. 'It's bound ter seem queer ter him. I don't hunderstand it myself—'

"He lapsed into silence, and smoked.

" 'I carn't understand 'ow it is ther Second Mate didn't 'appen to spot it,' Quoin said, in a puzzled voice.

"It seemed to me that Plummer nudged him to be quiet. It looked as if Plummer shared the Second Mate's opinion, and the idea made me savage. But Stubbins's next remark drew my attention.

" 'I don't hunderstand it,' he said, again; speaking with deliberation. 'All ther same, ther Second should have savvied enough not to have slung you hoff ther look-hout.'

"He nodded his head, slowly, keeping his gaze fixed on my face.

" 'How do you mean?' I asked, puzzled; yet with a vague sense that the man understood more, perhaps, than I had hitherto thought.

" 'I mean what's ther Second so blessed cock-sure about?' he said.

"He took a draw at his pipe, removed it, and leant forward somewhat, over his bunk-board.

" 'Didn't he say nothin' ter you, after you came hoff ther look-hout?' he asked.

" 'Yes,' I replied; 'he spotted me going aft. He told me I was getting to imagining things too much. He said I'd better come forrard and get a sleep.'

" 'An' what did you say?'

" 'Nothing. I came forrard.'

" 'Why didn't you bloomin' well harsk him if he weren't doin' ther imaginin' trick when he sent us chasin' hup ther main, hafter that bogy-man of his ?'

" 'I never thought of it,' I told him.

" 'Well, yer ought ter have.'

"He paused, and sat up in his bunk, and asked for a match.

"As I passed him my box, Quoin looked up from his game.

" 'It might 'ave been a stowaway, yer know. Yer carn't say as it's ever been proved as it wasn't.'

"Stubbins passed the box back to me, and went on without noticing Quoin's remark:—

" 'Told you to go an' have a snooze, did he? I don't hunderstand what he's bluffin' at.'

" 'How do you mean, bluffing?' I asked.

"He nodded his head, sagely.

" 'It's my hidea he knows you saw that light, just as bloomin' well as I do.'

"Plummer looked up from his game, at this speech; but said nothing.

" 'Then *you* don't doubt that I really saw it?' I asked, with a certain surprise.

" 'Not me,' he remarked, with assurance. 'You hain't likely ter make that kind of mistake three times runnin'.'

" 'No,' I said. 'I *know* I saw the light, right enough; but'—I hesitated a moment—'it's blessed queer.'

" 'It *is* blessed queer!' he agreed. 'It's damned queer! An' there's a lot of other damn queer things happenin' aboard this packet lately.'

"He was silent for a few seconds. Then he spoke suddenly:—

" 'It's not nat'ral, I'm damned sure of that much.'

"He took a couple of draws at his pipe, and in the momentary silence, I caught Jaskett's voice, above us. He was hailing the poop.

" 'Red light on the starboard quarter, Sir,' I heard him sing out.

" 'There you are,' I said, with a jerk of my head. 'That's about where that packet I spotted ought to be by now. She couldn't cross our bows, so she up helm, and let us pass, and now she's hauled up again and gone under our stern.'

"I got up from the chest, and went to the door, the other three following. As we stepped out on deck, I heard the Second Mate shouting out, away aft, to know the whereabouts of the light.

" 'By Jove! Stubbins,' I said. 'I believe the blessed thing's gone again.'

"We ran to the starboard side, in a body, and looked over; but there was no sign of a light in the darkness astern.

" 'I carn't say as *I* see any light,' said Quoin.

"Plummer said nothing.

"I looked up at the fo'cas'le head. There, I could faintly distinguish the outlines of Jaskett. He was standing by the starboard rail, with his hands up, shading his eyes, evidently staring towards the place where he had last seen the light.

" 'Where's she got to, Jaskett?' I called out.

" 'I can't say, mate,' he answered. 'It's the most 'ellishly funny thing ever I've comed across. She were there as plain as me 'att one minnit, an' ther next she were gone— clean gone.'

"I turned to Plummer.

" 'What do you think about it, *now*?' I asked him.

" 'Well,' he said. 'I'll admit I thought at first 'twere somethin' an' nothin'. I thought yer was mistaken; but it seems yer did see somethin'.'

"Away aft, we heard the sound of steps, along the deck.

" 'Ther Second's comin' forrard for a hexplanation, Jaskett,' Stubbins sung out. 'You'd better go down an' change yer breeks.'

"The Second Mate passed us, and went up the starboard ladder.

" 'What's up now, Jaskett?' he said, quickly. 'Where is this light? Neither the 'prentice nor I can see it!'

" 'Ther dam thing's clean gone, Sir,' Jaskett replied.

" 'Gone!' the Second Mate said. 'Gone! What do you mean?'

" 'She were there one minnit, Sir, as plain as me 'att, an' ther next, she'd gone.'

" 'That's a dam silly yarn to tell me!' the Second replied. 'You don't expect me to believe it, do you?'

" 'It's Gospel trewth any'ow, Sir,' Jaskett answered. 'An' Jessop seen it just ther same.'

"He seemed to have added that last part as an afterthought. Evidently, the old beggar had changed his opinion as to my need for sleep.

" 'You're an old fool, Jaskett,' the Second said, sharply. 'And that idiot Jessop has been putting things into your silly old head.'

" 'He paused, an instant. Then he continued:—

" 'What the devil's the matter with you all, that you've taken to this sort of game? You know very well that you saw no light! I sent Jessop off the look-out, and then you must go and start the same game.'

" 'We 'aven't—' Jaskett started to say; but the Second silenced him.

" 'Stow it!' he said, and turned and went down the ladder, passing us quickly, without a word.

" 'Doesn't look to *me*, Stubbins,' I said, 'as though the Second did believe we've seen the light.'

" 'I hain't so sure,' he answered. 'He's a puzzler.'

"The rest of the watch passed away quietly; and at eight bells I made haste to turn-in, for I was tremendously tired.

"When we were called again for the four to eight watch on deck, I learnt that one of the men in the Mate's watch had seen a light, soon after we had gone below, and had reported it, only for it to disappear immediately. This, I found, had happened twice, and the Mate had got so wild (being under the impression that the man was playing the fool) that he had nearly come to blows with him—finally ordering him off the look-out, and sending another man up in his place. If this last man saw the light, he took good care not to let the Mate know; so that the matter had ended there.

"And then, on the following night, before we had ceased to talk about the matter of the vanishing lights, something else occurred that temporarily drove from my mind all memory of the mist, and the extraordinary, blind atmosphere it had seemed to usher.

◆▸◆◂◆

IX

The Man Who Cried for Help

IT WAS, AS I have said, on the following night that something further happened. And it brought home pretty vividly to me, if not to any of the others, the sense of a personal danger aboard.

"We had gone below for the eight to twelve watch, and my last impression of the weather at eight o'clock, was that the wind was freshening. There had been a great bank of cloud rising astern, which had looked as if it were going to breeze up still more.

"At a quarter to twelve, when we were called for our twelve to four watch on deck, I could tell at once, by the sound, that there was a fresh breeze blowing; at the same time, I heard the voices of the men in the other watch, singing out as they hauled on the ropes. I caught the rattle of canvas in the wind, and guessed that they were taking the royals off her. I looked at my watch, which I always kept hanging in my bunk. It showed the time to be just after the quarter; so that, with luck, we should escape having to go up to the sails.

"I dressed quickly, and then went to the door to look at the weather. I found that the wind had shifted from the starboard quarter, to right aft; and, by the look of the sky, there seemed to be a promise of more, before long.

"Up aloft, I could make out faintly the fore and mizzen royals, flapping in the wind. The main had been left for a while longer. In the fore rigging, Jacobs, the Ordinary Seaman in the Mate's watch, was following another of the men aloft to the sail. The Mate's two 'prentices were already up at the mizzen. Down on deck, the rest of the men were busy clearing up the ropes.

"I went back to my bunk, and looked at my watch—the time was only a few minutes off eight bells; so I got my oilskins ready, for it looked like rain, outside. As I was doing this, Jock went to the door for a look.

" 'What's it doin', Jock?' Tom asked, getting out of his bunk, hurriedly.

" 'I'm thinkin' maybe it's goin' to blow a wee, and ye'll be needin' yer' oilskins,' Jock answered.

"When eight bells went, and we mustered aft for roll-call, there was a considerable delay, owing to the Mate refusing to call the roll until Tom (who, as usual, had only turned out of his bunk at the last minute) came aft to answer his name. When, at last, he did come, the Second and the Mate joined in giving him a good dressing down for a lazy sojer; so that several minutes passed before we were on our way forrard again. This was a small enough matter in itself, and yet really terrible in its consequence to one of our number; for, just as we reached the fore rigging, there was a shout aloft, loud above the noise of the wind, and the next moment, something crashed down into our midst, with a great, slogging thud—something bulky and weighty, that struck full upon Jock, so that he went down with a loud, horrible, ringing 'ugg,' and never said a word. From the whole crowd of us there went up a yell of fear, and then, with one accord, there was a run for the lighted fo'cas'le. I am not ashamed to say that I ran with the rest. A blind, unreasoning fright had seized me, and I did not stop to think.

"Once in the fo'cas'le and the light, there was a reaction. We all stood and looked blankly at one another for a few moments. Then some one asked a question, and there was a general murmur of denial. We all felt ashamed, and someone reached up, and unhooked the lantern on the port side. I did the same with the starboard one; and there was a quick movement towards the doors. As we streamed out on deck, I caught the sound of the Mates' voices. They had evidently come down from off the poop to find out what had happened; but it was too dark to see their whereabouts.

" 'Where the hell have you all got to?' I heard the Mate shout.

"The next instant, they must have seen the light from our lanterns; for I heard their footsteps, coming along the deck at a run. They came the starboard side, and just abaft the fore rigging, one of them stumbled and fell over something. It was the First Mate who had tripped. I knew this by the cursing that came directly afterwards. He picked himself up, and, apparently without stopping to see what manner of thing it was that he had fallen over, made a rush to the pinrail. The Second Mate ran into the circle of light thrown by our lanterns, and stopped, dead—eyeing us doubtfully. I am not surprised at this, *now*, nor at the behaviour of the Mate, the following instant; but at that time, I must say I could not conceive what had come to them, particularly the First Mate. He came out at us from the darkness with a rush and a roar like a bull, and brandishing a belaying-pin. I had failed to take into account the scene which his eyes must have shown him:— The whole crowd of men in the fo'cas'le—both watches—pouring out on to the deck in utter confusion, and greatly excited, with a couple of fellows at their head, carrying lanterns. And before this, there had been the cry aloft and the crash down on deck, followed by the shouts of the frightened crew, and the sounds of many feet running. He may well have taken the cry for a signal, and our actions for something not far short of mutiny. Indeed, his words told us that this was his very thought.

" 'I'll knock the face off the first man that comes a step further aft!' he shouted, shaking the pin in my face. 'I'll show yer who's master here! What the hell do yer mean by this? Get forrard into yer kennel!'

"There was a low growl from the men at that last remark, and the old bully stepped back a couple of paces.

" 'Hold on, you fellows!' I sung out. 'Shut up a minute!'

" 'Mr. Tulipson!' I called out to the Second, who had not been able to get a word in edgeways, 'I don't know what the devil's the matter with the First Mate; but he'll not find it pay to talk to a crowd like ours, in that sort of fashion, or there'll be ructions aboard.'

" 'Come! come! Jessop! This won't do! I can't have you talking like that about the Mate!' he said, sharply. 'Let me know what's to-do, and then go forrard again, the lot of you.'

" 'We'd have told you at first, Sir,' I said, 'only the Mate wouldn't give any of us a chance to speak. There's been an awful accident, Sir. Something's fallen from aloft, right onto Jock—'

"I stopped suddenly; for there was a loud crying aloft.

" 'Help! help! help!' some one was shouting, and then it rose from a shout into a scream.

" 'My God! Sir,' I shouted. 'That's one of the men up at the fore royal!'

" 'Listen!' ordered the Second Mate. 'Listen!'

"Even as he spoke, it came again—broken and, as it were, in gasps.

"'Help! …Oh! …. God! …Oh! …Help! H-e-l-p!'

"Abruptly, Stubbins's voice struck in.

" 'Hup with us, lads! By God! hup with us!' and he made a spring into the fore rigging. I shoved the handle of the lantern between my teeth, and followed. Plummer was coming; but the Second Mate pulled him back.

" 'That's sufficient,' he said. 'I'm going,' and he came up after me.

"We went over the foretop, racing like fiends. The light from the lantern prevented me from seeing to any distance in the darkness; but, at the crosstrees, Stubbins, who was some ratlines ahead, shouted out all at once, and in gasps:—

" 'They're fightin' …like …hell!'

" 'What?' called the Second Mate, breathlessly.

"Apparently, Stubbins did not hear him; for he made no reply. We cleared the crosstrees, and climbed into the r'gallant rigging. The wind was fairly fresh up there, and overhead, there sounded the flap, flap of sailcloth flying in the wind; but since we had left the deck, there had been no other sound from above.

"Now, abruptly, there came again a wild crying from the darkness over us. A strange, wild medley it was of screams for help, mixed up with violent, breathless curses.

"Beneath the royal yard, Stubbins halted, and looked down to me.

" 'Hurry hup… with ther… lantern… Jessop!' he shouted, catching his breath between the words. 'There'll be… murder done… hin a minute!'

"I reached him, and held the light up for him to catch. He stooped, and took it from me. Then, holding it above his head, he went a few ratlines higher. In this manner, he reached to a level with the royal yard. From my position, a little below him, the lantern seemed but to throw a few straggling, flickering rays along the spar; yet they showed me something. My first glance had been to wind'ard, and I had seen at once, that there was nothing on the weather yard arm. From there my gaze went to leeward. Indistinctly, I saw something upon the yard, that clung, struggling. Stubbins bent towards it with the light; thus I saw it more clearly. It was Jacobs, the Ordinary Seaman. He had his right arm tightly round the yard; with the other, he appeared to be fending himself from something on the other side of him, and further out upon the yard. At times, moans and gasps came from him, and sometimes curses. Once, as he appeared to be dragged partly from his hold, he screamed like a woman. His whole attitude suggested stubborn despair. I can scarcely tell you how this extraordinary sight affected me. I seemed to stare at it without realising that the affair was a real happening.

"During the few seconds which I had spent staring and breathless, Stubbins had climbed round the after side of the mast, and now I began again to follow him.

"From his position below me, the Second had not been able to see the thing that was occurring on the yard, and he sung out to me to know what was happening.

" 'It's Jacobs, Sir,' I called back. 'He seems to be fighting with some one to looard of him. I can't see very plainly yet.'

"Stubbins had got round onto the lee foot-rope, and now he held the lantern up, peering, and I made my way quickly alongside of him. The Second Mate followed; but instead of getting down on to the foot-rope, he got on the yard, and stood there holding on to the tie. He sung out for one of us to pass him up the lantern, which I did, Stubbins handing it to me. The Second held it out at arm's length, so that it lit up the lee part of the yard. The light showed through the darkness, as far as to where Jacobs struggled so weirdly. Beyond him, nothing was distinct.

"There had been a moment's delay while we were passing the lantern up to the Second Mate. Now, however, Stubbins and I moved out slowly along the foot-rope. We went slowly; but we did well to go at all, with any show of boldness; for the whole business was so abominably uncanny. It seems impossible to convey truly to you, the strange scene on the royal yard. You may be able to picture it to yourselves. The Second Mate standing upon the spar, holding the lantern; his body swaying with each roll of the ship, and his head craned forward as he peered along the yard. On our left, Jacobs, mad, fighting, cursing, praying, gasping; and outside of him, shadows and the night.

"The Second Mate spoke, abruptly.

" 'Hold on a moment!' he said. Then:—

" 'Jacobs!' he shouted. 'Jacobs, do you hear me?'

"There was no reply, only the continual gasping and cursing.

" 'Go on,' the Second Mate said to us. 'But be careful. Keep a tight hold!'

"He held the lantern higher, and we went out cautiously.

"Stubbins reached the Ordinary, and put his hand on his shoulder, with a soothing gesture.

" 'Steady hon now, Jacobs,' he said. 'Steady hon.'

"At his touch, as though by magic, the young fellow calmed down, and Stubbins—reaching round him—grasped the jackstay on the other side.

" 'Get a hold of him your side, Jessop,' he sung out. 'I'll get this side.'

"This, I did, and Stubbins climbed round him.

" 'There hain't no one here,' Stubbins called to me; but his voice expressed no surprise.

" 'What!' sung out the Second Mate. 'No one there! Where's Svensen, then?'

"I did not catch Stubbins's reply; for suddenly, it seemed to me that I saw something shadowy at the extreme end of the yard, out by the lift. I stared. It rose up, upon the yard, and I saw that it was the figure of a man. It grasped at the lift, and commenced to swarm up, quickly. It passed diagonally above Stubbins's head, and reached down a vague hand and arm.

" 'Look out! Stubbins!' I shouted. 'Look out!'

" 'What's hup now?' he called, in a startled voice. At the same instant, his cap went whirling away to leeward.

" 'Damn ther wind!' he burst out.

"Then, all at once, Jacobs, who had only been giving an occasional moan, commenced to shriek and struggle.

" 'Hold fast hon ter him!' Stubbins yelled. 'He'll be throwin' hisself hoff ther yard.'

"I put my left arm round the Ordinary's body—getting hold of the jackstay on the other side. Then I looked up. Above us, I seemed to see something dark and indistinct, that moved rapidly up the lift.

" 'Keep tight hold of him, while I get a gasket,' I heard the Second Mate sing out.

"A moment later there was a crash, and the light disappeared.

" 'Damn and set fire to the sail!' shouted the Second Mate.

"I twisted round, somewhat, and looked in his direction. I could dimly make him out on the yard. He had evidently been in the act of getting down on to the foot-rope, when the lantern was smashed. From him, my gaze jumped to the lee rigging. It seemed that I made out some shadowy thing stealing down through the darkness; but I could not be sure; and then, in a breath, it had gone.

" 'Anything wrong, Sir?' I called out.

" 'Yes,' he answered. 'I've dropped the lantern. The blessed sail knocked it out of my hand!'

" 'We'll be all right, Sir,' I replied. 'I think we can manage without it. Jacobs seems to be quieter now.'

" 'Well, be careful as you come in,' he warned us.

" 'Come on, Jacobs,' I said. 'Come on; we'll go down on deck.'

" 'Go along, young feller,' Stubbins put in. 'You're right now. We'll take care of you.' And we started to guide him along the yard.

"He went willingly enough; though without saying a word. He seemed like a child. Once or twice he shivered; but said nothing.

"We got him in to the lee rigging. Then, one going beside him, and the other keeping below, we made our way slowly down on deck. We went very slowly—so slowly, in fact, that the Second Mate—who had stayed a minute to shove the gasket round the lee side of the sail—was almost as soon down.

" 'Take Jacobs forrard to his bunk,' he said, and went away aft to where a crowd of the men, one with a lantern, stood round the door of an empty berth under the break of the poop on the starboard side.

"We hurried forrard to the fo'cas'le. There we found all in darkness.

" 'They're haft with Jock, and Svensen.' Stubbins had hesitated an instant before saying the name.

" 'Yes,' I replied. 'That's what it must have been, right enough.'

" 'I kind of knew it all ther time,' he said.

"I stepped in through the doorway, and struck a match. Stubbins followed, guiding Jacobs before him, and, together, we got him into his bunk. We covered him up with his blankets, for he was pretty shivery. Then we came out. During the whole time, he had not spoken a word.

"As we went aft, Stubbins remarked that he thought the business must have made him a bit dotty.

" 'It's driven him clean barmy,' he went on. 'He don't hunderstand a word that's said ter him.'

" 'He may be different in the morning,' I answered.

"As we neared the poop, and the crowd of waiting men, he spoke again:—

" 'They've put 'em hinter ther Second's hempty berth.'

" 'Yes,' I said. 'Poor beggars.'

"We reached the other men, and they opened out, and allowed us to get near the door. Several of them asked in low tones, whether Jacobs was all right, and I told them, Yes; not saying anything then about his condition.

"I got close up to the doorway, and looked into the berth. The lamp was lit, and I could see, plainly. There were two bunks in the place, and a man had been laid in each. The Skipper was there, leaning up against a bulkshead. He looked worried; but was silent—seeming to be mooding in his own thoughts. The Second Mate was busy with a couple of flags, which he was spreading over the bodies. The First Mate was talking, evidently telling him something; but his tone was so low that I caught his words, only with difficulty. It struck me that he seemed pretty subdued. I got parts of his sentences in patches, as it were.

" '...broken,' I heard him say. 'And the Dutchman....'

" 'I've seen him,' the Second Mate said, shortly.

" 'Two, straight off the reel,' said the Mate. '...three in....'

"The Second made no reply.

" 'Of course, yer know... accident.' The First Mate went on.

" 'Is it!' the Second said, in a queer voice.

"I saw the Mate glance at him, in a doubtful sort of way; but the Second was covering poor old Jock's dead face, and did not appear to notice his look.

" 'It—it—' the Mate said, and stopped.

"After a moment's hesitation, he said something further, that I could not catch; but there seemed a lot of funk in his voice.

"The Second Mate appeared not to have heard him; at any rate, he made no reply; but bent, and straightened out a corner of the flag over the rigid figure in the lower bunk. There was a certain niceness in his action which made me warm towards him.

" 'He's white!' I thought to myself.

"Out loud, I said:—

" 'We've put Jacobs into his bunk, Sir.'

"The Mate jumped; then whizzed round, and stared at me as though I had been a ghost. The Second Mate turned also; but before he could speak, the Skipper took a step towards me.

" 'Is he all right?' he asked.

" 'Well, Sir,' I said. 'He's a bit queer; but I think it's possible he may be better, after a sleep.'

" 'I hope so, too,' he replied, and stepped out on deck. He went towards the starboard poop ladder, walking slowly. The Second went and stood by the lamp, and the Mate, after a quick glance at him, came out and followed the Skipper up on to the poop. It occurred to me then, like a flash, that the man had stumbled upon a portion of the *truth*. This accident coming so soon after that other! It was evident that, in his mind, he had connected them. I recollected the fragments of his remarks to the Second Mate. Then, those many minor happenings that had cropped up at different times, and at which he had sneered. I wondered whether he would begin to comprehend their significance—their beastly, sinister significance.

" 'Ah! Mr. Bully-Mate,' I thought to myself. 'You're in for a bad time if you've begun to understand.'

"Abruptly, my thoughts jumped to the vague future before us.

" 'God help us!' I muttered.

"The Second Mate, after a look round, turned down the wick of the lamp, and came out, closing the door after him.

" 'Now, you men,' he said to the Mate's watch, 'get forrard; we can't do anything more. You'd better go and get some sleep.'

" 'i, i, Sir,' they said, in a chorus.

"Then, as we all turned to go forrard, he asked if any one had relieved the look-out.

" 'No, Sir,' answered Quoin.

" 'Is it yours?' the Second asked.

" 'Yes, Sir,' he replied.

" 'Hurry up and relieve him then,' the Second said.

" 'i, i, Sir,' the man answered, and went forrard with the rest of us.

"As we went, I asked Plummer who was at the wheel.

" 'Tom,' he said.

"As he spoke, several spots of rain fell, and I glanced up at the sky. It had become thickly clouded.

" 'Looks as if it were going to breeze up,' said.

" 'Yes,' he replied. 'We'll be shortenin' 'er down 'fore long.'

" 'May be an all-hands job,' I remarked.

" 'Yes,' he answered again. ' 'Twon't be no use their turnin'-in, if it is.'

"The man who was carrying the lantern, went into the fo'cas'le, and we followed.

" 'Where's ther one, belongin' to our side?' Plummer asked.

" 'Got smashed hupstairs,' answered Stubbing.

" ' 'ow were that?' Plummer inquired.

"Stubbins hesitated.

" 'The Second Mate dropped it,' I replied. 'The sail hit it, or something.'

"The men in the other watch seemed to have no immediate intention of turning-in; but sat in their bunks, and around on the chests. There was a general lighting of pipes, in the midst of which there came a sudden moan from one of the bunks in the forepart of the fo'cas'le—a part that was always a bit gloomy, and was more so now, on account of our having only one lamp.

" 'Wot's that?' asked one of the men belonging to the other side.

" 'S—sh !' said Stubbins. 'It's him.'

" ' 'oo?' inquired Plummer. 'Jacobs?'

" 'Yes,' I replied. 'Poor devil!'

" 'Wot were 'appenin' w'en yer got hup *ther?*' asked the man on the other side, indicating with a jerk of his head, the fore royal.

"Before I could reply, Stubbins jumped up from his sea-chest.

" 'Ther Second Mate's whistlin'!' he said. 'Come hon,' and he ran out on deck.

"Plummer, Jaskett and I followed quickly. Outside, it had started to rain pretty heavily. As we went, the Second Mate's voice came to us through the darkness.

" 'Stand by the main royal clewlines and buntlines,' I heard him shout, and the next instant came the hollow thutter of the sail as he started to lower away.

"In a few minutes we had it hauled up.

" 'Up and furl it, a couple of you,' he sung out.

"I went towards the starboard rigging; then I hesitated. No one else had moved.

"The Second Mate came among us.

" 'Come on now, lads,' he said. 'Make a move. It's got to be done.'

"Still, no one stirred, and no one answered.

" 'I'll go,' I said. 'If some one else will come.'

"Tammy came across to me.

" 'I'll come,' he volunteered, in a nervous voice.

" 'No, by God, no!' said the Second Mate, abruptly. He jumped into the main rigging himself. 'Come along, Jessop!' he shouted.

"I followed him; but I was astonished. I had fully expected him to get on to the other fellows' tracks like a ton of bricks. It had not occurred to me that he was making allowances. I was simply puzzled then; but afterwards it dawned upon me.

"No sooner had I followed the Second Mate, than, straightway, Stubbins, Plummer, and Jaskett came up after us at a run.

"About half-way to the maintop, the Second Mate stopped, and looked down.

" 'Who's that coming up below you, Jessop?' he asked.

"Before I could speak, Stubbins answered:—

" 'It's me, Sir, an' Plummer an' Jaskett.'

" 'Who the devil told you to come *now*? Go straight down, the lot of you!'

" 'We're comin' hup ter keep you company, Sir,' was his reply.

"At that, I was confident of a burst of temper from the Second; and yet, for the second time within a couple of minutes I was wrong. Instead of cursing Stubbins, he, after a moment's pause, went on up the rigging, without another word, and the rest of us followed. We reached the royal, and made short work of it; indeed, there were sufficient of us to have eaten it. When we had finished, I noticed that the Second Mate remained on the yard until we were all in the rigging. Evidently, he had determined to take a full share of any risk there might be; but I took care to keep pretty close to him; so as to be on hand if anything happened; yet we reached the deck again, without anything having occurred. I have said, without anything having occurred; but I am not really correct in this; for, as the Second Mate came down over the cross-trees, he gave a short, abrupt cry.

" 'Anything wrong, Sir?' I asked.

" 'No—o !' he said. 'Nothing! I banged my knee.'

"And yet *now*, I believe he was lying. For, that same watch, I was to hear men giving just such cries; but, God knows, they had reason enough.

X

Hands That Plucked

Directly we reached the deck, the Second Mate gave the order:—

" 'Mizzen t'gallant clewlines and buntlines,' and led the way up on to the poop. He went and stood by the haulyards, ready to lower away. As I walked across to the starboard clewline, I saw that the Old Man was on deck, and as I took hold of the rope, I heard him sing out to the Second Mate.

" 'Call all hands to shorten sail, Mr. Tulipson.'

" 'Very good, Sir,' the Second Mate replied. Then he raised his voice:—

" 'Go forrard, you, Jessop, and call all hands to shorten sail. You'd better give them a call in the bosun's place, as you go.'

" 'i, i, Sir,' I sung out, and hurried off.

"As I went, I heard him tell Tammy to go down and call the Mate.

"Reaching the fo'cas'le, I put my head in through the starboard doorway, and found some of the men beginning to turn-in.

" 'It's all hands on deck, shorten sail,' I sung out.

"I stepped inside.

" 'Just wot I said,' grumbled one of the men.

" 'They don't damn well think we're goin' aloft to-night, after what's happened?' asked another.

" 'We've been up to the main royal,' I answered. 'The Second Mate went with us.'

" 'Wot?' said the first man. 'Ther Second Mate hisself?'

" 'Yes,' I replied. 'The whole blooming watch went up.'

" 'An' wot 'appened?' he asked.

" 'Nothing,' I said. 'Nothing at all. We just made a mouthful apiece of it, and came down again.'

" 'All the same,' remarked the second man, 'I don't fancy goin' upstairs, after what's happened.'

" 'Well,' I replied. 'It's not a matter of fancy. We've got to get the sail off her, or there'll be a mess. One of the 'prentices told me the glass is falling.'

" 'Come erlong, boys. We've got ter du it,' said one of the older men, rising from a chest, at this point. 'What's it duin' outside, mate?'

" 'Raining,' I said. 'You'll want your oilskins.'

"I hesitated a moment before going on deck again. From the bunk forrard among the shadows, I had seemed to hear a faint moan.

" 'Poor beggar!' I thought to myself.

"Then the old chap who had last spoken, broke in upon my attention.

" 'It's awl right, mate!' he said, rather testily. 'Yer needn't wait. We'll be out in er minit.'

" 'That's all right. I wasn't thinking about you lot,' I replied, and walked forrard to Jacobs' bunk. Some time before, he had rigged up a pair of curtains, cut out of an old sack, to keep off the draught. These, some one had drawn, so that I had to pull them aside to see him. He was lying on his back, breathing in a queer, jerky fashion. I could not see his face, plainly; but it seemed rather pale, in the half-light.

" 'Jacobs,' I said. 'Jacobs, how do you feel now?' but he made no sign to show that he had heard me. And so, after a few moments, I drew the curtains to again, and left him.

" 'What like does 'e seem?' asked one of the fellows, as I went towards the door.

" 'Bad,' I said. 'Damn bad! I think the Steward ought to be told to come and have a look at him. I'll mention it to the Second when I get a chance.'

"I stepped out on deck, and ran aft again to give them a hand with the sail. We got it hauled up, and then went forrard to the fore t'gallant. And, a minute later, the other watch were out, and, with the Mate, were busy at the main.

"By the time the main was ready for making fast, we had the fore hauled up, so that now all three t'gallants were in the ropes, and ready for stowing. Then came the order:—

" 'Up aloft and furl!'

" 'Up with you, lads,' the Second Mate said. 'Don't let's have any hanging back this time.'

"Away aft by the main, the men in the Mate's watch seemed to be standing in a clump by the mast; but it was too dark to see clearly. I heard the Mate start to curse; then there came a growl, and he shut up.

" 'Be handy, men! be handy!' the Second Mate sung out.

"At that, Stubbins jumped into the rigging.

" 'Come hon!' he shouted. 'We'll have ther bloomin' sail fast, an' down hon deck again before they're started.'

"Plummer followed; then Jaskett, I, and Quoin who had been called down off the look-out to give a hand.

" 'That's the style, lads!' the Second sung out, encouragingly. Then he ran aft to the Mate's crowd. I heard him and the Mate talking to the men, and presently, when we were going over the foretop, I made out that they were beginning to get into the rigging.

"I found out, afterwards, that as soon as the Second Mate had seen them off the deck, he went up to the mizzen t'gallant, along with the four 'prentices.

"On our part, we made our way slowly aloft, keeping one hand for ourselves and the other for the ship, as you can fancy. In this manner we had gone as far as the crosstrees, at least, Stubbins, who was first, had; when, all at once, he gave out just another such cry as had the Second Mate a little earlier, only that in his case he followed it by turning round and blasting Plummer.

" 'You might have blarsted well sent me flyin' down hon deck,' he shouted. 'If you bl—dy well think it's a joke, try it hon some one else—'

" 'It wasn't me!' interrupted Plummer. 'I 'aven't touched yer. 'oo the 'ell are yer swearin' at?'

" 'At you—!' I heard him reply; but what more he may have said, was lost in a loud shout from Plummer.

" 'What's up, Plummer?' I sung out. 'For God's sake, you two, don't get fighting, up aloft!'

"But a loud, frightened curse was all the answer he gave. Then straightway, he began to shout at the top of his voice, and in the lulls of his noise, I caught the voice of Stubbins, cursing savagely.

" 'They'll come down with a run!' I shouted, helplessly. 'They'll come down as sure as nuts.'

"I caught Jaskett by the boot.

" 'What are they doing? What are they doing?' I sung out. 'Can't you see?' I shook his leg as I spoke. But at my touch, the old idiot—as I thought him at the moment—began to shout in a frightened voice:—

"Oh! oh! help! hel—!'

" 'Shut up!' I bellowed. 'Shut up, you old fool! If you won't do anything, let me get past you!"

"Yet he only cried out the more. And then, abruptly, I caught the sound of a frightened clamour of men's voices, away down somewhere about the maintop— curses, cries of fear, even shrieks, and above it all, someone shouting to go down on deck:—

" 'Get down! get down! down! down! Blarst—' The rest was drowned in a fresh outburst of hoarse crying in the night.

"I tried to get past old Jaskett; but he was clinging to the rigging, sprawled onto it, is the best way to describe his attitude, so much of it as I could see in the darkness. Up above him, Stubbins and Plummer still shouted and cursed, and the shrouds quivered and shook, as though the two were fighting desperately.

"Stubbins seemed to be shouting something definite; but whatever it was, I could not catch.

"At my helplessness, I grew angry, and shook and prodded Jaskett, to make him move.

" 'Damn you, Jaskett!' I roared. 'Damn you for a funky old fool! Let me get past! Let me get past, will you!'

"But, instead of letting me pass, I found that he was beginning to make his way down. At that, I caught him by the slack of his trousers, near the stern, with my right hand, and with the other, I got hold of the after shroud somewhere above his left hip; by these means, I fairly hoisted myself up onto the old fellow's back. Then, with my right, I could reach to the forrard shroud, over his right shoulder, and having got a grip, I shifted my left to a level with it; at the same moment, I was able to get my foot on to the splice of a ratline and so give myself a further lift. Then I paused an instant, and glanced up.

" 'Stubbins! Stubbins!' I shouted. 'Plummer! Plummer!'

"And even as I called, Plummer's foot—reaching down through the gloom—alighted full on my upturned face. I let go from the rigging with my right hand, and struck furiously at his leg, cursing him for his clumsiness. He lifted his foot, and in the same instant a sentence from Stubbins floated down to me, with a strange distinctness:—

" *'For God's sake tell 'em ter get down hon deck!'* he was shouting.

"Even as the words came to me, something in the darkness gripped my waist. I made a desperate clutch at the rigging with my disengaged right hand, and it was well for me that I secured the hold so quickly; for the same instant, I was wrenched at with a brutal ferocity that appalled me. I said nothing, but lashed out into the night with my left foot. It is queer, but I cannot say with certainty that I struck anything; I was too downright desperate with funk, to be sure; and yet it seemed to me that my foot encountered something soft, that gave under the blow. It may have been nothing more than an imagined sensation; yet I am inclined to think otherwise; for, instantly, the hold about my waist was released; and I commenced to scramble down, clutching the shrouds pretty desperately.

"I have only a very uncertain remembrance of that which followed. Whether I slid over Jaskett, or whether he gave way to me, I cannot tell. I know only that I reached the deck, a blind whirl of fear and excitement, and the next thing I remember, I was among a crowd of shouting, half-mad sailor-men.

XI

The Search for Stubbins

IN A CONFUSED WAY, I was conscious that the Skipper and the Mates were down among us, trying to get us into some state of calmness. Eventually they succeeded, and we were told to go aft to the Saloon door, which we did in a body. Here, the Skipper himself served out a large tot of rum to each of us. Then, at his orders, the Second Mate called the roll.

"He called over the Mate's watch first, and everyone answered. Then he came to ours, and he must have been much agitated; for the first name he sung out was Jock's.

"Among us there came a moment of dead silence, and I noticed the wail and moan of the wind aloft, and the flap, flap of the three unfurled t'gallan's'ls.

"The Second Mate called the next name, hurriedly:—

" 'Jaskett,' he sung out.

" 'Sir,' Jaskett answered.

" 'Quoin.'

" 'Yes, Sir.'

" 'Jessop.'

" 'Sir,' I replied.

" 'Stubbins.'

"There was no answer.

" 'Stubbins,' again called the Second Mate.

"Again there was no reply.

" 'Is Stubbins here?—any one!' The Second's voice sounded sharp and anxious.

"There was a moment's pause. Then one of the men spoke:—

" 'He's not here, Sir.'

" 'Who saw him last?' the Second asked.

"Plummer stepped forward into the light that streamed through the Saloon doorway. He had on neither coat nor cap, and his shirt seemed to be hanging about him in tatters.

" 'It were me, Sir,' he said.

"The Old Man, who was standing next to the Second Mate, took a pace towards him, and stopped and stared; but it was the Second who spoke.

" 'Where?' he asked.

" ' 'e were just above me, in ther crosstrees, when, when—' the man broke off short.

" 'Yes! yes!' the Second Mate replied. Then he turned to the Skipper.

" 'Someone will have to go up, Sir, and see—' He hesitated.

" 'But—' said the Old Man, and stopped.

"The Second Mate cut in.

" 'I shall go up, for one, Sir,' he said, quietly.

"Then he turned back to the crowd of us.

" 'Tammy,' he sung out. 'Get a couple of lamps out of the lamp-locker.'

" 'i, i, Sir,' Tammy replied, and ran off.

" 'Now,' said the Second Mate, addressing us, 'I want a couple of men to jump aloft along with me, and take a look for Stubbins.'

"Not a man replied. I would have liked to step out and offer; but the memory of that horrible clutch was with me, and for the life of me, I could not summon up the courage.

" 'Come! come, men!' he said. 'We can't leave him up there. We shall take lanterns. Who'll come now?'

"I walked out to the front. I was in a horrible funk; but, for very shame, I could not stand back any longer.

" 'I'll come with you, Sir,' I said, not very loud, and feeling fairly twisted up with nervousness.

" 'That's more the tune, Jessop !' he replied, in a tone that made me glad I had stood out.

"At this point, Tammy came up, with the lights. He brought them to the Second, who took one, and told him to give the other to me. The Second Mate held his light above his head, and looked round at the hesitating men.

" 'Now, men!' he sung out. 'You're not going to let Jessop and me go up alone. Come along, another one or two of you! Don't act like a damned lot of cowards!'

"Quoin stood out, and spoke for the crowd.

" 'I dunno as we're actin' like cowyards, Sir; but just look at '*im*,' and he pointed at Plummer, who still stood full in the light from the Saloon doorway.

" 'What sort of a Thing is it as 'as done that, Sir?' he went on. 'An' then yer arsks us ter go up agen! It aren't likely as we're in a 'urry.'

"The Second Mate looked at Plummer, and surely, as I have before mentioned, the poor beggar was in a state; his ripped-up shirt was fairly flapping in the breeze that came through the doorway.

"The Second looked; yet he said nothing. It was as though the realisation of Plummer's condition had left him without a word more to say. It was Plummer himself who finally broke the silence.

" 'I'll come with yer, Sir,' he said. 'Only yer ought ter 'ave more light than them two lanterns. 'Twon't be no use, unless we 'as plenty ei light.'

"The man had grit; and I was astonished at his offering to go, after what he must have gone through. Yet, I was to have even a greater astonishment; for, abruptly, the Skipper—who all this time had scarcely spoken—stepped forward a pace, and put his hand on the Second Mate's shoulder.

" 'I'll come with you, Mr. Tulipson,' he said.

"The Second Mate twisted his head round, and stared at him a moment, in astonishment. Then he opened his mouth.

" 'No, Sir; I don't think—' he began.

" 'That's sufficient, Mr. Tulipson,' the Old Man interrupted. 'I've made up my mind.'

"He turned to the First Mate, who had stood by without a word.

" 'Mr. Grainge,' he said. 'Take a couple of the 'prentices down with you, and pass out a box of blue-lights and some flare-ups.'

"The Mate answered something, and hurried away into the Saloon, with the two 'prentices in his watch. Then the Old Man spoke to the men.

" 'Now, men!' he began. 'This is no time for dilly-dallying. The Second Mate and I will go aloft, and I want about half a dozen of you to come along with us, and carry lights. Plummer and Jessop here, have volunteered. I want four or five more of you. Step out now, some of you!'

"There was no hesitation whatever, now; and the first man to come forward was Quoin. After him followed three of the Mate's crowd, and then old Jaskett.

" 'That will do; that will do,' said the Old Man.

"He turned to the Second Mate.

" 'Has Mr. Grainge come with those lights yet?' he asked, with a certain irritability.

" 'Here, Sir,' said the First Mate's voice, behind him in the Saloon doorway. He had the box of blue-lights in his hands, and behind him came the two boys carrying the flares.

"The Skipper took the box from him, with a quick gesture, and opened it.

" 'Now, one of you men, come here,' he ordered.

"One of the men in the Mate's watch, ran to him.

"He took several of the lights from the box, and handed them to the man.

" 'See here,' he said. 'When we go aloft, you get into the foretop, and keep one of these going all the time, do you hear?'

" 'Yes, Sir,' replied the man.

" 'You know how to strike them?' the Skipper asked, abruptly.

" 'Yes, Sir,' he answered.

"The Skipper sung out to the Second Mate:—

" 'Where's that boy of yours—Tammy, Mr. Tulipson?'

" 'Here, Sir,' said Tammy, answering for himself.

"The Old Man took another light from the box.

" 'Listen to me, boy!' he said. 'Take this, and stand by on the forrard deck house.

When we go aloft, you must give us a light until the man gets his going in the top. You understand?'

" 'Yes, Sir,' answered Tammy, and took the light.

" 'One minute!' said the Old Man, and stooped and took a second light from the box. 'Your first light may go out before we're ready. You'd better have another, in case it does.'

"Tammy took the second light, and moved away.

" 'Those flares all ready for lighting there, Mr. Grainge?' the Captain asked.

" 'All ready, Sir,' replied the Mate.

"The Old Man pushed one of the blue-lights into his coat pocket, and stood upright.

" 'Very well,' he said. 'Give each of the men one apiece. And just see that they all have matches.'

"He spoke to the men particularly:—

" 'As soon as we are ready, the other two men in the Mate's watch will get up into the cranelines, and keep their flares going there. Take your paraffin tins with you. When we reach the upper topsail, Quoin and Jaskett will get out on to the yardarms, and show their flares there. Be careful to keep your lights away from the sails. Plummer and Jessop will come up with the Second Mate and myself. Does every man clearly understand?'

" 'Yes, Sir,' said the men in a chorus.

"A sudden idea seemed to occur to the Skipper, and he turned, and went through the doorway into the Saloon. In about a minute, he came back, and handed something to the Second Mate, that shone in the light from the lanterns. I saw that it was a revolver, and he held another in his other hand, and this I saw him put into his side pocket.

"The Second Mate held the pistol a moment, looking a bit doubtful.

" 'I don't think, Sir—' he began. But the Skipper cut him short.

" 'You don't know!' he said. 'Put it in your pocket.'

"Then he turned to the First Mate.

" 'You will take charge of the deck, Mr. Grainge, while we're aloft,' he said.

" 'i, i, Sir,' the Mate answered, and sung out to one of his 'prentices to take the blue-light box back into the cabin.

"The Old Man turned, and led the way forrard. As we went, the light from the two lanterns shone upon the decks, showing the litter of the t'gallant gear. The ropes were foul of one another in a regular 'bunch o' buffers.' This had been caused, I suppose, by the crowd trampling over them in their excitement, when they reached the deck. And then, suddenly, as though the sight had waked me up to a more vivid comprehension, you know, it came to me new and fresh, how damned strange was the whole business…. I got a little touch of despair, and asked myself what was going to be the end of all these beastly happenings. You can understand?

"Abruptly, I heard the Skipper shouting, away forrard. He was singing out to Tammy to get up on to the house with his blue-light. We reached the fore rigging, and, the same instant, the strange, ghastly flare of Tammy's blue-light burst out into the night, causing every rope, sail, and spar to jump out weirdly.

"I saw now that the Second Mate was already in the starboard rigging, with his lantern. He was shouting to Tammy to keep the drip from his light, clear of the staysail, which was stowed upon the house. Then, from somewhere on the port side, I heard the Skipper shout to us to hurry.

" 'Smartly now, you men,' he was saying. 'Smartly now.'

"The man who had been told to take up a station in the foretop, was just behind the Second Mate. Plummer was a couple of ratlines lower.

"I caught the Old Man's voice again.

" 'Where's Jessop with that other lantern?' I heard him shout.

" 'Here, Sir,' I sung out.

" 'Bring it over this side,' he ordered. 'You don't want the two lanterns on one side.'

"I ran round the fore side of the house. Then I saw him. He was in the rigging, and making his way smartly aloft. One of the Mate's watch and Quoin were with him. This, I saw as I came round the house. Then I made a jump, gripped the sherpole, and swung myself up onto the rail. And then, all at once, Tammy's blue-light went out, and there came, what seemed by contrast, pitchy darkness. I stood where I was—one foot on the rail, and my knee upon the sherpole. The light from my lantern seemed no more than a sickly yellow glow against the gloom, and higher, some forty or fifty feet, and a few ratlines below the futtock rigging on the starboard side, there was another glow of yellowness in the night. Apart from these, all was blackness. And then from above—high above—there wailed down through the darkness a weird, sobbing cry. What it was, I do not know; but it sounded horrible.

"The Skipper's voice came down, jerkily.

" 'Smartly with that light, boy!' he shouted. And the blue glare blazed out again, almost before he had finished speaking.

"I stared up at the Skipper. He was standing where I had seen him before the light went out, and so were the two men. As I looked, he commenced to climb again. I glanced across to starboard. Jaskett, and the other man in the Mate's watch, were about midway between the deck of the house and the foretop. Their faces showed extraordinarily pale in the dead glare of the blue-light. Higher, I saw the Second Mate in the futtock rigging, holding his light up over the edge of the top. Then he went further, and disappeared. The man with the blue-lights followed, and also vanished from view. On the port side, and more directly above me, the Skipper's feet were just stepping out of the futtock shrouds. At that, I made haste to follow.

"Then, suddenly, when I was close under the top, there came from above me the sharp flare of a blue-light, and almost in the same instant, Tammy's went out.

"I glanced down at the decks. They were filled with flickering, grotesque shadows cast by the dripping light above. A group of the men stood by the port galley door—their faces upturned and pale and unreal under the gleam of the light. Then I was in the futtock rigging, and a moment afterwards, standing in the top, beside the Old Man. He was shouting to the men who had gone out on the cranelines. It seemed that the man on the port side was bungling; but at last—nearly a minute after the other man had lit his flare—he got his going. In that time, the man in the top had lit his second blue-light, and we were ready to get into the top-mast rigging. First, however, the Skipper leant over the after side of the top, and sung out to the First Mate to send a man up on to the fo'cas'le head with a flare. The Mate replied, and then we started again, the Old Man leading.

"Fortunately, the rain had ceased, and there seemed to be no increase in the wind; indeed, if anything, there appeared to be rather less; yet what there was drove the flames of the flare-ups out into occasional, twisting serpents of fire at least a yard long.

"About half-way up the topmast rigging, the Second Mate sung out to the Skipper, to know whether Plummer should light his flare; but the Old Man said he had better wait until we reached the crosstrees, as then he could get out away from the gear to where there would be less danger of setting fire to anything.

" We neared the crosstrees, and the Old Man stooped and sung out to me to pass him the lantern by Quoin. A few ratlines more, and both he and the Second Mate stopped almost simultaneously, holding their lanterns as high as possible, and peered up into the darkness.

" 'See any signs of him, Mr. Tulipson?' the Old Man asked.

" 'No, Sir,' replied the Second. 'Not a sign.'

"He raised his voice.

" 'Stubbins,' he sung out. 'Stubbins, are you there?'

"We listened; but nothing came to us beyond the blowing moan of the wind, and the flap, flap of the bellying t'gallant above.

"The Second Mate climbed over the crosstrees, and Plummer followed. The man got out by the royal backstay, and lit his flare. By its light we could see, plainly; but there was no vestige of Stubbins, so far as the light went.

" 'Get out onto the yard-arms with those flares, you two men,' shouted the Skipper. 'Be smart now! Keep them away from the sail!'

"The men got on to the foot-ropes—Quoin on the port, and Jaskett on the starboard, side. By the light from Plummer's flare, I could see them clearly, as they lay out upon the yard. It occurred to me that they went gingerly—which is no surprising thing. And then, as they drew near to the yard-arms, they passed beyond the brilliance of the light; so that I could not see them clearly. A few seconds passed, and then the light from Quoin's flare streamed out upon the wind; yet nearly a minute went by, and there was no sign of Jaskett's.

"Then out from the semi-darkness at the starboard yard-arm, there came a curse from Jaskett, followed almost immediately by a noise of something vibrating.

" 'What's up?' shouted the Second Mate. 'What's up, Jaskett?'

" 'It's ther foot-rope, Sir-r-r!' he drew out the last word into a sort of gasp.

"The Second Mate bent quickly, with the lantern. I craned round the after side of the topmast, and looked.

" 'What is the matter, Mr. Tulipson?' I heard the Old Man singing out.

"Out on the yard arm, Jaskett began to shout for help, and then, all at once, in the light from the Second Mate's lantern, I saw that the starboard foot-rope on the upper topsail yard was being violently shaken—savagely shaken, is perhaps a better word. And then, almost in the same instant, the Second Mate shifted the lantern from his right to his left hand. He put the right into his pocket and brought out his gun with a jerk. He extended his hand and arm, as though pointing at something a little below the yard. Then a quick flash spat out across the shadows, followed immediately by a sharp, ringing crack. In the same moment, I saw that the footrope ceased to shake.

" 'Light your flare! Light your flare, Jaskett!' the Second shouted. 'Be smart now!'

"Out at the yard-arm there came the splutter of a match, and then, straightway, a great spurt of fire as the flare took light.

" 'That's better, Jaskett. You're all right now!' the Second Mate called out to him.

" 'What was it, Mr. Tulipson?' I heard the Skipper ask.

"I looked up, and saw that he had sprung across to where the Second Mate was standing. The Second Mate explained to him; but he did not speak loud enough for me to catch what he said.

"I had been struck by Jaskett's attitude, when the light of his flare had first revealed him. He had been crouched with his right knee cocked over the yard, and his left leg down between it and the foot-rope, while his elbows had been crooked over the yard for support as he was lighting the flare. Now, however, he had slid both feet back on to the foot-rope, and was lying on his belly, over the yard, with the flare held a little below the head of the sail. It was thus, with the light being on the fore side of the sail, that I saw a small hole a little below the foot-rope, through which a ray of the light shone. It was undoubtedly the hole which the bullet from the Second Mate's revolver had made in the sail.

"Then I heard the Old Man shouting to Jaskett.

" 'Be careful with that flare there!' he sung out. 'You'll be having that sail scorched!'

"He left the Second Mate, and came back on to the port side of the mast.

"To my right, Plummer's flare seemed to be dwindling. I glanced up at his face through the smoke. He was paying no attention to it; instead, he was staring up above his head.

" 'Shove some paraffin on to it, Plummer,' I called to him. 'It'll be out in a minute.'

"He looked down quickly to the light, and did as I suggested. Then he held it out at arm's length, and peered up again into the darkness.

" 'See anything?' asked the Old Man, suddenly observing his attitude.

"Plummer glanced at him, with a start.

" 'It's ther r'yal, Sir,' he explained. 'It's all adrift.'

" 'What!' said the Old Man.

"He was standing a few ratlines up the t'gallant rigging, and he bent his body outwards to get a better look.

" 'Mr. Tulipson!' he shouted. 'Do you know that the royal's all adrift?'

" 'No, Sir,' answered the Second Mate. 'If it is, it's more of this devilish work!"

" 'It's adrift right enough,' said the Skipper, and he and the Second went a few ratlines higher, keeping level with one another.

"I had now got above the crosstrees, and was just at the Old Man's heels.

"Suddenly, he shouted out:—

" 'There he is! —Stubbins! Stubbins!'

" 'Where, Sir?' asked the Second, eagerly. 'I can't see him!'

" 'There! there!' replied the Skipper, pointing.

"I leant out from the rigging, and looked up along his back, in the direction his finger indicated. At first, I could see nothing; then, slowly, you know, there grew upon my sight a dim figure crouching upon the bunt of the royal, and partly hidden by the mast. I stared, and gradually it came to me that there was a couple of them, and further out upon the yard, a hump that might have been anything, and was only visible indistinctly amid the flutter of the canvas.

" 'Stubbins!' the Skipper sung out. 'Stubbins, come down out of that! Do you hear me?'

"But no one came, and there was no answer.

" 'There's two—' I began; but he was shouting again:—

" 'Come down out of that! Do you damned well hear me?'

"Still there was no reply.

" 'I'm hanged if I can see him at all, Sir!' the Second Mate called out from his side of the mast.

" 'Can't see him!' said the Old Man, now thoroughly angry. 'I'll soon let you see him!'

"He bent down to me with the lantern.

" 'Catch hold, Jessop,' he said, which I did.

"Then he pulled the blue-light from his pocket, and as he was doing so, I saw the Second peek round the back side of the mast at him. Evidently, in the uncertain light, he must have mistaken the Skipper's action; for, all at once, he shouted out in a frightened voice:—

" 'Don't shoot, Sir! For God's sake, don't shoot!'

" 'Shoot be damned!' exclaimed the Old Man. 'Watch!'

"He pulled off the cap of the light.

" 'There's two of them, Sir,' I called again to him.

" 'What!' he said in a loud voice, and at the same instant he rubbed the end of the light across the gap, and it burst into fire.

"He held it up so that it lit the royal yard like day, and straightway, a couple of shapes dropped silently from the royal on to the t'gallant yard. At the same moment, the humped something, midway out upon the yard, rose up. It ran in to the mast, and I lost sight of it.

" ' —God!' I heard the Skipper gasp, and he fumbled in his side pocket.

"I saw the two figures which had dropped on to the t'gallant, run swiftly along the yard—one to the starboard and the other to the port yard-arms.

"On the other side of the mast, the Second Mate's pistol cracked out twice, sharply. Then, from over my head the Skipper fired twice, and then again; but with what effect, I could not tell. Abruptly, as he fired his last shot, I was aware of an indistinct Something, gliding down the starboard royal backstay. It was descending full upon Plummer, who, all unconscious of the thing, was staring towards the t'gallant yard.

" 'Look out above you, Plummer!' I almost shrieked.

" 'What? where?' he called, and grabbed at the stay, and waved his flare, excitedly.

"Down on the upper topsail yard, Quoin's and Jaskett's voices rose simultaneously, and in the identical instant, their flares went out. Then Plummer shouted, and his light went utterly. There were left only the two lanterns, and the blue-light held by the Skipper, and that, a few seconds afterwards, finished and died out.

"The Skipper and the Second Mate were shouting to the men upon the yard, and I heard them answer, in shaky voices. Out on the crosstrees, I could see, by the light from my lantern, that Plummer was holding in a dazed fashion to the backstay.

" 'Are you all right, Plummer?' I called.

" 'Yes,' he said, after a little pause; and then he swore.

" 'Come in off that yard, you men!' the Skipper was singing out. 'Come in! come in!'

"Down on deck, I heard some one calling; but could not distinguish the words. Above me, pistol in hand, the Skipper was glancing about, uneasily.

" 'Hold up that light, Jessop,' he said. 'I can't see!'

"Below us, the men got off the yard, into the rigging.

" 'Down on deck with you!' ordered the Old Man. 'As smartly as you can!'

" 'Come in off there, Plummer!' sung out the Second Mate. 'Get down with the others!'

" 'Down with you, Jessop!' said the Skipper, speaking rapidly. 'Down with you!'

"I got over the crosstrees, and he followed. On the other side, the Second Mate was level with us. He had passed his lantern to Plummer, and I caught the glint of his revolver in his right hand. In this fashion, we reached the top. The man who had been stationed there with the blue-lights, had gone. Afterwards, I found that he went down on deck as soon as they were finished. There was no sign of the man with the flare on the starboard craneline. He also, I learnt later, had slid down one of the backstays on to the deck, only a very short while before we reached the top. He swore that a great black shadow of a man had come suddenly upon him from aloft. When I heard that, I remembered the thing I had seen descending upon Plummer. Yet the man who had gone out upon the port craneline—the one who had bungled with the lighting of his flare—was still where we had left him; though his light was burning now but dimly.

" 'Come in out of that, *you!*' the Old Man sung out. 'Smartly now, and get down on deck!'

" 'i, i, Sir,' the man replied, and started to make his way in.

"The Skipper waited until he had got into the main rigging, and then he told me to get down out of the top. He was in the act of following, when, all at once, there rose a loud outcry on deck, and then came the sound of a man screaming.

" 'Get out of my way, Jessop!' the Skipper roared, and swung himself down alongside of me.

"I heard the Second Mate shout something from the starboard rigging. Then we were all racing down as hard as we could go. I had caught a momentary glimpse of a man running from the doorway on the port side of the fo'cas'le. In less than half a minute we were upon the deck, and among a crowd of the men who were grouped round something. Yet, strangely enough, they were not looking at the thing among them; but away aft at something in the darkness.

" 'It's on the rail!' cried several voices.

" 'Overboard!' called somebody, in an excited voice. 'It's jumped over the side!'

" 'Ther' wer'n't nothin'!' said a man in the crowd.

" 'Silence!' shouted the Old Man. 'Where's the Mate? What's happened?'

" 'Here, Sir,' called the First Mate, shakily, from near the centre of the group. 'It's Jacobs, Sir. He—he—'

" 'What!' said the Skipper. 'What!'

" 'He—he's—he's dead—I think!' said the First Mate, in jerks.

" 'Let me see,' said the Old Man, in a quieter tone.

"The men had stood to one side to give him room, and he knelt beside the man upon the deck.

" 'Pass the lantern here, Jessop,' he said.

"I stood by him, and held the light. The man was lying face downwards on the deck. Under the light from the lantern, the Skipper turned him over and looked at him.

" 'Yes,' he said, after a short examination. 'He's dead.'

"He stood up and regarded the body a moment, in silence. Then he turned to the Second Mate, who had been standing by, during the last couple of minutes.

" 'Three!' he said, in a grim undertone.

"The Second Mate nodded, and cleared his voice.

"He seemed on the point of saying something; then he turned and looked at Jacobs, and said nothing.

" 'Three,' repeated the Old Man. 'Since eight bells!'

"He stooped and looked again at Jacobs.

" 'Poor devil! poor devil!' he muttered.

"The Second Mate grunted some of the huskiness out of his throat, and spoke.

" 'Where must we take him?' he asked, quietly. 'The two bunks are full.'

" 'You'll have to put him down on the deck by the lower bunk,' replied the Skipper.

"As they carried him away, I heard the Old Man make a sound that was almost a groan. The rest of the men had gone forrard, and I do not think he realised that I was standing by him.

" 'My God! O, my God!' he muttered, and began to walk slowly aft.

"He had cause enough for groaning. There were three dead, and Stubbins had gone utterly and completely. We never saw him again.

XII

The Council

A FEW MINUTES LATER, the Second Mate came forrard again. I was still standing near the rigging, holding the lantern, in an aimless sort of way.

" 'That you, Plummer?' he asked.

" 'No, Sir,' I said. 'It's Jessop.'

" 'Where's Plummer, then?' he inquired.

" 'I don't know, Sir,' I answered. 'I expect he's gone forrard. Shall I go and tell him you want him?'

" 'No, there's no need,' he said. 'Tie your lamp up in the rigging—on the sherpole there. Then go and get his, and shove it up on the starboard side. After that you'd better go aft and give the two 'prentices a hand in the lamp locker.'

" 'i, i, Sir,' I replied, and proceeded to do as he directed. After I had got the light from Plummer, and lashed it up to the starboard sherpole, I hurried aft. I found Tammy and the other 'prentice in our watch, busy in the locker, lighting lamps.

" 'What are we doing?' I asked.

" 'The Old Man's given orders to lash all the spare lamps we can find, in the rigging, so as to have the decks light,' said Tammy. 'And a damned good job too!'

"He handed me a couple of the lamps, and took two himself.

" 'Come on,' he said, and stepped out on deck. 'We'll fix these in the main rigging, and then I want to talk to you.'

" 'What about the mizzen?' I inquired.

" 'Oh,' he replied. 'He' (meaning the other 'prentice) 'will see to that. Anyway, it'll be daylight directly.'

"We shoved the lamps up on the sherpoles—two on each side. Then he came across to me.

" 'Look here, Jessop!' he said, without any hesitation. 'You'll have to jolly well tell the Skipper and the Second Mate all you know about all this.'

" 'How do you mean?' I asked.

" 'Why, that it's something about the ship herself that's the cause of what's happened,' he replied. 'If you'd only explained to the Second Mate when I told you to, this might never have been!'

" 'But I don't *know*,' I said. 'I may be all wrong. It's only an idea of mine. I've no proofs—'

" 'Proofs!' he cut in with. 'Proofs! what about tonight? We've had all the proofs ever I want!'

"I hesitated before answering him.

" 'So have I, for that matter,' I said, at length. 'What I mean is, I've nothing that the Skipper and the Second Mate would consider as proofs. They'd never listen seriously to me.'

" 'They'd listen fast enough,' he replied. 'After what's happened this watch, they'd listen to anything. Anyway, it's jolly well your duty to tell them!'

" 'What could they do, anyway?' I said, despondently. 'As things are going, we'll all be dead before another week is over, at this rate.'

" 'You tell them,' he answered. 'That's what you've got to do. If you can only get them to realise that you're right, they'll be glad to put into the nearest port, and send us all ashore.'

"I shook my head.

" 'Well, anyway, they'll have to do something,' he replied, in answer to my gesture. 'We can't go round the Horn, with the number of men we've lost. We haven't enough to handle her, if it comes on to blow.'

" 'You've forgotten, Tammy,' I said. 'Even if I could get the Old Man to believe I'd got at the truth of the matter, he couldn't do anything. Don't you see, if I'm right, we couldn't even see the land, if we made it. We're like blind men....'

" 'What on earth do you mean?' he interrupted. 'How do you make out we're like blind men? Of course we could see the land—'

" 'Wait a minute! wait a minute!' I said. 'You don't understand. Didn't I tell you?'

" 'Tell what?' he asked.

" 'About the ship I spotted,' I said. 'I thought you knew!'

" 'No,' he said. 'When?'

" 'Why,' I replied. 'You know when the Old Man sent me away from the wheel?'

" 'Yes,' he answered. 'You mean in the morning watch, day before yesterday?'

" 'Yes,' I said. 'Well, don't you know what was the matter?'

" 'No,' he replied. 'That is, I heard you were snoozing at the wheel, and the Old Man came up and caught you.'

" 'That's all a damned silly yarn!' I said. And then I told him the whole truth of the affair. After I had done that, I explained my idea about it, to him.

" 'Now you see what I mean?' I asked.

" 'You mean that this strange atmosphere—or whatever it is—we're in, would not allow us to see another ship?' he asked, a bit awestruck.

" 'Yes,' I said. 'But the point I wanted you to see, is that if we can't see another vessel, even when she's quite close, then, in the same way, we shouldn't be able to see land. To all intents and purposes we're blind. Just you think of it! We're out in the middle of the briny, doing a sort of eternal blind man's hop. The Old Man couldn't put into port, even if he wanted to. He'd run us bang on shore, without our ever seeing it.'

" 'What are we going to do, then?' he asked, in a despairing sort of way. 'Do you mean to say we can't do anything? Surely something can be done! It's terrible!'

" 'For perhaps a minute, we walked up and down, in the light from the different lanterns. Then he spoke again.

" 'We might be run down, then,' he said, 'and never even see the other vessel?'

" 'It's possible,' I replied. 'Though, from what I saw, it's evident that *we're* quite visible; so that it would be easy for them to see us, and steer clear of us, even though we couldn't see them.'

" 'And we might run into something, and never see it?' he asked me, following up the train of thought.

" 'Yes,' I said. 'Only there's nothing to stop the other ship from getting out of our way.'

" 'But if it wasn't a vessel?' he persisted. 'It might be an iceberg, or a rock, or even a derelict.'

" 'In that case,' I said, putting it a bit flippantly, naturally, 'we'd probably damage it.'

"He made no answer to this, and for a few moments, we were quiet.

"Then he spoke abruptly, as though the idea had come suddenly to him.

" 'Those lights the other night!' he said. 'Were they a ship's lights?'

"'Yes,' I replied. 'Why?'

" 'Why,' he answered. 'Don't you see, if they were really lights, we *could* see them?'

" 'Well, I should think I ought to know that,' I replied. 'You seem to forget that the Second Mate slung me off the look-out for daring to do that very thing.'

" 'I don't mean that,' he said. 'Don't you see that if we could see them at all, it showed that the atmosphere-thing wasn't round us then?'

" 'Not necessarily,' I answered. 'It may have been nothing more than a rift in it; though, of course, I may be all wrong. But, anyway, the fact that the lights disappeared almost as soon as they were seen, shows that it was very much round the ship.'

"That made him feel a bit the way I did, and when next he spoke, his tone had lost its hopefulness.

" 'Then you think it'll be no use telling the Second Mate and the Skipper anything?' he asked.

" 'I don't know,' I replied. 'I've been thinking about it, and it can't do any harm. I've a very good mind to.'

" 'I should,' he said. 'You needn't be afraid of anybody laughing at you, now. It might do some good. You've seen more than anyone else.'

"He stopped in his walk, and looked round.

"Wait a minute,' he said, and ran aft a few steps. I saw him look up at the break of the poop; then he came back.

" 'Come along now,' he said. 'The Old Man's up on the poop, talking to the Second Mate. You'll never get a better chance.'

"Still I hesitated; but he caught me by the sleeve, and almost dragged me to the lee ladder.

" 'All right,' I said, when I got there. 'All right, I'll come. Only I'm hanged if I know what to say when I get there.'

" 'Just tell them you want to speak to them,' he said. 'They'll ask what you want, and then you spit out all you know. They'll find it interesting enough.'

" 'You'd better come too,' I suggested. 'You'll be able to back me up in lots of things,'

" 'I'll come, fast enough,' he replied. 'You go up.'

"I went up the ladder, and walked across to where the Skipper and the Second Mate stood talking earnestly, by the rail. Tammy kept behind. As I came near to them, I caught two or three words; though I attached no meaning then to them. They were: '…send for him.' Then the two of them turned and looked at me, and the Second Mate asked what I wanted.

" 'I want to speak to you and the Old M—Captain, Sir,' I answered.

" 'What is it, Jessop?' the Skipper inquired.

" 'I scarcely know how to put it, Sir,' I said. 'It's—it's about these—these things.'

" 'What things? Speak out, man,' he said.

" 'Well, Sir,' I blurted out. 'There's some dreadful thing or things come aboard this ship, since we left port.'

"I saw him give one quick glance at the Second Mate, and the Second looked back.

"Then the Skipper replied.

" 'How do you mean, come aboard?' he asked.

" 'Out of the sea, Sir,' I said. 'I've seen them. So's Tammy, here.'

" 'Ah!' he exclaimed, and it seemed to me, from his face, that he was understanding something better. 'Out of the sea!'

"Again he looked at the Second Mate; but the Second was staring at me.

" 'Yes, Sir,' I said. 'It's the *ship*. She's not safe! I've watched. I think I understand a bit; but there's a lot I don't.'

"I stopped. The Skipper had turned to the Second Mate. The Second nodded, gravely. Then I heard him mutter, in a low voice, and the Old Man replied; after which he turned to me again.

" 'Look here, Jessop,' he said. 'I'm going to talk straight to you. You strike me as being a cut above the ordinary shellback, and I think you've sense enough to hold your tongue.'

" 'I've got my mate's ticket, Sir,' I said, simply.

"Behind me, I heard Tammy give a little start. He had not known about it until then.

"The Skipper nodded.

" 'So much the better,' he answered. 'I may have to speak to you about that, later on.'

"He paused, and the Second Mate said something to him, in an undertone.

" 'Yes,' he said, as though in reply to what the Second had been saying. Then he spoke to me again.

" 'You've seen things come out of the sea, you say?' he questioned. 'Now just tell me all you can remember, from the very beginning.'

"I set to, and told him everything in detail, commencing with the strange figure that had stepped aboard out of the sea, and continuing my yarn, up to the things that had happened in that very watch.

"I stuck well to solid facts; and now and then he and the Second Mate would look at one another, and nod. At the end, he turned to me with an abrupt gesture.

" 'You still hold, then, that you saw a ship the other morning, when I sent you from the wheel?' he asked.

" 'Yes, Sir,' I said. 'I most certainly do.'

" 'But you know there wasn't any!' he said.

" 'Yes, Sir,' I replied, in an apologetic tone. 'There was; and, if you will let me, I believe that I can explain it a bit.'

" 'Well,' he said. 'Go on.'

"Now that I knew he was willing to listen to me in a serious manner, all my funk of telling him had gone, and I went ahead and told him my ideas about the mist, and the thing it seemed to have ushered, you know. I finished up, by telling him how Tammy had worried me to come and tell what I knew.

" 'He thought then, Sir,' I went on, 'that you might wish to put into the nearest port; but I told him that I didn't think you could, even if you wanted to.'

" 'How's that?' he asked, profoundly interested.

" 'Well, Sir,' I replied. 'If we're unable to see other vessels, we shouldn't be able to see the land. You'd be piling the ship up, without ever seeing where you were putting her.'

"This view of the matter, affected the Old Man in an extraordinary manner; as it did, I believe, the Second Mate. And neither spoke for a moment. Then the Skipper burst out.

" 'By Gad! Jessop,' he said. 'If you're right, the Lord have mercy on us.'

"He thought for a couple of seconds. Then he spoke again, and I could see that he was pretty well twisted up:—

" 'My God ! …if you're right!'

"The Second Mate spoke.

" 'The men mustn't know, Sir,' he warned him. 'It'd be a mess if they did!'

" 'Yes,' said the Old Man.

"He spoke to me.

" 'Remember that, Jessop,' he said. 'Whatever you do, don't go yarning about this, forrard.'

" No, Sir,' I replied.

" 'And you too, boy,' said the Skipper. 'Keep your tongue between your teeth. We're in a bad enough mess, without your making it worse. Do you hear?'

" 'Yes, Sir,' answered Tammy.

"The Old Man turned to me again.

" 'These things, or creatures that you say come out of the sea,' he said. 'You've never seen them, except after nightfall?' he asked.

" 'No, Sir,' I replied. 'Never.'

"He turned to the Second Mate.

" 'So far as I can make out, Mr. Tulipson,' he remarked, 'the danger seems to be only at night.'

" 'It's always been at night, Sir,' the Second answered.

"The Old Man nodded.

" 'Have you anything to propose, Mr. Tulipson?' he asked.

" 'Well, Sir,' replied the Second Mate. 'I think you ought to have her snugged down every night, before dark!'

"He spoke with considerable emphasis. Then he glanced aloft, and jerked his head in the direction of the unfurled t'gallants.

" 'It's a damned good thing, Sir,' he said, 'that it didn't come on to blow any harder.'

"The Old Man nodded again.

" 'Yes,' he remarked. 'We shall have to do it; but God knows when we'll get home!'

" 'Better late than not at all,' I heard the Second mutter, under his breath.

"Out loud, he said:—

" 'And the lights, Sir?'

" 'Yes,' said the Old Man. 'I will have lamps in the rigging every night, after dark.'

" 'Very good, Sir,' assented the Second. Then he turned to us.

" 'It's getting daylight, Jessop,' he remarked, with a glance at the sky. 'You'd better take Tammy with you, and shove those lamps back again into the locker.'

" 'i, i, Sir,' I said, and went down off the poop with Tammy.

XIII

The Shadow in the Sea

WHEN EIGHT BELLS WENT, at four o'clock, and the other watch came on deck to relieve us, it had been broad daylight for some time. Before we went below, the Second Mate had the three t'gallants set; and now that it was light, we were pretty curious to have a look aloft, especially up the fore; and Tom, who had been up to overhaul the gear, was questioned a lot, when he came down, as to whether there were any signs of anything queer up there. But he told us there was nothing unusual to be seen.

"At eight o'clock, when we came on deck for the eight to twelve watch, I saw the Sailmaker coming forrard along the deck, from the Second Mate's old berth. He had his rule in his hand, and I knew he had been measuring the poor beggars in there, for their burial outfit. From breakfast time until near noon, he worked, shaping out three canvas wrappers from some old sailcloth. Then, with the aid of the Second Mate and one of the hands, he brought out the three dead chaps on to the after hatch, and there sewed them up, with a few lumps of holy stone at their feet. He was just finishing, when eight bells went, and I heard the Old Man tell the Second Mate to call all hands aft for the burial. This was done, and one of the gangways unshipped.

"We had no decent grating big enough, so they had to get off one of the hatches, and use it instead. The wind had died away during the morning, and the sea was almost a calm—the ship lifting ever so slightly to an occasional glassy heave. The only sounds that struck on the ear were the soft, slow rustle and occasional shiver of the sails, and the continuous and monotonous creak, creak of the spars and gear at the gentle movements of the vessel. And it was in this solemn half-quietness that the Skipper read the burial service.

"They had put the Dutchman first upon the hatch (I could tell him by his stumpiness), and when at last the Old Man gave the signal, the Second Mate tilted his end, and he slid off, and down into the dark.

" 'Poor old Dutchie,' I heard one of the men say, and I fancy we all felt a bit like that.

"Then they lifted Jacobs on to the hatch, and when he had gone, Jock. When Jock was lifted, a sort of sudden shiver ran through the crowd. He had been a favourite in a quiet way, and I know I felt, all at once, just a bit queer. I was standing by the rail, upon the after bollard, and Tammy was next to me; while Plummer stood a little behind. As the Second Mate tilted the hatch for the last time, a little, hoarse chorus broke from the men:—

" 'S'long, Jock! So long, Jock!'

"And then, at the sudden plunge, they rushed to the side to see the last of him as he went downwards. Even the Second Mate was not able to resist this universal feeling, and he, too, peered over. From where I had been standing, I had been able to see the body take the water, and now, for a brief couple of seconds, I saw the white of the canvas, blurred by the blue of the water, dwindle and dwindle in the extreme depth. Abruptly, as I stared, it disappeared—too abruptly, it seemed to me.

" 'Gone!' I heard several voices say, and then our watch began to go slowly forrard, while one or two of the other, started to replace the hatch.

"Tammy pointed, and nudged me.

" 'See, Jessop,' he said. 'What is it?'

" 'What?' I asked.

" 'That queer shadow,' he replied. 'Look!'

"And then I saw what he meant. It was something big and shadowy, that appeared to be growing clearer. It occupied the exact place—so it seemed to me—in which Jock had disappeared.

" 'Look at it!' said Tammy, again. 'It's getting bigger!'

"He was pretty excited, and so was I.

"I was peering down. The thing seemed to be rising out of the depths. It was taking shape. As I realised what the shape was, a queer, cold funk took me.

" 'See,' said Tammy. 'It's just like the shadow of a ship!'

"And it was. The shadow of a ship rising out of the unexplored immensity beneath our keel. Plummer, who had not yet gone forrard, caught Tammy's last remark, and glanced over.

" 'What's 'e mean?' he asked.

" 'That!' replied Tammy, and pointed.

"I jabbed my elbow into his ribs; but it was too late. Plummer had seen. Curiously enough, though, he seemed to think nothing of it.

" 'That ain't nothin', 'cept ther shadder er ther ship,' he said.

"Tammy, after my hint, let it go at that. But when Plummer had gone forrard with the others, I told him not to go telling everything round the decks, like that.

" 'We've got to be thundering careful!' I remarked. 'You know what the Old Man said, last watch!'

" 'Yes,' said Tammy. 'I wasn't thinking; I'll be careful next time.'

"A little way from me, the Second Mate was still staring down into the water. I turned, and spoke to him.

" 'What do you make it out to be, Sir?' I asked.

" 'God knows!' he said, with a quick glance round to see whether any of the men were about.

"He got down from the rail, and turned to go up onto the poop. At the top of the ladder, he leant over the break.

" 'You may as well ship that gangway, you two,' he told us. 'And mind, Jessop, keep your mouth shut about this.'

" 'i, i, Sir,' I answered.

" 'And you too, youngster!' he added, and went aft along the poop.

"Tammy and I were busy with the gangway, when the Second came back. He had brought the Skipper.

" 'Right under the gangway, Sir,' I heard the Second say, and he pointed down into the water.

"For a little while, the Old Man stared. Then I heard him speak.

" 'I don't see anything,' he said.

"At that, the Second Mate bent more forward and peered down. So did I; but the thing, whatever it was, had gone completely.

" 'It's gone, Sir,' said the Second. 'It was there right enough when I came for you.'

"About a minute later, having finished shipping the gangway, I was going forrard, when the Second's voice called me back.

" 'Tell the Captain what it was you saw just now,' he said, in a low voice.

" 'I can't say exactly, Sir,' I replied. 'But it seemed to me like the shadow of a ship, rising up through the water.'

" 'There, Sir,' remarked the Second Mate to the Old Man. 'Just what I told you.'

"The Skipper stared at me.

" 'You're quite sure?' he asked.

" 'Yes, Sir,' I answered. 'Tammy saw it, too.'

"I waited a minute. Then they turned to go aft. The Second was saying something.

" 'Can I go, Sir?' I asked.

" 'Yes, that will do, Jessop,' he said, over his shoulder. But the Old Man came back to the break, and spoke to me.

" 'Remember, not a word of this forrard!' he said.

" 'No, Sir,' I replied, and he went back to the Second Mate; while I walked forrard to the fo'cas'le to get something to eat.

" 'Your whack's in the kid, Jessop,' said Tom, as I stepped in over the washboard. 'An' I got your limejuice in my pannakin.'

" 'Thanks,' I said, and sat down.

"As I stowed away my grub, I took no notice of the chatter of the others. I was too stuffed with my own thoughts. That shadow of a vessel rising, you know, out of the profound deeps, had impressed me tremendously. It had not been imagination. Three of us had seen it—really four; for Plummer distinctly saw it; though he failed to recognise it as anything extraordinary.

"As you can understand, I thought a lot about this shadow of a vessel. But, I am sure, for a time, my ideas must just have gone in an everlasting, blind circle. And then I got another thought; for I got thinking of the figures I had seen aloft in the early morning; and I began to imagine fresh things. You see, that first thing that had come up over the side, had come *out of the sea*. And it had gone back. And now there was this shadow vessel-thing—ghost-ship I called it. It was a damned good name, too. And the dark, noiseless men.... I thought a lot on these lines. Unconsciously, I put a question to myself, aloud:—

" 'Were they the crew?'

" 'Eh?' said Jaskett, who was on the next chest.

"I took hold of myself, as it were, and glanced at him, in an apparently careless manner.

" 'Did I speak?' I asked.

" 'Yes, mate,' he replied, eyeing me, curiously. 'Yer said sumthin' about a crew.'

" 'I must have been dreaming,' I said; and rose up to put away my plate.

XIV

The Ghost Ships

At FOUR O'CLOCK, WHEN again we went on deck, the Second Mate told me to go on with a paunch mat I was making; while Tammy, he sent to get out his sinnet. I had the mat slung on the fore side of the mainmast, between it and the after end of the house; and, in a few minutes, Tammy brought his sinnet and yarns to the mast, and made fast to one of the pins.

" 'What do you think it was, Jessop?' he asked, abruptly, after a short silence.

"I looked at him.

" 'What do you think?' I replied.

" I don't know what to think,' he said. 'But I've a feeling that it's something to do with all the rest,' and he indicated aloft, with his head.

" 'I've been thinking, too,' I remarked.

" 'That it is?' he inquired.

" 'Yes,' I answered, and told him how the idea had come to me at my dinner, that the strange men-shadows which came aboard, might come from that indistinct vessel we had seen down in the sea.

" 'Good Lord!' he exclaimed, as he got my meaning.

"And then for a little, he stood and thought.

" 'That's where they live, you mean?' he said, at last, and paused again.

" 'Well,' I replied. 'It can't be the sort of existence *we* should call life.'

"He nodded, doubtfully.

" 'No,' he said, and was silent again.

"Presently, he put out an idea that had come to him.

" 'You *think*, then, that that—vessel has been with us for some time, if we'd only known?' he asked.

" 'All along,' I replied. 'I mean ever since these things started.'

" 'Supposing there are others,' he said, suddenly.

"I looked at him.

" 'If there are,' I said. 'You can pray to God that they won't stumble across us. It strikes me that whether they're ghosts, or not ghosts, they're blood-gutted pirates.'

" 'It seems horrible,' he said, solemnly, 'to be talking seriously like this, about— you know, about such things.'

" 'I've tried to stop thinking that way,' I told him. 'I've felt I should go cracked, if I didn't. There's damned queer things happen at sea, I know; but this isn't one of them.'

" 'It seems so strange and unreal, one moment, doesn't it?' he said. 'And the next, you *know* it's really true, and you can't under-stand why you didn't always know.

And yet they'd never believe, if you told them ashore about it.'

" 'They'd believe, if they'd been in this packet in the middle watch this morning,' I said.

" 'Besides,' I went on. 'They don't understand. We didn't.... I shall always feel different now, when I read that some packet hasn't been heard of.'

"Tammy stared at me.

" 'I've heard some of the old shellbacks talking about things,' he said. 'But I never took them really seriously.'

" 'Well,' I said. 'I guess we'll have to take this seriously. I wish to God we were home!'

" 'My God! so do I,' he said.

"For a good while after that, we both worked on in silence; but, presently, he went off on another tack.

" 'Do you think we'll really shorten her down every night before it gets dark?' he asked.

" 'Certainly,' I replied. 'They'll never get the men to go aloft at night, after what's happened.'

" 'But, but—supposing they *ordered* us aloft—' he began.

" 'Would you go?' I interrupted.

" 'No!' he said, emphatically. 'I'd jolly well be put in irons first!'

" 'That settles it, then,' I replied. 'You wouldn't go, nor would any one else.'

"At this moment the Second Mate came along.

" 'Shove that mat and that sinnet away, you two,' he said. 'Then get your brooms and clear up.'

" 'i, i, Sir,' we said, and he went on forrard.

" 'Jump on the house, Tammy,' I said. 'And let go the other end of this rope, will you?'

" 'Right,' he said, and did as I had asked him. When he came back, I got him to give me a hand to roll up the mat, which was a very large one.

" 'I'll finish stopping it,' I said. 'You go and put your sinnet away.'

" 'Wait a minute,' he replied, and gathered up a double handful of shakins from the deck, under where I had been working. Then he ran to the side.

" 'Here!' I said. 'Don't go dumping those. They'll only float, and the Second Mate or the Skipper will be sure to spot them.'

" 'Come here, Jessop!' he interrupted, in a low voice, and taking no notice of what I had been saying.

"I got up off the hatch, where I was kneeling. He was staring over the side.

" 'What's up?' I asked.

" 'For God's sake, hurry!' he said, and I ran, and jumped on to the spar, alongside of him.

" 'Look!' he said, and pointed with a handful of shakins, right down, directly beneath us.

"Some of the shakins dropped from his hand, and blurred the water, momentarily, so that I could not see. Then, as the ripples cleared away, I saw what he meant.

" 'Two of them!' he said, in a voice that was scarcely above a whisper. 'And there's another out there,' and he pointed again with the handful of shakins.

" 'There's another a little further aft,' I muttered.

" 'Where?—where?' he asked.

" 'There,' I said, and pointed.

" 'That's four,' he whispered. 'Four of them!'

"I said nothing; but continued to stare. They appeared to me to be a great way down in the sea, and quite motionless. Yet, though their outlines were somewhat blurred and indistinct, there was no mistaking that they were very like exact, though shadowy, representations of vessels. For some minutes we watched them, without speaking. At last Tammy spoke.

" 'They're real, right enough,' he said, in a low voice.

" 'I don't know,' I answered.

" 'I mean we weren't mistaken this morning,' he said.

" 'No,' I replied. 'I never thought we were.'

"Away forrard, I heard the Second Mate, returning aft. He came nearer, and saw us.

" 'What's up now, you two?' he called, sharply. 'This isn't clearing up!'

"I put out my hand to warn him not to shout, and draw the attention of the rest of the men.

"He took several steps towards me.

" 'What is it? what is it?' he said, with a certain irritability; but in a lower voice.

" 'You'd better take a look over the side, Sir,' I replied.

"My tone must have given him an inkling that we had discovered something fresh; for, at my words, he made one spring, and stood on the spar, alongside of me.

" 'Look, Sir,' said Tammy. 'There's four of them.'

" The Second Mate glanced down, saw something, and bent sharply forward.

" 'My God!' I heard him mutter, under his breath.

"After that, for some half-minute, he stared, without a word.

" 'There are two more out there, Sir,' I told him, and indicated the place with my finger.

"It was a little time before he managed to locate these, and when he did, he gave them only a short glance. Then he got down off the spar, and spoke to us.

" 'Come down off there,' he said, quickly. 'Get your brooms and clear up. Don't say a word!— It may be nothing.'

"He appeared to add that last bit, as an afterthought, and we both knew it meant nothing. Then he turned and went swiftly aft.

" 'I expect he's gone to tell the Old Man,' Tammy remarked, as we went forrard, carrying the mat and his sinnet.

" 'H'm,' I said, scarcely noticing what he was saying; for I was full of the thought of those four shadowy craft, waiting quietly down there.

"We got our brooms, and went aft. On the way, the Second Mate and the Skipper passed us. They went forrard to by the fore brace, and got upon the spar. I saw the Second point up at the brace, and he appeared to be saying something about the gear. I guessed that this was done purposely, to act as a blind, should any of the other men be looking. Then the Old Man glanced down over the side, in a casual sort of manner; so did the Second Mate. A minute or two later, they came aft, and went back, up on to the poop. I caught a glimpse of the Skipper's face as he passed me, on his return. He struck me as looking worried—bewildered, perhaps, would be a better word.

"Both Tammy and I were tremendously keen to have another look; but when at last we got a chance, the sky reflected so much on the water, we could see nothing below.

"We had just finished sweeping up when four bells went, and we cleared below for tea. Some of the men got chatting while they were grubbing.

" 'I 'ave 'eard,' remarked Quoin, 'as we're goin' ter shorten 'er down afore dark.'

" 'Eh?' said old Jaskett, over his pannakin of tea.

"Quoin repeated his remark.

" ' 'oo says so?' inquired Plummer.

" 'I 'eard it from ther Doc,' answered Quoin. ' 'e got it from ther Stooard.'

" ' 'ow would 'ee know?' asked Plummet.

" 'I dunno,' said Quoin. 'I 'spect 'e's 'eard 'em talkin' 'bout it arft.'

"Plummer turned to me.

" ' 'ave you 'eard anythin', Jessop?' he inquired.

" 'What, about shortening down?' I replied.

" 'Yes,' he said. 'Weren't ther Old Man talkin' ter yer, up on ther poop this mornin'?'

" 'Yes,' I answered. 'He said something to the Second Mate about shortening down; but it wasn't to me.'

" 'Ther y'are!' said Quoin. ' 'aven't I just said so?'

"At that instant, one of the chaps in the other watch, poked his head in through the starboard doorway.

" 'All hands shorten sail!' he sung out; at the same moment the Mate's whistle came sharp along the decks.

"Plummer stood up, and reached for his cap.

" 'Well,' he said. 'It's evydent they ain't goin' ter lose no more of us!'

"Then we went out on deck.

"It was a dead calm; but all the same, we furled the three royals, and then the three t'gallants. After that, we hauled up the main and foresail, and stowed them. The crossjack, of course, had been furled some time, with the wind being plumb aft.

"It was while we were up at the foresail, that the sun went over the edge of the horizon. We had finished stowing the sail, out upon the yard, and I was waiting for the others to clear in, and let me get off the foot-rope. Thus it happened that having nothing to do for nearly a minute, I stood watching the sun set, and so saw something that otherwise I should, most probably, have missed. The sun had dipped nearly half-way below the horizon, and was showing like a great, red dome of dull fire. Abruptly, far away on the starboard bow, a faint mist drove up out of the sea. It spread across the face of the sun, so that its light shone now as though it came through a dim haze of smoke. Quickly, this mist or haze grew thicker; but, at the same time, separating and taking strange shapes, so that the red of the sun struck through ruddily between them. Then, as I watched, the weird mistiness collected and shaped and rose into three towers. These became more definite, and there was something elongated beneath them. The shaping and forming continued, and almost suddenly I saw that the thing had taken on the shape of a great ship. Directly afterwards, I saw that it was moving. It had been broadside on to the sun. Now it was swinging. The bows came round with a stately movement, until the three masts bore in a line. It was heading directly towards us. It grew larger; but yet less distinct. Astern of it, I saw now that the sun had sunk to a mere line of light. Then, in the gathering dusk it seemed to me that the ship was sinking back into the ocean. The sun went beneath the sea, and the thing I had seen became merged, as it were, into the monotonous greyness of the coming night.

"A voice came to me from the rigging. It was the Second Mate's. He had been up to give us a hand.

" 'Now then, Jessop,' he was saying. 'Come along! come along!'

"I turned quickly, and realised that the fellows were nearly all off the yard.

" 'i, i, Sir,' I muttered, and slid in along the foot-rope, and went down on deck. I felt fresh dazed and frightened.

"A little later, eight bells went, and, after roll-call, I cleared up, on to the poop, to relieve the wheel. For a while as I stood at the wheel, my mind seemed blank, and incapable of receiving impressions. This sensation went, after a time, and I realised that there was a great stillness over the sea. There was absolutely no wind, and even the everlasting creak, creak of the gear seemed to ease off at times.

"At the wheel there was nothing whatever to do. I might just as well have been forrard, smoking in the fo'cas'le. Down on the maindeck, I could see the loom of the lanterns that had been lashed up to the sherpoles in the fore and main rigging.

Yet they showed less than they might, owing to the fact that they had been shaded on their after sides, so as not to blind the officer of the watch more than need be.

"The night had come down strangely dark, and yet of the dark and the stillness and the lanterns, I was only conscious in occasional flashes of comprehension. For, now that my mind was working, I was thinking chiefly of that queer, vast phantom of mist, I had seen rise from the sea, and take shape.

"I kept staring into the night, towards the West, and then all round me; for, naturally, the memory predominated that she had been coming towards us, when the darkness came, and it was a pretty disquieting sort of thing to think about. I had such a horrible feeling that something beastly was going to happen any minute.

"Yet, two bells came and went, and still all was quiet—strangely quiet, it seemed to me. And, of course, besides the queer, misty vessel I had seen in the West, I was all the time remembering the four shadowy craft lying down in the sea, under our port side. Every time I remembered them, I felt thankful for the lanterns round the maindeck, and I wondered why none had been put in the mizzen rigging. I wished to goodness that they had, and made up my mind I would speak to the Second Mate about it, next time he came aft. At the time, he was leaning over the rail across the break of the poop. He was not smoking, as I could tell; for had he been, I should have seen the glow of his pipe, now and then. It was plain to me that he was uneasy. Three times already he had been down on to the maindeck, prowling about. I guessed that he had been to look down into the sea, for any signs of those four grim craft. I wondered whether they would be visible at night.

"Suddenly, the time-keeper struck three bells, and the deeper notes of the bell forrard, answered them. I gave a start. It seemed to me that they had been struck close to my elbow. There was something unaccountably strange in the air that night. Then, even as the Second Mate answered the look-out's 'All's well,' there came the sharp whir and rattle of running gear, on the port side of the mainmast. Simultaneously, there was the shrieking of a parrel, up the main; and I knew that some one, or something, had let go the main topsail haulyards. From aloft there came the sound of something parting; then the crash of the yard as it ceased falling.

"The Second Mate shouted out something unintelligible, and jumped for the ladder. From the maindeck there came the sound of running feet, and the voices of the watch, shouting. Then I caught the Skipper's voice; he must have run out on deck, through the Saloon doorway.

" 'Get some more lamps! Get some more lamps!' he was singing out. Then he swore.

"He sung out something further. I caught the last two words.

" '…carried away,' they sounded like.

" 'No, Sir,' shouted the Second Mate. 'I don't think so.'

"A minute of some confusion followed; and then came the click of pawls. I could tell that they had taken the haulyards to the after capstan. Odd words floated up to me.

" '...all this water?' I heard in the Old Man's voice. He appeared to be asking a question.

" 'Can't say, Sir,' came the Second Mate's.

"There was a period of time, filled only by the clicking of the pawls and the sounds of the creaking parrel and the running gear. Then the Second Mate's voice came again.

" 'Seems all right, Sir,' I heard him say.

"I never heard the Old Man's reply; for in the same moment, there came to me a chill of cold breath at my back. I turned sharply, and saw something peering over the taffrail. It had eyes that reflected the binnacle light, weirdly, with a frightful, tigerish gleam; but beyond that, I could see nothing with any distinctness. For the moment, I just stared. I seemed frozen. It was so close. Then movement came to me, and I jumped to the binnacle and snatched out the lamp. I twitched round, and shone the light towards it. The thing, whatever it was, had come more forward over the rail; but now, before the light, it recoiled with a queer, horrible litheness. It slid back, and down, and so out of sight. I have only a confused notion of a wet, glistening something, and two vile eyes. Then I was running, crazy, towards the break of the poop. I sprang down the ladder, and missed my footing, and landed on my stern, at the bottom. In my left hand I held the still burning binnacle lamp. The men were putting away the capstan-bars; but at my abrupt appearance, and the yell I gave out at falling, one or two of them fairly ran backwards a short distance, in sheer funk, before they realised what it was.

"From somewhere further forrard, the Old Man and the Second Mate came running aft.

" 'What the devil's up now?' sung out the Second, stopping and bending to stare at me. 'What's to do, that you're away from the wheel?'

"I stood up and tried to answer him; but I was so shaken that I could only stammer.

" 'I—I—there—there—' I stuttered.

" 'Damnation!' shouted the Second Mate, angrily. 'Get back to the wheel!'

"I hesitated, and tried to explain.

" 'Do you damned well hear me?' he sung out.

" 'Yes, Sir; but—' I began.

" 'Get up on to the poop, Jessop!' he said.

"I went. I meant to explain, when he came up. At the top of the ladder, I stopped. I was not going back alone to that wheel. Down below, I heard the Old Man speaking.

" 'What on earth is it now, Mr. Tulipson?' he was saying.

"The Second Mate made no immediate reply; but turned to the men, who were evidently crowding near.

" 'That will do, men!' he said, somewhat sharply.

"I heard the watch start to go forrard. There came a mutter of talk from them. Then the Second Mate answered the Old Man. He could not have known that I was near enough to overhear him.

" 'It's Jessop, Sir. He must have seen something; but we mustn't frighten the crowd more than need be.'

" 'No,' said the Skipper's voice.

"They turned and came up the ladder, and I ran back a few steps, as far as the skylight. I heard the Old Man speak as they came up.

" 'How is it there are no lamps, Mr. Tulipson?' he said, in a surprised tone.

" 'I thought there would be no need up here, Sir,' the Second Mate replied. Then he added something about saving oil.

" 'Better have them, I think,' I heard the Skipper say.

" 'Very good, Sir,' answered the Second, and sung out to the time-keeper to bring up a couple of lamps.

"Then the two of them walked aft, to where I stood by the skylight.

" 'What are you doing, away from the wheel?' asked the Old Man, in a stern voice.

"I had collected my wits somewhat by now.

" 'I won't go, Sir, till there's a light,' I said.

"The Skipper stamped his foot, angrily; but the Second Mate stepped forward.

" 'Come! Come, Jessop!' he exclaimed. 'This won't do, you know! You'd better get back to the wheel without further bother.'

" 'Wait a minute,' said the Skipper, at this juncture. 'What objection have you to going back to the wheel?' he asked.

" 'I saw something,' I said. 'It was climbing over the taffrail, Sir—'

" 'Ah!' he said, interrupting me with a quick gesture. Then, abruptly: 'Sit down! sit down; you're all in a shake, man.'

"I flopped down on to the skylight seat. I was, as he had said, all in a shake, and the binnacle lamp was wobbling in my hand, so that the light from it went dancing here and there across the deck.

" 'Now,' he went on. 'Just tell us what you saw.'

"I told them, at length, and while I was doing so, the time-keeper brought up the lights and lashed one up on the sheer-pole in each rigging.

" 'Shove one under the spanker boom,' the Old Man sung out, as the boy finished lashing up the other two. 'Be smart now.'

" 'i, i, Sir,' said the 'prentice, and hurried off.

" 'Now then,' remarked the Skipper, when this had been done. 'You needn't be afraid to go back to the wheel. There's a light over the stern, and the Second Mate or myself will be up here all the time.'

"I stood up.

" 'Thank you, Sir,' I said, and went aft. I replaced my lamp in the binnacle, and took hold of the wheel; yet, time and again, I glanced behind, and I was very thankful when, a few minutes later, four bells went, and I was relieved.

"Though the rest of the chaps were forrard in the fo'cas'le, I did not go there. I shirked being questioned about my sudden appearance at the foot of the poop ladder; and so I lit my pipe and wandered about the maindeck. I did not feel particularly nervous, as there were now two lanterns in each rigging, and a couple standing upon each of the spare topmasts under the bulwarks.

"Yet, a little after five bells, it seemed to me that I saw a shadowy face peer over the rail, a little abaft the fore lanyards. I snatched up one of the lanterns from off the spar, and flashed the light towards it, whereupon there was nothing. Only, on my mind, more than my sight, I fancy, a queer knowledge remained of wet, peery eyes. Afterwards, when I thought about them, I felt extra beastly. I knew then how brutal they had been…. Inscrutable, you know. Once more in that same watch I had a somewhat similar experience, only in this instance it had vanished even before I had time to reach a light. And then came eight bells, and our watch below.

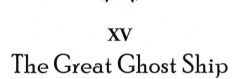

XV

The Great Ghost Ship

WHEN WE WERE CALLED again, at a quarter to four, the man who roused us out, had some queer information.

" 'Toppin's gone—clean vanished!' he told us, as we began to turn out. 'I never was in such a damned, hair-raisin' hooker as this here. It ain't safe to go about the bloomin' decks,'

" ' 'oo's gone?' asked Plummer, sitting up suddenly and throwing his legs over his bunk-board.

" 'Toppin, one of the 'prentices,' replied the man. 'We've been huntin' all over the bloomin' show. We're still at it—but they'll never find him,' he ended, with a sort of gloomy assurance.

" 'Oh, I dunno,' said Quoin. 'P'raps 'e's snoozin' somewheres 'bout.'

" 'Not him,' replied the man. 'I tell you we've turned everythin' upside down. He's not aboard the bloomin' ship.'

" 'Where was he when they last saw him?' I asked. 'Someone must know something, you know.'

" 'Keepin' time up on the poop,' he replied. 'The Old Man's nearly shook the life out of the Mate and the chap at the wheel. And they say they don't know nothin'.'

" 'How do you mean?' I inquired. 'How do you mean, nothing?'

" 'Well,' he answered. 'The youngster was there one minute, and then the next thing they knew, he'd gone. They've both sworn black an' blue that there wasn't a whisper. He's just disappeared off of the face of the bloomin' earth.'

"I got down onto my chest, and reached for my boots.

"Before I could speak again, the man was saying something fresh.

" 'See here, mates,' he went on. 'If things is goin' on like this, I'd like to know where you an' me'll be befor' long!'

" 'We'll be in 'ell,' said Plummer.

" 'I dunno as I like to think 'bout it,' said Quoin.

" 'We'll have to think about it!' replied the man. 'We've got to think a bloomin' lot about it. I've talked to our side, an' they're game.'

" 'Game for what?' I asked.

" 'To go an' talk straight to the bloomin' Capting,' he said, wagging his finger at me. 'It's make tracks for the nearest bloomin' port, an' don't you make no bloomin' mistake.'

"I opened my mouth to tell him that the probability was we should not be able to make it, even if he could get the Old Man to see the matter from his point of view. Then I remembered that the chap had no idea of the things I had seen, and *thought out*; so, instead, I said:—

" 'Supposing he won't?'

" 'Then we'll have to bloomin' well make him,' he replied.

" 'And when you got there,' I said. 'What then? You'd be jolly well locked up for mutiny.'

" 'I'd sooner be locked up,' he said. 'It don't kill you!'

"There was a murmur of agreement from the others, and then a moment of silence, in which, I know, the men were thinking.

"Jaskett's voice broke into it.

" 'I never thought at first as she was 'aunted—' he commenced; but Plummer cut in across his speech.

" 'We mustn't 'urt any one, yer know,' he said. 'That'd mean 'angin', an' they ain't been er bad crowd.'

" 'No,' assented every one, including the chap who had come to call us.

" 'All the same,' he added. 'It's got to be up hellum, an' shove her into the nearest bloomin' port.'

" 'Yes,' said every one, and then eight bells went, and we cleared out on deck.

"Presently, after roll-call—in which there had come a queer, awkward little pause at Toppin's name—Tammy came over to me. The rest of the men had gone forrard, and I guessed they were talking over mad plans for forcing the Skipper's hand, and making him put into port—poor beggars!

"I was leaning over the port rail, by the fore brace-block, staring down into the sea, when Tammy came to me. For perhaps a minute he said nothing. When at last he spoke, it was to say that the shadow vessels had not been there since daylight.

" 'What?' I said, in some surprise. 'How do you know?'

" 'I woke up when they were searching for Toppin,' he replied. 'I've not been asleep since. I came here, right away.' He began to say something further; but stopped short.

" 'Yes,' I said encouragingly.

" 'I didn't know—' he began, and broke off. He caught my arm. 'Oh, Jessop!' he exclaimed. 'What's going to be the end of it all? Surely something can be done?'

"I said nothing. I had a desperate feeling that there was very little we could do to help ourselves.

" 'Can't we do something?' he asked, and shook my arm. 'Anything's better than this! We're being murdered!'

"Still, I said nothing; but stared moodily down into the water. I could plan nothing; though I would get mad, feverish fits of thinking.

" 'Do you hear?' he said. He was almost crying.

" 'Yes, Tammy,' I replied. 'But I don't know! I don't know!'

" 'You don't know!' he exclaimed. 'You don't know! Do you mean we're just to give in, and be murdered, one after another?'

" 'We've done all we can,' I replied. 'I don't know what else we can do, unless we go below and lock ourselves in, every night.'

" 'That would be better than this,' he said. 'There'll be no one to go below, or anything else, soon!'

" 'But what if it came on to blow?' I asked. 'We'd be having the sticks blown out of her.'

" 'What if it came on to blow now?' he returned. 'No one would go aloft, if it were dark, you said, yourself! Besides, we could shorten her right down, first. I tell you, in a few days there won't be a chap alive aboard this packet, unless they jolly well do something!'

" 'Don't shout,' I warned him, 'You'll have the Old Man hearing you.' But the young beggar was wound up, and would take no notice.

" 'I will shout,' he replied. 'I want the Old Man to hear. I've a good mind to go up and tell him.'

"He started on a fresh tack.

" 'Why don't the men do something?' he began. 'They ought to damn well make the Old Man put us into port! They ought—'

" 'For goodness' sake, shut up, you little fool!' I said. 'What's the good of talking a lot of damned rot like that? You'll be getting yourself into trouble.'

" 'I don't care,' he replied. 'I'm not going to be murdered!'

" 'Look here,' I said. 'I told you before, that we shouldn't be able to see the land, even if we made it.'

" 'You've no proof,' he answered. 'It's only your idea.'

"'Well,' I replied. 'Proof, or no proof, the Skipper would only pile her up, if he tried to make the land, with things as they are now.'

" 'Let him pile her up,' he answered. 'Let him jolly well pile her up! That would be better than staying out here to be pulled over-board, or chucked down from aloft!'

" 'Look here, Tammy—' I began; but just then the Second Mate sung out for him, and he had to go. When he came back, I had started to walk to and from, across the fore side of the mainmast. He joined me, and after a minute, he started his wild talk again.

" 'Look here, Tammy,' I said, once more. 'It's no use your talking like you've been doing. Things are as they are, and it's no one's fault, and nobody can help it. If you want to talk sensibly, I'll listen; if not, then go and gas to some one else.'

"With that, I returned to the port side, and got upon the spar, again, intending to sit on the pinrail, and have a bit of a talk with him. Before sitting down, I glanced over, into the sea. The action had been almost mechanical; yet, after a few instants, I was in a state of the most intense excitement, and without withdrawing my gaze, I reached out and caught Tammy's arm, to attract his attention.

" 'My God!' I muttered. 'Look!'

" 'What is it?' he asked, and bent over the rail, beside me. And this is what we saw:— A little distance below the surface there lay a pale-coloured, slightly-domed disk. It seemed only a few feet down. Below it, we saw quite clearly, after a few moments' staring, the shadow of a royal-yard, and, deeper, the gear and standing-rigging of a great mast. Far down among the shadows, I thought, presently, that I could make out the immense, indefinite stretch of vast decks.

" 'My God!' whispered Tammy, and shut up. But presently, he gave out a short exclamation, as though an idea had come to him; and got down off the spar, and ran forrard on to the fo'cas'le head. He came running back, after a short look into the sea, to tell me that there was the truck of another great mast coming up there, a bit off the bow, to within a few feet of the surface of the sea.

"In the meantime, you know, I had been staring like mad down through the water at the huge, shadowy mast just below me. I had traced out bit by bit, until now, I could clearly see the jackstay, running along the top of the royal mast; and, you know, the royal itself was *set*.

"But, you know, what was getting at me more than anything, was a feeling that there was movement down in the water there, among the rigging. I *thought* I could actually see, at times, things moving and glinting faintly and rapidly to and fro in the gear. And once, I was practically certain that something was on the royal-yard, moving in to the mast; as though, you know, it might have come up the leech of the sail. And this way, I got a beastly feeling that there were things swarming down there.

"Unconsciously, I must have leant further and further out over the side, staring; and suddenly—good Lord! how I yelled—I overbalanced. I made a sweeping grab, and caught the fore brace, and with that, I was back in a moment upon the spar. In the same second, almost, it seemed to me that the surface of the water above the submerged truck was broken, and I am sure *now*, I saw something a moment in the air against the ship's side—a sort of shadow in the air; though I did not realise it at the time. Anyway, the next instant, Tammy gave out an awful scream, and was head downwards over the rail, in a second. I had an idea *then* that he was jumping overboard. I collared him by the waist of his britchers, and one knee, and then I had him down on the deck, and sat plump on him; for he was struggling and shouting all the time, and I was so breathless and shaken and gone to mush, I could not have trusted my hands to hold him. You see, I never thought *then* it was anything but some influence at work on him; and that he was trying to get loose to go over the side. But I know *now* that I saw the shadow-man that had him. Only, at the time, I was so mixed up, and with the one idea in my head, I was not really able to notice anything, properly. But, afterwards, I comprehended a bit (you can understand, can't you?) what I had seen at the time without taking in.

"And even now looking back, I know that the shadow was only like a faint-seen greyness in the daylight, against the whiteness of the decks, clinging against Tammy.

"And there was I, all breathless and sweating, and quivery with my own tumble, sitting on the little screeching beggar, and he fighting like a mad thing; so that I thought I should never hold him.

"And then I heard the Second Mate shouting, and there came running feet along the deck. Then many hands were pulling and hauling, to get me off him.

" 'Bl—dy cowyard!' sung out some one.

" 'Hold him! Hold him!' I shouted. 'He'll be overboard!'

"At that, they seemed to understand that I was not ill-treating the youngster; for they stopped manhandling me, and allowed me to rise; while two of them took hold of Tammy, and kept him safe.

" 'What's the matter with him?' the Second Mate was singing out. 'What's happened?'

" 'He's gone off his head, I think,' I said.

" 'What?' asked the Second Mate. But before I could answer him, Tammy ceased suddenly to struggle, and flopped down upon the deck.

" ' 'e's fainted,' said Plummer, with some sympathy. He looked at me, with a puzzled, suspicious air. 'What's 'appened? What's 'e been doin'?'

" 'Take him aft into the berth!' ordered the Second Mate, a bit abruptly. It struck me that he wished to prevent questions. He must have tumbled to the fact that we had seen something, about which it would be better not to tell the crowd.

"Plummer stooped to lift the boy.

" 'No,' said the Second Mate. 'Not you, Plummer. Jessop, you take him.' He turned to the rest of the men. 'That will do,' he told them, and they went forrard, muttering a little.

"I lifted the boy, and carried him aft.

" 'No need to take him into the berth,' said the Second Mate. 'Put him down on the after hatch. I've sent the other lad for some brandy.'

"When the brandy came, we dosed Tammy and soon brought him round. He sat up, with a somewhat dazed air. Otherwise, he seemed quiet and sane enough.

" 'What's up?' he asked. He caught sight of the Second Mate. 'Have I been ill, Sir?' he exclaimed.

" 'You're right enough now, youngster,' said the Second Mate. 'You've been a bit off. You'd better go and lie down for a bit.'

" 'I'm all right now, Sir,' replied Tammy. 'I don't think—'

" 'You do as you're told!' interrupted the Second. 'Don't always have to be told twice! If I want you, I'll send for you.'

"Tammy stood up, and made his way, in rather an unsteady fashion, into the berth. I fancy he was glad enough to lie down.

" 'Now then, Jessop,' exclaimed the Second Mate, turning to me. 'What's been the cause of all this? Out with it now, smart!'

"I commenced to tell him; but, almost directly, he put up his hand.

" 'Hold on a minute,' he said. 'There's the breeze!'

"He jumped up the port ladder, and sung out to the chap at the wheel. Then down again.

" 'Starboard fore brace,' he sung out. He turned to me. 'You'll have to finish telling me afterwards,' he said.

" 'i, i, Sir,' I replied, and went to join the other chaps at the braces.

"As soon as we were braced sharp up on the port tack, he sent some of the watch up to loose the sails. Then he sung out for me.

" 'Go on with your yarn now, Jessop,' he said.

"I told him about the great shadow vessel, and I said something about Tammy—I mean about my not being sure *now* whether he *had* tried to jump overboard.

Because, you see, I began to realise that I had seen the shadow; and I remembered the stirring of the water above the submerged truck. But the Second did not wait, of course, for any theories; but was away, like a shot, to see for himself. He ran to the side, and looked down. I followed, and stood beside him; yet, now that the surface of the water was blurred by the wind, we could see nothing.

" 'It's no good,' he remarked, after a minute. 'You'd better get away from the rail before any of the others see you. Just be taking those halyards aft to the capstan.'

"From then, until eight bells, we were hard at work getting the sail upon her, and when at last eight bells went, I made haste to swallow my breakfast, and get a sleep.

"At midday, when we went on deck for the afternoon watch, I ran to the side; but there was no sign of the great shadow ship. All that watch, the Second Mate kept me working at my paunch mat, and Tammy he put on to his sinnet, telling me to keep an eye on the youngster. But the boy was right enough; as I scarcely doubted now, you know; though—a most unusual thing—he hardly opened his lips the whole afternoon. Then at four o'clock, we went below for tea.

"At four bells, when we came on deck again, I found that the light breeze, which had kept us going during the day, had dropped, and we were only just moving. The sun was low down, and the sky clear. Once or twice, as I glanced across to the horizon, it seemed to me that I caught again that odd quiver in the air that had preceded the coming of the mist; and, indeed, on two separate occasions, I saw a thin wisp of haze drive up, apparently out of the sea. This was at some little distance on our port beam; otherwise, all was quiet and peaceful; and though I stared into the water, I could make out no vestige of that great shadow ship, down in the sea.

"It was some little time after six bells, that the order came for all hands to shorten sail for the night. We took in the royals and t'gallants, and then the three courses. It was shortly after this, that a rumour went round the ship that there was to be no look-out that night after eight o'clock. This naturally created a good deal of talk among the men; especially as the yarn went, that the fo'cas'le doors were to be shut and fastened as soon as it was dark, and that no one was to be allowed on deck.

" ' 'oo's goin' ter take ther wheels?' I heard Plummer ask.

" 'I s'pose they'll 'ave us take 'em as usual,' replied one of the men. 'One of ther officers is bound ter be on ther poop; so we'll 'ave company.'

"Apart from these remarks, there was a general opinion that—if it were true—it was a sensible act on the part of the Skipper. As one of the men said:—

" 'It ain't likely as there'll be any of us missin' in ther mornin', if we stays in our bunks all ther blessed night.'

"And soon after this, eight bells went.

◆▸ ◆ ◂◆

XVI

The Ghost Pirates

AT THE MOMENT WHEN eight bells actually went, I was in the fo'cas'le, talking to four of the other watch. Suddenly, away aft, I heard shouting, and then on the deck overhead, came the loud thudding of some one pomping with a capstan-bar. Straightway, I turned and made a run for the port doorway, along with the four other men. We rushed out through the doorway on to the deck. It was getting dusk; but that did not hide from me a terrible and extraordinary sight. All along the port rail there was a queer, undulating greyness, that moved downwards inboard, and spread over the decks. As I looked, I found that I saw more clearly, in a most extraordinary way. And, suddenly, all the moving greyness resolved into hundreds of strange men. In the half-light, they looked unreal and impossible, as though there had come upon us the inhabitants of some fantastic dream-world. My God! I thought I was mad. They swarmed in upon us in a great wave of murderous, living shadows. From some of the men who must have been going aft for roll-call, there rose into the evening air a loud, awful shouting.

" 'Aloft!' yelled someone; but, as I looked aloft, I saw that the horrible things were swarming there in scores and scores.

" 'Jesus Christ—!' shrieked a man's voice, cut short, and my glance dropped from aloft, to find two of the men who had come out from the fo'cas'le with me, rolling upon the deck. They were two indistinguishable masses that writhed here and there across the planks. The brutes fairly covered them. From them, came muffled little shrieks and gasps; and there I stood, and with me were the other two men. A man darted past us into the fo'cas'le, with two grey men on his back, and I heard them kill him. The two men by me, ran suddenly across the fore hatch, and up the starboard ladder on to the fo'cas'le head. Yet, almost in the same instant, I saw several of the grey men disappear up the other ladder. From the fo'cas'le head above, I heard the two men commence to shout, and this died away into a loud scuffling. At that, I turned to see whether I could get away. I stared round, hopelessly; and then with two jumps, I was on the pigsty, and from there upon the top of the deckhouse. I threw myself flat, and waited, breathlessly.

"All at once, it seemed to me that it was darker than it had been the previous moment, and I raised my head, very cautiously. I saw that the ship was enveloped in great billows of mist, and then, not six feet from me, I made out some one lying, face downwards. It was Tammy. I felt safer now that we were hidden by the mist, and I crawled to him. He gave a quick gasp of terror when I touched him; but when he saw who it was, he started to sob like a little kid.

" 'Hush!' I said. 'For God's sake be quiet!' But I need not have troubled; for the shrieks of the men being killed, down on the decks all around us, drowned every other sound.

"I knelt up, and glanced round and then aloft. Overhead, I could make out dimly the spars and sails, and now as I looked, I saw that the t'gallants and royals had been unloosed and were hanging in the buntlines. Almost in the same moment, the terrible crying of the poor beggars about the decks, ceased; and there succeeded an awful silence, in which I could distinctly hear Tammy sobbing. I reached out, and shook him.

" 'Be quiet! Be quiet!' I whispered, intensely. 'THEY'LL hear us!'

"At my touch and whisper, he struggled to become silent; and then, overhead, I saw the six yards being swiftly mastheaded. Scarcely were the sails set, when I heard the swish and flick of gaskets being cast adrift on the lower yards, and realised that ghostly things were at work there.

"For a minute or so there was silence, and I made my way cautiously to the after end of the house, and peered over. Yet, because of the mist, I could see nothing. Then, abruptly, from behind me, came a single wail of sudden pain and terror from Tammy. It ended instantly in a sort of choke. I stood up in the mist and ran back to where I had left the kid; but he had gone. I stood dazed. I felt like shrieking out loud. Above me, I heard the flaps of the courses being tumbled off the yards. Down upon the decks, there were the noises of a multitude working in a weird, inhuman silence. Then came the squeal and rattle of blocks and braces aloft. They were squaring the yards.

"I remained standing. I watched the yards squared, and then I saw the sails fill suddenly. An instant later, the deck of the house upon which I stood, became canted forrard. The slope increased, so that I could scarcely stand, and I grabbed at one of the wire-winches. I wondered, in a stunned sort of way, what was happening. Almost directly afterwards, from the deck on the port side of the house, there came a sudden, loud, human scream; and immediately, from different parts of the decks there rose, afresh, some most horrible shouts of agony from odd men. This grew into an intense screaming that shook my heart up; and there came again a noise of desperate, brief fighting. Then a breath of cold wind seemed to play in the mist, and I could see down the slope of the deck. I looked below me, towards the bows. The jibboom was plunged right into the water, and, as I stared, the bows disappeared into the sea. The deck of the house became a wall to me, and I was swinging from the winch, which was now above my head. I watched the ocean lip over the edge of the fo'cas'le head, and rush down on to the maindeck, roaring into the empty fo'cas'le. And still all around me came the crying of the lost sailormen. I heard something strike the corner of the house above me, with a dull thud, and then I saw Plummer plunge down into the flood beneath. I remembered that he had been at the wheel. The next instant, the water had leapt to my feet; there came a drear chorus of bubbling screams, a roar of waters, and I was going swiftly down into the darkness. I let go of the winch, and struck out madly, trying to hold my breath. There was a loud singing in my ears. It grew louder. I opened my mouth. I felt I was dying. And then, thank God! I was at the surface, breathing. For the moment, I was blinded with the water, and my agony of breathlessness. Then, growing easier, I brushed the water from my eyes, and so, not three hundred yards away, I made out a large ship, floating almost motionless. At first, I could scarcely believe I saw aright. Then, as I realised that indeed there was yet a chance of living, I started to swim towards you.

"You know the rest—"

"And you think—?" said the Captain, interrogatively, and stopped short.

"No," replied Jessop. "I don't think, I *know*. None of us *think*. It's a gospel fact. People *talk* about queer things happening at sea; but this isn't one of them. This is one of the *real* things. You've all seen queer things; perhaps more than I have. It depends. But they don't go down in the log. These kinds of things never do. This one won't; at least, not as it's really happened."

He nodded his head, slowly, and went on, addressing the Captain more particularly.

"I'll bet," he said, deliberately, "that you'll enter it in the log-book, something like this:—

" 'May 18th. Lat.—S. Long.—W. 2 p.m. Light winds from the South and East. Sighted a full-rigged ship on the starboard bow. Overhauled her in the first dog-watch. Signalled her; but received no response. During the second dog-watch she steadily refused to communicate. About eight bells, it was observed that she seemed to be settling by the head, and a minute later she foundered suddenly, bows foremost, with all her crew. Put out a boat and picked up one of the men, an A.B. by the name of Jessop. He was quite unable to give any explanation of the catastrophe.'

"And you two," he made a gesture at the First and Second Mates, "will probably sign your names to it, and so will I, and perhaps one of your A.B.'s. Then when we get home they'll print a report of it in the newspapers, and people will talk about unseaworthy ships. Maybe some of the experts will talk rot about rivets and defective plates and so forth."

He laughed, cynically. Then he went on.

"And, you know, when you come to think of it, there's no one except our own selves will ever know how it happened—really. The shellbacks don't count. They're only 'beastly, drunken brutes of *common sailors*'—Poor devils! No one would think of taking anything they said, as anything more than a damned cuffer. Besides, the beggars only tell these things when they're half boozed. They wouldn't then (for fear of being laughed at), only they're not responsible—"

He broke off, and looked round at us.

The Skipper and the two Mates nodded their heads, in silent assent.

Appendix
The Silent Ship

I'M THE THIRD MATE of the *Sangier*, the vessel that picked up Jessop, you know; and he's asked us to write a short note of what we saw from our side, and sign it. The Old Man's set me on to the job, as he says I can put it better than he can.

Well, it was in the first dog-watch that we came up with her, the *Mortzestus* I mean; but it was in the second dog-watch that it happened. The Mate and I were on the poop watching her. You see, we'd signalled her, and she'd not taken any notice, and that seemed queer, as we couldn't have been more than three or four hundred yards off her port beam, and it was a fine evening; so that we could almost have had a tea-fight, if they'd seemed a pleasant crowd. As it was, we called them a set of sulky swine, and left it at that, though we still kept our hoist up.

All the same, you know, we watched her a lot; and I remember, even then I thought it queer how quiet she was. We couldn't hear even her bell go, and I spoke to the Mate about it, and he said he'd been noticing the same thing.

Then, about six bells, they shortened her right down to top-sails; and I can tell you that made us stare more than ever, as any one can imagine. And I remember we noticed then, especially, that we couldn't hear a single sound from her, even when the haulyards were let go; and, you know, without the glass, I saw their Old Man singing out something; but we didn't get a sound of it, and we *should* have been able to hear every word.

Then, just after eight bells, the thing Jessop's told us about, happened. Both the Mate and the Old Man said they could see men going up her side, a bit indistinct, you know, because it was getting dusk; but the Second Mate and I half thought we did, and half thought we didn't; but there was something queer; we all knew that; and it looked like a sort of movey mist along her side. I know I felt pretty funny; but it wasn't the sort of thing, of course, to be too sure and serious about until you *were* sure.

After the Mate and the Captain had said they saw the men boarding her, we began to hear sounds from her; very queer at first, and rather like a phonograph makes when it's getting up speed. Then the sounds came properly from her, and we heard them shouting and yelling; and, you know, I don't know even now just what I really thought. I was all so queer and mixed.

The next thing I remember, there was a thick mist round the ship; and then all the noise was shut off, as if it were all the other side of a door. But we could still see her masts and spars and sails above the misty stuff; and both the Captain and the Mate said they could see men aloft; and I thought I could; but the Second Mate wasn't sure. All the same, though, the sails were all loosed in about a minute, it seemed, and the yards mastheaded. We couldn't see the courses above the mist; but Jessop says they were loosed too, and sheeted home, along with the upper sails. Then we saw the yards squared, and I saw the sails fill bang up with; and yet, you know, ours were slatting.

The next thing was the one that hit me more than anything. Her masts took a cant forrard, and then I saw her stern come up out of the mist that was round her. Then, all in an instant, we could hear sounds from the vessel again. And I tell you, the men didn't seem to be shouting, but screaming. Her stern went higher. It was most extraordinary to look at; and then she went plunk down, head foremost, right bang into the mist-stuff.

It's all right what Jessop says, and when we saw him swimming (I was the one who spotted him) we got out a boat quicker than a wind-jammer ever got out a boat before, I should think.

The Captain and the Mate and the Second and I are all going to sign this.

(Signed)

WILLIAM NAWSTON, *Master.*
J. E. G. ADAMS, *First Mate.*
ED. BROWN, *Second Mate.*
JACK T. EVAN, *Third Mate.*

A Tropical Horror

W E ARE A HUNDRED and thirty days out from Melbourne, and for three weeks we have lain in this sweltering calm.

It is midnight, and our watch on deck until four a.m. I go out and sit on the hatch. A minute later, Joky, our youngest 'prentice, joins me for a chatter. Many are the hours we have sat thus and talked in the night watches; though, to be sure, it is Joky who does the talking. I am content to smoke and listen, giving an occasional grunt at seasons to show that I am attentive.

Joky has been silent for some time, his head bent in meditation. Suddenly he looks up, evidently with the intention of making some remark. As he does so, I see his face stiffen with a nameless horror. He crouches back, his eyes staring past me at some unseen fear. Then his mouth opens. He gives forth a strangulated cry and topples backward off the hatch, striking his head against the deck. Fearing I know not what, I turn to look.

Great Heavens! Rising above the bulwarks, seen plainly in the bright moonlight, is a vast slobbering mouth a fathom across. From the huge dripping lips hang great tentacles. As I look the Thing comes further over the rail. It is rising, rising, higher and higher. There are no eyes visible; only that fearful slobbering mouth set on the tremendous trunk-like neck; which, even as I watch, is curling inboard with the stealthy celerity of an enormous eel. Over it comes in vast heaving folds. Will it never end? The ship gives a slow, sullen roll to starboard as she feels the weight. Then the tail, a broad, flat-shaped mass, slips over the teak rail and falls with a loud slump on to the deck.

For a few seconds the hideous creature lies heaped in writhing, slimy coils. Then, with quick, darting movements, the monstrous head travels along the deck. Close by the mainmast stand the harness casks, and alongside of these a freshly opened cask of salt beef with the top loosely replaced. The smell of the meat seems to attract the monster, and I can hear it sniffing with a vast indrawing breath. Then those lips open, displaying four huge fangs; there is a quick forward motion of the head, a sudden crashing, crunching sound, and beef and barrel have disappeared. The noise brings one of the ordinary seamen out of the fo'cas'le. Coming into the night, he can see nothing for a moment. Then, as he gets further aft, he *sees*, and with horrified cries rushes forward. Too late! From the mouth of the Thing there flashes forth a long, broad blade of glistening white, set with fierce teeth. I avert my eyes, but cannot shut out the sickening "Glut! Glut!" that follows.

The man on the look-out, attracted by the disturbance, has witnessed the tragedy, and flies for refuge into the fo'cas'le, flinging to the heavy iron door after him.

The carpenter and sailmaker come running out from the half-deck in their drawers. Seeing the awful Thing, they rush aft to the cabin with shouts of fear. The Second Mate, after one glance over the break of the poop, runs down the companion-way with the Helmsman after him. I can hear them barring the scuttle, and abruptly I realise that I am on the maindeck alone.

So far I have forgotten my own danger. The past few minutes seem like a portion of an awful dream. Now, however, I comprehend my position and, shaking off the horror that has held me, turn to seek safety. As I do so my eyes fall upon Joky, lying huddled and senseless with fright where he has fallen. I cannot leave him there. Close by stands the empty half-deck—a little steel-built house with iron doors. The lee one is hooked open. Once inside I am safe.

Up to the present the Thing has seemed to be unconscious of my presence. Now, however, the huge barrel-like head sways in my direction; then comes a muffled bellow, and the great tongue flickers in and out as the brute turns and swirls aft to meet me. I know there is not a moment to lose, and, picking up the helpless lad, I make a run for the open door. It is only distant a few yards, but that awful shape is coming down the deck to me in great wreathing coils. I reach the house and tumble in with my burden; then out on deck again to unhook and close the door. Even as I do so something white curls round the end of the house. With a bound I am inside and the door is shut and bolted. Through the thick glass of the ports I see the Thing sweep round the house, in vain search for me.

Joky has not moved yet; so, kneeling down, I loosen his shirt collar and sprinkle some water from the breaker over his face. While I am doing this I hear Morgan shout something; then comes a great shriek of terror, and again that sickening "Glut! Glut!"

Joky stirs uneasily, rubs his eyes, and sits up suddenly.

"Was that Morgan shouting—?" He breaks off with a cry. "Where are we? I have had such awful dreams!"

At this instant there is a sound of running footsteps on the deck and I hear Morgan's voice at the door.

"Tom, open—!"

He stops abruptly and gives an awful cry of despair. Then I hear him rush forward. Through the porthole, I see him spring into the fore rigging and scramble madly aloft. Something steals up after him. It shows white in the moonlight. It wraps itself around his right ankle. Morgan stops dead, plucks out his sheath-knife, and hacks fiercely at the fiendish thing. It lets go, and in a second he is over the top and running for dear life up the t'gallant rigging.

A time of quietness follows, and presently I see that the day is breaking. Not a sound can be heard save the heavy gasping breathing of the Thing. As the sun rises higher the creature stretches itself out along the deck and seems to enjoy the warmth. Still no sound, either from the men forward or the officers aft. I can only suppose that they are afraid of attracting its attention. Yet, a little later, I hear the report of a pistol away aft, and looking out I see the serpent raise its huge head as though listening. As it does so I get a good view of the fore part, and in the daylight see what the night has hidden.

There, right about the mouth, is a pair of little pig-eyes, that seem to twinkle with a diabolical intelligence. It is swaying its head slowly from side to side; then, without warning, it turns quickly and looks right in through the port. I dodge out of sight; but not soon enough. It has seen me, and brings its great mouth up against the glass.

I hold my breath. My God! If it breaks the glass! I cower, horrified. From the direction of the port there comes a loud, harsh, scraping sound. I shiver. Then I remember that there are little iron doors to shut over the ports in bad weather. Without a moment's waste of time I rise to my feet and slam to the door over the port. Then I go round to the others and do the same. We are now in darkness, and I tell Joky in a whisper to light the lamp, which, after some fumbling, he does.

About an hour before midnight I fall asleep. I am awakened suddenly some hours later by a scream of agony and the rattle of a water-dipper. There is a slight scuffling sound; then that soul-revolting "Glut! Glut!"

I guess what has happened. One of the men forrard has slipped out of the fo'cas'le to try and get a little water. Evidently he has trusted to the darkness to hide his movements. Poor beggar! He has paid for his attempt with his life!

After this I cannot sleep, though the rest of the night passes quietly enough. Towards morning I doze a bit, but wake every few minutes with a start. Joky is sleeping peacefully; indeed, he seems worn out with the terrible strain of the past twenty-four hours. About eight a.m. I call him, and we make a light breakfast off the dry ship's biscuit and water. Of the latter happily we have a good supply. Joky seems more himself, and starts to talk a little—possibly somewhat louder than is safe; for, as he chatters on, wondering how it will end, there comes a tremendous blow against the side of the house, making it ring again. After this Joky is very silent. As we sit there I cannot but wonder what all the rest are doing, and how the poor beggars forrard are faring, cooped up without water, as the tragedy of the night has proved.

Towards noon, I hear a loud bang, followed by a terrific bellowing. Then comes a great smashing of woodwork, and the cries of men in pain. Vainly I ask myself what has happened. I begin to reason. By the sound of the report it was evidently something much heavier than a rifle or pistol, and judging from the mad roaring of the Thing, the shot must have done some execution. On thinking it over further, I become convinced that, by some means, those aft have got hold of the small signal cannon we carry, and though I know that some have been hurt, perhaps killed, yet a feeling of exultation seizes me as I listen to the roars of the Thing, and realise that it is badly wounded, perhaps mortally. After a while, however, the bellowing dies away, and only an occasional roar, denoting more of anger than aught else, is heard.

Presently I become aware, by the ship's canting over to starboard, that the creature has gone over to that side, and a great hope springs up within me that possibly it has had enough of us and is going over the rail into the sea. For a time all is silent and my hope grows stronger. I lean across and nudge Joky, who is sleeping with his head on the table. He starts up sharply with a loud cry.

"Hush!" I whisper hoarsely. "I'm not certain, but I do believe it's gone."

Joky's face brightens wonderfully, and he questions me eagerly. We wait another hour or so, with hope ever rising. Our confidence is returning fast. Not a sound can we hear, not even the breathing of the Beast. I get out some biscuits, and Joky, after rummaging in the locker, produces a small piece of pork and a bottle of ship's vinegar. We fall to with a relish. After our long abstinence from food the meal acts on us like wine, and what must Joky do but insist on opening the door, to make sure the Thing has gone. This I will not allow, telling him that at least it will be safer to open the iron port-covers first and have a look out. Joky argues, but I am immovable. He becomes excited. I believe the youngster is lightheaded. Then, as I turn to unscrew one of the after-covers, Joky makes a dash at the door. Before he can undo the bolts I have him, and after a short struggle lead him back to the table. Even as I endeavour to quieten him there comes at the starboard door—the door that Joky has tried to open—a sharp, loud sniff, sniff, followed immediately by a thunderous grunting howl and a foul stench of putrid breath sweeps in under the door. A great trembling takes me, and were it not for the Carpenter's tool-chest I should fall. Joky turns very white and is violently sick, after which he is seized by a hopeless fit of sobbing.

Hour after hour passes, and, weary to death, I lie down on the chest upon which I have been sitting, and try to rest.

It must be about half-past two in the morning, after a somewhat longer doze, that I am suddenly awakened by a most tremendous uproar away forrard—men's voices shrieking, cursing, praying; but in spite of the terror expressed, so weak and feeble; while in the midst, and at times broken off short with that hellishly suggestive "Glut! Glut!" is the unearthly bellowing of the Thing. Fear incarnate seizes me, and I can only fall on my knees and pray. Too well I know what is happening.

Joky has slept through it all, and I am thankful.

Presently, under the door there steals a narrow ribbon of light, and I know that the day has broken on the second morning of our imprisonment. I let Joky sleep on. I will let him have peace while he may. Time passes, but I take little notice. The Thing is quiet, probably sleeping. About midday I eat a little biscuit and drink some of the water. Joky still sleeps. It is best so.

A sound breaks the stillness. The ship gives a slight heave, and I know that once more the Thing is awake. Round the deck it moves, causing the ship to roll perceptibly. Once it goes forrard—I fancy to again explore the fo'cas'le. Evidently it finds nothing, for it returns almost immediately. It pauses a moment at the house, then goes on further aft. Up aloft, somewhere in the fore-rigging, there rings out a peal of wild laughter, though sounding very faint and far away. The Horror stops suddenly. I listen intently, but hear nothing save a sharp creaking beyond the after end of the house, as though a strain had come upon the rigging.

A minute later I hear a cry aloft, followed almost instantly by a loud crash on deck that seems to shake the ship. I wait in anxious fear. What is happening? The minutes pass slowly. Then comes another frightened shout. It ceases suddenly. The suspense has become terrible, and I am no longer able to bear it. Very cautiously I open one of the after port-covers, and peep out to see a fearful sight. There, with its tail upon the deck and its vast body curled round the mainmast, is the monster, its head above the topsail yard, and its great claw-armed tentacle waving in the air. It is the first proper sight that I have had of the Thing. Good Heavens! It must weigh a hundred tons! Knowing that I shall have time, I open the port itself, then crane my head out and look up. There on the extreme end of the lower topsail yard I see one of the able seamen. Even down here I note the staring horror of his face. At this moment he sees me and gives a weak, hoarse cry for help. I can do nothing for him. As I look the great tongue shoots out and licks him off the yard, much as might a dog a fly off the window-pane.

Higher still, but happily out of reach, are two more of the men. As far as I can judge they are lashed to the mast above the royal yard. The Thing attempts to reach them, but after a futile effort it ceases, and starts to slide down, coil on coil, to the deck. While doing this I notice a great gaping wound on its body some twenty feet above the tail.

I drop my gaze from aloft and look aft. The cabin door is torn from its hinges, and the bulkhead—which, unlike the half-deck, is of teak wood—is partly broken down. With a shudder I realise the cause of those cries after the cannon-shot. Turning I screw my head round and try to see the foremast, but cannot. The sun, I notice, is low, and the night is near. Then I draw in my head and fasten up both port and cover.

How will it end? Oh! how will it end?

After a while Joky wakes up. He is very restless, yet though he has eaten nothing during the day I cannot get him to touch anything.

Night draws on. We are too weary—too dispirited to talk. I lie down, but not to sleep…. Time passes.

A ventilator rattles violently somewhere on the maindeck, and there sounds constantly that slurring, gritty noise. Later I hear a cat's agonised howl, and then again all is quiet. Some time after comes a great splash alongside. Then, for some hours all is silent as the grave. Occasionally I sit up on the chest and listen, yet never a whisper of noise comes to me. There is an absolute silence, even the monotonous creak of the gear has died away entirely, and at last a real hope is springing up within me. That splash, this silence—surely I am justified in hoping. I do not wake Joky this time. I will prove first for myself that all is safe. Still I wait. I will run no unnecessary risks. After a time I creep to the after-port and will listen; but there is no sound. I put up my hand and feel at the screw, then again I hesitate, yet not for long. Noiselessly I begin to unscrew the fastening of the heavy shield. It swings loose on its hinge, and I pull it back and peer out. My heart is beating madly. Everything seems strangely dark outside. Perhaps the moon has gone behind a cloud. Suddenly a beam of moonlight enters through the port, and goes as quickly. I stare out. Something moves. Again the light streams in, and now I seem to be looking into a great cavern, at the bottom of which quivers and curls something palely white.

My heart seems to stand still! It is the Horror! I start back and seize the iron port-flap to slam it to. As I do so, something strikes the glass like a steam ram, shatters it to atoms, and flicks past me into the berth. I scream and spring away. The port is quite filled with it. The lamp shows it dimly. It is curling and twisting here and there. It is as thick as a tree, and covered with a smooth slimy skin. At the end is a great claw, like a lobster's, only a thousand times larger. I cower down into the farthest corner…. It has broken the tool-chest to pieces with one click of those frightful mandibles. Joky has crawled under a bunk. The Thing sweeps round in my direction. I feel a drop of sweat trickle slowly down my face—it tastes salty. Nearer comes that awful death…. Crash! I roll over backwards. It has crushed the water breaker against which I leant, and I am rolling in the water across the floor. The claw drives up, then down, with a quick uncertain movement, striking the deck a dull, heavy blow, a foot from my head. Joky gives a little gasp of horror. Slowly the Thing rises and starts feeling its way round the berth. It plunges into a bunk and pulls out a bolster, nips it in half and drops it, then moves on. It is feeling along the deck. As it does so it comes across a half of the bolster. It seems to toy with it, then picks it up and takes it out through the port….

A wave of putrid air fills the berth. There is a grating sound, and something enters the port again—something white and tapering and set with teeth. Hither and thither it curls, rasping over the bunks, ceiling, and deck, with a noise like that of a great saw at work. Twice it flickers above my head, and I close my eyes. Then off it goes again. It sounds now on the opposite side of the berth and nearer to Joky. Suddenly the harsh, raspy noise becomes muffled, as though the teeth were passing across some soft substance. Joky gives a horrid little scream, that breaks off into a bubbling, whistling sound. I open my eyes. The tip of the vast tongue is curled tightly round something that drips, then is quickly withdrawn, allowing the moonbeams to steal again into the berth. I rise to my feet. Looking round, I note in a mechanical sort of way the wrecked state of the berth—the shattered chests, dismantled bunks, and something else—

"Joky!" I cry, and tingle all over.

There is that awful Thing again at the port. I glance round for a weapon. I will revenge Joky. Ah! there, right under the lamp, where the wreck of the Carpenter's chest strews the floor, lies a small hatchet. I spring forward and seize it. It is small, but so keen—so keen! I feel its razor edge lovingly. Then I am back at the port. I stand to one side and raise my weapon. The great tongue is feeling its way to those fearsome remains. It reaches them. As it does so, with a scream of "Joky! Joky!" I strike savagely again and again and again, gasping as I strike; once more, and the monstrous mass falls to the deck, writhing like a hideous eel. A vast, warm flood rushes in through the porthole. There is a sound of breaking steel and an enormous bellowing. A singing comes in my ears and grows louder—louder. Then the berth grows indistinct and suddenly dark.

Extract from the log of the steamship *Hispaniola*.

June 24. —Lat. —N. Long. —W. 11 a.m. —Sighted four-masted barque about four points on the port bow, flying signal of distress. Ran down to her and sent a boat aboard. She proved to be the *Glen Doon*, homeward bound from Melbourne to London. Found things in a terrible state. Decks covered with blood and slime. Steel deck-house stove in. Broke open door, and discovered youth of about nineteen in last stage of inanition, also part remains of boy about fourteen years of age. There was a great quantity of blood in the place, and a huge curled-up mass of whitish flesh, weighing about half a ton, one end of which appeared to have been hacked through with a sharp instrument. Found forecastle door open and hanging from one hinge. Doorway bulged, as though something had been forced through. Went inside. Terrible state of affairs, blood everywhere, broken chests, smashed bunks, but no men nor remains. Went aft again and found youth showing signs of recovery. When he came round, gave the name of Thompson. Said they had been attacked by a huge serpent— thought it must have been sea-serpent. He was too weak to say much, but told us there were some men up the mainmast. Sent a hand aloft, who reported them lashed to the royal mast, and quite dead. Went aft to the cabin. Here we found the bulkhead smashed to pieces, and the cabin-door lying on the deck near the after-hatch. Found body of Captain down lazarette, but no officers. Noticed amongst the wreckage part of the carriage of a small cannon. Came aboard again.

Have sent the Second Mate with six men to work her into port. Thompson is with us. He has written out his version of the affair. We certainly consider that the state of the ship, as we found her, bears out in every respect his story.

(Signed)

WILLIAM NORTON, *Master*
TOM BRIGGS, *1st Mate*

The Sea Horses

"An' we's under the sea, b'ys,
Where the Wild Horses go,
Horses wiv tails
As big as ole whales
All jiggin' around in a row,
An' when you ses Whoa!
Them divvels *does* go!"

How was it you caught my one, Granfer?" asked Nebby, as he had asked the same question any time during the past week, whenever his burly, blue-guernseyed grandfather crooned out the old Ballade of the Sea-Horses, which, however, he never carried past the portion given above.

"Like as he was a bit weak, Nebby b'y; an' I gev him a smart clip wiv the axe, 'fore he could bolt off," explained his grandfather, lying with inimitable gravity and relish.

Nebby dismounted from his curious-looking go-horse, by the simple method of dragging it forward from between his legs. He examined its peculiar, unicorn-like head, and at last put his finger on a bruised indentation in the black paint that covered the nose.

" 'S that where you welted him, Granfer?" he asked, seriously.

"Aye," said his Granfer Zacchy, taking the strangely-shaped go-horse, and examining the contused paint. "Aye, I shore hit 'm a turrible welt."

"Are he dead, Granfer?" asked the boy.

"Well," said the burly old man, feeling the go-horse all over with an enormous finger and thumb, "betwixt an' between, like." He opened the cleverly hinged mouth, and looked at the bone teeth with which he had fitted it, and then squinted earnestly, with one eye, down the red-painted throat. "Aye," he repeated, "betwixt an' between, Nebby. Don't you never let 'm go to water, b'y; for he'd maybe come alive ag'in, an' ye'd lose 'm sure."

Perhaps old Diver-Zacchy, as he was called in the little sea-village, was thinking that water would prove unhealthy to the glue, with which he had fixed-on the big bonito's tail, at what he termed the starn-end of the curious looking beast. He had cut the whole thing out of a nice, four-foot by ten-inch piece of soft, knotless yellow pine; and, to the rear, he had attached, thwart-ship, the aforementioned bonito's tail; for the thing was no ordinary horse, as you may think; but a *gen-u-ine* (as Zacchy described it) Sea-Horse, which he had brought up from the sea bottom for his small grandson, whilst following his occupation as diver.

The animal had taken him many a long hour to carve, and had been made during his spell-ohs, between dives, aboard the diving-barge. The creature itself was a combined production of his own extremely fertile fancy, plus his small grandson's Faith. For Zacchy had manufactured unending and peculiar stories of what he saw daily at the bottom of the sea, and during many a winter's evening, Nebby had "cut boats" around the big stove, whilst the old man smoked and yarned the impossible yarns that were so marvellously real and possible to the boy. And of all the tales that the old diver told in his whimsical fashion, there was none that so stirred Nebby's feelings as the one about the Sea-Horses.

At first it had been but a scrappy and a fragmentary yarn, suggested, as like as not, by the old ballade which Zacchy so often hummed, half-unconsciously. But Nebby's constant questionings had provided so many suggestions for fresh additions, that at last it took nearly the whole of a long evening for the Tale of the Sea-Horses to be told properly, from where the first Horse was seen by Zacchy, eatin' sea-grass as nat'rel as ye like, to where Zacchy had seen li'l Martha Tullet's b'y ridin' one like a reel cow-puncher; and from that tremendous effort of imagination, the Horse Yarn had speedily grown to include every child that wended the Long Road out of the village.

"Shall I go ridin' them Sea-Horses, Granfer, when I dies?" Nebby had asked, earnestly.

"Aye," Granfer Zacchy had replied, absently, puffing at his corn-cob. "Aye, like's not, Nebby. Like as not."

"Mebbe I'll die middlin' soon, Granfer?" Nebby had suggested, longingly. "There's plenty li'l boys dies 'fore they gets growed up."

"Husht! b'y! Husht!" Granfer had said, wakening suddenly to what the child was saying.

Later, when Nebby had many times betrayed his exceeding high requirement of death, that he might ride the Sea-Horses all round his Granfer at work on the sea-bottom, old Zacchy had suddenly evolved a less drastic solution of the difficulty.

"I'll ketch ye one, Nebby, sure," he said, "an' ye kin ride it round the kitchen."

The suggestion pleased Nebby enormously, and practically nullified his impatience regarding the date of his death, which was to give him the freedom of the sea and all the Sea-Horses therein.

For a long month, old Zacchy was met each evening by a small and earnest boy, desirous of learning whether he had "catched one" that day, or not. Meanwhile, Zacchy had been dealing honestly with that four-foot by ten-inch piece of yellow pine, already described. He had carved out his notion of what might be supposed to constitute a veritable Sea-Horse, aided in his invention by Nebby's illuminating questions as to whether Sea-Horses had tails like a real horse or like real fishes; did they wear horse-shoes; did they bite?

These were three points upon which Nebby's curiosity was definite; and the results were definite enough in the finished work; for Granfer supplied the peculiar creature with "reel" bone teeth and a workable jaw; two squat, but prodigious legs, near what he termed the "bows"; whilst to the "starn" he affixed the bonito-tail which has already had mention, setting it the way Dame Nature sets it on the bonito, that is, "thwart-ships," so that its two flukes touched the ground when the go-horse was in position, and thus steadied it admirably with this hint taken direct from the workmanship of the Great Carpenter.

There came a day when the horse was finished and the last coat of paint had dried smooth and hard. That evening, when Nebby came running to meet Zacchy, he was aware of his Grandfather's voice in the dusk, shouting:—"Whoa, Mare! Whoa, Mare!" followed immediately by the cracking of a whip.

Nebby shrilled out a call, and raced on, mad with excitement, towards the noise. He knew instantly that at last Granfer had managed to catch one of the wily Sea-Horses. Presumably the creature was somewhat intractable; for when Nebby arrived, he found the burly form of Granfer straining back tremendously upon stout reins, which Nebby saw vaguely in the dusk were attached to a squat, black monster:—

"Whoa, Mare!" roared Granfer, and lashed the air furiously with his whip. Nebby shrieked delight, and ran round and round, whilst Granfer struggled with the animal.

"Hi! Hi! Hi!" shouted Nebby, dancing from foot to foot. "Ye've catched 'm, Granfer! Ye've catched 'm, Granfer!"

"Aye," said Granfer, whose struggles with the creature must have been prodigious; for he appeared to pant. "She'll go quiet now, b'y. Take a holt!" And he handed the reins and the whip over to the excited, but half-fearful Nebby. "Put y'r hand on 'er,

Neb," said old Zacchy. "That'll quiet 'er."

Nebby did so, a little nervously, and drew away in a moment.

"She's all wet 's wet!" he cried out.

"Aye," said Granfer, striving to hide the delight in his voice. "She 'm straight up from the water, b'y."

This was quite true; it was the final artistic effort of Granfer's imagination; he had dipped the horse overside, just before leaving the diving barge. He took his towel from his pocket, and wiped the horse down, hissing as he did so.

"Now, b'y," he said, "welt 'er good, an' make her take ye home."

Nebby straddled the go-horse, made an ineffectual effort to crack the whip, shouted:—"Gee-up! Gee-up!" And was off—two small, lean bare legs twinkling away into the darkness at a tremendous rate, accompanied by shrill and recurrent "Gee-ups!"

Granfer Zacchy stood in the dusk, laughing happily, and pulled out his pipe. He filled it slowly, and as he applied the light, he heard the galloping of the horse, returning. Nebby dashed up, and circled his Granfer in splendid fashion, singing in a rather breathless voice:—

"An' we's under the sea, b'ys,
Where the Wild Horses go,
Horses wiv tails
As big as ole whales
All jiggin' around in a row,
An' when you ses Whoa!
Them debbils *does* go!"

And away he went again at the gallop.

This had happened a week earlier; and now we have Nebby questioning Granfer Zacchy as to whether the Sea-Horse is really alive or dead.

"Should think they has Sea-Horses 'n heaven, Granfer?" said Nebby, thoughtfully, as he once more straddled the go-horse.

"Sure," said Granfer Zacchy.

"Is Martha Tullet's li'l b'y gone to heaven?" asked Nebby.

"Sure," said Granfer again, as he sucked at his pipe.

Nebby was silent a good while, thinking. It was obvious that he confused heaven with the Domain of the Sea-Horses; for had not Granfer himself seen Martha Tullet's li'l b'y riding one of the Sea-Horses? Nebby had told Mrs. Tullet about it; but she had only thrown her apron over her head, and cried, until at last Nebby had stolen away, feeling rather dumpy.

"Has you ever seed any angels wiv wings on the Sea-Horses, Granfer?" Nebby asked, presently; determined to have further information with which to assure his ideas.

"Aye," said Granfer Zacchy. "Shoals of 'em. Shoals of 'em, b'y."

Nebby was greatly pleased.

"Could they ride some, Granfer?" he questioned.

"Sure," said old Zacchy, reaching for his pouch.

"As good 's me?" asked Nebby, anxiously.

"Middlin' near. Middlin' near, b'y," said Granfer Zacchy. "Why, Neb," he continued, waking up with a sudden relish to the full possibilities of the question, "thar's some of them lady ayngels as c'ud do back-somersaults an' never take a throw, b'y."

It is to be feared that Granfer Zacchy's conception of a lady angel had been formed during odd visits to the circus. But Nebby was duly impressed, and bumped his head badly the same day, trying to achieve the rudiments of a back-somersault.

2

Some evenings later, Nebby came running to meet old Zacchy, with an eager question:—

"Has you seed Jane Melly's li'l gel ridin' the Horses, Granfer?" he asked, earnestly.

"Aye," said Granfer. Then, realising suddenly what the question portended:—

"What's wrong wiv Mrs. Melly's wee gel?" he queried.

"Dead," said Nebby, calmly. "Mrs. Kay ses it's the fever come to the village again, Granfer."

Nebby's voice was cheerful; for the fever had visited the village some months before, and Granfer Zacchy had taken Nebby to live on the barge, away from danger of infection. Nebby enjoyed it all enormously, and had often prayed God since to send another fever, with its attendant possibilities of life again aboard the diving-barge.

"Shall we live in the barge, Granfer?" he asked, as he swung along with the old man.

"Maybe! Maybe!" said old Zacchy, absently, in a somewhat troubled voice.

Granfer left Nebby in the kitchen, and went on up the village to make inquiries; the result was that he packed Nebby's clothes and toys into a well-washed sugar-bag, and the next day took the boy down to the barge, to live. But whereas Granfer walked, carrying the sack of gear, Nebby rode all the way, most of it at an amazing gallop. He even rode daringly down the narrow, rail-less gang-plank. It is true that Granfer Zacchy took care to keep close behind, in as unobtrusive a fashion as possible; but of this, or the need of such watchfulness, Nebby was most satisfactorily ignorant. He was welcomed in the heartiest fashion by Ned, the pump-man, and Binny, who attended to the air-pipe and life-line when Granfer Zacchy was down below.

3

Life aboard the diving-barge was a very happy time for Nebby. It was a happy time also for Granfer Zacchy and his two men; for the child, playing constantly in their midst, brought back to them an adumbration of their youth. There was only one point upon which there arose any trouble, and that was Nebby's forgetfulness, in riding across the air-tube, when he was exercising his Sea-Horse.

Ned, the pump-man, had spoken very emphatically to Nebby on this point, and Nebby had promised to remember; but, as usual, soon forgot. They had taken the barge outside the bar, and anchored her over the buoy that marked Granfer's submarine operations. The day was gloriously fine, and so long as the weather remained fixed, they meant to keep the barge out there, merely sending the little punt ashore for provisions.

To Nebby, it was all just splendid! When he was not riding his Sea-Horse, he was talking to the men, or waiting at the gangway eagerly for Granfer's great copper head-piece to come up out of the water, as the air-tube and life-line were slowly drawn aboard. Or else his shrill young voice was sure to be heard, as he leant over the rail and peered into the depths below, singing:—

"An' we's under the sea, b'ys,
Where the Wild Horses go,
Horses wiv tails
As big as ole whales
All jiggin' around in a row,
An' when you ses Whoa!
Them debbils *does* go!"

Possibly, he considered it as some kind of charm with which to call the Sea-Horses up to view.

Each time the boat went ashore, it brought sad news, that first this and then that one had gone the Long Road; but it was chiefly the children that interested Nebby. Each time that his Granfer came up out of the depths, Nebby would dance round him impatiently, until the big helmet was unscrewed; then would come his inevitable, eager question:—Had Granfer seen Carry Andrew's li'l gel; or had Granfer seen Marty's li'l b'y riding the Sea-Horses? And so on.

"Sure," Granfer would reply; though, several times, it was his first intimation that the child mentioned had died; the news having reached the barge through some passing boat, whilst he was on the sea-bottom.

4

"Look you, Nebby!" shouted Ned, the pump-man, angrily. "I'll shore break that horse of yours up for kindlin' next time you goes steppin' on the air-pipe."

It was all too true; Nebby had forgotten, and done it again; but whereas, generally, he took Ned's remonstrances in good part, and promised better things, he stood now, looking with angry defiance at the man. The suggestion that his Sea-Horse was made of wood, bred in him a tempest of bitterness. Never for one moment to himself had he allowed so horrible a thought to enter his own head; not even when, in a desperate charge, he had knocked a chip off the nose of the Sea-Horse, and betrayed the merciless wood below. He had simply refused to look particularly at the place; his fresh, child's imagination allowing him presently to grow assured again that all was well; that he truly rode a "gen-u-ine" Sea-Horse. In his earnestness of determined make-believe, he had even avoided showing Granfer Zacchy the place, and asking him to mend it, much as he wanted it mended. Granfer always mended his toys for him; but *this* could not be mended. It was a *real* Sea-Horse; not a toy. Nebby resolutely averted his thoughts from the possibility of any other Belief; though it is likely that such mental processes were more subconscious than conscious.

And now, Ned had said the deadly thing, practically in so many naked words. Nebby trembled with anger and a furious mortification of his pride of Sea-Horse-Ownership. He looked round swiftly for the surest way to avenge the brutish insult, and saw the air-pipe; the thing around which the bother had been made. Yes, that would make Ned angry! Nebby turned his strange steed, and charged straight away back at the pipe. There, with an angry and malicious deliberateness, he halted, and made the big front hoofs of his extraordinary monster, stamp upon the air-pipe.

"You young devil!" roared Ned, scarcely able to believe the thing he saw. "You young devil!"

Nebby continued to stamp the big hoofs upon the pipe, glaring with fierce, defiant, blue eyes at Ned. Whereupon, Ned's patience arose and departed, and Ned himself arrived bodily in haste and with considerable vigour. He gave one kick, and the Sea-Horse went flying across the deck, and crashed into the low bulwarks. Nebby screamed; but it was far more a scream of tremendous anger, than of fear.

"I'll heave the blamed thing over the side!" said Ned, and ran to complete his dreadful sacrilege. The following instant, something clasped his right leg, and small, distinctly sharp teeth bit his bare shin, below the up-rolled trousers. Ned yelled, and sat rapidly and luridly upon the deck, in a fashion calculated to shock his system, in every sense of the word.

Nebby had loosed from him, the instant his bite had taken effect; and now he was nursing and examining the black monster of his dreams and waking moments. He knelt there, near the bulwarks, looking with burning eyes of anger and enormous distress at the effects of Ned's great kick; for Ned wore his bluchers on his bare feet. Ned himself still endured a sitting conjunction with the deck; he had not yet finished expressing himself; not that Nebby was in the least interested…anger and distress had built a wall of fierce indifference about his heart. He desired chiefly Ned's death.

If Ned, himself, had been less noisy, he would have heard Binny even earlier than he did; for that sane man had jumped to the air-pump, luckily for Granfer Zacchy, and was now, as he worked, emptying his soul of most of its contents upon the derelict Ned. As it was, Ned's memory and ears did duty together, and he remembered that he had committed the last crime in the Pump-man's Calendar…he had left the pump, whilst his diver was still below water. Powder ignited in quite a considerable quantity beneath him, could scarcely have moved Ned more speedily. He gave out one yell, and leaped for the pump; at the same instant he discovered that Binny was there, and his gasp of relief was as vehement as prayer. He remembered his leg, and concluded his journey to the pump, with a limp. Here, with one hand he pumped, whilst with the other, he investigated Nebby's teeth-marks. He found that the skin was barely broken; but it was his temper that most needed mending; and, of course, it had been very naughty of Nebby to attempt such a familiarity.

Binny was drawing in the life-line and air-pipe; for Granfer Zacchy was ascending the long rope-ladder, that led up from the sea-bottom, to learn what had caused the unprecedented interruption of his air-supply.

It was a very angry Granfer who, presently, having heard a fair representation of the facts, applied a wet but horny hand to Nebby's anatomy, in a vigorous and decided manner. Yet Nebby neither cried nor spoke; he merely clung on tightly to the Sea-Horse; and Granfer whacked on. At last Granfer grew surprised at the continued absence of remonstrance on Nebby's part, and turned that young man the other end about, to discover the wherefore of so determined a silence.

Nebby's face was very white, and tears seemed perilously near; yet even the nearness of these, did not in any way detract from the expression of unutterable defiance that looked out at Granfer and all the world, from his face. Granfer regarded him for a few moments with earnest attention and doubt, and decided to cease whipping that atom of blue-eyed stubbornness. He looked at the Sea-Horse that Nebby clutched so tightly, in his silence, and perceived the way to make Nebby climb down…Nebby must go and beg Ned's pardon for trying to eat him (Granfer smothered a chuckle), or else the Sea-Horse would be taken away.

Nebby's face, however, showed no change, unless it was that the blue eyes shone with a fiercer defiance, which dried out of them that suspicion of tears. Granfer pondered over him, and had a fresh idea. He would take the Sea-Horse back again to the bottom of the sea; and it would then come alive once more and swim away, and Nebby would never see it again, if Nebby did not go at once to Ned and beg Ned's pardon, that very minute. Granfer was prodigiously stern.

There came, perhaps, the tiniest flash of fright into the blue eyes; but it was blurred with unbelief; and, anyway, it had no power at that stage of Nebby's temper to budge him from his throne of enormous anger. He decided, with that fierce courage of the burner of boats, that if Granfer did truly do such a dreadful thing, he (Nebby) would "kneel down proper" and pray God to kill Ned. An added relish of vengeance came to his child's mind…. He would kneel down in front of Ned; he would pray to God "out loud." Ned should thus learn beforehand that he was doomed.

In that moment of inspired Intention, Nebby became trebly fixed into his Aura of Implacable Anger. He voiced his added grimness of heart in the most tremendous words possible:—

"It's wood!" said Nebby, glaring at Granfer, in a kind of fierce, sick, horrible triumph. "It carn't come back alive again!"

Then he burst into tears, at this dreadful act of disillusionment, and wrenching himself free from Granfer's gently-detaining hand, he dashed away aft, and down the scuttle into the cuddy, where for an hour he hid himself under a bunk, and refused, in dreary silence, any suggestion of dinner.

After dinner, however, he emerged, tear-stained but unbroken. He had brought the Sea-Horse below with him; and now, as the three men watched him, unobtrusively, from their seats around the little cuddy-table, it was plain to them that Nebby had some definite object in view, which he was attempting to mask under an attitude of superb but ineffectual casualness.

"B'y," said Granfer Zacchy, in a very stern voice, "come you an' beg Ned's pard'n, or I'll shore take th' Sea-Horse down wiv me, an' you'll never see 'm no more, an' I'll never ketch ye another, Nebby."

Nebby's reply was an attempted dash for the scuttle-ladder; but Granfer reached out a long arm, that might have been described as possessing the radius of the small cuddy. As a result, Nebby was put with his face in a corner, whilst Granfer Zacchy laid the Sea-Horse across his knees, and stroked it meditatively, as he smoked a restful after-dinner pipe.

Presently, he knocked out his pipe, and, reaching round, brought Nebby to stand at his knee.

"Nebby, b'y," he said, in his grave, kindly fashion, "go you an' beg Ned's pard'n, an' ye shall hev this right back to play wiv."

But Nebby had not been given time yet to ease himself clear of the cloud of his indignation; and even as he stood there by Granfer, he could see the great bruise in the paint, where Ned's blucher had taken effect; and the broken fluke of the tail, that had been smashed when the poor Sea-Horse brought-up so violently against the low bulwarks of the barge.

"Ned's a wicked pig man!" said Nebby, with a fresh intensity of anger against the pump-hand.

"Hush, b'y!" said Granfer, with real sternness. "Ye've had fair chance to come round, an' ye've not took it, an' now I'll read ye a lesson as ye'll shore mind!"

He stood up, and put the Sea-Horse under his arm; then, with one hand on Nebby's shoulder, he went to the ladder, and so in a minute they were all on the deck of the barge. Presently, Granfer was once more transformed from a genial and burly giant, into an indiarubber-covered and dome-ended monster. Then, with a slowness and solemnity befitting so terrible an execution of justice, Granfer made a fathom, or so, of spunyarn fast about the Sea-Horse's neck, whilst Nebby looked on, white-faced.

When this was accomplished, Granfer stood up and marched with ponderous steps to the side, the Sea-Horse under his arm. He began to go slowly down the wooden rungs of the rope-ladder, and presently there were only his shoulders and copper-headpiece visible. Nebby stared down in an anguish; he could see the Sea-Horse vaguely. It seemed to waggle in the crook of Granfer's arm. It was surely about to swim away. Then Granfer's shoulders, and finally his great copper head disappeared from sight, and there was soon only the slight working of the ladder, and the paying out of the air-pipe and life-line, to tell that any one was down there in all that greyness of the water-dusk; for Granfer had often explained to Nebby that it was always "evenin' at th' sea-bottom."

Nebby sobbed once or twice, in a dry, horrid way in his throat; then, for quite half an hour, he lay flat on his stomach in the gangway, silent and watchful, staring down into the water. Several times he felt *quite* sure he saw something swimming with a queer, waggling movement, a little under the water; and presently he started to sing in a low voice:—

"An' we's under the sea, b'ys,
Where the Wild Horses go,
Horses wiv tails
As big as ole whales
All jiggin' around in a row,
An' when you ses Whoa!
Them debbils *does* go!"

But it seemed to have no power to charm the Sea-Horse up to the surface; and he fell silent, after singing it through, maybe a dozen times. He was waiting for Granfer. He had a vague hope, which grew, that Granfer had meant to tie it up with the spunyarn, so that it could not swim away; and perhaps Granfer would bring it up with him when he came. Nebby felt that he would really beg Ned's pardon, if only Granfer brought the Sea-Horse up with him again.

A little later, there came the signal that Granfer was about to ascend, and Nebby literally trembled with excitement, as the lifeline and air-pipe came in slowly, hand over hand. He saw the big dome of the helmet come vaguely into view, with the line of the air-pipe leading down at the usual "funny" angle, right into the top of the dome (it was an old type of helmet). Then the helmet broke the water, and Nebby could not see anything, because the "rimples" on the water stopped him seeing. Granfer's big shoulders came into view, and then sufficient of him for Nebby to see that the Sea-Horse was truly not with him. Nebby whitened. Granfer had *really* let the Sea-Horse go. As a matter of fact, Granfer Zacchy had tethered the Sea-Horse to some tough marine weed-rootlets at the sea-bottom, so as to prevent it floating traitorously to the surface; but to Nebby it was plain only that the Sea-Horse had truly "come alive" and swum away.

Granfer stepped on to the deck, and Binny eased off the great helmet, whilst Ned ceased his last, slow revolution of the pump-handle.

It was at this moment that Nebby faced round on Ned, with a white, set, little face, in which his blue eyes literally burned. Ned was surely doomed in that instant! And then, even in the Moment of his Intention, Nebby heard Granfer say to Binny:—

"Aye, I moored it wiv the spunyarn safe enough."

Nebby's anger lost its deadliness abruptly, under the sudden sweet chemistry of hope. He oscillated an instant between a new, vague thought, and his swiftly-lessening requirement of vengeance. The new, vague thought became less vague, and he swayed the more toward it; and so, in a moment had rid himself of his Dignity, and run across to Granfer Zacchy:—

"Has it comed alive, Granfer?" he asked, breathlessly, with the infinite eagerness and expectancy of a child.

"Aye!" said Granfer Zacchy, with apparent sternness. "Ye've sure lost it now, b'y. 'Tis swimmin' an' swimmin' roun' an' roun' all the time."

Nebby's eyes shone with sudden splendour, as the New Idea took now a most definite form in his young brain.

Granfer, looking at him with eyes of tremendous sternness, was quite non-plussed at the harmless effect of his expectedly annihilative news concerning the final and obvious lostness of the Sea-Horse. Yet, Nebby said never a word to give Granfer an inkling of the stupendous plan that was settling fast in his daring child's-mind. He opened his mouth once or twice upon a further question; then relapsed into the safety of silence again, as though instinctively realising that he might ask something that would make Granfer suspicious.

Presently, Nebby had stolen away once more to the gangway, and there, lying on his stomach, he began again to look down into the sea. His anger now was almost entirely submerged in the great, glorious New Idea, that filled him with such tremendous exaltation that he could scarcely lie quiet, or cease from singing aloud at the top of his voice.

A few moments earlier, he had meant to "kneel down proper" and pray God "out loud" for Ned to be killed quickly and painfully; but now all was changed. Though, in an indifferent sort of way, in his healthily-savage child's-mind, he did not *forgive* Ned....Ned's sin had, of course, been unforgivable, presumably "for ever and ever and ever"—Certainly until to-morrow! Meanwhile, Nebby never so much as thought of him, except it might be as one whose bewilderment should presently be the last lustre of the glory of his (Nebby's) proposed achievement. Not that Nebby thought it all out like this into separate ideas; but it was all there in that young and surging head...in what I might term a Chaos of Determination, buoying up (as it might be a lonesome craft) one clear, vigorous Idea.

Granfer Zacchy went down twice more before evening, and each time that he returned, Nebby questioned him earnestly as to the doings of the Sea-Horse; and each time, Granfer told the same tale (in accents of would-be sternness) that the Sea-Horse was "jest swimmin' roun' an' roun'; an' maybe ye wish now ye'd begged Ned's pardon, when ye was bid!"

But, in his heart, Granfer decided that the Sea-Horse might be safely re-caught on the morrow.

5

That night, when the three men were asleep in the little cuddy, Nebby's small figure slipped noiselessly out of the bunk that lay below Granfer Zacchy's. He flitted silently to the ladder, and stole up into the warm night, his shirt (a quaint cut-down of Granfer's) softly flicking his lean, bare legs, as he moved through the darkness, along the barge's decks.

Nebby came to a stop where Granfer's diving-suit was hung up carefully on the "frame"; but this was not what Nebby wanted. He stooped to the bottom of the "frame," and pulled up the small hatch of a square locker, where reposed the big, domed, copper helmet, glimmering dully in the vague starlight.

Nebby reached into the locker, and lugged the helmet out bodily, hauling with both hands upon the air-pipe. He carried it across clumsily to the gangway, the air-pipe unreeling off the winch, with each step that he took.

He found the helmet too clumsy and rotund to lift easily on to his own curly head, and so, after an attempt or two, evolved the method of turning the helmet upon its side, and then kneeling down and thrusting his head into it; after which, with a prodigious effort, he rose victoriously to his knees, and began to fumble himself backwards over the edge of the gangway, on to the wooden rungs of Granfer's rope-ladder, which had not been hauled up. He managed a firm foot-hold with his left foot, and then with his right; and so began to descend, slowly and painfully, the great helmet rocking clumsily on his small shoulders.

His right foot touched the water at the fourth rung, and he paused, bringing the other foot down beside the first. The water was pleasantly warm, and Nebby hesitated only a very little while, ere he ventured the next step. Then he stopped again, and tried to look down into the water. The action swayed the big helmet backwards, so that—inside of it—Nebby's delightfully impudent little nose received a bang that made his determined blue eyes water. He loosed his left hand from the ladder, holding on with his right, and tried to push the clumsy helmet forward again into place.

He was, as you will understand, up to his knees in the water, and the rung, on which he perched, was slippery with that peculiar slipperiness, that wood and water together know so well how to breed. One of Nebby's bare feet slipped, and immediately the other. The great helmet gave a prodigious wobble, and completed the danger; for the sudden strain wrenched his grip from the rope between the rungs. There was a muffled little cry inside the helmet, and Nebby swung a small, desperate hand through the darkness towards the ladder; but it was too late; he was falling. There was a splash; not a very big splash for so big a boy's-heart and courage; and no one heard it, or the little bubbling squeak that came out of the depths of the big copper helmet. And then, in a moment, there was only the vaguely disturbed surface of the water, and the air-pipe was running out smoothly and swiftly off the drum.

6

It was in the strange, early-morning light, when the lemon and gold-of-light of dawn was in the grey East, that Granfer discovered the thing which had happened. With the wakefulness that is so often an asset of healthy age, he had turned-out in the early hours, to fill his pipe, and had discovered that Nebby's bunk was empty.

He went swiftly up the small ladder. On the deck, the out-trailed air-pipe whispered its tale in silence, and Granfer rushed to it, shouting in a dreadful voice for Binny and Ned, who came bounding up, sleepily, in their heavy flannel drawers.

They hauled in the air-pipe, swiftly but carefully; but when the great dome of the helmet came up to them, there was no Nebby; only, tangled from the thread of one of the old-fashioned thumb-screws, they found several golden, curly strands of Nebby's hair.

Granfer, his great muscular hands trembling, began to get into his rubber suit, the two men helping him, wordless. Within a hundred and fifty seconds, he was dwindling away down under the quiet sea that spread, all grey and lemon-hued and utterly calm, in the dawn. Ned was turning the pump-handle, and wiping his eyes undisguisedly from time to time with the back of one hairy, disengaged hand. Binny, who was of a sterner type, though no less warm-hearted, was grimly silent, giving his whole attention to the air-pipe and the life-line; his hand delicate upon the line, awaiting the signal. He could tell from the feel and the coming-up and going-out of the pipe and the line, that Granfer Zacchy was casting round and round, in ever largening circles upon the sea-bottom.

All that day, Granfer quartered the sea-bottom; staying down so long each time, that at last Binny and Ned were forced to remonstrate. But the old man turned on them, and snarled in a kind of speechless anger and agony that forced them to be silent and let him go his own gait.

For three days, Granfer continued his search, the sea remaining calm; but found nothing. On the fourth day, Granfer Zacchy was forced to take the barge in over the bar; for the wind breezed up hard out of the North, and blew for a dreary and savage fortnight, each day of which found Granfer, with Binny and Ned, searching the shore for the "giving up" of the sea. But the sea had one of its secret moods, and gave up nothing.

At the end of the fortnight of heavy weather, it fell calm, and they took the barge out again, to start once more their daily work. There was little use now in searching further for the boy. The barge was moored again over the old spot, and Granfer descended; and the first thing he saw in the grey half-light of the water, was the Sea-Horse, still moored securely by the length of spunyarn to the rootlets of heavy weed at the sea-bottom.

The sight of the creature, gave old Zacchy a dreadful feeling; it was, at once, so familiar of Nebby, as to give him the sensation and unreasoning impression that the "b'y" must be surely close at hand; and yet, at the same time, the grotesque, inanimate creature was the visible incarnation of the Dire Cause of the unspeakable loneliness and desolation that now possessed his old heart so utterly. He glared at it, through the thick glass of his helmet, and half raised his axe to strike at it. Then, with a sudden revulsion, he reached out, and pulled the silent go-horse to him, and hugged it madly, as if, indeed, it were the boy himself.

Presently, old Granfer Zacchy grew calmer, and turned to his work; yet a hundred times, he would find himself staring round in the watery twilight towards it—staring eagerly and unreasoningly, and actually listening, inside his helmet, for sounds that the eternal silence of the sea might never bring through its dumb waters, that are Barriers of Silence about the lonesome diver in the strange underworld of the waters. And then, realising freshly that there was no longer One who might make the so-craved-for sounds, Granfer would turn again, grey-souled and lonely, to his work. Yet, in a while, he would be staring and listening once more.

In the course of days, old Zacchy grew calmer and more resigned; yet he kept the motionless Sea-Horse tethered, in the quiet twilight of the water, to the weed-rootlets at the sea-bottom. And more and more, he grew to staring round at it; and less and less did it seem a futile or an unreasonable thing to do.

In weeks, the habit grew to such an extent, that he had ceased to be aware of it. He prolonged his hours under water, out of all reason, so far as his health was concerned; and turned queerly "dour" when Ned and Binny remonstrated with him, warning him not to stay down so long, or he would certainly have to pay the usual penalty.

Only once did Granfer say a word in explanation, and then it was obviously an unintentional remark, jerked out of him by the intensity of his feelings:—

"Like as I feel 'm nigh me, w'en I'm below," he had muttered, in a half coherent fashion. And the two men understood; for it was just what they had vaguely supposed. They had no reply to make; and the matter dropped.

Generally now, on descending each morning, Granfer would stop near the Sea-Horse, and "look it over." Once, he discovered that the bonito-tail had come unglued; but this he remedied neatly, by lashing it firmly into position with a length of roping-twine. Sometimes, he would pat the head of the horse, with one great hand, and mutter a quite unconscious:—"Whoa, mare!" as it bobbed silently under his touch. Occasionally, as he swayed heavily past it, in his clumsy dress, the slight swirl of the water in his "wake" would make the Horse slue round uncannily towards him; and thereafter, it would swing and oscillate for a brief time, slowly back into quietness; the while that Granfer would stand and watch it, unconsciously straining his ears, in that place of no-sound.

Two months passed in this way, and Granfer was vaguely aware that his health was failing; but the knowledge brought no fear to him; only the beginnings of an indefinite contentment—a feeling that maybe he would be "soon seein' Nebby." Yet the thought was never definitely conscious; nor ever, of course, in any form, phrased. Yet it had its effect, in the vague contentment which I have hinted at, which brought a new sense of ease round Granfer's heart; so that, one day, as he worked, he found himself crooning unconsciously the old Ballade of the Sea Horses.

He stopped on the instant, all an ache with memory; then turned and peered towards the Sea-Horse, which loomed, a vague shadow, silent in the still water. It had seemed to him in that moment, that he had heard a subtle echo of his crooned song, in the quiet deeps around him. Yet, he saw nothing, and presently assured himself that he heard nothing; and so came round again upon his work.

A number of times in the early part of that day, old Granfer caught himself crooning the old Ballade, and each time he shut his lips fiercely on the sound, because of the ache of memory that the old song bred in him; but, presently, all was forgotten in an intense listening; for, abruptly, old Zacchy was sure that he heard the song, coming from somewhere out of the eternal twilight of the waters. He slued himself round, trembling, and stared towards the Sea-Horse; but there was nothing new to be seen, neither was he any more sure that he had ever heard anything.

Several times this happened, and on each occasion Granfer would heave himself round ponderously in the water, and listen with an intensity that had in it, presently, something of desperateness.

In the late afternoon of that day, Granfer again heard something; but refused now to credit his hearing, and continued grimly at work. And then, suddenly, there was no longer any room for doubt…a shrill, sweet child's voice was singing, somewhere among the grey twilights far to his back. He heard it with astounding clearness, helmet and surrounding water notwithstanding. It was a sound, indeed, that he would have heard through all the Mountains of Eternity. He stared round, shaking violently.

The sound appeared to come from the greyness that dwelt away beyond a little wood of submarine growths, that trailed up their roots, so hushed and noiseless, out of a near-by vale in the sea-bottom.

As Granfer stared, everything about him darkened into a wonderful and rather dreadful Blackness. This passed, and he was able to see again; but somehow, as it might be said, newly. The shrill, sweet, childish singing had ceased; but there was something beside the Sea-Horse…a little, agile figure, that caused the Sea-Horse to bob and bound at its moorings. And, suddenly, the little figure was astride the Sea-Horse, and the Horse was free, and two twinkling legs urged it across the sea-bottom towards Granfer.

Granfer thought that he stood up, and ran to meet the boy; but Nebby dodged him, the Sea-Horse curvetting magnificently; and immediately Nebby began to gallop round and round Granfer, singing:—

"An' we's under the sea, b'ys,
Where the Wild Horses go,
Horses wiv tails
As big as ole whales
All jiggin' around in a row,
An' when you ses Whoa!
Them debbils *does* go!"

The voice of the blue-eyed mite was ineffably gleeful; and abruptly, tremendous youth invaded Granfer, and a glee beyond all understanding.

7

On the deck of the barge, Ned and Binny were in great doubt and trouble. The weather had been growing heavy and threatening, during all the late afternoon; and now it was culminating in a tremendous, black squall, which was coming swiftly down upon them.

Time after time, Binny had attempted to signal Granfer Zacchy to come up; but

Granfer had taken a turn with his life-line round a hump of rock that protruded out of the sea-bottom; so that Binny was powerless to do aught; for there was no second set of diving gear aboard.

All that the two men could do, was to wait, in deep anxiety, keeping the pump going steadily, and standing-by for the signal that was never to come; for by that time, old Granfer Zacchy was sitting very quiet and huddled against the rock, round which he had hitched to prevent Binny from signalling him, as Binny had become prone to do, when Granfer stayed below, out of all reason and wisdom.

And all the time, Ned kept the un-needed pump going, and far down in the grey depth, the air came out in a continual series of bubbles, around the big copper helmet. But Granfer was breathing an air of celestial sweetness, all unwotting and un-needing of the air that Ned laboured faithfully to send to him.

The squall came down in a fierce haze of rain and foam, and the ungainly old craft swung round, jibbing heavily at her kedge-rope, which gave out a little twanging sound, that was lost in the roar of the wind. The unheard twanging of the rope, ended suddenly in a dull thud, as it parted; and the bluff old barge fell off, broadside on to the weight of the squall. She drifted with astonishing rapidity, and the life-line and the air-pipe flew out, with a buzz of the unwinding drums, and parted, with two differently toned reports, that were plain in an instant's lull in the roaring of the squall.

Binny had run forrard to the bows, to try to get over another kedge; but now he came racing aft again, shouting. Ned still pumped on mechanically, with a look of dull, stunned horror in his eyes; the pump driving a useless jet of air through the broken remnant of the air-pipe. Already, the barge was a quarter of a mile to leeward of the diving-ground, and the men could do no more than hoist the foresail, and try to head her in safely over the bar, which was now right under their lee.

Down in the sea, old Granfer Zacchy had altered his position; the jerk upon the air-pipe had done that. But Granfer was well enough content; not only for the moment; but for Eternity; for as Nebby rode so gleefully round and round him, there had come a change in all things; there were strange and subtle lights in all the grey twilights of the deep, that seemed to lead away and away into stupendous and infinitely beautiful distances.

"Is you listenin', Granfer?" Old Zacchy heard Nebby say; and discovered suddenly that Nebby was insisting that he should race him across the strangely glorified twilights, that bounded them now eternally.

"Sure, b'y," said Granfer Zacchy, undismayed; and Nebby wheeled his charger.

"Gee-Up!" shouted Nebby, excitedly, and his small legs began to twinkle ahead in magnificent fashion; with Granfer running a cheerful and deliberate second.

And so passed Granfer Zacchy and Nebby into the Land where little boys may ride Sea-Horses for ever, and where Parting becomes one of the Lost Sorrows.

And Nebby led the way at a splendid gallop; maybe, for all that I have any right to know, to the very Throne of the Almighty, singing, shrill and sweet:—

> "An we's under the sea, b'ys,
> Where the Wild Horses go,
> Horses wiv tails
> As big as ole whales
> All jiggin' around in a row,
> An' when you ses Whoa!
> Them debbils *does* go!"

And overhead (was it *only* a dozen fathoms!) there rushed the white-maned horses of the sea, mad with the glory of the storm, and tossing ruthless from crest to crest, a wooden go-horse, from which trailed a length of broken spunyarn.

The Searcher
of the End House

❖◆❖

I T WAS STILL EVENING, as I remember, and the four of us, Jessop, Arkright, Taylor and I, looked disappointedly at Carnacki, where he sat silent in his great chair.

We had come in response to the usual card of invitation, which—as you know—we have come to consider as a sure prelude to a good story; and now, after telling us the short incident of the Three Straw Platters, he had lapsed into a contented silence, and the night not half gone, as I have hinted.

However, as it chanced, some pitying fate jogged Carnacki's elbow, or his memory, and he began again, in his queer level way:—

"The 'Straw Platters' business reminds me of the 'Searcher' Case, which I have sometimes thought might interest you. It was some time ago, in fact a deuce of a long time ago, that the thing happened; and my experience of what I might term 'curious' things was very small indeed.

"I was living with my Mother, when it occurred, in a small house just outside of Appledorn, on the South Coast. The house was the last of a row of detached cottage-villas, I might call them, each house standing in its own garden; and very dainty little places they were, exceedingly old, and most of them smothered in roses; and all, you know, with those quaint, leaded windows, and the doors built of genuine oak. You must just try to picture them for the sake of their complete niceness.

"Now I must remind you at the beginning, that my Mother and I had lived in that little house for two years, and in the whole of that time there had not been a single thing peculiar to worry us.

"And then, you know, something happened.

"It was about two o'clock one morning, just as I was finishing some letters, that I heard the door of my Mother's bedroom open, and she came to the top of the stairs, and knocked on the banisters.

" 'All right, dear,' I called; for I supposed that she was merely reminding me that I should have been in bed long ago; then I heard her go back to her room, and I hurried my work, for fear that she should lie awake, until she had heard me safe up to my room.

"When I was finished, I lit my candle, put out the lamp, and went upstairs. As I came opposite to the door of my Mother's room, I saw that it was open, and called good-night to her, very softly, and asked whether I should close the door.

"As there was no answer, I knew that she had dropped over again to sleep, and I closed the door very gently, and turned into my room, just across the passage. As I did so, I had a momentary, half-aware sense that there was a faint, peculiar, disagreeable odour in the passage; but it was not until the following night that I *realised* that I had seemed to smell something that offended me. You follow me, don't you? I mean, it is so often like that—one suddenly knows about a thing that really recorded itself on one's consciousness, perhaps a year before.

"The next morning at breakfast, I mentioned casually to my Mother that she had 'dropped-off', and that I had shut her door for her. But, to my surprise, she assured me that she had never been out of her room. I reminded her about the two raps that she had given upon the banister; but she was still certain that I must be mistaken; and in the end I teased her that she had got so accustomed to my bad habit of sitting up late, that she had come to call me in her sleep. Of course, she denied this, and I let the matter drop; but I was more than a little puzzled, and did not know whether to believe my own explanation, or to take the Mater's, which was to put the noises to the blame of mice, and the open door to the fact that she may not have properly latched it when she went to bed. I suppose, away in the subconscious part of me, I had a stirring of less reasonable-seeming thoughts; but certainly, I had no knowledge of real uneasiness at that time.

"Then, the next night there came a further development, for about two-thirty a.m., I heard my Mother's door open, exactly as on the previous night, and immediately afterward she rapped sharply, on the banister, as it seemed to me. I stopped my work a moment, and called up to her that I would not be long; but as she made no reply, and I did not hear her go back to bed, I had a quick wonder whether she might not be doing it in her sleep, after all, just as I had said.

"With the thought, I stood up, and taking the lamp from the table, began to go towards the door, which was open into the passage. And then, you know, I got a sudden nasty sort of thrill; for it came to me, all at once, that my Mother never knocked, when I had sat up too late, but called. But you will understand that I was not really frightened in any way; only vaguely uneasy, and pretty sure that she must be really doing the thing in her sleep.

"I went up the stairs quickly, and when I had come to the top, my Mother was not there; but her door was open. I had a little bewildered sense that she must have gone quietly back to bed, after all, without my hearing her; but, for all that I thought I believed this, I was pretty quick into her room. Yet, when I got there, she was sleeping quietly and naturally; for the vague sense of trouble in me was sufficiently strong to make me go over to look at her, to make certain.

"When I was sure that she was perfectly right in every way, I was still a little bothered; but much more inclined to believe that my suspicion was right and that she had got quietly back to bed in her sleep, without waking to know what she had been doing. This was the most reasonable thing to think, as you must see.

"And then, it came to me, suddenly, that there was a vague, queer, mildewy smell in the room; and it was in that instant that I became aware that I had smelt the same strange, uncertain smell the night before, in the passage, as you remember.

"I was definitely uneasy now, and began quietly to search my Mother's room; though with no aim or clear thought of anything, except to assure myself that there was nothing in the room. And all the time, you know, I never *expected really* to find anything; only that my uneasiness had to be reassured.

"In the middle of my search round, my Mother woke up, and of course I had to explain. I told her about her door opening, and then the knocks on the banister, and that I had come up and found her asleep. I said nothing about the smell, which was not very distinct; but told her that the thing happening twice had made me a bit nervous, and possibly fanciful, and that I thought I would take a look about, just to feel satisfied.

"I have thought since then that the reason I made no mention of the smell, was not only that I did not want to make my Mother feel frightened—for I was scarcely that way myself—but because I had a vague half-knowledge that I associated the smell with fancies too indefinite and peculiar to bear talking about. You will understand that I am able *now* to analyse and put the thing into words; but *then* I did not even know my chief reason for saying nothing; let alone appreciate its possible significance. You follow me?

"It was my Mother, after all, who put part of my vague sensations into words:—

" 'What a disagreeable smell,' she exclaimed, and was silent a moment, looking at me. Then:— 'You feel that there's something wrong,' still looking at me, very quiet, you know; but with a little, questioning, nervous note of expectancy.

" 'I don't know,' I said. 'I can't understand it, unless you've really been walking about in your sleep.'

" 'But the smell,' she said.

" 'Yes,' I replied. 'That's what puzzles me, too. I'll have a walk through the house; though I don't suppose it's anything.'

"I lit her candle, and then taking the lamp, I went through the two other bedrooms, and afterwards all over the house, including the three underground cellars, which I found a little trying to the nerves.

"Then I went back to my Mother, and told her that there was really nothing to bother about; and, you know, in the end, we talked ourselves into believing that it was nothing. My Mother would not agree that she might have been sleep-walking; but she was ready to put the door opening, down to the fault of the latch, which certainly snicked very lightly. As for the knocks, they might be the old warped woodwork of the house, cracking a bit, or a mouse rattling a piece of loose plaster. The smell was a little more difficult to explain; but finally we agreed that it might easily be the queer night-smell of the moist earth, coming in through the window of my Mother's room, from the back garden, or—for that matter—from the little church-yard beyond the big wall at the bottom of the garden.

"And so, at last, we quietened down, and finally I went off to bed, and had some sleep.

"I think this is certainly a good lesson on the way in which we humans can delude ourselves; for there was not one of these explanations that my reason could really accept. You just try to imagine yourselves in the same circumstances, and you will see how absurd our attempts to explain the happenings really were.

"In the morning, when I came down to breakfast, we talked it all over again, and whilst we agreed that it was strange, we also agreed that we had begun to imagine queer things in the backs of our minds, which now we felt half ashamed to admit. I think this is very funny, when you come to look into it; but it's absurdly human.

"And then, you know, that night, my Mother's door was slammed once violently, just after midnight.

"I caught up the lamp, and when I reached her door, I found it shut. I opened it quickly and went in, to find my Mother lying with her eyes open, and rather nervous; having been waked by the slam of the door. But what upset me more than anything, was the fact that there was·a simply brutal smell in the passage and in her room.

"Whilst I was asking her whether she was all right, a door slammed twice downstairs; and you can imagine how it made me feel. My Mother and I looked at one another; and then I lit her candle, and taking the poker from the fender, went downstairs with the lamp, feeling really horribly nervous. The culminative effect of so many queer little things was getting hold of me; and all the *apparently* reasonable explanations seemed abjectly futile.

"The horrible smell seemed to be very strong in the downstairs passage; also in the front room and the cellars; but chiefly in the passage. However, I made a very thorough search of the house, and when I had finished, I knew that all the lower windows and doors had been properly shut and fastened, and that there was certainly no living thing in the house, beyond our two selves.

"Then I went upstairs again to my Mother's room, and we talked the thing over for an hour or more, and in the end came to the conclusion that we might, after all, be reading too much into a number of little things; but, you know, inside of us, we did not believe this. You just think!

"Later, when we had talked ourselves into a more comfortable state of mind, I said good night, and went off to bed; and presently managed to get to sleep.

"Then, in the early hours of the morning, whilst it was still dark, I was waked by a loud noise. You can imagine that it made me feel rather queer, after the little unexplained things that had been happening; and I sat up pretty quick in bed, and listened. And then, downstairs, I heard:—bang, bang, bang, one door after another being slammed; at least, that is the impression that the sounds gave me.

"I jumped out of bed, with a tingle and shiver of sudden fright on me; and at the same moment, as I lit my candle, my door was pushed slowly open; you see, I had not latched it, so as to feel that my Mother was not shut off from me in any way.

" 'Who's there!' I shouted out, in a voice about twice as deep as natural, and with that queer breathlessness, that a sudden fright so often gives one. 'Who's there!'

"Then I heard my Mother saying:—

" 'It's me, Thomas. Whatever *is* happening downstairs?'

"She was in the room, by this, and I saw that she had her bedroom poker in one hand, and her candle in the other. I could have smiled at her, if it had not been for the extraordinary sounds downstairs; for, you know, she was such a little woman; but with heaps of pluck.

"I got into my slippers, and reached down an old sword-bayonet from the wall. Then I picked up my candle, and begged my Mother not to come; but I knew it would be little use, if she had made up her mind; and she had, with the result that she acted as a sort of rearguard for me, during our search. I know, in some ways, selfishly, I was very glad to have her with me.

"By this time, the door-slamming had ceased, and there seemed, probably because of the sheer contrast, to be a simply beastly silence in the house. However, I led the way, holding my candle high, and keeping the sword-bayonet handy.

"When we got downstairs, I saw that all the room doors were wide open; and when we had made a thorough search, and found the outer doors and the windows all secured, I tell you, I wondered whether the noises had been made by the doors at all. Of one thing only we were able to make sure, and that was that there was no living thing in the house, beside ourselves. But everywhere, in the whole house, there seemed the taint of that extraordinarily horrible smell.

"Of course, it was absurd to try to 'make-believe' any longer. There was something strange about the house; and as soon as it was daylight, I set my Mother to packing. After breakfast, I saw her off by train to one of my aunts, with a wire in advance, to prepare them.

"Then I set to work to try to clear up this mystery. I went first to the landlord, and told him all the circumstances. From him, I found that twelve or fifteen years back, the house had got rather a curious name from three or four tenants; with the result that it had remained empty for a long while; and in the end he had let it at a low rent to a Captain Tobias, on the one condition that the Captain should hold his tongue, if he saw anything peculiar. The Landlord's idea—as he told me frankly—was to free the house from these tales of 'something queer', by keeping a tenant in it, and then to sell it for the best price he could get.

"However, when Captain Tobias left, after a ten years' tenancy, there was no longer any 'talk' about the house; so that when we came and offered to take it on a five years' lease, he had jumped at the chance. This was the whole story; at least, so he gave me to understand. When I pressed him for details of the supposed peculiar happenings in the house, all those years back, he said that the tenants had talked about a woman who was always going about the house at night. Some tenants never saw anything; but others would not stay the first month's tenancy.

"One thing the landlord was particular to point out, that no tenant had ever complained about knockings, or doors slamming. As for the smell, he seemed positively indignant about it; but why, I don't suppose he quite knew himself, except that he probably had some vague feeling that it was an indirect accusation on my part that the drains were not right.

"In the end, I suggested that he should come down that evening and spend the night with me. He agreed at once, especially as I told him that I intended to keep the whole business quiet, and try to get really to the bottom of the curious happenings; for he was very anxious to keep the rumour of the haunting from getting about again.

"About three o'clock that afternoon, he came down, and we made a thorough search of the house, which, however, showed us nothing unusual. Afterwards, the Landlord made one or two tests, which showed him that the drainage was in perfect order; and after that, we made our preparations for sitting up all night.

"First, we borrowed two policemen's dark lanterns from the station near by, where the Superintendent and I were very friendly; and as soon as it was really dusk, the Landlord went up to his house for his gun. I had the sword-bayonet that I have told you about; and when the Landlord got back, we sat talking in my study until nearly midnight.

"Then we lit the lanterns and went upstairs on to the landing, where I brought a small table and a couple of chairs out of one of the bedrooms. We put the lanterns and the gun and bayonet handy on the table; then I shut and sealed the bedroom-doors; after which we took our seats, and turned off the lights.

"From then, until two o'clock, nothing happened; but a little after two, as I found by holding my watch near to the faint glow of the closed lanterns, I had a time of quite extraordinary nervousness. At last I bent towards the Landlord, and whispered to him that I had a queer feeling that something was about to happen, and to be ready with his lantern. At the same time, I reached out towards mine. In the very instant that I made this movement, the night which filled the passage seemed to become suddenly of a dull violet colour; not, mind you, as if a light had been shone; but as if the natural blackness of the night had changed colour, as I might say from the inside. Do you understand what I am trying to tell you? And then, coming through this violet night, through this violet-coloured gloom, came a little naked child, running. In an extraordinary way, the child seemed not to be distinct from the surrounding gloom; but almost as if it were a concentration of that extraordinary atmosphere; almost—can you understand?—as if that gloomy colour which had changed the night, came from the child. It seems impossible to make clear to you; but try to take hold of what I'm saying.

"The child went past me, running, quite naturally, as a chubby human child might run; only in an absolute and inconceivable silence. I remember that it was a very small child, and must have passed under the table; but I saw it through the table, as if the table had been only a slightly darker shadow than the coloured gloom. In the same instant, I saw that a fluctuating shimmer of violet light outlined the metal of the gun-barrels and the blade of the sword-bayonet, making them seem like faint shapes of glimmering light, floating unsupported where the table-top should have shown solid.

"Now, curiously, as I saw these things, I was subconsciously aware that I heard the anxious breathing of the Landlord, quite clear and laboured, close to my elbow, where he waited nervously with his hands on the lantern. And, you know, I realised in that moment that he saw nothing; but waited in the darkness, for my warning to come true.

"Even as I took heed of these minor things, I saw the child jump to one side, and hide behind some half-seen object, that was certainly nothing belonging to the passage. I stared, intently, with a most extraordinary thrill of expectant wonder, and fright making goose-flesh of my back. And even as I stared, I solved for myself the less important problem of what two black clouds were that hung over a part of the table. I think it is very curious and interesting, that double working of the mind, often so much more apparent during times of stress. The two black clouds came from two faintly shining shapes, which I knew must be the metal of the lanterns; and the things that looked black to the sight with which I was then seeing, could be nothing else but what to normal human sight is known as light. This phenomenon I have always remembered. I have twice seen a somewhat similar thing, in that Dark Light Case, and in that trouble of Maetheson's, which you know about.

"Even as I understood this matter of the lights, I was looking to my left, to understand why the child was hiding. And suddenly, I heard the Landlord shout out:— 'The woman!' But I saw nothing. I had a vague, disagreeable sense that something repugnant was near to me, and I was aware in the same moment that the Landlord was gripping my arm in a hard, frightened grip. Then I was staring back to where the child had hidden. I saw the child peeping out from behind its hiding-place, seeming to be looking up the passage; but whether in fear or not, I could not tell. Then it came out, and ran headlong away, through the place where should have been the wall of my Mother's bedroom; but the sense with which I was seeing these things, showed me the wall only as a vague, upright shadow, unsubstantial. And immediately the child was lost to me, in the dull violet gloom. At the same time, I felt the Landlord press back against me, as if something passed too close to him; and he gave out again a hoarse little cry:— 'The Woman! The Woman!' and turned the shade clumsily from off his lantern, which seemed to let loose instantly a great fan-shaped jet of blackness across the violet-coloured gloom. But I had seen no Woman. Abruptly, the violet tint went out of the night, and the fan-shaped jet of blackness became plain to me as the funnel of light from the landlord's lantern. I saw that the passage showed empty, as he shone the beam of his light jerkily to and fro; but chiefly in the direction of the doorway of my Mother's room.

"He was still clutching my arm, and had risen to his feet; and now, mechanically and almost slowly, I picked up my own lantern and turned on the light. I shone it, a little dazedly, at the seals upon the doors; but none was broken; then I sent the light to and fro, up and down the passage; but there was nothing there; and I looked at the Landlord, who was saying something in a rather incoherent fashion. As my light passed over his face, I noted, in a stupid sort of way, that it was drenched with sweat.

"Then my wits became more handleable, and I began to catch the drift of his words:— 'Did you see her? Did you see her?' he was saying, over and over again. I found myself telling him, in quite a level voice, that I had not seen any woman. He became more coherent then, and told me that he had seen a Woman come from the end of the passage, and go right past us; but he could not describe her, except that she kept stopping and looking about her, and had even peered at the wall, close beside him, as if looking for something. But what seemed to trouble him most, was that she had not seemed to see him, at all. He repeated this so often, that in the end I told him, in an absurd sort of way, that he ought to be very glad that she had not. You can imagine what my nerves felt like. What did it all mean? was the one question; and somehow I was not so frightened, as utterly bewildered. I had seen less then, than since; and knew less of possible and actual dangers. The chief effect of what I had seen, was to make me feel adrift from all my anchorages of Reason.

"What did it mean? He had seen a Woman, searching for something. I had not seen this Woman. *I* had seen a Child, running away, and hiding from Something or Someone. *He* had not seen this Child, or the other things—only the Woman. And *I* had not seen her. What did it all mean?

"I had said nothing yet to the Landlord about the Child. I had been too bewildered in the first few moments; and afterwards, I realised immediately that it would be futile to attempt to explain it to him. He was already frightened and stupid, with the thing that he had seen; and not the kind of man to understand. All this went through my mind very quickly, as we stood there, shining the lanterns to and fro; and as a result, I said nothing of what I had seen. And all the time, intermingled with this streak of practical reasoning, I was questioning to myself, what did it all mean; what was the Woman searching for, and what was the Child running from? You can understand the multitude of vague minor questions that kept rising.

"And suddenly, as I stood there, bewildered and nervous, and making random answers to the Landlord, a door was violently slammed downstairs; and directly I caught the horrible reek of which I have told you before.

" 'There!' I said to the Landlord, and caught his arm, in my turn. 'And the Smell! The Smell, do *you* smell it?'

"He looked at me, stupidly, so that I shook him, with a sort of nervous anger.

" 'Yes,' he said, at last, in a queer voice, and trying to shine the light from his shaking lantern at the stair-head.

" 'Come on!' I said, and picked up my bayonet; and he came, carrying his gun awkwardly. I think he came, more because he was afraid to be left alone, than because he had any pluck left, poor beggar. I never sneer at that kind of funk, at least very seldom; for when it takes hold of you, it makes rags of your courage, as I know.

"I began to go downstairs, shining my light over the banisters into the lower passage, and afterwards at the doors to see whether they were shut; for I had closed and latched them, leaning a corner of a mat up against each door, so that I should know which had been opened, in the event of anything happening.

"I saw at once that none of the doors had been opened; then I paused and threw the beam of my light down alongside of the stairway, so as to see the mat that I had leaned against the door at the top of the cellar stairs. In a moment, I got a horrid thrill; for the mat was flat. I waited a couple of seconds, shining my light to and fro in the passage. Then, holding pretty solid on to my courage, I went down the remainder of the stairs.

"As I came to the bottom step, I saw suddenly that there were wet patches all up and down the passage. I shone my lantern on to one of them. It was the imprint of a wet foot on the black oak floor; not an ordinary footprint, but a queer, soft, flabby, spreading imprint, that gave me an extraordinary feeling of horror.

"Backward and forward I flashed the light over the impossible footprints, and saw them everywhere. And suddenly I saw that they led to each of the closed doors. I felt something touch my back, and glanced round swiftly, to find that the Landlord had come down close to me, almost pressing against me, in his fear.

" 'It's all right,' I said, but in a rather breathless whisper, meaning to put a little courage into him; for I could feel that he was shaking through all his body. And then, you know, even as I tried to get him steadied enough to be of some use, his gun went off with a tremendous bang and knocked the seat clean out of one of the hall chairs. He jumped, and yelled with sheer terror; and I swore at the top of my voice, because of the shock.

" 'For God's sake give it to me!' I said, and slipped the gun from his hand; in the same instant there was a sound of running footsteps up the garden path, and immediately the flash of a bull's-eye lantern upon the fanlight over the front door. Then the door was tried, and directly afterwards there came a thundering knocking, which told me that the policeman on the beat had heard the shot, and run up to see what was wrong.

"I went quickly to the door, and opened it. Fortunately the Constable knew me well, and when I had beckoned him in, I was able to explain matters in a very short time.

"Whilst I was doing this, Inspector Johnstone, whose round lay that way, came up the path, having missed the officer, and seen the lights and the open door. I told him as briefly as possible what had happened; but nothing about the Child or the Woman; for it would have seemed too fantastic for him to notice seriously. Then I showed him the queer, wet footprints and how they went towards the closed doors. I explained quickly about the mats, and how that the one against the cellar door was flat, which showed that the door must have been opened.

"The Inspector nodded, and told the Constable to draw his staff and guard the door. He asked then for the hall lamp to be lit; after which he took the policeman's lantern, and led the way into the front room. He paused with the door wide open, and threw the light all round; then jumped into the room, and looked behind the door; there was no one there; nor had I expected that there would be anyone; but all over the polished oak floor, between the scattered rugs, went the marks of those horrible spreading footprints; and the whole room was tainted with the disgusting smell.

"The Inspector searched carefully but quickly, and then came out and went into the middle room, using the same precautions. You can imagine just how beastly it was going into those rooms. There was nothing, of course, in the middle one, or in the kitchen and pantry; but everywhere went the wet footmarks about all the rooms, showing plain wherever there was clear woodwork or oilcloth; and always wherever we went there was the smell.

"The Inspector ceased from his search, and spent a minute in trying whether the mats would really fall flat when the doors were open, or merely ruckle upward again, in such a way as to appear that they had been untouched. But in each case, the mats fell flat, and remained so.

" 'Most extraordinary!' I heard Inspector Johnstone mutter to himself. Then he went towards the cellar door. He had inquired at first whether there were any windows to the cellars, and when he knew there was no way out, except by the door, he had left this part of the search to the last.

"As Johnstone came up to the door, the policeman made a motion of salute, and said something in a low voice; and something in the tone made me flick my light across him. I saw then that the man was very white, and he looked scared and bewildered.

" 'What?' said Johnstone, impatiently. 'Speak up!'

" 'A woman come along 'ere, sir, and went through this 'ere door,' said the Constable, clearly, but with that curious monotonous intonation that you sometimes get from an unintelligent human who is badly frightened.

" 'What!' shouted the Inspector.

" 'A woman come along 'ere, sir, and went through this 'ere door,' said the man, monotonously.

"The Inspector caught the man by the shoulder, and deliberately smelt his breath.

" 'No!' he said. And then sarcastically:— 'I hope you held the door open politely for the lady.'

" 'The door weren't opened, sir,' said the man, simply.

" 'Are you mad—' began Johnstone.

" 'No,' said the Landlord's voice from the back, and speaking steadily enough. 'I saw the woman upstairs.' It was evident that he had got back his control again.

" 'I'm afraid, Inspector Johnstone,' I said, 'that there's more in this than you think. I certainly saw something very extraordinary upstairs.'

"The Inspector seemed about to say something; but, instead, he turned again to the door, and flashed his light down and round about the mat. I saw then that the strangely horrible footmarks came straight up to the cellar door; and the last print showed *under* the door; yet the policeman said the door had not been opened.

"And suddenly, without any intention, or realisation of what I was saying, I said to the Landlord:—

" 'What were the feet like?'

"I received no answer; for the Inspector was ordering the Constable to open the cellar door, and the man was not obeying. Johnstone repeated the order, and at last, in a queer automatic way, the man obeyed, and pushed the door open. The disgusting smell beat up at us, in a great wave of horror, and the Inspector came backward a step.

" 'My God!' he said, and went forward again, and shone his light down the steps; but there was nothing visible, only that on each step showed the unnatural footprints.

" 'The Inspector brought the beam of the light vividly on to the top step; and there, clear in the light, there was something small, moving. The Inspector bent to look, and the policeman and I with him. Now I don't want to disgust you; but the thing was a maggot. The Policeman backed suddenly out of the doorway.

" 'The churchyard,' he said, '…at the back of the 'ouse.'

" 'Silence!' said Johnstone, with a queer break in the word, and I knew that at last he was frightened. He put his lantern into the doorway, and shone it from step to step, following the footprints down into the darkness; then he stepped back from the open doorway, and we all gave back with him. He looked round, and I had a feeling that he was looking for a weapon of some kind.

" 'Your gun,' I said to the Landlord, and he brought it from the front hall, and passed it over to the Inspector, who took it and ejected the empty shell from the right barrel. He held out his hand for a live cartridge, which the Landlord brought from his pocket. Then he loaded the gun and snapped the breech. He turned to the Constable:—

" 'Come on,' he said, and moved towards the cellar doorway.

" 'I ain't comin', sir,' said the policeman, very white in the face.

"With a sudden blaze of passion, the Inspector took the man by the scruff, and hove him bodily down into the darkness, and he went downward, screaming. The Inspector followed him instantly, with his lantern and the gun; and I after the Inspector, with the bayonet ready. Behind me, I heard the Landlord come, stumbling nervously.

At the bottom of the stairs, the Inspector was helping the policeman to his feet, where he stood swaying a moment, in a bewildered manner; then the Inspector went into the front cellar, and his man followed him in a quiet, stupid fashion; but evidently no longer with any thought of running away from anything we might find dangerous or horrible.

"We all crowded into the front cellar, flashing our lights to and fro, over the place. Inspector Johnstone was examining the floor, and I saw that the footmarks went round the cellar, into each of the corners, and across and across the floor. And I thought suddenly of the Child that was running away from Something. Do you realise the thing that I was seeing vaguely?

"We went out of the front cellar, in a body, for there was nothing to be found. In the next, the footprints went everywhere in that same queer erratic fashion, as of something or someone searching for something, or following some blind scent.

"In the third cellar the prints ended at the shallow well that had been the old water-supply of the little house. The well was full to the brim, and the water so clear that the pebbly bottom was plain to be seen, as we shone the lights into the water. The search came to an abrupt *end,* and we stood about the well, looking at one another, in an absolute, horrible quiet.

"Johnstone made another examination of the footprints; then he shone his light again into the clear shallow water, searching each inch of the plainly-seen bottom; but there was nothing there. The cellar was heavy with the dreadful smell; and we all stood silent, turning the beams of our lamps constantly to and fro around the cellar.

"The Inspector looked up from his search of the well; and nodded quietly across at me; and with his sudden, dumb acknowledgment that our belief was now his belief, the smell in the cellar seemed to grow more dreadful, and to be, as it were, a menace—the material evidence that some monstrous thing was there with us, invisible.

" 'I think—' began the Inspector, and shone his light towards the stairway. With the hint, the Constable's restraint went utterly, and he ran for the stairs, making a queer sound in his throat.

"The Landlord followed, at a quick walk, and then the Inspector and I. He waited a single instant for me, and we went up together, treading on the same steps, and with our lights held backwards. At the top, I slammed and locked the stair door, and wiped my forehead. By Jove! my hands were shaking.

"The Inspector asked me to give his man a glass of whisky, and then he shunted him out on to his beat. He stayed a short while with the Landlord and me, and it was arranged that he would join us the following night, and watch the Well with us from midnight until daylight. When he left us, the dawn was just coming in; and the Landlord and I locked up the house and went over to his own place for a sleep.

"In the afternoon, the Landlord and I returned to the house, to make arrangements for the night. He was very quiet, and I felt that he was to be relied on, now that he had been 'salted', as it were, with his fright of the previous night.

"We opened all the doors and windows, and blew the house through thoroughly; and in the meanwhile, we lit all the lamps we could find, and took them down into the cellars, where we set them all about, so as to have light everywhere. Then we carried down three chairs and a table, and put them in the cellar where the well was sunk. After that, we stretched thin piano wire across the cellar floor, at such a height that it should trip anything moving about in the dark.

"When this was done, I went through the house with the Landlord, and sealed every window and door in the place, excepting only the front-door and the door at the top of the cellar stairs.

"In the meanwhile, a local wire-smith was making something to my order; and when the Landlord and I had finished tea at his house, we went down to see how the smith was getting on.

"We found the thing completed. It looked rather like a huge parrot's cage, without any bottom, made of heavy-gauge wire, and about seven feet high. It was exactly three feet in diameter. Fortunately, I had remembered to have it made longitudinally in two halves, or else we should never have got it through the doorways and down the cellar stairs.

I told the wire-smith to bring the cage up to the house right away, so that he could fit the two halves rigidly together for me; and as we returned, I called in at an ironmongers, where I bought some thin hemp rope and an iron rack-pulley, like those used in Lancashire for hauling up the ceiling clothes-racks, which you find in every house and cottage. I bought also a couple of pitchforks.

" 'We shan't want to touch it,' I said to the Landlord; and he nodded, looking rather white all at once, but saying nothing.

"As soon as the cage had arrived, and been fitted together rigidly in the cellar, I sent away the smith; and the Landlord and I suspended it exactly over the well, into which it just fitted easily. In the end, and after a lot of trouble, we managed to hang it so perfectly central from the rope over the iron pulley, that when hoisted to the ceiling, and dropped, it went every time plunk into the well, like a candle-extinguisher. When we had got this finally arranged, I hoisted it up once more, to the ready position, and made the rope fast to a heavy wooden pillar, which stood in the middle of the cellar, near to the table.

"By ten o'clock I had everything arranged, with the two pitchforks and the two police lanterns; also some whisky and sandwiches on the table; and underneath, I had several buckets full of disinfectant.

"A little after eleven o'clock, there was a knock at the front door, and when I went, I found that Inspector Johnstone had arrived, and brought with him one of his plain-clothes men. You will understand how pleased I was to see that there would be this addition to our watch; for he looked a tough, nerveless man, brainy and collected; just the man I should have picked to help us with the horrible job I felt pretty sure we should have to do that night.

"When the inspector and the detective had entered, I shut and locked the front door; then, while the Inspector held the light, I sealed the door carefully, with tape and wax. At the head of the cellar stairs, I shut and locked that door also, behind us, and sealed it in the same way.

"As we entered the cellar, I warned Johnstone and his man to be careful not to trip over the wires; and then, as I saw his surprise at my arrangements, I began to explain my ideas and intentions, to all of which he listened with a very strong approval. I was pleased to see also that the detective was nodding his head, as I talked, in a way that showed he appreciated all my precautions.

"Both Johnstone and his man had brought police lanterns with them, and these they put on the table, by the two that we had borrowed from the station. As he put his lantern down, the inspector picked up one of the pitch-forks, and balanced it in his hand; then looked at me, and nodded.

" 'The best thing,' he said. 'I only wish you'd got two more.'

"Then we all took our seats, the detective getting a washing-stool from the corner of the cellar, as we had brought down only three chairs. From then, until a quarter to twelve, we talked quietly, whilst we made a light supper of whisky and sandwiches; after which, we cleared everything off the table, excepting the lanterns and the pitch-forks. One of the latter, I handed to the Inspector; the other I took myself, and, then, having set my chair so as to be handy to the rope which lowered the cage into the well, I went round the cellar and put out every lamp.

"I groped my way back to my chair, and arranged the pitchfork and the dark lantern ready to my hand; after which I suggested that everyone should keep an absolute silence throughout the watch. I asked, also, that no lantern should be turned on, until I gave the word.

"I put my watch on the table, where a faint glow from my lantern made me able to see the time. For an hour nothing happened, and everyone kept an absolute silence, except for an occasional uneasy movement.

"About half-past one, however, I was conscious again of the same extraordinary and peculiar nervousness, which I had felt on the previous night. I put my hand out quickly, and eased the hitched rope from around the pillar. The Inspector seemed aware of the movement; for I saw the faint light from his lantern, move a little, as if he had suddenly taken hold of it, in readiness.

"About a minute later, I became aware that there was a change in the colour of the night in the cellar, and it grew slowly violet-tinged upon my eyes. I glanced to and fro, quickly, in the new darkness, and even as I looked, I was conscious that the violet colour of the night deepened. In the direction of the well, but seeming to be at a great distance beyond, there was, as it were, a nucleus to the night; and the nucleus came swiftly towards us, appearing to come through a great space, almost in a single moment. It came near, and I saw again, as on the previous occasion, that it was a little naked child, running, and seeming to be *of* the violet night in which it ran.

"The child came with a natural running movement, exactly as I have already described it; but in a silence so peculiarly intense, that it was as if it brought the silence with it. I don't suppose you understand what I am trying to tell you; but I cannot make it clearer. Seemingly, about half-way between the well and the table, the child turned swiftly, and looked back at something invisible to me; and suddenly it went down into a crouching attitude, and seemed to be hiding behind something shadowy that showed vaguely; but, you know, there was nothing there, except the bare floor of the cellar; nothing, I mean, in our world.

"About this time I remember thinking to myself in a queerly collected way that I could hear the breathing of the three other men, with a wonderful distinctness; and also the tick of my watch upon the table seemed to sound as loud and as slow as the tick of one of those old grandfather's clocks. And, you know, I knew that none of the others saw what I was seeing.

"Abruptly, the Landlord, who was next to me, let out his breath with a little hissing sound; and I knew that something was visible to him. There came a creak from the table, and I had a feeling that the Inspector was leaning forward, looking at something that I could not see. The Landlord reached out his hand through the darkness, and fumbled a moment to catch my arm:—

" 'The Woman!' he whispered, close to my ear. 'Over by the well.'

"I stared hard in that direction; but saw nothing, except that perhaps the violet colour of the night seemed a little duller just there.

'I looked back quickly to the shadow where the child was hiding. I saw that it was peering backward from the hiding-place. And suddenly it rose and ran straight for the middle of the table, which showed only as a vague shadow half-way between my eyes and the unseen floor. As the child ran under the table, I saw that the steel prongs of my pitch-fork were glimmering with a violet, fluctuating light. A little way off, there showed high up in the gloom, the vaguely shining outline of the other fork, so that I knew the Inspector had it raised in his hand, ready. There was no doubt but that he saw something. On the table, the metal of the five lanterns shone with the same strange glowing; and about each lantern there was a little cloud of absolute blackness, where the phenomenon that is light to our natural eyes, came through the fittings; and through each complete blackness, the metal of each lantern showed plain, as might a cat's-eye stone in a nest of black cotton-wool.

"Just beyond the table, the Child paused again, and stood, seeming to oscillate a little upon its feet, which gave me a queer impression that it was lighter and vaguer than a cloud; and yet, in the same moment, another part of me seemed to know that it was to me, as something that might be beyond thick, invisible glass, and subject to conditions and forces that I was vacant to comprehend. In some ways, I might say that the impression left, was as if I had looked through thick, plate-glass windows at someone out in a strong wind; and all the time I could not hear or know of the wind, except by seeing the person rocked by it. Do I get the thing in any way clear to you ?

"The Child was looking back again, and my gaze went the same way. I stared across the cellar, and saw the cage hanging clear in the violet light, every wire and tie outlined with a glimmering of strange light; above it there was a little space of gloom, and then the dull shining of the iron pulley which I had screwed into the ceiling.

"I stared in a bewildered, abnormal sort of way, round the cellar; there were thin lines of vague fire crossing the floor in all directions; and suddenly I remembered the piano-wire that the Landlord and I had stretched. But there was nothing else to be seen, except that near the table there were indistinct glimmerings of light, and at the far end the outline of a dull-glowing revolver, evidently in the detective's pocket. I remember having felt a subconscious satisfaction, as my brain reasoned out this trifle in a queer automatic fashion. On the table, near to me, there was a little shapeless collection of the light; and this I knew, after an instant's uninterested consideration, to be the steel portions of the works of my watch.

"I had looked several times round the lost confines of the cellar, and at the child, whilst I was deciding these trifles; and had found it still in that attitude of looking at something. But now, suddenly, it ran clear away to my right into a great distance, and was nothing more than a slightly deeper coloured nucleus far off in the strange coloured night.

"Beside me, the Landlord gave out a queer little cry, and twisted over against me, as if to avoid something. From the Inspector there came a sharp breathing sound, as if he had been suddenly drenched with cold water. And abruptly the violet colour went out of the night, and the sense of distance and space; and I was conscious of the nearness of something monstrous and repugnant, that made me sweat.

"There was a tense silence, and the blackness of the cellar seemed absolute, with only the faint glow about each of the lanterns on the table. Then, in the dark and the silence, there sounded a faint tinkle of water from the well, as if something were rising noiselessly out of it, and the water running back off it with a gentle tinkling. In the same instant, there came to me a sudden waft of the disgusting smell.

"I gave a sharp cry of warning to the Inspector, and loosed the rope. There came instantly the sharp splash of the cage entering the water; and then, with a quick, stiff, frightened movement, I opened the shutter of my lantern, and shone the light at the cage, shouting to the others to do the same.

"As my light struck the cage, I saw that about two feet of it projected from the top of the well, and there was something protruded up out of the water, into the cage. I stared, with a feeling that I recognised the thing; and then, as the other lanterns were opened, I saw that it was a leg of mutton. The thing was held by a brawny fist and arm, which were rising out of the water; and I stood there, utterly stiff and bewildered, to see what was coming. In a moment there rose into view a great bearded face, that I felt sure in that grim instant was the face of a drowned man, long dead. Then the face opened at the mouth-part, and spluttered and coughed. Another big hand came into view, and wiped the water from the eyes, which were blinked rapidly, and then fixed themselves into a stare at the lights.

"From the Detective there came a sudden shout:—

" 'Captain Tobias!' he shouted, and the Inspector echoed him, and instantly they burst into loud roars of laughter.

"The Inspector and the Detective ran across the cellar to the cage; and I followed, still bewildered. The man in the cage was keeping the leg of mutton as far away from him, as possible, and holding his nose.

" 'Lift thig dam trap, quig!' he shouted in a stifled voice; but the Inspector and the Detective simply doubled before him, and tried to hold their noses, whilst they laughed, and the light from their lanterns went dancing all over the place.

" 'Quig! Quig!' said the man in the cage, still holding his nose, and trying to speak plainly.

"Then Johnstone and the Detective stopped laughing, and lifted the cage. The man in the well threw the leg across the cellar and turned swiftly to go down into the well; but the two officers were too quick for him, and had him out in a twinkling; then whilst they held him, dripping upon the floor, the Inspector jerked his thumb in the direction of the offending leg, and the Landlord, having got the keys from me, harpooned it with one of the pitch-forks, ran it upstairs and so into the open air.

"In the meanwhile, I had given the man from the well a stiff tot of whisky; for which he thanked me with a cheerful nod, and having emptied the glass at a draught, held out his hand for the bottle, which he finished, as if it had been so much water.

"Now, as you will be guessing, this Captain Tobias who had appeared from the well, was the very man who had been the previous tenant. In the course of the talk that followed, I learned the reason why Captain Tobias had been forced to leave the house. He had been wanted by the police for certain smuggling, and had undergone imprisonment; having been released only a couple of weeks earlier.

"He had returned home, to find us tenants of his old home. He had then entered the house through the well, the walls of which were not continued right to the bottom (this I will deal with later); and gone upstairs by a little stairway in my cellar wall, which opened at the top through a panel beside my Mother's bedroom. This panel was opened, by revolving the left doorpost of the bedroom door, with the result that the bedroom door always became unlatched, in the process of opening the panel.

"The Captain complained, without any bitterness, that the panel had warped, and that each time he opened it, it made a loud cracking noise. This had been evidently what I mistook for raps. He would not give his reason for entering the house; but it was pretty obvious that he had hidden something, which he wanted to get. However, as he found it impossible to enter the house, without the risk of being caught, he decided to try to drive us out, relying on the bad reputation of the place, and his own artistic efforts as a ghost. I must say he succeeded.

"He intended then to rent the house again, as before; when he would, of course, have plenty of time to get whatever he had hidden. Moreover, no doubt the house suited him admirably; for there was a passage—as he showed me afterwards—connecting the dummy well with the crypt of the church beyond the garden wall; and these, in turn, were connected with certain caves in the cliffs, which went down to the beach beyond the church.

"In the course of his talk, Captain Tobias offered to take the house off my hands; and as this suited me perfectly, for I was just about 'stalled' with it, and also satisfied the Landlord, it was decided that no steps should be taken against him; and that the whole business be hushed up.

"I asked the Captain whether there was really anything queer about the house; whether he had ever seen anything. He said yes, that he had twice seen a woman going about the house at night. You can imagine how we all looked at one another, when he said that. The Captain told us that she never bothered him, and that he had only seen her the two times; and on each occasion it had been just after a narrow escape from the Revenue People, and when he had been rather badly frightened; that is, I ought to add, so far as a man of his type was capable of feeling fright.

"Captain Tobias was a cute man; for he had seen how I had leaned the mats up against the doors; and after entering the rooms, and walking all about them, so as to leave the foot-marks of an old pair of wet woollen slippers everywhere, he had deliberately put the mats back as he found them, as he left each room.

"The maggot which had dropped from his infernal leg-of-mutton, had been an accident, and beyond even his horrific planning; but he was hugely delighted to learn how it had affected us.

"The faint, mouldy smell which I had smelled, before the leg-abomination, was probably from the little, closed stairway, when the Captain had opened the panel; at least, this was the conclusion I came to when he took me through, to show it to me. The door-slamming was also another of his contributions.

"Now I come to the end of the Captain's ghost-play; and to the difficulty of trying to explain the other peculiar things. In the first place, it is obvious to you that there was something genuinely strange in the house; which made itself manifest as a Woman. So many people had seen this Woman, under different circumstances, that it is impossible to put the thing down to fancy; at the same time it must seem extraordinary that people should live years in the house, and see nothing; whilst the policeman saw the Woman, before he had been twenty minutes in the place; also the Landlord, the Detective, and the Inspector all saw her.

"I have thought a great deal about this, and I can only suppose that *fear* was in every case the key, as I might say, which opened the senses to an awareness of the presence of the Woman. The policeman was a nervy, highly-strung man, and he got frightened. When he became frightened, he was able to see the Woman. The same reasoning applies all round. *I* saw nothing, until I became really frightened; then I saw, not the Woman, but a Child, running away from Something or Someone. However, I will touch on that later. In short, until a very strong degree of fear was present, the person was not capable of being affected by the Force which made Itself evident, as a Woman. I don't think I can put it clearer than this. I think my theory explains why some tenants were never aware of anything strange in the house, whilst others left immediately. The more sensitive they were, the less would be the degree of fear necessary to make them aware of the Force present in the house. This is a peculiar and interesting point.

"The curious shining of all the metal objects in the cellar, had been visible only to me. The cause, naturally, I do not know; neither do I know why I alone was able to see the shining."

"The Child," I said. "Can you explain that part at all, Carnacki… why *you* didn't see the Woman, and why *they* didn't see the Child. Was it merely the same Force, appearing differently to different people?"

"No," said Carnacki. "I can't explain that. But I am quite sure in my own mind that the Woman and the Child were not only two complete and different entities; but also that they were not even in quite the same planes of Existence.

"It is impossible to put the thing into words, because language is not enough developed yet, to have produced words with sufficiently exact shades of meaning to enable me to tell you just what I do know. At the time that the thing occurred, I was quite unable to understand it, even slightly. Yet, later I gained a vague insight into certain possibilities.

"To give you the root-idea of the matter, it is held in the Sigsand MS. that a child 'still-born' is 'snatched back bye thee Haggs'. This is crude; but may yet contain an elemental truth. But, before I attempt to make this clearer, let me tell you a thought that has often been mine. It may be that physical birth is but a secondary process; and that, prior to the possibility, the Mother Spirit searches for, until it finds, the small Element—the primal Ego or Child's soul. It may be that a certain waywardness would cause Such to strive to evade capture by the Mother-Spirit. It may have been such a thing as this, that I saw. I have always tried to think so; but it is impossible to ignore the sense of repulsion that I felt when the unseen Woman went past me. This repulsion carries forward the idea suggested in the Sigsand MS., that primarily a *still-born* child is thus (eliminating obvious physical causes) because its ego or spirit has been snatched back, by the 'Haggs'. In other words, by certain of the Monstrosities of the Outer Circle. The thought is inconceivably terrible, and probably the more so because it is so fragmentary. It leaves us with the conception of a child's soul adrift half-way between two lives, and running through by-ways of Eternity from Something incredible and inconceivable (because not understood) to our senses.

"The thing is beyond further discussion; for it is futile to attempt to discuss a thing, to any purpose, of which one has a conception so fragmentary as this. There is one thought, which is often mine. Perhaps there is a Mother-Spirit— No, it's no use trying to get that into words."

"And the well?" said Arkright. "How did the Captain get in from the other side?"

"As I said before," answered Carnacki. "The side-walls of the well did not reach to the bottom; so that you had only to dip down into the water, and come up again on the other side of the wall, under the cellar floor, and so climb into the hidden passage. Of course, the water was the same height on both sides of the walls. Don't ask me who made the well-entrance or the little stairway; for I don't know. The house was very old, as I have told you; and that sort of thing was useful in the wild old days."

"And the Child," I said, coming back to the thing which chiefly interested me. "You would say that the birth must have occurred in that house; and in this way, one might suppose the house to have become *en rapport*, if I can use the word in that way, with the Forces that produced the tragedy?"

"Yes," replied Carnacki. "That is, supposing we take the suggestion of the Sigsand MS., to account for the phenomenon."

"There may be other houses—" I began.

"There are," said Carnacki, and stood up.

"Out you go," he said, genially, using the familiar formula. And in five minutes we were on the Embankment, going thoughtfully to our various homes.

The Stone Ship

❖◆❖

R um things!— Of course there are rum things happen at sea— As rum as ever there were. I remember when I was in the *Alfred Jessop*, a small barque, whose owner was her skipper, we came across a most extraordinary thing.

We were twenty days out from London, and well down into the tropics. It was before I took my ticket, and I was in the fo'cas'le. The day had passed without a breath of wind, and the night found us with all the lower sails up in the buntlines.

Now, I want you to take good note of what I am going to say:—

When it was dark in the second dog-watch, there was not a sail in sight; not even the far off smoke of a steamer, and no land nearer than Africa, about a thousand miles to the Eastward of us.

It was our watch on deck from eight to twelve midnight, and my look-out from eight to ten. For the first hour, I walked to and fro across the break of the fo'cas'le head, smoking my pipe and just listening to the quiet.... Ever heard the kind of silence you can get away out at sea? You need to be in one of the old-time wind-jammers, with all the lights dowsed, and the sea as calm and quiet as some queer plain of death. And then you want a pipe and the lonesomeness of the fo'cas'le head, with the caps'n to lean against while you listen and think. And all about you, stretching out into the miles, only and always the enormous silence of the sea, spreading out a thousand miles every way into the everlasting, brooding night. And not a light anywhere, out on all the waste of waters; nor ever a sound, as I have told, except the faint moaning of the masts and gear, as they chafe and whine a little to the occasional invisible roll of the ship.

And suddenly, across all this silence, I heard Jensen's voice from the head of the starboard steps, say:—

"Did you hear *that*, Duprey?"

"What?" I asked, cocking my head up. But as I questioned, I heard what he heard—the constant sound of running water, for all the world like the noise of a brook running down a hill-side. And the queer sound was surely not a hundred fathoms off our port bow!

"By gum!" said Jensen's voice, out of the darkness. "That's damned sort of funny!"

"Shut up!" I whispered, and went across, in my bare feet, to the port rail, where I leaned out into the darkness, and stared towards the curious sound.

The noise of a brook running down a hill-side continued, where there was no brook for a thousand sea-miles in any direction.

"What is it?" said Jensen's voice again, scarcely above a whisper now. From below him, on the maindeck, there came several voices questioning:— "Hark!" "Stow the talk!" "…there!" "Listen!" "Lord love us, what is it?" …And then Jensen muttering to them to be quiet.

There followed a full minute, during which we all heard the brook, where no brook could ever run; and then, out of the night there came a sudden hoarse incredible sound:—ooaaze, oooaze, arrrr, arrrr, oooaze—a stupendous sort of croak, deep and somehow abominable, out of the blackness. In the same instant, I found myself sniffing the air. There was a queer rank smell, stealing through the night.

"Forrard there on the look-out!" I heard the Mate singing out, away aft. "Forrard there! What the blazes are you doing!"

I heard him come clattering down the port ladder from the poop, and then the sound of his feet at a run along the maindeck. Simultaneously, there was a thudding of bare feet, as the watch below came racing out of the fo'cas'le beneath me.

"Now then! Now then! Now then!" shouted the Mate, as he charged up on to the fo'cas'le head. "What's up?"

"It's something off the port bow, Sir," I said. "Running water! And then that sort of howl…. Your night-glasses," I suggested.

"Can't see a thing," he growled, as he stared away through the dark. "There's a sort of mist. Phoo! what a devil of a stink!"

"Look!" said someone down on the maindeck. "What's that?"

I saw it in the same instant, and caught the Mate's elbow.

"Look, Sir," I said. "There's a light there, about three points off the bow. It's moving."

The Mate was staring through his night-glasses, and suddenly he thrust them into my hands:—

"See if you can make it out," he said, and forthwith put his hands round his mouth, and bellowed into the night:— "Ahoy there! Ahoy there! Ahoy there!" his voice going out lost into the silence and darkness all around. But there came never a comprehensible answer, only all the time the infernal noise of a brook running out there on the sea, a thousand miles from any brook of earth; and away on the port bow, a vague shapeless shining.

I put the glasses to my eyes, and stared. The light was bigger and brighter, seen through the binoculars; but I could make nothing of it, only a dull, elongated shining, that moved vaguely in the darkness, apparently a hundred fathoms or so, away on the sea.

"Ahoy there! Ahoy there!" sung out the Mate again. Then, to the men below:— "Quiet there on the maindeck!"

There followed about a minute of intense stillness, during which we all listened; but there was no sound, except the constant noise of water running steadily.

I was watching the curious shining, and I saw it flick out suddenly at the Mate's shout. Then in a moment I saw three dull lights, one under the other, that flicked in and out intermittently.

"Here, give me the glasses!" said the Mate, and grabbed them from me.

He stared intensely for a moment; then swore, and turned to me:—

"What do you make of them?" he asked, abruptly.

"I don't know, Sir," I said. "I'm just puzzled. Perhaps it's electricity, or something of that sort."

"Oh hell!" he replied, and leant far out over the rail, staring. "Lord!" he said, for the second time, "what a stink!"

As he spoke, there came a most extraordinary thing; for there sounded a series of heavy reports out of the darkness, seeming in the silence, almost as loud as the sound of small cannon.

"They're shooting!" shouted a man on the main-deck, suddenly.

The Mate said nothing; only he sniffed violently at the night air. "By Gum!" he muttered, "what is it?"

I put my hand over my nose; for there was a terrible, charnel-like stench filling all the night about us.

"Take my glasses, Duprey," said the Mate, after a few minutes further watching. "Keep an eye over yonder. I'm going to call the Captain."

He pushed his way down the ladder, and hurried aft. About five minutes later, he returned forrard with the Captain and the Second and Third Mates, all in their shirts and trousers.

"Anything fresh, Duprey?" asked the Mate.

"No, Sir," I said, and handed him back his glasses. "The lights have gone again, and I think the mist is thicker. There's still the sound of running water out there."

The Captain and the three Mates stood some time along the port rail of the fo'cas'le head, watching through their night-glasses, and listening. Twice the Mate hailed; but there came no reply.

There was some talk, among the officers; and I gathered that the Captain was thinking of investigating.

"Clear one of the life-boats, Mr. Gelt," he said, at last. "The glass is steady; there'll be no wind for hours yet. Pick out half a dozen men. Take 'em out of either watch, if they want to come. I'll be back when I've got my coat."

"Away aft with you, Duprey, and some of you others," said the Mate. "Get the cover off the port life-boat, and bail her out."

" 'i, 'i, Sir," I answered, and went away aft with the others.

We had the boat into the water within twenty minutes, which is good time for a wind-jammer, where boats are generally used as storage receptacles for odd gear.

I was one of the men told off to the boat, with two others from our watch, and one from the starboard.

The Captain came down the end of the main tops'l halyards into the boat, and the Third after him. The Third took the tiller, and gave orders to cast off.

We pulled out clear of our vessel, and the Skipper told us to lie on our oars for a moment while he took his bearings. He leant forward to listen, and we all did the same. The sound of the running water was quite distinct across the quietness; but it struck me as seeming not so loud as earlier.

I remember now, that I noticed how plain the mist had become—a sort of warm, wet mist; not a bit thick; but just enough to make the night very dark, and to be visible, eddying slowly in a thin vapour round the port side-light, looking like a red cloudiness swirling lazily through the red glow of the big lamp.

There was no other sound at this time, beyond the sound of the running water; and the Captain, after handing something to the Third Mate, gave the order to give-way.

I was rowing stroke, and close to the officers, and so was able to see dimly that the Captain had passed a heavy revolver over to the Third Mate.

"Ho!" I thought to myself, "so the Old Man's a notion there's really something dangerous over there."

I slipped a hand quickly behind me, and felt that my sheath knife was clear.

We pulled easily for about three or four minutes, with the sound of the water growing plainer somewhere ahead in the darkness; and astern of us, a vague red glowing through the night and vapour, showed where our vessel was lying.

We were rowing easily, when suddenly the bow-oar muttered "G'lord!" Immediately afterwards, there was a loud splashing in the water on his side of the boat.

"What's wrong in the bows, there?" asked the Skipper, sharply.

"There's somethin' in the water, Sir, messing round my oar," said the man.

I stopped rowing, and looked round. All the men did the same. There was a further sound of splashing, and the water was driven right over the boat in showers. Then the bow-oar called out:— "There's somethin' got a holt of my oar, Sir!"

I could tell the man was frightened; and I knew suddenly that a curious nervousness had come to me—a vague, uncomfortable dread, such as the memory of an ugly tale will bring, in a lonesome place. I believe every man in the boat had a similar feeling. It seemed to me in that moment, that a definite, muggy sort of silence was all round us, and this in spite of the sound of the splashing, and the strange noise of the running water somewhere ahead of us on the dark sea.

"It's let go the oar, Sir!" said the man.

Abruptly, as he spoke, there came the Captain's voice in a roar:— "Back water all!" he shouted. "Put some beef into it now! Back all! Back all!... Why the devil was no lantern put in the boat! Back now! Back! Back!"

We backed fiercely, with a will; for it was plain that the Old Man had some good reason to get the boat away pretty quickly. He was right, too; though, whether it was guess-work, or some kind of instinct that made him shout out at that moment, I don't know; only I am sure he could not have seen anything in that absolute darkness.

As I was saying, he was right in shouting to us to back; for we had not backed more than half a dozen fathoms, when there was a tremendous splash right ahead of us, as if a house had fallen into the sea; and a regular wave of sea-water came at us out of the darkness, throwing our bows up, and soaking us fore and aft.

"Good Lord!" I heard the Third Mate gasp out. "What the devil's that?"

"Back all! Back! Back!" the Captain sung out again.

After some moments, he had the tiller put over, and told us to pull. We gave way with a will, as you may think, and in a few minutes were alongside our own ship again.

"Now then, men," the Captain said, when we were safe, aboard, "I'll not order any of you to come; but after the Steward's served out a tot of grog each, those who are willing, can come with me, and we'll have another go at finding out what devil's work is going on over yonder."

He turned to the Mate, who had been asking questions:—

"Say, Mister," he said, "it's no sort of thing to let the boat go without a lamp aboard. Send a couple of the lads into the lamp locker, and pass out a couple of the anchor-lights, and that deck bull's-eye, you use at nights for clearing up the ropes."

He whipped round on the Third:— "Tell the Steward to buck up with that grog, Mr. Andrews," he said, "and while you're there, pass out the axes from the rack in my cabin."

The grog came along a minute later; and then the Third Mate with three big axes from out the cabin rack.

"Now then, men," said the Skipper, as we took our tots off, "those who are coming with me, had better take an axe each from the Third Mate. They're mighty good weapons in any sort of trouble."

We all stepped forward, and he burst out laughing, slapping his thigh.

"That's the kind of thing I like!" he said. "Mr. Andrews, the axes won't go round. Pass out that old cutlass from the Steward's pantry. It's a pretty hefty piece of iron!"

The old cutlass was brought, and the man who was short of an axe, collared it. By this time, two of the 'prentices had filled (at least we supposed they had filled them!) two of the ship's anchor-lights; also they had brought out the bull's-eye lamp we used when clearing up the ropes on a dark night. With the lights and the axes and the cutlass, we felt ready to face anything, and down we went again into the boat, with the Captain and the Third Mate after us.

"Lash one of the lamps to one of the boat-hooks, and rig it over the bows," ordered the Captain.

This was done, and in this way the light lit up the water for a couple of fathoms ahead of the boat; and made us feel less that something could come at us without our knowing. Then the painter was cast off, and we gave way again toward the sound of the running water, out there in the darkness.

I remember now that it struck me that our vessel had drifted a bit; for the sounds seemed farther away. The second anchor-light had been put in the stern of the boat, and the Third Mate kept it between his feet, while he steered. The Captain had the bull's-eye in his hand, and was pricking up the wick with his pocket-knife.

As we pulled, I took a glance or two over my shoulder; but could see nothing, except the lamp making a yellow halo in the mist round the boat's bows, as we forged ahead. Astern of us, on our quarter, I could see the dull red glow of our vessel's port light. That was all, and not a sound in all the sea, as you might say, except the roll of our oars in the rowlocks, and somewhere in the darkness ahead, that curious noise of water running steadily; now sounding, as I have said, fainter and seeming farther away.

"It's got my oar again, Sir!" exclaimed the man at the bow oar, suddenly, and jumped to his feet. He hove his oar up with a great splashing of water, into the air, and immediately something whirled and beat about in the yellow halo of light over the bows of the boat. There was a crash of breaking wood, and the boat-hook was broken. The lamp soused down into the sea, and was lost. Then, in the darkness, there was a heavy splash, and a shout from the bow-oar:— "It's gone, Sir. It's loosed off the oar!"

"Vast pulling, all!" sung out the Skipper. Not that the order was necessary; for not a man was pulling. He had jumped up, and whipped a big revolver out of his coat pocket.

He had this in his right hand, and the bull's-eye in his left. He stepped forrard smartly over the oars from thwart to thwart, till he reached the bows, where he shone his light down into the water.

"My word!" he said. "Lord in Heaven! Saw anyone ever the like!"

And I doubt whether any man ever did see what we saw then; for the water was thick and living for yards round the boat with the hugest eels I ever saw before or after.

"Give way, men," said the Skipper, after a minute. "Yon's no explanation of the almighty queer sounds out yonder we're hearing this night. Give way, lads!"

He stood right up in the bows of the boat, shining his bull's-eye from side to side, and flashing it down on the water.

"Give way, lads!" he said again. "They don't like the light, that'll keep them from the oars. Give way steady now. Mr. Andrews, keep her dead on for the noise out yonder."

We pulled for some minutes, during which I felt my oar plucked at twice; but a flash of the Captain's lamp seemed sufficient to make the brutes loose hold.

The noise of the water running, appeared now quite near sounding. About this time, I had a sense again of an added sort of silence to all the natural quietness of the sea. And I had a return of the curious nervousness that had touched me before. I kept listening intensely, as if I expected to hear some other sound than the noise of the water. It came to me suddenly that I had the kind of feeling one has in the aisle of a large cathedral. There was a sort of echo in the night—an incredibly faint reduplicating of the noise of our oars.

"Hark!" I said, audibly; not realising at first that I was speaking aloud. "There's an echo—"

"That's it!" the Captain cut in, sharply. "I thought I heard something rummy!"

"…I thought I heard something rummy," said a thin ghostly echo, out of the night "…thought I heard something rummy" "…heard something rummy." The words went muttering and whispering to and fro in the night about us, in rather a horrible fashion.

"Good Lord!" said the Old Man, in a whisper.

We had all stopped rowing, and were staring about us into the thin mist that filled the night. The Skipper was standing with the bull's-eye lamp held over his head, circling the beam of light round from port to starboard, and back again.

Abruptly, as he did so, it came to me that the mist was thinner. The sound of the running water was very near; but it gave back no echo.

"The water doesn't echo, Sir," I said. "That's dam funny!"

"That's dam funny," came back at me, from the darkness to port and starboard, in a multitudinous muttering. "…Dam funny!…funny…eeey!"

"Give way!" said the Old Man, loudly. "I'll bottom this!"

"I'll bottom this… Bottom this… this!" The echo came back in a veritable rolling of unexpected sound. And then we had dipped our oars again, and the night was full of the reiterated rolling echoes of our rowlocks.

Suddenly the echoes ceased, and there was, strangely, the sense of a great space about us, and in the same moment the sound of the water running, appeared to be directly before us, but somehow up in the air.

"Vast rowing!" said the Captain, and we lay on our oars, staring round into the darkness ahead. The Old Man swung the beam of his lamp upwards, making circles with it in the night, and abruptly I saw something looming vaguely through the thinner-seeming mist.

"Look, Sir," I called to the Captain. "Quick, Sir, your light right above you! There's something up there!"

The Old Man flashed his lamp upwards, and found the thing I had seen. But it was too indistinct to make anything of, and even as he saw it, the darkness and mist seemed to wrap it about.

"Pull a couple of strokes, all!" said the Captain. "Stow your talk, there in the boat!… Again!… That'll do! Vast pulling!"

He was sending the beam of his lamp constantly across that part of the night where we had seen the thing, and suddenly I saw it again.

"There, Sir!" I said, quickly, "A little to starboard with the light."

He flicked the light swiftly to the right, and immediately we all saw the thing plainly—a strangely made mast, standing up there out of the mist, and looking like no spar I had ever seen.

It seemed now that the mist must lie pretty low on the sea in places; for the mast stood up out of it plainly for several fathoms; but, lower, it was hidden in the mist, which, I thought, seemed heavier now all round us; but thinner, as I have said, above.

"Ship ahoy!" sung out the Skipper, suddenly. "Ship ahoy, there!" But for some moments there came never a sound back to us except the constant noise of the water running, not a score yards away; and then, it seemed to me that a vague echo beat back at us out of the mist, oddly:—"Ahoy! Ahoy! Ahoy!"

"There's something hailing us, Sir," said the Third Mate.

Now, that "something" was significant. It showed the sort of feeling that was on us all.

"That's na ship's mast as ever I've seen!" I heard the man next to me mutter. "It's got a unnatcheral look."

"Ahoy there!" shouted the Skipper again, at the top of his voice. "Ahoy there!"

With the suddenness of a clap of thunder there burst out at us a vast, grunting:—oooaze; arrrr; arrrr; oooaze—a volume of sound so great that it seemed to make the loom of the oar in my hand vibrate.

"Good Lord!" said the Captain, and levelled his revolver into the mist; but he did not fire.

I had loosed one hand from my oar, and gripped my axe. I remember thinking that the Skipper's pistol wouldn't be much use against whatever thing made a noise like that.

"It wasn't ahead, Sir," said the Third Mate, abruptly, from where he sat and steered. "I think it came from somewhere over to starboard."

"Damn this mist!" said the Skipper. "Damn it! What a devil of a stink! Pass that other anchor-light forrard."

I reached for the lamp, and handed it to the next man, who passed it on.

"The other boat-hook," said the Skipper; and when he'd got it, he lashed the lamp to the hook end, and then lashed the whole arrangement upright in the bows, so that the lamp was well above his head.

"Now," he said. "Give way gently! And stand by to back-water, if I tell you…. Watch my hand, Mister," he added to the Third Mate. "Steer as I tell you."

We rowed a dozen slow strokes, and with every stroke, I took a look over my shoulder. The Captain was leaning forward under the big lamp, with the bull's-eye in one hand and his revolver in the other. He kept flashing the beam of the lantern up into the night.

"Good Lord!" he said, suddenly. "Vast pulling."

We stopped, and I slewed round on the thwart, and stared.

He was standing up under the glow of the anchor-light, and shining the bull's-eye up at a great mass that loomed dully through the mist. As he flicked the light to and fro over the great bulk, I realised that the boat was within some three or four fathoms of the hull of a vessel.

"Pull another stroke," the Skipper said, in a quiet voice, after a few minutes of silence. "Gently now! Gently!… Vast pulling!"

I slewed round again on my thwart and stared. I could see part of the thing quite distinctly now, and more of it, as I followed the beam of the Captain's lantern. She was a vessel right enough; but such a vessel as I had never seen. She was extraordinarily high out of the water, and seemed very short, and rose up into a queer mass at one end. But what puzzled me more, I think, than anything else, was the queer look of her sides, down which water was streaming all the time.

"That explains the sound of the water running," I thought to myself; "but what on earth is she built of?"

You will understand a little of my bewildered feelings, when I tell you that as the beam of the Captain's lamp shone on the side of this queer vessel, it showed stone everywhere—as if she were built out of stone. I never felt so dumb-founded in my life.

"She's stone, Cap'n!" I said. "Look at her, Sir!" I realised, as I spoke, a certain horribleness, of the unnatural…. A stone ship, floating out there in the night in the midst of the lonely Atlantic!

"She's stone," I said again, in that absurd way in which one reiterates, when one is bewildered.

"Look at the slime on her!" muttered the man next but one forrard of me. "She's a proper Davy Jones ship. By gum! she stinks like a corpse!"

"Ship ahoy!" roared the Skipper, at the top of his voice. "Ship ahoy! Ship ahoy!"

His shout beat back at us, in a curious, dank, yet metallic, echo, something the way one's voice sounds in an old disused quarry.

"There's no one aboard there, Sir," said the Third Mate. "Shall I put the boat alongside?"

"Yes, shove her up, Mister," said the Old Man. "I'll bottom this business. Pull a couple of strokes, aft there! In bow, and stand by to fend off."

The Third Mate laid the boat alongside, and we unshipped our oars. Then, I leant forward over the side of the boat, and pressed the flat of my hand upon the stark side of the ship. The water that ran down her side, sprayed out over my hand and wrist in a cataract; but I did not think about being wet, for my hand was pressed solid upon stone…. I pulled my hand back with a queer feeling.

"She's stone, right enough, Sir," I said to the Captain.

"We'll soon see what she is," he said. "Shove your oar up against her side, and shin up. We'll pass the lamp up to you as soon as you're aboard. Shove your axe in the back of your belt. I'll cover you with my gun, till you're aboard."

" 'i, 'i, Sir," I said; though I felt a bit funny at the thought of having to be the first aboard that dam rummy craft.

I put my oar upright against her side, and took a spring up it from the thwart, and in a moment I was grabbing over my head for her rail, with every rag on me soaked through with the water that was streaming down her, and spraying out over the oar and me.

I got a firm grip of the rail, and hoisted my head high enough to look over; but I could see nothing… what with the darkness, and the water in my eyes.

I knew it was no time for going slow, if there were danger aboard; so I went in over that rail in one spring, my boots coming down with a horrible, ringing, hollow stony sound on her decks. I whipped the water out of my eyes and the axe out of my belt, all in the same moment; then I took a good stare fore and aft; but it was too dark to see anything.

"Come along, Duprey!" shouted the Skipper. "Collar the lamp."

I leant out sideways over the rail, and grabbed for the lamp with my left hand, keeping the axe ready in my right, and staring inboard; for I tell you, I was just mortally afraid in that moment of what might be aboard of her.

I felt the lamp-ring with my left hand, and gripped it. Then I switched it aboard, and turned fair and square to see where I'd gotten.

Now, you never saw such a packet as that, not in a hundred years, nor yet two hundred, I should think. She'd got a rum little maindeck, about forty feet long, and then came a step about two feet high, and another bit of a deck, with a little house on it.

That was the after end of her; and more I couldn't see, because the light of my lamp went no farther, except to show me vaguely the big, cocked-up stern of her, going up into the darkness. I never saw a vessel made like her; not even in an old picture of old-time ships.

Forrard of me, was her mast—a big lump of a stick it was too, for her size. And here was another amazing thing, the mast of her looked just solid stone.

"Funny, isn't she, Duprey?" said the Skipper's voice at my back, and I came round on him with a jump.

"Yes," I said. "I'm puzzled. Aren't you, Sir?"

"Well," he said, "I am. If we were like the shellbacks they talk of in books, we'd be crossing ourselves. But, personally, give me a good heavy Colt, or the hefty chunk of steel you're cuddling."

He turned from me, and put his head over the rail.

"Pass up the painter, Jales," he said, to the bow-oar. Then to the Third Mate:—

"Bring 'em all up, Mister. If there's going to be anything rummy, we may as well make a picnic party of the lot…. Hitch that painter round the cleet yonder, Duprey," he added to me. "It looks good solid stone!… That's right. Come along."

He swung the thin beam of his lantern fore and aft, and then forrard again.

"Lord!" he said. "Look at that mast. It's stone. Give it a whack with the back of your axe, man; only remember she's apparently a bit of an old-timer! So go gently."

I took my axe short, and tapped the mast, and it rang dull, and solid, like a stone pillar. I struck it again, harder, and a sharp flake of stone flew past my cheek. The Skipper thrust his lantern close up to where I'd struck the mast.

"By George," he said, "she's absolutely a stone ship—solid stone, afloat here out of Eternity, in the middle of the wide Atlantic…. Why! She must weigh a thousand tons more than she's buoyancy to carry. It's just impossible…. It's—"

He turned his head quickly, at a sound in the darkness along the decks. He flashed his light that way, across and across the after decks; but we could see nothing.

"Get a move on you in the boat!" he said sharply, stepping to the rail and looking down. "For once I'd really prefer a little more of your company…." He came round like a flash. "Duprey, what was that?" he asked in a low voice.

"I certainly heard something, Sir," I said. "I wish the others would hurry. By Jove! Look! What's that—"

"Where?" he said, and sent the beam of his lamp to where I pointed with my axe.

"There's nothing," he said, after circling the light all over the deck. "Don't go imagining things. There's enough solid unnatural fact here, without trying to add to it."

There came the splash and thud of feet behind, as the first of the men came up over the side, and jumped clumsily into the lee scuppers, which had water in them. You see she had a cant to that side, and I supposed the water had collected there.

The rest of the men followed, and then the Third Mate. That made six men of us, all well armed; and I felt a bit more comfortable, as you can think.

"Hold up that lamp of yours, Duprey, and lead the way," said the Skipper. "You're getting the post of honour this trip!"

" 'i, 'i, Sir," I said, and stepped forward, holding up the lamp in my left hand, and carrying my axe half way down the haft, in my right.

"We'll try aft, first," said the Captain, and led the way himself, flashing the bull's-eye to and fro. At the raised portion of the deck, he stopped.

"Now," he said, in his queer way, "let's have a look at this…. Tap it with your axe, Duprey…. Ah!" he added, as I hit it with the back of my axe. "That's what we call stone at home, right enough. She's just as rum as anything I've seen while I've been fishing. We'll go on aft and have a peep into I the deck-house. Keep your axes handy, men."

We walked slowly up to the curious little house, the deck rising to it with quite a slope. At the foreside of the little deck-house, the Captain pulled up, and shone his bull's-eye down at the deck. I saw that he was looking at what was plainly the stump of the after mast. He stepped closer to it, and kicked, it with his foot; and it gave out the same dull, solid note that the foremast had done. It was obviously a chunk of stone.

I held up my lamp so that I could see the upper part of the house more clearly. The fore-part had two square window-spaces in it; but there was no glass in either of them; and the blank darkness within the queer little place, just seemed to stare out at us.

And then I saw something suddenly… a great shaggy head of red hair was rising slowly into sight, through the port window, the one nearest to us.

"My God! What's that, Cap'n?" I called out. But it was gone, even as I spoke.

"What?" he asked, jumping at the way I had sung out.

"At the port window, Sir," I said. "A great red-haired head. It came right up to the window-place; and then it went in a moment."

The Skipper stepped right up to the little dark window, and pushed his lantern through into the blackness. He flashed the light round; then withdrew the lantern.

"Bosh, man!" he said. "That's twice you've got fancying things. Ease up your nerves a bit!"

"I did see it!" I said, almost angrily. "It was like a great red-haired head…."

"Stow it, Duprey!" he said, though not sneeringly. "The house is absolutely empty. Come round to the door, if the Infernal Masons that built her, went in for doors! Then you'll see for yourself. All the same, keep your axes ready, lads. I've a notion there's something pretty queer aboard here."

We went up round the after-end of the little house, and here we saw what appeared to be a door.

The Skipper felt at the queer, odd-shapen handle, and pushed at the door; but it had stuck fast.

"Here, one of you!" he said, stepping back. "Have a whack at this with your axe. Better use the back."

One of the men stepped forward, and we stood away to give him room. As his axe struck, the door went to pieces with exactly the same sound that a thin slab of stone would make, when broken.

"Stone!" I heard the Captain mutter, under his breath. " By Gum! What *is* she?"

I did not wait for the Skipper. He had put me a bit on edge, and I stepped bang in through the open doorway, with the lamp high, and holding my axe short and ready; but there was nothing in the place, save a stone seat running all round, except where the doorway opened on to the deck.

"Find your red-haired monster?" asked the Skipper, at my elbow.

I said nothing. I was suddenly aware that he was all on the jump with some inexplicable fear. I saw his glance going everywhere about him. And then his eye caught mine, and he saw that I realised. He was a man almost callous to fear, that is the fear of danger in what I might call any normal sea-faring shape. And this palpable nerviness affected me tremendously. He was obviously doing his best to throttle it; and trying all he knew to hide it. I had a sudden warmth of understanding for him, and dreaded lest the men should realise his state. Funny that I should be able at that moment to be aware of anything but my own bewildered fear and expectancy of intruding upon something monstrous at any instant. Yet I describe exactly my feelings, as I stood there in the house.

"Shall we try below, Sir?" I said, and turned to where a flight of stone steps led down into an utter blackness, out of which rose a strange, dank scent of the sea... an imponderable mixture of brine and darkness.

"The worthy Duprey leads the van!" said the Skipper; but I felt no irritation now. I knew that he must cover his fright, until he had got control again; and I think he felt, somehow, that I was backing him up. I remember now that I went down those stairs into that unknowable and ancient cabin, as much aware in that moment of the Captain's state, as of that extraordinary thing I had just seen at the little window, or of my own half-funk of what we might see any moment.

The Captain was at my shoulder, as I went, and behind him came the Third Mate, and then the men, all in single file; for the stairs were narrow.

I counted seven steps down, and then my foot splashed into water on the eighth. I held the lamp low, and stared. I had caught no glimpse of a reflection, and I saw now that this was owing to a curious, dull, greyish scum that lay thinly on the water, seeming to match the colour of the stone which composed the steps and bulksheads.

"Stop!" I said. "I'm in water!"

I let my foot down slowly, and got the next step. Then sounded with my axe, and found the floor at the bottom. I stepped down and stood up to my thighs in water.

"It's all right, Sir," I said, suddenly whispering. I held my lamp up, and glanced quickly about me. "It's not deep. There's two doors here…."

I whirled my axe up as I spoke; for, suddenly, I had realised that one of the doors was open a little. It seemed to move, as I stared, and I could have imagined that a vague undulation ran towards me, across the dull scum-covered water.

"The door's opening!" I said, aloud, with a sudden sick feeling. "Look out!"

I backed from the door, staring; but nothing came. And abruptly, I had control of myself; for I realised that the door was not moving. It had not moved at all. It was simply ajar.

"It's all right, Sir," I said. "It's not opening."

I stepped forward again a pace towards the doors, as the Skipper and the Third Mate came down with a jump, splashing water all over me.

The Captain still had the "nerves" on him, as I think I could feel, even then; but he hid it well.

"Try the door, Mister. I've jumped my dam lamp out!" he growled to the Third Mate; who pushed at the door on my right; but it would not open beyond the nine or ten inches it was fixed ajar.

"There's this one here, Sir," I whispered, and held my lantern up to the closed door that lay to my left.

"Try it," said the Skipper, in an undertone. We did so, but it also was fixed. I whirled my axe suddenly, and struck the door heavily in the centre of the main panel, and the whole thing crashed into flinders of stone, that went with hollow sounding splashes into the darkness beyond.

"Goodness!" said the Skipper, in a startled voice; for my action had been so instant and unexpected. He covered his lapse, in a moment, by the warning:—

"Look out for bad air!" But I was already inside with the lamp, and holding my axe handily. There was no bad air; for right across from me, was a split clean through the ship's side, that I could have put my two arms through, just above the level of the scummy water.

The place I had broken into, was a cabin, of a kind; but seemed strange and dank, and too narrow to breathe in; and wherever I turned, I saw stone. The Third Mate and the Skipper gave simultaneous expressions of disgust at the wet dismalness of the place.

"It's all stone," I said, and brought my axe hard against the front of a sort of squat cabinet, which was built into the after bulkshead. It caved in, with a crash of splintered stone.

"Empty!" I said, and turned instantly away.

The Skipper and the Third Mate, with the men who were now peering in at the door, crowded out; and in that moment, I pushed my axe under my arm, and thrust my hand into the burst stone-chest. Twice I did this, with almost the speed of lightning, and shoved what I had seen, into the side-pocket of my coat. Then, I was following the others; and not one of them had noticed a thing. As for me, I was quivering with excitement, so that my knees shook; for I had caught the unmistakable gleam of gems; and had grabbed for them in that one swift instant.

I wonder whether anyone can realise what I felt in that moment. I knew that, if my guess were right, I had snatched the power in that one miraculous moment, that would lift me from the weary life of a common shellback, to the life of ease that had been mine during my early years. I tell you, in that instant, as I staggered almost blindly out of that dark little apartment, I had no thought of any horror that might be held in that incredible vessel, out there afloat on the wide Atlantic.

I was full of the one blinding thought, that possibly I was *rich*! And I wanted to get somewhere by myself as soon as possible, to see whether I was right. Also, if I could, I meant to get back to that strange cabinet of stone, if the chance came; for I knew that the two handfuls I had grabbed, had left a lot behind.

Only, whatever I did, I must let no one guess; for then I should probably lose everything, or have but an infinitesimal share doled out to me, of the wealth that I believed to be in those glittering things there in the side-pocket of my coat.

I began immediately to wonder what other treasures there might be aboard; and then, abruptly, I realised that the Captain was speaking to me:—

"The light, Duprey, damn you!" he was saying, angrily, in a low tone. "What's the matter with you! Hold it up."

I pulled myself together, and shoved the lamp above my head. One of the men was swinging his axe, to beat in the door that seemed to have stood so eternally ajar; and the rest were standing back, to give him room. Crash! went the axe, and half the door fell inward, in a shower of broken stone, making dismal splashes in the darkness. The man struck again, and the rest of the door fell away, with a sullen slump into the water.

"The lamp," muttered the Captain. But I had hold of myself once more, and I was stepping forward slowly through the thigh-deep water, even before he spoke.

I went a couple of paces in through the black gape of the doorway, and then stopped and held the lamp so as to get a view of the place. As I did so, I remember how the intense silence struck home on me. Every man of us must surely have been holding his breath; and there must have been some heavy quality, either in the water, or in the scum that floated on it, that kept it from rippling against the sides of the bulksheads, with the movements we had made.

At first, as I held the lamp (which was burning badly), I could not get its position right to show me anything, except that I was in a very large cabin for so small a vessel. Then I saw that a table ran along the centre, and the top of it was no more than a few inches above the water. On each side of it, there rose the backs of what were evidently two rows of massive, olden looking chairs. At the far end of the table, there was a huge, immobile, humped something.

I stared at this for several moments; then I took three slow steps forward, and stopped again; for the thing resolved itself, under the light from the lamp, into the figure of an enormous man, seated at the end of the table, his face bowed forward upon his arms. I was amazed, and thrilling abruptly with new fears and vague impossible thoughts. Without moving a step, I held the light nearer at arm's length....

The man was of stone, like everything in that extraordinary ship.

"That foot!" said the Captain's voice, suddenly cracking. "Look at that foot!" His voice sounded amazingly startling and hollow in that silence, and the words seemed to come back sharply at me from the vaguely seen bulksheads.

I whipped my light to starboard, and saw what he meant—a huge human foot was sticking up out of the water, on the right hand side of the table. It was enormous. I have never seen so vast a foot. And it also was of stone.

And then, as I stared, I saw that there was a great head above the water, over by the bulkshead.

"I've gone mad!" I said, out loud, as I saw something else, more incredible.

"My God! Look at the hair on the head!" said the Captain.... "It's growing! It's growing!" His voice cracked again.

"Look at it! It's growing!" he called out once more.

I was looking. On the great head, there was becoming visible a huge mass of red hair, that was surely and unmistakably rising up, as we watched it.

"It's what I saw at the window!" I said. "It's what I saw at the window! I told you I saw it!"

"Come out of that, Duprey," said the Third Mate, quietly.

"Let's get out of here!" muttered one of the men. Two or three of them called out the same thing; and then, in a moment, they began a mad rush up the stairway.

I stood dumb, where I was. The hair rose up in a horrible living fashion on the great head, waving and moving. It rippled down over the forehead, and spread abruptly over the whole gargantuan stone face, hiding the features completely. Suddenly, I swore at the thing madly, and I hove my axe at it. Then I was backing crazily for the door, slumping the scum as high as the deck-beams, in my fierce haste. I reached the stairs, and caught at the stone rail, that was modelled like a rope; and so hove myself up out of the water. I reached the little deck-house, where

I had seen the great head of hair. I jumped through the doorway, out on to the decks, and I felt the night air sweet on my face…. Goodness! I ran forward along the decks. There was a Babel of shouting in the waist of the ship, and a thudding of feet running. Some of the men were singing out, to get into the boat; but the Third Mate was shouting that they must wait for me.

"He's coming," called someone. And then I was among them.

"Turn that lamp up, you idiot," said the Captain's voice. "This is just where we want light!"

I glanced down, and realised that my lamp was almost out. I turned it up, and it flared, and began again to dwindle.

"Those damned boys never filled it," I said. "They deserve their necks breaking."

The men were literally tumbling over the side, and the Skipper was hurrying them.

"Down with you into the boat," he said to me. "Give me the lamp. I'll pass it down. Get a move on you!"

The Captain had evidently got his nerve back again. This was more like the man I knew. I handed him the lamp, and went over the side. All the rest had now gone, and the Third Mate was already in the stern, waiting.

As I landed on the thwart, there was a sudden, strange noise from aboard the ship—a sound, as if some stone object were trundling down the sloping decks, from aft. In that one moment, I got what you might truly call the "horrors." I seemed suddenly able to believe incredible possibilities.

"The stone men!" I shouted. "Jump, Captain! Jump! Jump!" The vessel seemed to roll oddly.

Abruptly, the Captain yelled out something, that not one of us in the boat understood. There followed a succession of tremendous sounds, aboard the ship, and I saw his shadow swing out huge against the thin mist, as he turned suddenly with the lamp. He fired twice with his revolver.

"The hair!" I shouted. "Look at the hair!"

We all saw it—the great head of red hair that we had seen grow visibly on the monstrous stone head, below in the cabin. It rose above the rail, and there was a moment of intense stillness, in which I heard the Captain gasping. The Third Mate fired six times at the thing, and I found myself fixing an oar up against the side of that abominable vessel, to get aboard.

As I did so, there came one appalling crash, that shook the stone ship fore and aft, and she began to cant up, and my oar slipped and fell into the boat. Then the Captain's voice screamed something in a choking fashion above us. The ship lurched forward, and paused. Then another crash came, and she rocked over towards us; then away from us again. The movement away from us, continued, and the round of the vessel's bottom showed, vaguely. There was a smashing of glass above us, and the dim glow of light aboard, vanished. Then the vessel fell clean over from us, with a giant splash. A huge wave came at us, out of the night, and half filled the boat.

The boat nearly capsized, then righted and presently steadied.

"Captain!" shouted the Third Mate. "Captain!" But there came never a sound; only presently, out of all the night, a strange murmuring of waters.

"Captain!" he shouted once more; but his voice just went lost and remote into the darkness.

"She's foundered!" I said.

"Out oars," sung out the Third. "Put your backs into it. Don't stop to bail!"

For half an hour we circled the spot slowly. But the strange vessel had indeed foundered and gone down into the mystery of the deep sea, with her mysteries.

Finally we put about, and returned to the *Alfred Jessop*.

Now, I want you to realise that what I am telling you is a plain and simple tale of fact. This is no fairy tale, and I've not done yet; and I think this yarn should prove to you that some mighty strange things do happen at sea, and always will while the world lasts. It's the home of all the mysteries; for it's the one place that is really difficult for humans to investigate. Now just listen:—

The Mate had kept the bell going, from time to time, and so we came back pretty quickly, having as we came, a strange repetition of the echoey reduplication of our oar-sounds; but we never spoke a word; for not one of us wanted to hear those beastly echoes again, after what we had just gone through. I think we all had a feeling that there was something a bit hellish abroad that night.

We got aboard, and the Third explained to the Mate what had happened; but he would hardly believe the yarn. However, there was nothing to do, but wait for daylight; so we were told to keep about the deck, and keep our eyes and ears open.

One thing the Mate did, showed he was more impressed by our yarn, than he would admit. He had all the ship's lanterns lashed up round the decks, to the sheerpoles; and he never told us to give up either the axes or the cutlass.

It was while we were keeping about the decks, that I took the chance to have a look at what I had grabbed. I tell you, what I found, made me nearly forget the Skipper, and all the rummy things that had happened. I had twenty-six stones in my pocket and four of them were diamonds, respectively 9, 11, 13½ and 17 carats in weight, uncut, that is. I know quite something about diamonds. I'm not going to tell you how I learnt what I know; but I would not have taken a thousand pounds for the four, as they lay there, in my hand. There was also a big, dull stone, that looked red inside. I'd have dumped it over the side, I thought so little of it; only, I argued that it must be something, or it would never have been among that lot. Lord! but I little knew what I'd got; not then. Why, the thing was as big as a fair-sized walnut. You may think it funny that I thought of the four diamonds first; but you see, I *know* diamonds when I see them. They're things I understand; but I never saw a ruby, in the rough, before or since. Good Lord! And to think I'd have thought nothing of heaving it over the side!

You see, a lot of the stories were not anything much; that is, not in the modern market. There were two big topazes, and several onyx and cornelians—nothing much. There were five hammered slugs of gold about two ounces each they would be. And then a prize—one winking green devil of an emerald. You've got to know an emerald to look for the "eye" of it, in the rough; but it is there—the eye of some hidden devil staring up at you. Yes, I'd seen an emerald before, and I knew I held a lot of money in that one stone alone.

And then I remembered what I'd missed, and cursed myself for not grabbing a third time. But that feeling lasted only a moment. I thought of the beastly part that had been the Skipper's share; while there I stood safe under one of the lamps, with a fortune in my hands. And then, abruptly, as you can understand, my mind was filled with the crazy wonder and bewilderment of what had happened. I felt how absurdly ineffectual my imagination was to comprehend anything understandable out of it all, except that the Captain had certainly gone, and I had just as certainly had a piece of impossible luck.

Often, during that time of waiting, I stopped to take a look at the things I had in my pocket; always careful that no one about the decks should come near me, to see what I was looking at.

Suddenly the Mate's voice came sharp along the decks:—

"Call the Doctor, one of you," he said. "Tell him to get the fire in and the coffee made."

" 'i, 'i, Sir," said one of the men; and I realised that the dawn was growing vaguely over the sea.

Half an hour later, the "Doctor" shoved his head out of the galley doorway, and sung out that coffee was ready.

The watch below turned out, and had theirs with the watch on deck, all sitting along the spar that lay under the port rail.

As the daylight grew, we kept a constant watch over the side; but even now we could see nothing; for the thin mist still hung low on the sea.

"Hear that?" said one of the men, suddenly. And, indeed, the sound must have been plain for half a mile round.

"Ooaaze, ooaaze, arrr, arrrr, oooaze—"

"By George!" said Tallett, one of the other watch; "that's a beastly sort of thing to hear."

"Look!" I said. "What's that out yonder?"

The mist was thinning under the effect of the rising sun, and tremendous shapes seemed to stand towering half-seen, away to port. A few minutes passed, while we stared. Then, suddenly, we heard the Mate's voice:—

"All hands on deck!" he was shouting, along the decks.

I ran aft a few steps.

"Both watches are out, Sir," I called.

"Very good!" said the Mate. "Keep handy all of you. Some of you have got the axes. The rest had better take a caps'n-bar each, and stand-by till I find what this devilment is, out yonder."

" 'i, 'i, Sir," I said, and turned forrard. But there was no need to pass on the Mate's orders; for the men had heard, and there was a rush for the capstan-bars, which are a pretty hefty kind of cudgel, as any sailorman knows. We lined the rail again, and stared away to port.

"Look out, you sea-divvils," shouted Timothy Galt, a huge Irishman, waving his bar excitedly, and peering over the rail into the mist, which was steadily thinning, as the day grew.

Abruptly there was a simultaneous cry:— *"Rocks!"* shouted everyone.

I never saw such a sight. As at last the mist thinned, we could see them. All the sea to port was literally cut about with far-reaching reefs of rock. In places the reefs lay just submerged; but in others they rose into extraordinary and fantastic rock-spires, and arches, and islands of jagged rock.

"Jehoshaphat!" I heard the Third Mate shout. "Look at that, Mister! Look at that! Lord! how did we take the boat through that, without stoving her!"

Everything was so still for the moment, with all the men just staring and amazed, that I could hear every word come along the decks.

"There's sure been a submarine earthquake somewhere," I heard the First Mate say. "The bottom of the sea's just riz up here, quiet and gentle, during the night; and God's mercy we aren't now a-top of one of those ornaments out there."

And then, you know, I saw it all. Everything that had looked mad and impossible, began to be natural; though it was, none the less, all amazing and wonderful.

There had been during the night, a slow lifting of the sea-bottom, owing to some action of the Internal Pressures. The rocks had risen so gently that they had made never a sound; and the stone ship had risen with them out of the deep sea. She had evidently lain on one of the submerged reefs, and so had seemed to us to be just afloat in the sea. And she accounted for the water we heard running. She was naturally bung-full, as you might say, and took longer to shed the water than she did to rise. She had probably some biggish holes in her bottom. I began to get my "soundings" a bit, as I might call it in sailor talk. The natural wonders of the sea, beat all made-up yarns that ever were!

The Mate sung out to us to man the boat again, and told the Third Mate to take her out to where we lost the Skipper, and have a final look round, in case there might be any chance to find the Old Man's body anywhere about.

"Keep a man in the bows to look out for sunk rocks, Mister," the Mate told the

Third, as we pulled off. "Go slow. There'll be no wind yet awhile. See if you can fix up what made those noises, while you're looking round."

We pulled right across about thirty fathoms of clear water, and in a minute we were between two great arches of rock. It was then I realised that the reduplicating of our oar-roll was the echo from these on each side of us. Even in the sunlight, it was queer to hear again that same strange cathedral echoey sound that we had heard in the dark.

We passed under the huge arches, all hung with deep-sea slime. And presently we were heading straight for a gap, where two low reefs swept in to the apex of a huge horseshoe. We pulled for about three minutes, and then the Third gave the word to vast pulling.

"Take the boat-hook, Duprey," he said, "and go forrard, and see we don't hit anything."

" 'i, 'i, Sir," I said, and drew in my oar.

"Give way again gently!" said the Third; and the boat moved forward for another thirty or forty yards.

"We're right on to a reef, Sir," I said, presently, as I stared down over the bows. I sounded with the boat-hook. "There's about three feet of water, Sir," I told him.

"Vast pulling," ordered the Third. "I reckon we are right over the rock, where we found that rum packet last night." He leant over the side, and stared down.

"There's a stone cannon on the rock, right under the bows of the boat," I said. Immediately afterwards I shouted:—

"There's the hair, Sir! There's the hair! It's on the reef. There's two! There's three! There's one on the cannon!"

"All right! All right, Duprey! Keep cool," said the Third Mate. "I can see them. You've enough intelligence not to be superstitious now the whole thing's explained. They're some kind of big-hairy sea-caterpillar. Prod one with your boat-hook."

I did so; a little ashamed of my sudden bewilderment. The thing whipped round like a tiger, at the boat-hook. It lapped itself round and round the boat-hook, while the hind portions of it kept gripped to the rock, and I could no more pull the boat-hook from its grip, than fly; though I pulled till I sweated.

"Take the point of your cutlass to it, Varley," said the Third Mate. "Jab it through."

The bow-oar did so, and the brute loosed the boat-hook, and curled up round a chunk of rock, looking like a great ball of red hair.

I drew the boat-hook up, and examined it.

"Goodness!" I said. "That's what killed the Old Man—one of those things! Look at all those marks in the wood, where it's gripped it with about a hundred legs."

I passed the boat-hook aft to the Third Mate to look at.

"They're about as dangerous as they can be, Sir, I reckon," I told him. "Makes you think of African centipedes, only these are big and strong enough to kill an elephant, I should think."

"Don't lean all on one side of the boat!" shouted the Third Mate, as the men stared over. "Get back to your places. Give way, there!... Keep a good look out for any signs of the ship or the Captain, Duprey."

For nearly an hour, we pulled to and fro over the reef; but we never saw either the stone ship or the Old Man again. The queer craft must have rolled off into the profound depths that lay on each side of the reef.

As I leant over the bows, staring down all that long while at the submerged rocks, I was able to understand almost everything, except the various extraordinary noises.

The cannon made it unmistakably clear that the ship which had been hove up from the sea-bottom, with the rising of the reef, had been originally a normal enough wooden vessel of a time far removed from our own. At the sea-bottom, she had evidently undergone some natural mineralising process, and this explained her stony appearance. The stone men had been evidently humans who had been drowned in her cabin, and their swollen tissues had been subjected to the same natural process, which, however, had also deposited heavy encrustations upon them, so that their size, when compared with the normal, was prodigious.

The mystery of the hair, I had already discovered; but there remained, among other things, the tremendous bangs we had heard. These were, possibly, explained later, while we were making a final examination of the rocks to the Westward, prior to returning to our ship. Here we discovered the burst and swollen bodies of several extraordinary deep-sea creatures, of the eel variety. They must have had a girth, in life, of many feet, and the one that we measured roughly with an oar, must have been quite forty feet long. They had, apparently, burst on being lifted from the tremendous pressure of the deep sea, into the light air pressure above water, and hence might account for the loud reports we had eoard; though, personally, I incline to think these loud bangs were more probably caused by the splitting of the rocks under new stresses.

As for the roaring sounds, I can only conclude that they were caused by a peculiar species of grampus-like fish, of enormous size, which we found dead and hugely distended on one of the rocky masses. This fish must have weighed at least four or five tons, and when prodded with a heavy oar, there came from its peculiar snout-shaped mouth, a low, hoarse sound, like a weak imitation of the tremendous sounds we had heard during the past night.

Regarding the apparently carved handrail, like a rope up the side of the cabin stairs, I realise that this had undoubtedly been actual rope at one time.

Recalling the heavy, trundling sounds aboard, just after I climbed down into the boat, I can only suppose that these were made by some stone object, possibly a fossilised gun-carriage, rolling down the decks, as the ship began to slip off the rocks, and her bows sank lower in the water.

The varying lights must have been the strongly phosphorescent bodies of some of the deep-sea creatures, moving about on the upheaved reefs. As for the giant splash that occurred in the darkness ahead of the boat, this must have been due to some large portion of heaved-up rock, overbalancing and rolling back into the sea.

No one aboard ever learnt about the jewels. I took care of that! I sold the ruby badly, so I've heard since; but I do not grumble even now. Twenty-three thousand pounds I had for it alone, from a merchant in London. I learned afterwards he made double that on it; but I don't spoil my pleasure by grumbling. I wonder often how the stones and things came where I found them; but she carried guns, as I've told, I think; and there's rum doings happen at sea; yes, by George!

The smell—oh that I guess was due to heaving all that deep-sea slime up for human noses to smell at.

This yarn is, of course, known in nautical circles, and was briefly mentioned in the old *Nautical Mercury* of 1879. The series of volcanic reefs (which disappeared in 1883) were charted under the name of the "*Alfred Jessop* Shoals and Reefs"; being named after our Captain who discovered them and lost his life on them.

The Voice in the Night

◆→ ← ◆

I t was a dark, starless night. We were becalmed in the Northern Pacific. Our exact position I do not know; for the sun had been hidden during the course of a weary, breathless week, by a thin haze which had seemed to float above us, about the height of our mastheads, at whiles descending and shrouding the surrounding sea.

With there being no wind, we had steadied the tiller, and I was the only man on deck. The crew, consisting of two men and a boy, were sleeping forrard in their den; while Will—my friend, and the master of our little craft—was aft in his bunk on the port side of the little cabin.

Suddenly, from out of the surrounding darkness, there came a hail:—

"Schooner, ahoy!"

The cry was so unexpected that I gave no immediate answer, because of my surprise.

It came again—a voice curiously throaty and inhuman, calling from somewhere upon the dark sea away on our port broadside:—

"Schooner, ahoy!"

"Hullo!" I sung out, having gathered my wits somewhat. "What are you? What do you want?"

"You need not be afraid," answered the queer voice, having probably noticed some trace of confusion in my tone. "I am only an old—man."

The pause sounded oddly; but it was only afterwards that it came back to me with any significance.

"Why don't you come alongside, then?" I queried somewhat snappishly; for I liked not his hinting at my having been a trifle shaken.

"I—I—can't. It wouldn't be safe. I—" The voice broke off, and there was silence.

"What do you mean?" I asked, growing more and more astonished. "Why not safe? Where are you?"

I listened for a moment; but there came no answer. And then, a sudden indefinite suspicion, of I knew not what, coming to me, I stepped swiftly to the binnacle, and took out the lighted lamp. At the same time, I knocked on the deck with my heel to waken Will. Then I was back at the side, throwing the yellow funnel of light out into the silent immensity beyond our rail. As I did so, I heard a slight, muffled cry, and then the sound of a splash, as though some one had dipped oars abruptly. Yet I cannot say that I saw anything with certainty; save, it seemed to me, that with the first flash of the light, there had been something upon the waters, where now there was nothing.

"Hullo, there!" I called. "What foolery is this!"

But there came only the indistinct sounds of a boat being pulled away into the night.

Then I heard Will's voice, from the direction of the after scuttle:—

"What's up, George?"

"Come here, Will!" I said.

"What is it?" he asked, coming across the deck.

I told him the queer thing which had happened. He put several questions; then, after a moment's silence, he raised his hands to his lips, and hailed:

"Boat, ahoy!"

From a long distance away, there came back to us a faint reply, and my companion repeated his call. Presently, after a short period of silence, there grew on our hearing the muffled sound of oars; at which Will hailed again.

This time there was a reply:—

"Put away the light."

"I'm damned if I will," I muttered; but Will told me to do as the voice bade, and I shoved it down under the bulwarks.

"Come nearer," he said, and the oar-strokes continued. Then, when apparently some half-dozen fathoms distant, they again ceased.

"Come alongside," exclaimed Will. "There's nothing to be frightened of aboard here!"

"Promise that you will not show the light?"

"What's to do with you," I burst out, "that you're so infernally afraid of the light?"

"Because—" began the voice, and stopped short.

"Because what?" I asked, quickly.

Will put his hand on my shoulder.

"Shut up a minute, old man," he said, in a low voice. "Let me tackle him."

He leant more over the rail.

"See here, Mister," he said, "this is a pretty queer business, you coming upon us like this, right out in the middle of the blessed Pacific. How are we to know what sort of a hanky-panky trick you're up to? You say there's only one of you. How are we to know, unless we get a squint at you—eh? What's your objection to the light, anyway?"

As he finished, I heard the noise of the oars again, and then the voice came; but now from a greater distance, and sounding extremely hopeless and pathetic.

" I am sorry—sorry! I would not have troubled you, only I am hungry, and—so is she."

The voice died away, and the sound of the oars, dipping irregularly, was borne to us.

"Stop!" sung out Will. "I don't want to drive you away. Come back! We'll keep the light hidden, if you don't like it."

He turned to me:—

"It's a damned queer rig, this; but I think there's nothing to be afraid of?"

There was a question in his tone, and I replied.

"No, I think the poor devil's been wrecked around here, and gone crazy."

The sound of the oars drew nearer.

"Shove that lamp back in the binnacle," said Will; then he leaned over the rail, and listened. I replaced the lamp, and came back to his side. The dipping of the oars ceased some dozen yards distant.

"Won't you come alongside now?" asked Will in an even voice. "I have had the lamp put back in the binnacle."

"I—I cannot," replied the voice. "I dare not come nearer. I dare not even pay you for the—the provisions."

"That's all right," said Will, and hesitated. "You're welcome to as much grub as you can take—" Again he hesitated.

"You are very good," exclaimed the voice. "May God, Who understands everything, reward you—" It broke off huskily.

"The—the lady?" said Will, abruptly. "Is she—"

"I have left her behind upon the island," came the voice.

"What island?" I cut in.

"I know not its name," returned the voice. "I would to God—!" it began, and checked itself as suddenly.

"Could we not send a boat for her?" asked Will at this point.

"No!" said the voice, with extraordinary emphasis. "My God! No!" There was a moment's pause; then it added, in a tone which seemed a merited reproach:—

"It was because of our want I ventured— Because her agony tortured me."

"I am a forgetful brute," exclaimed Will. "Just wait a minute, whoever you are, and I will bring you up something at once."

In a couple of minutes he was back again, and his arms were full of various edibles. He paused at the rail.

"Can't you come alongside for them?" he asked.

"No—I *dare not*," replied the voice, and it seemed to me that in its tones I detected a note of stifled craving—as though the owner hushed a mortal desire. It came to me then in a flash, that the poor old creature out there in the darkness, was *suffering* for actual need of that which Will held in his arms; and yet, because of some unintelligible dread, refraining from dashing to the side of our little schooner, and receiving it. And with the lightning-like conviction, there came the knowledge that the Invisible was not mad; but sanely facing some intolerable horror.

"Damn it, Will!" I said, full of many feelings, over which predominated a vast sympathy. "Get a box. We must float off the stuff to him in it."

This we did—propelling it away from the vessel, out into the darkness, by means of a boathook. In a minute, a slight cry from the Invisible came to us, and we knew that he had secured the box.

A little later, he called out a farewell to us, and so heartful a blessing, that I am sure we were the better for it. Then, without more ado, we heard the ply of oars across the darkness.

"Pretty soon off," remarked Will, with perhaps just a little sense of injury.

"Wait," I replied. "I think somehow he'll come back. He must have been badly needing that food."

"And the lady," said Will. For a moment he was silent; then he continued:—

"It's the queerest thing ever I've tumbled across, since I've been fishing."

"Yes," I said, and fell to pondering.

And so the time slipped away—an hour, another, and still Will stayed with me; for the queer adventure had knocked all desire for sleep out of him.

The third hour was three parts through, when we heard again the sound of oars across the silent ocean.

"Listen!" said Will, a low note of excitement in his voice.

"He's coming, just as I thought," I muttered.

The dipping of the oars grew nearer, and I noted that the strokes were firmer and longer. The food had been needed.

They came to a stop a little distance off the broadside, and the queer voice came again to us through the darkness:—

"Schooner, ahoy!"

"That you?" asked Will.

"Yes," replied the voice. "I left you suddenly; but—but there was great need."

"The lady?" questioned Will.

"The—lady is grateful now on earth. She will be more grateful soon in—in heaven."

Will began to make some reply, in a puzzled voice; but became confused, and broke off short. I said nothing. I was wondering at the curious pauses, and, apart from my wonder, I was full of a great sympathy.

The voice continued:—

"We—she and I, have talked, as we shared the result of God's tenderness and yours—"

Will interposed; but without coherence.

"I beg of you not to—to belittle your deed of Christian charity this night," said the voice. "Be sure that it has not escaped His notice."

It stopped, and there was a full minute's silence. Then it came again:—

"We have spoken together upon that which—which has befallen us. We had thought to go out, without telling any, of the terror which has come into our—lives. She is with me in believing that to-night's happenings are under a special ruling, and that it is God's wish that we should tell to you all that we have suffered since—since—"

"Yes?" said Will, softly.

"Since the sinking of the *Albatross*."

"Ah!" I exclaimed, involuntarily. "She left Newcastle for 'Frisco some six months ago, and hasn't been heard of since."

"Yes," answered the voice. "But some few degrees to the North of the line she was caught in a terrible storm, and dismasted. When the day came, it was found that she was leaking badly, and, presently, it falling to a calm, the sailors took to the boats, leaving—leaving a young lady—my fiancée—and myself upon the wreck.

"We were below, gathering together a few of our belongings, when they left. They were entirely callous, through fear, and when we came up upon the decks, we saw them only as small shapes afar off upon the horizon. Yet we did not despair, but set to work and constructed a small raft. Upon this we put such few matters as it would hold, including a quantity of water and some ship's biscuit. Then, the vessel being very deep in the water, we got ourselves on to the raft, and pushed off.

"It was later, when I observed that we seemed to be in the way of some tide or current, which bore us from the ship at an angle; so that in the course of three hours, by my watch, her hull became invisible to our sight, her broken masts remaining in view for a somewhat longer period. Then, towards evening, it grew misty, and so through the night. The next day we were still encompassed by the mist, the weather remaining quiet.

"For four days, we drifted through this strange haze, until, on the evening of the fourth day, there grew upon our ears the murmur of breakers at a distance. Gradually it became plainer, and, somewhat after midnight, it appeared to sound upon either hand at no very great space. The raft was raised upon a swell several times, and then we were in smooth water, and the noise of the breakers was behind.

"When the morning came, we found that we were in a sort of great lagoon; but of this we noticed little at the time; for close before us, through the enshrouding mist, loomed the hull of a large sailing-vessel. With one accord, we fell upon our knees and thanked God; for we thought that here was an end to our perils. We had much to learn.

"The raft drew near to the ship, and we shouted on them, to take us aboard; but none answered. Presently, the raft touched against the side of the vessel, and, seeing a rope hanging downwards, I seized it and began to climb. Yet I had much ado to make my way up, because of a kind of grey, lichenous fungus, which had seized upon the rope, and which blotched the side of the ship, lividly.

"I reached the rail, and clambered over it, on to the deck. Here, I saw that the decks were covered, in great patches, with the grey masses, some of them rising into nodules several feet in height; but at the time, I thought less of this matter than of the possibility of there being people aboard the ship. I shouted; but none answered. Then I went to the door below the poopdeck. I opened it, and peered in. There was a great smell of staleness, so that I knew in a moment that nothing living was within, and with the knowledge, I shut the door quickly; for I felt suddenly lonely.

"I went back to the side, where I had scrambled up. My—my sweetheart was still sitting quietly upon the raft. Seeing me look down, she called up to know whether there were any aboard of the ship. I replied that the vessel had the appearance of having been long deserted; but that if she would wait a little, I would see whether there was anything in the shape of a ladder, by which she could ascend to the deck. Then we would make a search through the vessel together. A little later, on, the opposite side of the decks, I found a rope side-ladder. This I carried across, and a minute afterwards, she was beside me.

"Together, we explored the cabins and apartments in the after-part of the ship; but nowhere was there any sign of life. Here and there, within the cabins themselves, we came across odd patches of that queer fungus; but this, as my sweetheart said, could be cleansed away.

"In the end, having assured ourselves that the after portion of the vessel was empty, we picked our ways to the bows, between the ugly grey nodules of that strange growth; and here we made a further search, which told us that there was indeed none aboard but ourselves.

"This being now beyond any doubt, we returned to the stern of the ship, and proceeded to make ourselves as comfortable as possible. Together, we cleared out and cleaned two of the cabins; and, after that, I made examination whether there was anything eatable in the ship. This I soon found was so, and thanked God in my heart for His goodness. In addition to this, I discovered the whereabouts of the freshwater pump, and having fixed it, I found the water drinkable, though somewhat unpleasant to the taste.

"For several days, we stayed aboard the ship, without attempting to get to the shore. We were busily engaged in making the place habitable. Yet even thus early, we became aware that our lot was even less to be desired than might have been imagined; for though, as a first step, we scraped away the odd patches of growth that studded the floors and walls of the cabins and saloon, yet they returned almost to their original size within the space of twenty-four hours, which not only discouraged us, but gave us a feeling of vague unease.

"Still, we would not admit ourselves beaten, so set to work afresh, and not only scraped away the fungus, but soaked the places where it had been, with carbolic, a can-full of which I had found in the pantry. Yet, by the end of the week, the growth had returned in full strength, and, in addition, it had spread to other places, as though our touching it had allowed germs from it to travel elsewhere.

"On the seventh morning, my sweetheart woke to find a small patch of it growing on her pillow, close to her face. At that, she came to me, so soon as she could get her garments upon her. I was in the galley at the time, lighting the fire for breakfast.

" 'Come here, John,' she said, and led me aft. When I saw the thing upon her pillow, I shuddered, and then and there we agreed to go right out of the ship, and see whether we could not fare to make ourselves more comfortable ashore.

"Hurriedly, we gathered together our few belongings, and even among these, I found that the fungus had been at work; for one of her shawls had a little lump of it growing near one edge. I threw the whole thing over the side, without saying anything to her.

"The raft was still alongside; but it was too clumsy to guide, and I lowered down a small boat that hung across the stern, and in this we made our way to the shore. Yet, as we drew near to it, I became gradually aware that here the vile fungus, which had driven us from the ship, was growing riot. In places it rose into horrible, fantastic mounds, which seemed almost to quiver, as with a quiet life, when the wind blew across them. Here and there, it took on the forms of vast fingers, and in others it just spread out flat and smooth and treacherous. Odd places, it appeared as grotesque stunted trees, seeming extraordinarily kinked and gnarled— The whole quaking vilely at times.

"At first, it seemed to us that there was no single portion of the surrounding shore which was not hidden beneath the masses of the hideous lichen; yet, in this, I found we were mistaken; for somewhat later, coasting along the shore at a little distance, we descried a smooth white patch of what appeared to be fine sand, and there we landed. It was not sand. What it was, I do not know. All that I have observed, is that upon it, the fungus will not grow; while everywhere else, save where the sand-like earth wanders oddly, path-wise, amid the grey desolation of the lichen, there is nothing but that loathsome greyness.

"It is difficult to make you understand how cheered we were to find one place that was absolutely free from the growth, and here we deposited our belongings. Then we went back to the ship for such things as it seemed to us we should need. Among other matters, I managed to bring ashore with me one of the ship's sails, with which I constructed two small tents, which, though exceedingly rough-shaped, served the purposes for which they were intended. In these, we lived and stored our various necessities, and thus for a matter of some four weeks, all went smoothly and without particular unhappiness. Indeed, I may say with much of happiness—for—for we were together.

"It was on the thumb of her right hand, that the growth first showed. It was only a small circular spot, much like a little grey mole. My God! how the fear leapt to my heart when she showed me the place. We cleansed it, between us, washing it with carbolic and water. In the morning of the following day, she showed her hand to me again. The grey warty thing had returned. For a little while, we looked at one another in silence. Then, still wordless, we started again to remove it. In the midst of the operation, she spoke suddenly.

" 'What's that on the side of your face, Dear!' Her voice was sharp with anxiety. I put my hand up to feel.

" 'There! Under the hair by your ear. —A little to the front a bit." My finger rested upon the place, and then I knew.

" 'Let us get your thumb done first,' I said. And she submitted, only because she was afraid to touch me until it was cleansed. I finished washing and disinfecting her thumb, and then she turned to my face. After it was finished, we sat together and talked awhile of many things; for there had come into our lives sudden, very terrible thoughts. We were, all at once, afraid of something worse than death. We spoke of loading the boat with provisions and water, and making our way out on to the sea; yet we were helpless, for many causes, and—and the growth had attacked us already. We decided to stay. God would do with us what was His will. We would wait.

"A month, two months, three months passed, and the places grew somewhat, and there had come others. Yet we fought so strenuously with the fear, that its headway was but slow, comparatively speaking.

"Occasionally, we ventured off to the ship for such stores as we needed. There, we found that the fungus grew persistently. One of the nodules on the maindeck became soon as high as my head.

"We had now given up all thought or hope of leaving the island. We had realised that it would be unallowable to go among healthy humans, with the thing from which we were suffering.

"With this determination and knowledge in our minds, we knew that we should have to husband our food and water; for we did not know, at that time, but that we should possibly live for many years.

"This reminds me that I have told you that I am an old man. Judged by years this is not so. But—but—"

He broke off; then continued somewhat abruptly:—

"As I was saying, we knew that we should have to use care in the matter of food. But we had no idea then how little food there was left, of which to take care. It was a week later, that I made the discovery that all the other bread tanks—which I had supposed full—were empty, and that (beyond odd tins of vegetables and meat, and some other matters) we had nothing on which to depend, but the bread in the tank which I had already opened.

"After learning this, I bestirred myself to do what I could, and set to work at fishing in the lagoon; but with no success. At this, I was somewhat inclined to feel desperate, until the thought came to me to try outside the lagoon, in the open sea.

"Here, at times, I caught odd fish; but, so infrequently, that they proved of but little help in keeping us from the hunger which threatened. It seemed to me that our deaths were likely to come by hunger, and not by the growth of the thing which had seized upon our bodies.

"We were in this state of mind when the fourth month wore out. Then I made a very horrible discovery. One morning, a little before midday, I came off from the ship, with a portion of the biscuits which were left. In the mouth of her tent, I saw my sweetheart sitting, eating something.

" 'What is it, my Dear?' I called out as I leapt ashore. Yet, on hearing my voice, she seemed confused, and, turning, slyly threw something towards the edge of the little clearing. It fell short, and, a vague suspicion having arisen within me, I walked across and picked it up. It was a piece of the grey fungus.

"As I went to her, with it in my hand, she turned deadly pale; then a rose red.

"I felt strangely dazed and frightened.

" 'My Dear! My Dear!' I said, and could say no more. Yet, at my words, she broke down and cried bitterly. Gradually, as she calmed, I got from her the news that she had tried it the preceding day, and—and liked it. I got her to promise on her knees not to touch it again, however great our hunger. After she had promised, she told me that the desire for it had come suddenly, and that, until the moment of desire, she had experienced nothing towards it, but the most extreme repulsion.

"Later in the day, feeling strangely restless, and much shaken with the thing which I had discovered, I made my way along one of the twisted paths—formed by the white, sand-like substance—which led among the fungoid growth. I had, once before, ventured along there; but not to any great distance. This time, being involved in perplexing thought, I went much further than hitherto.

"Suddenly, I was called to myself, by a queer hoarse sound on my left. Turning quickly, I saw that there was movement among an extraordinarily shaped mass of fungus, close to my elbow. It was swaying uneasily, as though it possessed life of its own. Abruptly, as I stared, the thought came to me that the thing had a grotesque resemblance to the figure of a distorted human creature. Even as the fancy flashed into my brain, there was a slight, sickening noise of tearing, and I saw that one of the branch-like arms was detaching itself from the surrounding grey masses, and coming towards me. The head of the thing—a shapeless grey ball, inclined in my direction. I stood stupidly, and the vile arm brushed across my face. I gave out a frightened cry, and ran back a few paces. There was a sweetish taste upon my lips, where the thing had touched me. I licked them, and was immediately filled with an inhuman desire. I turned and seized a mass of the fungus. Then more, and—more. I was insatiable. In the midst of devouring, the remembrance of the morning's discovery swept into my mazed brain. It was sent by God. I dashed the fragment I held, to the ground. Then, utterly wretched and feeling a dreadful guiltiness, I made my way back to the little encampment.

"I think she knew, by some marvellous intuition which love must have given, so soon as she set eyes on me. Her quiet sympathy made it easier for me, and I told her of my sudden weakness; yet omitted to mention the extraordinary thing which had gone before. I desired to spare her all unnecessary terror.

"But, for myself, I had added an intolerable knowledge, to breed an incessant terror in my brain; for I doubted not but that I had seen the end of one of those men who had come to the island in the ship in the lagoon; and in that monstrous ending, I had seen our own.

"Thereafter, we kept from the abominable food, though the desire for it had entered into our blood. Yet, our drear punishment was upon us; for, day by day, with monstrous rapidity, the fungoid growth took hold of our poor bodies. Nothing we could do would check it materially, and so—and so—we who had been human, became—Well, it matters less each day. Only—only we had been man and maid!

"And day by day, the fight is more dreadful, to withstand the hunger-lust for the terrible lichen.

"A week ago we ate the last of the biscuit, and since that time I have caught three fish. I was out here fishing to-night, when your schooner drifted upon me out of the mist. I hailed you. You know the rest, and may God, out of His great heart, bless you for your goodness to a—a couple of poor outcast souls."

There was the dip of an oar—another. Then the voice came again, and for the last time, sounding through the slight surrounding mist, ghostly and mournful.

"God bless you! Good-bye!"

"Good-bye," we shouted together, hoarsely, our hearts full of many emotions.

I glanced about me. I became aware that the dawn was upon us.

The sun flung a stray beam across the hidden sea; pierced the mist dully, and lit up the receding boat with a gloomy fire. Indistinctly, I saw something nodding between the oars. I thought of a sponge—a great, grey nodding sponge— The oars continued to ply. They were grey—as was the boat—and my eyes searched a moment vainly for the conjunction of hand and oar. My gaze flashed back to the—head. It nodded forward as the oars went backward for the stroke. Then the oars were dipped, the boat shot out of the patch of light, and the—the thing went nodding into the mist.

Eloi Eloi Lama Sabachthani

✦ • ✦

D ally, Whitlaw and I were discussing the recent stupendous explosion which had occurred in the vicinity of Berlin. We were marvelling concerning the extraordinary period of darkness that had followed, and which had aroused so much newspaper comment, with theories galore.

The papers had got hold of the fact that the War Authorities had been experimenting with a new explosive, invented by a certain chemist, named Baumoff, and they referred to it constantly as "The New Baumoff Explosive".

We were in the Club, and the fourth man at our table was John Stafford, who was professionally a medical man, but privately in the Intelligence Department. Once or twice, as we talked, I had glanced at Stafford, wishing to fire a question at him; for he had been acquainted with Baumoff. But I managed to hold my tongue; for I knew that if I asked out pointblank, Stafford (who's a good sort, but a bit of an ass as regards his almost ponderous code-of-silence) would be just as like as not to say that it was a subject upon which he felt he was not entitled to speak.

Oh, I know the old donkey's way; and when he had once said that, we might just make up our minds never to get another word out of him on the matter, as long as we lived. Yet, I was satisfied to notice that he seemed a bit restless, as if he were on the itch to shove in his oar; by which I guessed that the papers we were quoting had got things very badly muddled indeed, in some way or other, at least as regarded his friend Baumoff. Suddenly, he spoke:

"What unmitigated, wicked piffle!" said Stafford, quite warm. "I tell you it is wicked, this associating of Baumoff's name with war inventions and such horrors.

He was the most intensely poetical and earnest follower of the Christ that I have ever met; and it is just the brutal Irony of Circumstance that has attempted to use one of the products of his genius for a purpose of Destruction. But you'll find they won't be able to use it, in spite of their having got hold of Baumoff's formula. As an explosive it is not practicable. It is, shall I say, too impartial; there is no way of controlling it.

"I know more about it, perhaps, than any man alive; for I was Baumoff's greatest friend, and when he died, I lost the best comrade a man ever had. I need make no secret about it to you chaps. I was 'on duty' in Berlin, and I was deputed to get in touch with Baumoff. The government had long had an eye on him; he was an Experimental Chemist, you know, and altogether too jolly clever to ignore. But there was no need to worry about him. I got to know him, and we became enormous friends; for I soon found that *he* would never turn his abilities towards any new war-contrivance; and so, you see, I was able to enjoy my friendship with him, with a comfy conscience—a thing our chaps are not always able to do in their friendships. Oh, I tell you, it's a mean, sneaking, treacherous sort of business, ours; though it's necessary; just as some odd man, or other, has to be a hangsman. There's a number of unclean jobs to be done to keep the Social Machine running!

"I think Baumoff was the most enthusiastic *intelligent* believer in Christ that it will be ever possible to produce. I learned that he was compiling and evolving a treatise of most extraordinary and convincing proofs in support of the more inexplicable things concerning the life and death of Christ. He was, when I became acquainted with him, concentrating his attention particularly upon endeavouring to show that the Darkness of the Cross, between the sixth and the ninth hours, was a very real thing, possessing a tremendous significance. He intended at one sweep to smash utterly all talk of a timely thunderstorm or any of the other more or less inefficient theories which have been brought forward from time to time to explain the occurrence away as being a thing of no particular significance.

"Baumoff had a pet aversion, an atheistic Professor of Physics, named Hautch, who—using the 'marvellous' element of the life and death of Christ, as a fulcrum from which to attack Baumoff's theories—smashed at him constantly, both in his lectures and in print. Particularly did he pour bitter unbelief upon Baumoff's upholding that the Darkness of the Cross was anything more than a gloomy hour or two, magnified into blackness by the emotional inaccuracy of the Eastern mind and tongue.

"One evening, some time after our friendship had become very real, I called on Baumoff, and found him in a state of tremendous indignation over some article of the Professor's which attacked him brutally; using his theory of the *Significance* of the

'Darkness', as a target. Poor Baumoff! It was certainly a marvellously clever attack; the attack of a thoroughly trained, well-balanced Logician. But Baumoff was something more; he was Genius. It is a title few have any rights to; but it was his!

"He talked to me about his theory, telling me that he wanted to show me a small experiment, presently, bearing out his opinions. In his talk, he told me several things that interested me extremely. Having first reminded me of the fundamental fact that light is conveyed to the eye through the means of that indefinable medium, named the Aether, he went a step further, and pointed out to me that, from an aspect which more approached the primary, Light was a vibration of the Aether, of a certain definite number of waves per second, which possessed the power of producing upon our retina the sensation which we term Light.

"To this, I nodded; being, as of course is everyone, acquainted with so well-known a statement. From this, he took a quick, mental stride, and told me that an ineffably vague, but measurable, darkening of the atmosphere (greater or smaller according to the personality-force of the individual) was always evoked in the immediate vicinity of the human, during any period of great emotional stress.

"Step by step, Baumoff showed me how his research had led him to the conclusion that this queer darkening (a million times too subtle to be apparent to the eye) could be produced only through something which had power to disturb or temporally interrupt or break up the Vibration of Light. In other words, there was, at any time of unusual emotional activity, some disturbance of the Aether in the immediate vicinity of the person suffering, which had some effect upon the Vibration of Light, interrupting it, and producing the aforementioned infinitely vague darkening.

" 'Yes?' I said, as he paused, and looked at me, as if expecting me to have arrived at a certain definite deduction through his remarks. 'Go on.'

" 'Well,' he said, 'don't you see, the subtle darkening around the person suffering, is greater or less, according to the personality of the suffering human. Don't you?'

" 'Oh!' I said, with a little gasp of astounded comprehension, 'I see what you mean. You—you mean that if the agony of a person of ordinary personality can produce a faint disturbance of the Aether, with a consequent faint darkening, then the Agony of Christ, possessed of the Enormous Personality of the Christ, would produce a terrific disturbance of the Aether, and therefore, it might chance, of the Vibration of Light, and that this is the true explanation of the Darkness of the Cross; and that the fact of such an extraordinary and apparently unnatural and improbable Darkness having been recorded is not a thing to weaken the Marvel of Christ. But one more unutterably wonderful, infallible proof of His God-like power? Is that it? Is it? Tell me?'

"Baumoff just rocked on his chair with delight, beating one fist into the palm of his other hand, and nodding all the time to my summary. How he *loved* to be understood; as the Searcher always craves to be understood.

" 'And now,' he said, 'I'm going to show you something.'

"He took a tiny, corked test-tube out of his waistcoat pocket, and emptied its contents (which consisted of a single, grey-white grain, about twice the size of an ordinary pin's head) on to his dessert plate. He crushed it gently to powder with the ivory handle of a knife, then damped it gently, with a single minim of what I supposed to be water, and worked it up into a tiny patch of grey-white paste. He then took out his gold tooth-pick, and thrust it into the flame of a small chemist's spirit lamp, which had been lit since dinner as a pipe-lighter. He held the gold tooth-pick in the flame, until the narrow, gold blade glowed white hot.

" 'Now look!' he said, and touched the end of the tooth-pick against the infinitesimal patch upon the dessert plate. There came a swift little violet flash, and suddenly I found that I was staring at Baumoff through a sort of transparent darkness, which faded swiftly into a black opaqueness. I thought at first this must be the complementary effect of the flash upon the retina. But a minute passed, and we were still in that extraordinary darkness.

" 'My Gracious! Man! What is it?' I asked, at last.

"His voice explained then, that he had produced, through the medium of chemistry, an exaggerated effect which simulated, to some extent, the disturbance in the Aether produced by waves thrown off by any person during an emotional crisis or agony. The waves, or vibrations, sent out by his experiment produced only a partial simulation of the effect he wished to show me—merely the temporary interruption of the Vibration of Light, with the resulting darkness in which we both now sat.

" 'That stuff,' said Baumoff, 'would be a tremendous explosive, under certain conditions.'

I heard him puffing at his pipe, as he spoke, but instead of the glow of the pipe shining out visible and red, there was only a faint glare that wavered and disappeared in the most extraordinary fashion.

" 'My Goodness!' I said, 'when's this going away? And I stared across the room to where the big kerosene lamp showed only as a faintly glimmering patch in the gloom; a vague light that shivered and flashed oddly, as though I saw it through an immense gloomy depth of dark and disturbed water.

" 'It's all right,' Baumoff's voice said from out of the darkness. 'It's going now; in five minutes the disturbance will have quieted, and the waves of light will flow off evenly from the lamp in their normal fashion. But, whilst we're waiting, isn't it immense, eh?'

" 'Yes,' I said. 'It's wonderful; but it's rather unearthly, you know.'

" 'Oh, but I've something much finer to show you,' he said. 'The real thing. Wait another minute. The darkness is going. See! You can see the light from the lamp now quite plainly. It looks as if it were submerged in a boil of waters, doesn't it? that are growing clearer and clearer and quieter and quieter all the time.'

"It was as he said; and we watched the lamp, silently, until all signs of the disturbance of the light-carrying medium had ceased. Then Baumoff faced me once more.

" 'Now,' he said. 'You've seen the somewhat casual effects of just crude combustion of that stuff of mine. I'm going to show you the effects of combusting it in the human furnace, that is, in my own body; and then, you'll see one of the great wonders of Christ's death reproduced on a miniature scale.'

"He went across to the mantelpiece, and returned with a small, 120 minim glass and another of the tiny, corked test-tubes, containing a single grey-white grain of his chemical substance. He uncorked the test-tube, and shook the grain of substance into the minim glass, and then, with a glass stirring-rod, crushed it up in the bottom of the glass, adding water, drop by drop as he did so, until there were sixty minims in the glass.

" 'Now!' he said, and lifting it, he drank the stuff. 'We will give it thirty-five minutes,' he continued; 'then, as carbonization proceeds, you will find my pulse will increase, as also the respiration, and presently there will come the darkness again, in the subtlest, strangest fashion; but accompanied now by certain physical and psychic phenomena, which will be owing to the fact that the vibrations it will throw off, will be blent into what I might call the emotional-vibrations, which I shall give off in my distress. These will be enormously intensified, and you will possibly experience an extraordinarily interesting demonstration of the soundness of my more theoretical reasonings. I tested it by myself last week' (He waved a bandaged finger at me), 'and I read a paper to the Club on the results. They are very enthusiastic, and have promised their co-operation in the big demonstration I intend to give on next Good Friday—that's seven weeks off, to-day.'

"He had ceased smoking; but continued to talk quietly in this fashion for the next thirty-five minutes. The Club to which he had referred was a peculiar association of men, banded together under the presidentship of Baumoff himself, and having for their appellation the title of—so well as I can translate it —'The Believers And Provers Of Christ'. If I may say so, without any thought of irreverence, they were, many of them, men fanatically crazed to uphold the Christ. You will agree later, I think, that I have not used an incorrect term, in describing the bulk of the members of this extraordinary club, which was, in its way, well worthy of one of the religio-maniacal extrudences which have been forced into temporary being by certain of the more religiously-emotional minded of our cousins across the water.

"Baumoff looked at the clock; then held out his wrist to me. 'Take my pulse,' he said, 'it's rising fast. Interesting data, you know.'

"I nodded, and drew out my watch. I had noticed that his respirations were increasing; and I found his pulse running evenly and strongly at 105. Three minutes later, it had risen to 175, and his respirations to 41. In a further three minutes, I took his pulse again, and found it running at 203, but with the rhythm regular. His respirations were then 49. He had, as I knew, excellent lungs, and his heart was sound. His lungs, I may say, were of exceptional capacity, and there was at this stage no marked dyspnoea. Three minutes later I found the pulse to be 227, and the respiration 54.

'You've plenty of red corpuscles, Baumoff!' I said. 'But I hope you're not going to overdo things.'

"He nodded at me, and smiled; but said nothing. Three minutes later, when I took the last pulse, it was 233, and the two sides of the heart were sending out unequal quantities of blood, with an irregular rhythm. The respiration had risen to 67 and was becoming shallow and ineffectual, and dyspnoea was becoming very marked. The small amount of arterial blood leaving the left side of the heart betrayed itself in the curious bluish and white tinge of the face.

" 'Baumoff!' I said, and began to remonstrate; but he checked me, with a queerly invincible gesture.

" 'It's all right!' he said, breathlessly, with a little note of impatience. 'I know what I'm doing all the time. You must remember I took the same degree as you in medicine.'

"It was quite true. I remembered then that he had taken his M.D. in London; and this in addition to half a dozen other degrees in different branches of the sciences in his own country. And then, even as the memory reassured me that he was not acting in ignorance of the possible danger, he called out in a curious, breathless voice:

" 'The Darkness! It's beginning. Take note of every single thing. Don't bother about me. I'm all right!'

"I glanced swiftly round the room. It was as he had said. I perceived it now. There appeared to be an extraordinary quality of gloom growing in the atmosphere of the room. A kind of bluish gloom, vague, and scarcely, as yet, affecting the transparency of the atmosphere to light.

"Suddenly, Baumoff did something that rather sickened me. He drew his wrist away from me, and reached out to a small metal box, such as one sterilizes a hypodermic in. He opened the box, and took out four rather curious looking drawing-pins, I might call them, only they had spikes of steel fully an inch long, whilst all around the rim of the heads (which were also of steel) there projected downward, parallel with the central spike, a number of shorter spikes, maybe an eighth of an inch long.

"He kicked off his pumps; then stooped and slipped his socks off, and I saw that he was wearing a pair of linen inner-socks.

" 'Antiseptic!' he said, glancing at me. 'Got my feet ready before you came. No use running unnecessary risks.' He gasped as he spoke. Then he took one of the curious little steel spikes.

" 'I've sterilized them,' he said; and therewith, with deliberation, he pressed it in up to the head into his foot between the second and third branches of the dorsal artery.

" 'For God's sake, what are you doing!' I said, half rising from my chair.

" 'Sit down!' he said, in a grim sort of voice. 'I can't have any interference. I want you simply to observe; keep note of *everything*. You ought to thank me for the chance, instead of worrying me, when you know I shall go my own way all the time.'

"As he spoke, he had pressed in the second of the steel spikes up to the hilt in his left instep, taking the same precaution to avoid the arteries. Not a groan had come from him; only his face betrayed the effect of this additional distress.

" 'My dear chap!' he said, observing my upsetness. 'Do be sensible. I know exactly what I'm doing. There simply *must be distress*, and the readiest way to reach that condition is through physical pain.' His speech had becomes a series of spasmodic words, between gasps, and sweat lay in great clear drops upon his lip and forehead. He slipped off his belt and proceeded to buckle it round both the back of his chair and his waist; as if he expected to need some support from falling.

" 'It's wicked!' I said. Baumoff made an attempt to shrug his heaving shoulders, that was, in its way, one of the most piteous things that I have seen, in its sudden laying bare of the agony that the man was making so little of.

"He was now cleaning the palms of his hands with a little sponge, which he dipped from time to time in a cup of solution. I knew what he was going to do, and suddenly he jerked out, with a painful attempt to grin, an explanation of his bandaged finger. He had held his finger in the flame of the spirit lamp, during his previous experiment; but now, as he made clear in gaspingly uttered words, he wished to simulate as far as possible the actual conditions of the great scene that he had so much in mind. He made it so clear to me that we might expect to experience something very extraordinary, that I was conscious of a sense of almost superstitious nervousness.

" 'I wish you wouldn't, Baumoff!' I said.

" 'Don't—be—silly!' he managed to say. But the two latter words were more groans than words; for between each, he had thrust home right to the heads in the palms of his hands the two remaining steel spikes. He gripped his hands shut, with a sort of spasm of savage determination, and I saw the point of one of the spikes break through the back of his hand, between the extensor tendons of the second and third fingers. A drop of blood beaded the point of the spike. I looked at Baumoff's face; and he looked back steadily at me.

" 'No interference,' he managed to ejaculate. 'I've not gone through all this for nothing. I know—what—I'm doing. Look—it's coming. Take note—everything!'

"He relapsed into silence, except for his painful gasping. I realised that I must give way, and I stared round the room, with a peculiar commingling of an almost nervous discomfort and a stirring of very real and sober curiosity.

" 'Oh,' said Baumoff, after a moment's silence, 'something's going to happen. I can tell. Oh, wait—till I—I have my—big demonstration. I'll show that brute Hautch."

"I nodded; but I doubt that he saw me; for his eyes had a distinctly in-turned look, the iris was rather relaxed. I glanced away round the room again; there was a distinct occasional breaking up of the light-rays from the lamp, giving a coming-and-going effect.

"The atmosphere of the room was also quite plainly darker—heavy, with an extraordinary sense of gloom. The bluish tint was unmistakably more in evidence; but there was, as yet, none of that opacity which we had experienced before, upon simple combustion, except for the occasional, vague coming-and-going of the lamp-light.

"Baumoff began to speak again, getting his words out between gasps. 'Th'—this dodge of mine gets the—pain into the—the—right place. Right association of—of ideas—emotions—for—best —results. You follow me? Parallelising things—as— much as—possible. Fixing whole attention—on the—the death scene —'

"He gasped painfully for a few moments. 'We demonstrate truth of—of The Darkening; but—but there's psychic effect to be—looked for, through—results of parallelisation of—conditions. May have extraordinary simulation of—the *actual thing*. Keep note. Keep note.' Then, suddenly, with a clear, spasmodic burst: 'My God, Stafford, keep note of everything. Something's going to happen. Something— wonderful—Promise not—to bother me. I know—what I'm doing.'

"Baumoff ceased speaking, with a gasp, and there was only the labour of his breathing in the quietness of the room. As I stared at him, halting from a dozen things I needed to say, I realised suddenly that I could no longer see him quite plainly; a sort of wavering in the atmosphere, between us, made him seem momentarily unreal. The whole room had darkened perceptibly in the last thirty seconds; and as I stared around, I realised that there was a constant invisible swirl in the fast-deepening, extraordinary blue gloom that seemed now to permeate everything. When I looked at the lamp, alternate flashings of light and blue—darkness followed each other with an amazing swiftness.

" 'My God!' I heard Baumoff whispering in the half-darkness, as if to himself, 'how did Christ bear the nails!'

"I stared across at him, with an infinite discomfort, and an irritated pity troubling me; but I knew it was no use to remonstrate now. I saw him vaguely distorted through the wavering tremble of the atmosphere. It was somewhat as if I looked at him through convolutions of heated air; only there were marvellous waves of blue-blackness making gaps in my sight. Once I saw his face clearly, full of an infinite pain, that was somehow, seemingly, more spiritual than physical, and dominating everything was an expression of enormous resolution and concentration, making the livid, sweat-damp, agonized face somehow heroic and splendid.

"And then, drenching the room with waves and splashes of opaqueness, the vibration of his abnormally stimulated agony finally broke up the vibration of Light. My last, swift glance round, showed me, as it seemed, the invisible aether boiling and eddying in a tremendous fashion; and, abruptly, the flame of the lamp was lost in an extraordinary swirling patch of light, that marked its position for several moments, shimmering and deadening, shimmering and deadening; until, abruptly, I saw neither that glimmering patch of light, nor anything else. I was suddenly lost in a black opaqueness of night, through which came the fierce, painful breathing of Baumoff.

"A full minute passed; but so slowly that, if I had not been counting Baumoff's respirations, I should have said that it was five. Then Baumoff spoke suddenly, in a voice that was, somehow, curiously changed—a certain toneless note in it:

" 'My God!' he said, from out of the darkness, 'what must Christ have suffered!'

"It was in the succeeding silence, that I had the first realisation that I was vaguely afraid; but the feeling was too indefinite and unfounded, and I might say subconscious, for me to face it out. Three minutes passed, whilst I counted the almost desperate respirations that came to me through the darkness. Then Baumoff began to speak again, and still in that peculiarly altering voice:

" 'By Thy Agony and Bloody Sweat,' he muttered. Twice he repeated this. It was plain indeed that he had fixed his whole attention with tremendous intensity, in his abnormal state, upon the death scene.

"The effect upon me of his intensity was interesting and in some ways extraordinary. As well as I could, I analysed my sensations and emotions and general state of mind, and realised that Baumoff was producing an effect upon me that was almost hypnotic.

"Once, partly because I wished to get my level by the aid of a normal remark, and also because I was suddenly newly anxious by a change in the breath-sounds, I asked Baumoff how he was, my voice going with a peculiar and really uncomfortable blankness through that impenetrable blackness of opacity.

"He said: 'Hush! I'm carrying the Cross.' And, do you know, the effect of those simple words, spoken in that new, toneless voice, in that atmosphere of almost unbearable tenseness, was so powerful that, suddenly, with eyes wide open, I saw Baumoff clear and vivid against that unnatural darkness, carrying a Cross. Not, as the picture is usually shown of the Christ, with it crooked over the shoulder; but with the Cross gripped just under the cross-piece in his arms, and the end trailing behind, along rocky ground. I saw even the pattern of the grain of the rough wood, where some of the bark had been ripped away; and under the trailing end there was a tussock of tough wire-grass, that had been uprooted by the towing end, and dragged and ground along upon the rocks, between the end of the Cross and the rocky ground. I can see the thing now, as I speak. Its vividness was extraordinary; but it had come and gone like a flash, and I was sitting there in the darkness, mechanically counting the respirations; yet unaware that I counted.

"As I sat there, it came to me suddenly—the whole entire marvel of the thing that Baumoff had achieved. I was sitting there in a darkness which was an actual reproduction of the miracle of the Darkness of the Cross. In short, Baumoff had, by producing in himself an abnormal condition, developed an Energy of Emotion that must have almost, in its effects, paralleled the Agony of the Cross. And in so doing, he had shown from an entirely new and wonderful point, the indisputable truth of the stupendous personality and the enormous spiritual force of the Christ. He had evolved and made practical to the average understanding a proof that would make to live again the *reality* of that wonder of the world—*CHRIST*. And for all this, I had nothing but admiration of an almost stupefied kind.

"But, at this point, I felt that the experiment should stop. I had a strangely nervous craving for Baumoff to end it right there and then, and not to try to parallel the psychic conditions. I had, even then, by some queer aid of sub-conscious suggestion, a vague reaching-out-towards the danger of "monstrosity" being induced, instead of any actual knowledge gained.

"Baumoff!' I said. 'Stop it!'

"But he made no reply, and for some minutes there followed a silence, that was unbroken, save by his gasping breathing. Abruptly, Baumoff said, between his gasps: 'Woman—behold—thy—son.' He muttered this several times, in the same uncomfortably toneless voice in which he had spoken since the darkness became complete.

" 'Baumoff!' I said again. 'Baumoff! *Stop it!'* And as I listened for his answer, I was relieved to think that his breathing was less shallow. The abnormal demand for oxygen was evidently being met, and the extravagant call upon the heart's efficiency was being relaxed.

" 'Baumoff!' I said, once more. 'Baumoff! Stop it!"

"And, as I spoke, abruptly, I thought the room was shaken a little.

"Now, I had already as you will have realised, been vaguely conscious of a peculiar and growing nervousness. I think that is the word that best describes it, up to this moment. At this curious little shake that seemed to stir through the utterly dark room, I was suddenly more than nervous. I felt a thrill of actual and literal fear; yet with no sufficient cause of reason to justify me; so that, after sitting very tense for some long minutes, and feeling nothing further, I decided that I needed to take myself in hand, and keep a firmer grip upon my nerves. And then, just as I had arrived at this more comfortable state of mind, the room was shaken again, with the most curious and sickening oscillatory movement, that was beyond all comfort of denial.

" 'My God!' I whispered. And then, with a sudden effort of courage, I called: 'Baumoff! *For God's sake stop it!'*

"You've no idea of the effort it took to speak aloud into that darkness; and when I did speak, the sound of my voice set me afresh on edge. It went so empty and *raw* across the room; and somehow, the room seemed to be incredibly big. Oh, I wonder whether you realise how beastly I felt, without my having to make any further effort to tell you.

"And Baumoff never answered a word; but I could hear him breathing, a little fuller; though still heaving his thorax painfully, in his need for air. The incredible shaking of the room eased away; and there succeeded a spasm of quiet, in which I felt that it was my duty to get up and step across to Baumoff's chair. But I could not do it. Somehow, I would not have touched Baumoff then for any cause whatever. Yet, even in that moment, as now I know, I was not aware that I was *afraid* to touch Baumoff.

"And then the oscillations commenced again. I felt the seat of my trousers slide against the seat of my chair, and I thrust out my legs, spreading my feet against the carpet, to keep me from sliding off one way or the other on to the floor. To say I was afraid, was not to describe my state at all. I was terrified. And suddenly, I had comfort, in the most extraordinary fashion; for a single idea literally glazed into my brain, and gave me a reason to which to cling. It was a single line:

" 'Aether, the soul of iron and sundry stuffs' which Baumoff had once taken as a text for an extraordinary lecture on vibrations, in the earlier days of our friendship.

He had formulated the suggestion that, in embryo, Matter was, from a primary aspect, a localised vibration, traversing a closed orbit. These primary localised vibrations were inconceivably minute, but were capable, under certain conditions, of combining under the action of keynote-vibrations into secondary vibrations of a size and shape to be determined by a multitude of only guessable factors. These would sustain their new form, so long as nothing occurred to disorganise their combination or depreciate or divert their energy—their unity being partially determined by the inertia of the still Aether outside of the closed path which their area of activities covered. And such combination of the primary localised vibrations was neither more nor less than matter. Men and worlds, aye! and universes.

"And then he had said the thing that struck me most. He had said, that if it were possible to produce a vibration of the Aether of a sufficient energy, it would be possible to disorganise or confuse the vibration of matter. That, given a machine capable of creating a vibration of the Aether of a sufficient energy, he would engage to destroy not merely the world, but the whole universe itself, including heaven and hell themselves, if such places existed, and had such existence in a material form.

"I remember how I looked at him, bewildered by the pregnancy and scope of his imagination. And now his lecture had come back to me to help my courage with the sanity of reason. Was it not possible that the Aether disturbance which he had produced, had sufficient energy to cause some disorganisation of the vibration of matter, in the immediate vicinity, and had thus created a miniature quaking of the ground all about the house, and so set the house gently a-shake?

"And then, as this thought came to me, another and a greater, flashed into my mind. 'My God!' I said out loud into the darkness of the room. It explains one more mystery of the Cross, the disturbance of the Aether caused by Christ's Agony, disorganised the vibration of matter in the vicinity of the Cross, and there was then a small local earthquake, which opened the graves, and rent the veil, possibly by disturbing its supports. And, of course, the earthquake was an effect, and *not* a cause, as belittlers of the Christ have always insisted.

" 'Baumoff!' I called. 'Baumoff, you've proved another thing. Baumoff! Baumoff! Answer me. Are you all right?'

"Baumoff answered, sharp and sudden out of the darkness; but not to me:

" 'My God!' he said. 'My God!' His voice came out at me, a cry of veritable mental agony. He was suffering, in some hypnotic, induced fashion, something of the very agony of the Christ Himself.

" 'Baumoff!' I shouted, and forced myself to my feet. I heard his chair clattering, as he sat there and shook. 'Baumoff!'

An extraordinary quake went across the floor of the room, and I heard a creaking of the woodwork, and something fell and smashed in the darkness. Baumoff's gasps hurt me; but I stood there. I dared not go to him. I knew *then* that I was afraid of him—of his condition, or something I don't know what. But, oh, I was horribly afraid of him.

" 'Bau—' I began, but suddenly I was afraid even to speak to him. And I could not move. Abruptly, he cried out in a tone of incredible anguish:

" 'Eloi, Eloi, lama sabach*thani!'* But the last word changed in his mouth, from his dreadful hypnotic grief and pain, to a scream of simply infernal terror.

"And, suddenly, a horrible mocking voice roared out in the room, from Baumoff s chair: 'Eloi, Eloi, lama sabachthani!'

"Do you understand, the voice was not Baumoff's at all. It was not a voice of despair; but a voice sneering in an incredible, bestial, monstrous fashion. In the succeeding silence, as I stood in an ice of fear, I knew that Baumoff no longer gasped. The room was absolutely silent, the most dreadful and silent place in all this world. Then I bolted; caught my foot, probably in the invisible edge of the hearth-rug, and pitched headlong into a blaze of internal brain-stars. After which, for a very long time, certainly some hours, I knew nothing of any kind.

"I came back into this Present, with a dreadful headache oppressing me, to the exclusion of all else. But the Darkness had dissipated. I rolled over on to my side, and saw Baumoff and forgot even the pain in my head. He was leaning forward towards me; his eyes wide open, but dull. His face was enormously swollen, and there was, somehow, something *beastly* about him. He was dead, and the belt about him and the chair-back, alone prevented him from falling forward on to me. His tongue was thrust out of one corner of his mouth. I shall always remember how he looked. He was leering, like a human-beast, more than a man.

"I edged away from him, across the floor; but I never stopped looking at him, until I had got to the other side of the door, and closed between us. Of course, I got my balance in a bit, and went back to him; but there was nothing I could do.

"Baumoff died of heart-failure, of course, obviously! I should never be so foolish as to suggest to any sane jury that, in his extraordinary, self-hypnotised, defenseless condition, he was 'entered' by some Christ-apeing Monster of the Void. I've too much respect for my own claim to be a common-sensible man, to put forward such an idea with seriousness! Oh, I know I may seem to speak with a jeer; but what can I do but jeer at myself and all the world, when I dare not acknowledge, even secretly to myself, what my own thoughts are. Baumoff did, undoubtedly die of heart-failure; and, for the rest, how much was I hypnotised into believing. Only, there was over by the far wall, where it had been shaken down to the floor from a solidly fastened-up bracket, a little pile of glass that had once formed a piece of beautiful Venetian glassware. You remember that I heard something fall, when the room shook. Surely the room *did* shake? Oh, I must stop thinking. My head goes round.

"The explosive the papers are talking about. Yes, that's Baumoff's; that makes it all seem true, doesn't it? They had the darkness at Berlin, after the explosion. There is no getting away from *that*. The Government know only that Baumoff's formulae is capable of producing the largest quantity of gas, in the shortest possible time. That, in short, it is ideally *explosive*. So it is; but I imagine it will prove an explosive, as I have already said, and as experience has proved, a little too impartial in its action for it to create enthusiasm on either side of a battlefield. Perhaps this is but a mercy, in disguise; certainly a mercy, if Baumoff's theories as to the possibility of disorganising matter, be anywhere near to the truth.

"I have thought sometimes that there might be a more normal explanation of the dreadful thing that happened at the end. Baumoff *may* have ruptured a blood-vessel in the brain, owing to the enormous arterial pressure that his experiment induced; and the voice I heard and the mockery and the horrible expression and leer may have been nothing more than the immediate outburst and expression of the natural "obliqueness" of a deranged mind, which so often turns up a side of a man's nature and produces an inversion of character, that is the very complement of his normal state. And certainly, poor Baumoff's normal religious attitude was one of marvellous reverence and loyalty towards the Christ.

"Also, in support of this line of explanation, I have frequently observed that the voice of a person suffering from mental derangement is frequently wonderfully changed, and has in it often a very repellant and inhuman quality. I try to think that this explanation fits the case. But I can never forget that room. Never."

The Mystery
of the Derelict

❖ ◆ ❖

All the night had the four-masted ship, *Tarawak*, lain motionless in the drift of the Gulf Stream; for she had run into a "calm patch"—into a stark calm which had lasted now for two days and nights.

On every side, had it been light, might have been seen dense masses of floating gulf-weed, studding the ocean even to the distant horizon. In places, so large were the weed-masses that they formed long, low banks, that, by daylight, might have been mistaken for low-lying land.

Upon the lee side of the poop, Duthie, one of the 'prentices, leaned with his elbows upon the rail, and stared out across the hidden sea, to where in the Eastern horizon showed the first pink and lemon streamers of the dawn—faint, delicate streaks and washes of colour.

A period of time passed, and the surface of the leeward sea began to show—a great expanse of grey, touched with odd, wavering belts of silver. And everywhere the black specks and islets of the weed.

Presently, the red dome of the sun protruded itself into sight above the dark rim of the horizon; and, abruptly, the watching Duthie saw something—a great, shapeless bulk that lay some miles away to starboard, and showed black and distinct against the gloomy red mass of the rising sun.

"Something in sight to looard, Sir," he informed the Mate, who was leaning, smoking, over the rail that ran across the break of the poop. "I can't just make out what it is."

The Mate rose from his easy position, stretched himself, yawned, and came across to the boy.

"Whereabouts, Toby?" he asked, wearily, and yawning again.

"There, Sir," said Duthie—alias Toby— "broad away on the beam, and right in the track of the sun. It looks something like a big houseboat, or a haystack."

The Mate stared in the direction indicated, and saw the thing which puzzled the boy, and immediately the tiredness went out of his eyes and face.

"Pass me the glasses off the skylight, Toby," he commanded, and the youth obeyed.

After the Mate had examined the strange object through his binoculars for, maybe, a minute, he passed them to Toby, telling him to take a "squint," and say what he made of it.

"Looks like an old powder-hulk, Sir," exclaimed the lad, after a while, and to this description the Mate nodded agreement.

Later, when the sun had risen somewhat, they were able to study the derelict with more exactness. She appeared to be a vessel of an exceedingly old type, mastless, and upon the hull of which had been built a roof-like superstructure; the use of which they could not determine. She was lying just within the borders of one of the weed-banks, and all her side was splotched with a greenish growth.

It was her position, within the borders of the weed, that suggested to the puzzled Mate, how so strange and unseaworthy looking a craft had come so far abroad into the greatness of the ocean. For, suddenly, it occurred to him that she was neither more nor less than a derelict from the vast Sargasso Sea—a vessel that had, possibly, been lost to the world, scores and scores of years gone, perhaps hundreds. The suggestion touched the Mate's thoughts with solemnity, and he fell to examining the ancient hulk with an even greater interest, and pondering on all the lonesome and awful years that must have passed over her, as she had lain desolate and forgotten in that grim cemetery of the ocean.

Through all that day, the derelict was an object of the most intense interest to those aboard the *Tarawak*, every glass in the ship being brought into use to examine her. Yet, though within no more than some six or seven miles of her, the Captain refused to listen to the Mate's suggestions that they should put a boat into the water, and pay the stranger a visit; for he was a cautious man, and the glass warned him that a sudden change might be expected in the weather; so that he would have no one leave the ship on any unnecessary business. But, for all that he had caution, curiosity was by no means lacking in him, and his telescope, at intervals, was turned on the ancient hulk through all the day.

Then, it would be about six bells in the second dog watch, a sail was sighted astern, coming up steadily but slowly. By eight bells they were able to make out that a small barque was bringing the wind with her; her yards squared, and every stitch set. Yet the night had advanced apace, and it was nigh to eleven o'clock before the wind reached those aboard the *Tarawak*. When at last it arrived, there was a slight rustling and quaking of canvas, and odd creaks here and there in the darkness amid the gear, as each portion of the running and standing rigging took up the strain.

Beneath the bows, and alongside, there came gentle rippling noises, as the vessel gathered way; and so, for the better part of the next hour, they slid through the water at something less than a couple of knots in the sixty minutes.

To starboard of them, they could see the red light of the little barque, which had brought up the wind with her, and was now forging slowly ahead, being better able evidently than the big, heavy *Tarawak* to take advantage of so slight a breeze.

About a quarter to twelve, just after the relieving watch had been roused, lights were observed to be moving to and fro upon the small barque, and by midnight it was palpable that, through some cause or other, she was dropping astern.

When the Mate arrived on deck to relieve the Second, the latter officer informed him of the possibility that something unusual had occurred aboard the barque, telling of the lights about her decks,[1] and how that, in the last quarter of an hour, she had begun to drop astern.

On hearing the Second Mate's account, the First sent one of the 'prentices for his night-glasses, and, when they were brought, studied the other vessel intently, that is, so well as he was able through the darkness; for, even through the night-glasses, she showed only as a vague shape, surmounted by the three dim towers of her masts and sails.

Suddenly, the Mate gave out a sharp exclamation; for, beyond the barque, there was something else shown dimly in the field of vision. He studied it with great intentness, ignoring for the instant, the Second's queries as to what it was that had caused him to exclaim.

All at once, he said, with a little note of excitement in his voice:—

"The derelict! The barque's run into the weed around that old hooker!"

The Second Mate gave a mutter of surprised assent, and slapped the rail.

"That's it!" he said. "That's why we're passing her. And that explains the lights. If they're not fast in the weed, they've probably run slap into the blessed derelict!"

"One thing," said the Mate, lowering his glasses, and beginning to fumble for his pipe, "she won't have had enough way on her to do much damage."

The Second Mate, who was still peering through his binoculars, murmured an absent agreement, and continued to peer. The Mate, for his part, filled and lit his pipe, remarking meanwhile to the unhearing Second, that the light breeze was dropping.

Abruptly, the Second Mate called his superior's attention, and in the same instant, so it seemed, the failing wind died entirely away, the sails settling down into runkles, with little rustles and flutters of sagging canvas.

"What's up?" asked the Mate, and raised his glasses.

"There's something queer going on over yonder," said the Second. "Look at the lights moving about, and— Did you see *that*?"

The last portion of his remark came out swiftly, with a sharp accentuation of the last word.

"What?" asked the Mate, staring hard.

"They're shooting," replied the Second. "Look! There again!"

"Rubbish!" said the Mate, a mixture of unbelief and doubt in his voice.

With the falling of the wind, there had come a great silence upon the sea. And, abruptly, from far across the water, sounded the distant, dullish thud of a gun, followed almost instantly by several minute, but sharply defined, reports, like the cracking of a whip out in the darkness.

"Jove!" cried the Mate, "I believe you're right." He paused and stared. "There!" he said. "I saw the flashes then. They're firing from the poop, I believe…. I must call the Old Man."

He turned and ran hastily down into the saloon, knocked on the door of the Captain's cabin, and entered. He turned up the lamp, and, shaking his superior into wakefulness, told him of the thing he believed to be happening aboard the barque:—

"It's mutiny, Sir; they're shooting from the poop. We ought to do something—"
The Mate said many things, breathlessly; for he was a young man; but the Captain stopped him, with a quietly lifted hand.

"I'll be up with you in a minute, Mr. Johnson," he said, and the Mate took the hint, and ran up on deck.

Before the minute had passed, the Skipper was on the poop, and staring through his night-glasses at the barque and the derelict. Yet now, aboard of the barque, the lights had vanished, and there showed no more the flashes of discharging weapons—only there remained the dull, steady red glow of the port sidelight; and, behind it, the night-glasses showed the shadowy outline of the vessel.

The Captain put questions to the Mates, asking for further details.

"It all stopped while the Mate was calling you, Sir," explained the Second. "We could hear the shots quite plainly."

They seemed to be using a gun as well as their revolvers," interjected the Mate, without ceasing to stare into the darkness.

For a while the three of them continued to discuss the matter, whilst down on the maindeck the two watches clustered along the starboard rail, and a low hum of talk rose, fore and aft.

Presently, the Captain and the Mates came to a decision. If there had been a mutiny, it had been brought to its conclusion, whatever that conclusion might be, and no interference from those aboard the *Tarawak*, at that period, would be likely to do good. They were utterly in the dark—in more ways than one—and, for all they knew, there might not even have been any mutiny. If there had been a mutiny, and the mutineers had won, then they had done their worst; whilst if the officers had won, well and good. They had managed to do so without help. Of course, if the *Tarawak* had been a man-of-war with a large crew, capable of mastering any situation, it would have been a simple matter to send a powerful, armed boat's crew to inquire; but as she was merely a merchant vessel, undermanned, as is the modern fashion, they must go warily. They would wait for the morning, and signal. In a couple of hours it would be light. Then they would be guided by circumstances.

The Mate walked to the break of the poop, and sang out to the men:—

"Now then, my lads, you'd better turn in, the watch below, and have a sleep; we may be wanting you by five bells."

There was a muttered chorus of "i, i, Sir," and some of the men began to go forrard to the fo'cas'le; but others of the watch below remained, their curiosity overmastering their desire for sleep.

On the poop, the three officers leaned over the starboard rail, chatting in a desultory fashion, as they waited for the dawn. At some little distance hovered Duthie, who, as eldest 'prentice just out of his time, had been given the post of acting Third Mate.

Presently, the sky to starboard began to lighten with the solemn coming of the dawn. The light grew and strengthened, and the eyes of those in the *Tarawak* scanned with growing intentness that portion of the horizon where showed the red and dwindling glow of the barque's sidelight.

Then, it was in that moment when all the world is full of the silence of the dawn, something passed over the quiet sea, coming out of the East—a very faint, long-drawn-out, screaming, piping noise. It might almost have been the cry of a little wind wandering out of the dawn across the sea—a ghostly, piping skirl, so attenuated and elusive was it; but there was in it a weird, almost threatening note, that told the three on the poop it was no wind that made so dree and inhuman a sound.

The noise ceased, dying out in an indefinite, mosquito-like shrilling, far and vague and minutely shrill. And so came the silence again.

"I heard that, last night, when they were shooting," said the Second Mate, speaking very slowly, and looking first at the Skipper and then at the Mate. "It was when you were below, calling the Captain," he added.

"Ssh!" said the Mate, and held up a warning hand; but though they listened, there came no further sound; and so they fell to disjointed questionings, and guessed their answers, as puzzled men will. And ever and anon, they examined the barque through their glasses; but without discovering anything of note, save that, when the light grew stronger, they perceived that her jibboom had struck through the superstructure of the derelict, tearing a considerable gap therein.

Presently, when the day had sufficiently advanced, the Mate sung out to the Third, to take a couple of the 'prentices, and pass up the signal flags and the code book. This was done, and a "hoist" made; but those in the barque took not the slightest heed; so that finally the Captain bade them make up the flags and return them to the locker.

After that, he went down to consult the glass, and when he reappeared, he and the Mates had a short discussion, after which, orders were given to hoist out the starboard life-boat. This, in the course of half an hour, they managed; and, after that, six of the men and two of the 'prentices were ordered into her.

Then half a dozen rifles were passed down, with ammunition, and the same number of cutlasses. These were all apportioned among the men, much to the disgust of the two apprentices, who were aggrieved that they should be passed over; but their feelings altered when the Mate descended into the boat, and handed them each a loaded revolver, warning them, however, to play no "monkey tricks" with the weapons.

Just as the boat was about to push off, Duthie, the eldest 'prentice, came scrambling down the side ladder, and jumped for the after thwart. He landed, and sat down, laying the rifle which he had brought, in the stern; and, after that, the boat put off for the barque.

There were now ten in the boat, and all well armed, so that the Mate had a certain feeling of comfort that he would be able to meet any situation that was likely to arise.

After nearly an hour's hard pulling, the heavy boat had been brought within some two hundred yards of the barque, and the Mate sung out to the men to lie on their oars for a minute. Then he stood up and shouted to the people on the barque; but though he repeated his cry of "Ship ahoy!" several times, there came no reply.

He sat down, and motioned to the men to give way again, and so brought the boat nearer the barque by another hundred yards. Here, he hailed again; but still receiving no reply, he stooped for his binoculars, and peered for a while through them at the two vessels—the ancient derelict, and the modern sailing-vessel.

The latter had driven clean in over the weed, her stern being perhaps some two score yards from the edge of the bank. Her jibboom, as I have already mentioned, had pierced the green-blotched superstructure of the derelict, so that her cutwater had come very close to the grass-grown side of the hulk.

That the derelict was indeed a very ancient vessel, it was now easy to see; for at this distance the Mate could distinguish which was hull, and which superstructure. Her stern rose up to a height considerably above her bows, and possessed galleries, coming round the counter. In the window frames some of the glass still remained; but others were securely shuttered, and some missing, frames and all, leaving dark holes in the stern. And everywhere grew the dank, green growth, giving to the beholder a queer sense of repulsion. Indeed, there was that about the whole of the ancient craft, that repelled in a curious way—something elusive—a remoteness from humanity, that was vaguely abominable.

The Mate put down his binoculars, and drew his revolver, and, at the action, each one in the boat gave an instinctive glance to his own weapon. Then he sung out to them to give-way, and steered straight for the weed. The boat struck it, with something of a sog; and, after that, they advanced slowly, yard by yard, only with considerable labour.

They reached the counter of the barque, and the Mate held out his hand for an oar. This, he leaned up against the side of the vessel, and a moment later was swarming quickly up it. He grasped the rail, and swung himself aboard; then, after a swift glance fore and aft, gripped the blade of the oar, to steady it, and bade the rest follow as quickly as possible, which they did, the last man bringing up the painter with him, and making it fast to a cleat.

Then commenced a rapid search through the ship. In several places about the maindeck they found broken lamps, and aft on the poop, a shot-gun, three revolvers, and several capstan-bars lying about the poop-deck. But though they pried into every possible corner, lifting the hatches, and examining the lazarette, not a human creature was to be found—the barque was absolutely deserted.

After the first rapid search, the Mate called his men together; for there was an uncomfortable sense of danger in the air, and he felt that it would be better not to straggle. Then, he led the way forrard, and went up on to the t'gallant fo'cas'le head. Here, finding the port sidelight still burning, he bent over the screen, as it were mechanically, lifted the lamp, opened it, and blew out the flame; then replaced the affair on its socket.

After that, he climbed into the bows, and out along the jibboom, beckoning to the others to follow, which they did, no man saying a word, and all holding their weapons handily; for each felt the oppressiveness of the Incomprehensible about them.

The Mate reached the hole in the great superstructure, and passed inside, the rest following. Here they found themselves in what looked something like a great, gloomy barracks, the floor of which was the deck of the ancient craft. The superstructure, as seen from the inside, was a very wonderful piece of work, being beautifully shored and fixed; so that at one time it must have possessed immense strength; though now it was all rotted, and showed many a gape and rip. In one place, near the centre, or midships part, was a sort of platform, high up, which the Mate conjectured might have been used as a "look-out"; though the reason for the prodigious superstructure itself, he could not imagine.

Having searched the decks of this craft, he was preparing to go below, when, suddenly, Duthie caught him by the sleeve, and whispered to him, tensely, to listen. He did so, and heard the thing that had attracted the attention of the youth—it was a low, continuous, shrill whining that was rising from out of the dark hull beneath their feet, and, abruptly, the Mate was aware that there was an intensely disagreeable animal-like smell in the air. He had noticed it, in a subconscious fashion, when entering through the broken superstructure; but now, suddenly, he was *aware* of it.

Then, as he stood there hesitating, the whining noise rose all at once into a piping, screaming squeal, that filled all the space in which they were inclosed, with an awful, inhuman and threatening clamour. The Mate turned and shouted at the top of his voice to the rest, to retreat to the barque, and he, himself, after a further quick nervous glance round, hurried towards the place where the end of the barque's jibboom protruded in across the decks.

He waited, with strained impatience, glancing ever behind him, until all were off the derelict, and then sprang swiftly on to the spar that was their bridge to the other vessel. Even as he did so, the squealing died away into a tiny shrilling, twittering sound, that made him glance back; for the suddenness of the quiet was as effective as though it had been a loud noise. What he saw, seemed to him in that first instant so incredible and monstrous, that he was almost too shaken to cry out. Then he raised his voice in a shout of warning to the men, and a frenzy of haste shook him in every fibre, as he scrambled back to the barque, shouting ever to the men to get into the boat. For in that backward glance, he had seen the whole decks of the derelict a-move with living things—giant rats, thousands and tens of thousands of them; and so in a flash had come to an understanding of the disappearance of the crew of the barque.

He had reached the fo'cas'le head now, and was running for the steps, and behind him, making all the long slanting length of the jibboom black, were the rats, racing after him. He made one leap to the maindeck, and ran. Behind, sounded a queer, multitudinous pattering noise, swiftly surging upon him. He reached the poop steps, and as he sprang up them, felt a savage bite in his left calf. He was on the poop-deck now, and running with a stagger. A score of great rats leapt around him, and half a dozen hung grimly to his back, whilst the one that had gripped his calf, flogged madly from side to side as he raced on. He reached the rail, gripped it, and vaulted clean over and down into the weed.

The rest were already in the boat, and strong hands and arms hove him aboard, whilst the others of the crew sweated in getting their little craft round from the ship. The rats still clung to the Mate; but a few blows with a cutlass eased him of his murderous burden. Above them, making the rails and half-round of the poop black and alive, raced thousands of rats.

The boat was now about an oar's length from the barque, and, suddenly, Duthie screamed out that *they* were coming. In the same instant, nearly a hundred of the largest rats launched themselves at the boat. Most fell short, into the weed; but over a score reached the boat, and sprang savagely at the men, and there was a minute's hard slashing and smiting, before the brutes were destroyed.

Once more the men resumed their task of urging their way through the weed, and so in a minute or two, had come to within some fathoms of the edge, working desperately. Then a fresh terror broke upon them. Those rats which had missed their leap, were now all about the boat, and leaping in from the weed, running up the oars, and scrambling in over the sides, and, as each one got inboard, straight for one of the crew it went; so that they were all bitten and be-bled in a score of places.

There ensued a short but desperate fight, and then, when the last of the beasts had been hacked to death, the men lay once more to the task of heaving the boat clear of the weed.

A minute passed, and they had come almost to the edge, when Duthie cried out, to look; and at that, all turned to stare at the barque, and perceived the thing that had caused the 'prentice to cry out; for the rats were leaping down into the weed in black multitudes, making the great weed-fronds quiver, as they hurled themselves in the direction of the boat. In an incredibly short space of time, all the weed between the boat and the barque, was alive with the little monsters, coming at breakneck speed.

The Mate let out a shout, and, snatching an oar from one of the men, leapt into the stern of the boat, and commenced to thrash the weed with it, whilst the rest laboured infernally to pluck the boat forth into the open sea. Yet, despite their mad efforts, and the death-dealing blows of the Mate's great fourteen-foot oar, the black, living mass were all about the boat, and scrambling aboard in scores, before she was free of the weed. As the boat shot into the clear water, the Mate gave out a great curse, and, dropping his oar, began to pluck the brutes from his body with his bare hands, casting them into the sea. Yet, fast almost as he freed himself, others sprang upon him, so that in another minute he was like to have been pulled down, for the boat was alive and swarming with the pests, but that some of the men got to work with their cutlasses, and literally slashed the brutes to pieces, sometimes killing several with a single blow. And thus, in a while, the boat was freed once more; though it was a sorely wounded and frightened lot of men that manned her.

The Mate himself took an oar, as did all those who were able. And so they rowed slowly and painfully away from that hateful derelict, whose crew of monsters even then made the weed all of a-heave with hideous life.

From the *Tarawak* came urgent signals for them to haste; by which the Mate knew that the storm, which the Captain had feared, must be coming down upon the ship, and so he spurred each one to greater endeavour, until, at last they were under the shadow of their own vessel, with very thankful hearts, and bodies, bleeding, tired and faint.

Slowly and painfully, the boat's crew scrambled up the side-ladder, and the boat was hoisted aboard; but they had no time then to tell their tale; for the storm was upon them.

It came half an hour later, sweeping down in a cloud of white fury from the Eastward, and blotting out all vestiges of the mysterious derelict and the little barque which had proved her victim. And after that, for a weary day and night, they battled with the storm. When it passed, nothing was to be seen, either of the two vessels or of the weed which had studded the sea before the storm; for they had been blown many a score of leagues to the Westward of the spot, and so had no further chance—nor, I ween, inclination—to investigate further the mystery of that strange old derelict of a past time, and her habitants of rats.

Yet, many a time, and in many fo'cas'les has this story been told; and many a conjecture has been passed as to how came that ancient craft abroad there in the ocean. Some have suggested—as indeed I have made bold to put forth as fact—that she must have drifted out of the lonesome Sargasso Sea. And, in truth, I cannot but think this the most reasonable supposition. Yet, of the rats that evidently dwelt in her, I have no reasonable explanation to offer. Whether they were true ship's rats, or a species that is to be found in the weed-haunted plains and islets of the Sargasso Sea, I cannot say. It may be that they are the descendants of rats that lived in ships long centuries lost in the Weed Sea, and which have learned to live among the weed, forming new characteristics, and developing fresh powers and instincts. Yet, I cannot say; for I speak entirely without authority, and do but tell this story as it is told in the fo'cas'le of many an old-time sailing ship—that dark, brine-tainted place where the young men learn somewhat of the mysteries of the all mysterious sea.

[1] Unshaded lights are never allowed about the decks at night, as they are likely to blind the vision of the officer of the watch.

—W.H.H.

We Two and Bully Dunkan

◆━◆━◆

"**D**on't go, Miles," I said. "Better lose your pay-day. It seems he's got it in for you, and a common sailorman can do nothing against the after-guard."

"I'm going back, John," he told me. "I swore he'd not haze *me* out of the ship, and he shan't. He's belted the rest of the crew half silly, and they've bunked, without drawing a penny. Some of the poor devils even left their sea-chests. I expect he thinks I'm going to do the same; but he's mightily mistaken."

This was in 'Frisco. I had just run up against Miles, who had a badly swollen face, and an ugly scar over his right eyebrow.

"What is it?" I'd asked him. "Been a trip with a Yankee Skipper?"

"Just that, John," he answered me. "Bully Dunkan!"

"Goo' Lor'!" I said. "Were you drunk when you signed on?"

For no free, sober white-man ever sails with Bully Dunkan, not unless it's that or the hard and stony beach. That is just what it had been with poor old Miles; and he'd had a Number One rough time of it; for once, when he explained that he misliked the application of the Mate's heavy sea-boot to his rear anatomy, the Mate had promptly knocked him down, having first slipped a big brass knuckle-duster on his fist, to emphasise his accompanying and entirely unprintable remarks. This accounted for the scar over my old shipmate's eye.

The swollen face had been acquired at a later date; to be exact, about a week before the ship reached 'Frisco. It was what I might describe as the lingering physical memory of an efficiently dislocated jaw. The dislocation had been the personal and vigourous handiwork of Bully Dunkan himself. It appears that Miles, one afternoon, so far forgot his early training as to withhold the other cheek, during one of the Mate's attentive moods. In fact, I understand that Miles actually hit the man (Hogge by name and nature) so hearty a wallop with his fist, that he floored him on the maindeck. The next thing that poor Miles knew was, as he put it, stars. Old Bully Dunkan had come up behind him, wearing felt slippers, and hit him solidly with his fist, on the side of the jaw.

Bully Dunkan weighed two hundred pounds, in his stockings, and his title isn't a fancy one. So when Miles came round, in about ten minutes, and found the Bo'sun and Chips, the carpenter, trying to heave his jaw back into place, he wasn't surprised; but, as he told me, it hurt a lot; which I could believe, by the look of the swelling!

"Well," I told him, "you're a fool, if you try to make the trip back to Boston in her. He'll have it in pretty savage for you."

Miles, however, is a pig-headed brute, when he's fixed on anything; so when he just shook his head, I told him I would sacrifice my bones on the altar of friendship, and sign on for the return trip with him, just to look after him a bit!

"John," he said, in his solemn, earnest kind of way, "you're a friend to tie to. And I'll not try to persuade you not to come—not until you've heard the rest of what I've got to tell you:—

"When we were coming up from Sydney, through the Islands, the Old Man and the Mate went ashore one night in the boat. I was one of the boat's crew, and a chap, called Sandy Meg, was the other.

"We were told to stay by the boat, and lie just off the shore a bit. I thought it was a rummy business; and ugly too; for both the Skipper and the Mate had guns. They were loading them in the boat, while we were pulling ashore.

"Well, they'd been ashore about an hour, I should think, when Sandy Meg nudged me to listen. I heard what he meant, then; for there was a faint, far-off screaming, seeming about a mile or more away; and then there were several shots. I could swear to that.

" 'What do you make of it, Sandy?' I asked him; but he shook his head, and wouldn't answer. Poor devil; they had fairly beaten the bit of spirit out of him. Not that he was ever very wise.

"About half an hour later, I heard someone running, up among the trees; and then I saw the Mate and the Captain coming down to the bench at a run, and singing out to us to bring the boat ashore, smart.

"They fairly raced down the sands, and I could see they were carrying a packet between them; pretty heavy it seemed, and done up in some of that native matting. They hove this down into the bottom of the boat; and I swear it sounded like coin, packed tight. Then they shoved her out and scrambled in, yelling to us to give way, which we did, with the two of them double-banking the oars, and driving her out stern-first.

"We'd got out about three hundred yards, when a man came out of the woods, and ran down the shore, a white man, by the look of him in the moonlight; but, of course, that's half guessing. He knelt down near the edge of the water, and then there was a flash, and something knocked splinters off the port gunnel of the boat, and there was the bang of one of these old Martinis. I recognised the sound!

"By the time he'd loaded and fired twice more, we were too far away to get hurt. He never touched the boat, after that first shot. I saw several other men on the shore; but I suppose they can't have had anything to shoot with.

"Then we were heading away for the ship—she looked like a ghost out on the sea; too far away for the people ashore to recognise anything about her.

"Next day, when I was sent up to lace on the boat-cover, I saw something in the bottom, that made me stare. When I'd reached for it, I found it was a twenty-dollar gold piece. You'll remember the package they dumped into the bottom of the boat! Now what do you make of all that?"

"Ugly!" I said.

"Well," he told me, "*that's* one more reason why I'm going home to Boston in her. I've to get square for these" (he touched the scar and his jaw) "and I reckon the best way to get square with hogs of that kind, is to touch them right on their dollar-marks. Now, are you strong to come, as ever?"

"Stronger," I told him. "Only I guess we'll go heeled. There's sure to be some excitement coming to us this trip. Tell me, where is the lazarette trap—in the pantry, or in the big cabin?"

"Neither," said Miles. "Bully Dunkan sits on the grub hatch, as they say! The hatch of the lazarette is in his own cabin, and opens up under his table. It's no good thinking of that, John. And there's no getting in through the lazarette bulkshead, from the hold. She's stowed up with cargo, solid to the deck-beams. I've thought of all that. I've thought of things for hours at a time; but I can't see how to do it!"

"He drinks pretty heavily, doesn't he?" I asked.

"No," said Miles, "not for him, you know. I've never seen him stupid with it yet. And he sleeps so light, that we always have to go to the wheel on the port side of the poop. His cabin is on the starboard side, and he comes up raging, if anyone walks over his head."

"Do you happen to know what kind of irons they carry?" I asked.

"Yes," he told me. "They ironed Billy Duckworth. He went for the two of them, with an iron belaying-pin, after they had both been kicking him. They laid him out stiff; and ironed him down in the lazarette. Kept him there three days on water. He told me they've got big iron rings, let into the deck of the lazarette, and a chain and padlock. The way they fixed him up, was by handcuffing his two hands together, and then passing the chain over the handcuffs and through one of the rings in the deck, and padlocking him there, like a wild beast."

"Um!" I said; "and of course the lazarette's kept locked?"

"I don't know," he answered. "I don't see it matters anyway. It's not the lazarette that's going to be any use to us."

"Perhaps not," I said. "It certainly sounds a tough proposition. Let's go and have a drink."

II

Bully Dunkan signed me on, in a joyous mood, for him! But I had to ape to be half drunk, or he'd have smelled several kinds of a rat; for free, American white-men don't offer to go promiscuously to sea with him; unless they're either not sober, or they're on the rocks; and I wasn't ragged enough for that yarn to tally-up with appearances.

The ship was a wooden barque of about 500 tons, and Bully Dunkan carried no Second Mate; for the Bo'sun used to stand his watch for him, Marine Law Regulations or not!

The only two of the old crew who had not been run out of the ship, were Miles, and Sandy Meg, the rather soft-witted man who had been in the boat that night with Miles. I found that he had been made acting Steward, as the last man had been run out with the others. I daresay the arrangement suited Bully Dunkan very well; for he never raised Meg's wages, and as acting Steward he remained.

By good fortune, Miles and I were both picked in the same watch—the Mate's. Two days out at sea, there started the usual kind of Bully Dunkanism. One of the men, a big "Dutchman," in a foolish moment, imagined that his two hundred and fifty pounds of brawn and simplicity were the equivalent of Bully Dunkan's two hundred pounds of brawn and hell-fire. As a result, when Dunkan kicked the big Dutchman, the man turned on the Skipper, and held an enormous bony fist under his nose, just through that brief length of time that it took Bully Dunkan to realise the amazing fact.

"Shmell that!" said the huge Dutchman, in his sublime innocence.

Apparently there was something displeasing to the Skipper in the odour of the big Dutchman's homely fist; for he never said a word; but the crack he hit the Dutchman was heard by the watch below in the fo'cas'le.

There was no need for the Bully to accentuate his protest further; but being Bully Dunkan, he—well, he just Dunkanised, and jumped on the big man with his sea-boots, until I was almost angry enough to have interfered.

After all was over, however, the Dutchman was not really badly hurt. His ribs were like the ribs of a horse, and his spirit was like the spirit of a milch cow; and he was a first class sailorman. I have frequently seen them built on these lines, which are much approved by Skippers of the "Yankee Skipper" type.

I had a word with Miles, after this bit of bother.

"See here, Miles," I said, "if that unpleasant person aft, or his pet Hogge try that sort of game again on you, or attempt liberties with this particular American citizen who's talking to you, why then, my friend, we've both got to stick to each other, several degrees closer than the proverbial brother. And if one of us gets a taste of the irons, the other has got to go through it with him. Sumga? So keep those tools and oddments we got in 'Frisco, handy in your pockets, savvy?"

"Yes, John," said Miles, in his sober way. "I think I follow what's in your mind."

And at that I left it.

The next day, in the morning watch, I had an adventure with the Mate. Perhaps I ought to admit that the adventure was less of his seeking than mine; but, I thought perhaps certain plans I had in my head, might as well pass into action, early as late. And, in short, I sought trouble with both hands; so waste no pity on me; but give me what a Frenchman I once knew, called the liniment of your understanding.

I had been set to work on a paunch-mat, for chafing gear; and I decided that a smoke might be a soothing adjunct, to me; though I could hardly say truthfully that I expected the Mate would view it personally as a sedative. That I was right in this conclusion, I soon proved; for the Hogge, happening soon to come along the maindeck, let out a gasp as he came opposite to where I was working, foreside of the mainmast.

I pretended an entire innocence of anything unorthodox; but all the same, I slackened the bite I had on my pipe; for I was too far from a dentist, just at the moment.

The next thing I knew, the Mate (a hefty brute he was too), had made one jump for me. He gripped the pipe and tore it out of my mouth, with a violence that might have left a serious gap, had I not been prepared.

I turned slowly, and looked at him, as mildly as I could. He held the pipe in his fist, by the bowl; and seemed to be a little too full for words.

"Ah!" I said, "was it you who just removed my pipe?"

"Of all—" he began; and became incoherent....

"You shore got some nerve, you have!" was what he finally managed to reduce it to. This is, of course, a strictly expurgated quote.

"You ought *really* to be a little more careful," I explained. "I don't mind you borrowing my pipe; indeed I'll make you a gift of it; for I never care to smoke after other people; but you should really be a little more careful. You might have loosened one or more of my incisors, and dentists do make such awful charges."

"Say!" he shouted, and caught hold of his own throat, in a very ecstasy of deep feeling. "Say!" he shouted again. "Say!..."

He yelled it this time; and if I had never heard despair before, I should recognise it in future.

"I'm listening," I assured him, anxious to help him in every way. "Is it matches you want, or...."

But he relieved himself abruptly, with a remarkable exhibition of energy. In brief, he came for me, nearer mad than sane. I doubt whether anyone had ever spoken him fair and gentle before in all his rough, sinful life; and he was anxious to record his impressions—on me!

Now, I am not a big man; not when compared with the two-hundred-and-fifty pound Dutchman, or even the two-hundred pound Skipper, or the Hogge, who must weigh almost as much. I weigh a hundred and seventy-five pounds, stripped; but then I have fought in the ropes many a score of times, and I am rather unusually strong for a man of my weight; therefore, perhaps, you will understand why I was pleased to accept the Hogge's attentions in as warm a fashion as he could have wished.

He swung two mighty right and left hand punches at my head, which was certainly "not there" when the punches arrived; and he followed this by a second and a third right-and-left, right-and-left, grunting like a hogge, as he hit.

There was a clatter of feet, and good old Miles came racing up, to bear a hand; but I checked him.

"All right," I called out. "The Hogge and I are having a little argument." I slipped under the Mate's right, as I spoke. "Hark to him grunt!" I added, and shot my own right up under the man's unpleasant chin, with the lift of my shoulder under it. He went away from me, all loose, just as a man does who gets a punch of that kind. I went after him, with two steps, and hit him again, this time with a straight left-hand punch right below the point of the sternum.

As I hit, I was vaguely aware that someone had come at me, with a run, and Miles had jumped in between. The Mate concluded his falling movement and hit the deck. He lay as quiet as a tired babe, and I was able to glance round.

I saw that Miles and Bully Dunkan were mixing it, in the prettiest kind of a fight; only that Miles was no match for the Skipper, especially with his face and jaw still so tender, that a touch hurt like a blow.

The next thing I knew, poor old Miles was down and out, on the deck; and that two hundred pounds of Evil and Fight was charging me, in a silent ugly way that meant business.

Now, Captain Bully Dunkan could fight, and he knew how to use his hands; also he weighed almost two stones more than I do. But my years of ring-work stood for all that, and more. I slipped my head under his left drive, countering hard with my left on his nose; for I wished to daze and weaken him a bit, without knocking him out.

He had no *real* foot-work, and he was a little slow; but there was quite enough of the human hurricane to him, as he bored in at me, punching with right and left, to make me careful. I can quite believe that he must have proved a tough proposition for the average rough-and-ready fighter.

Bully Dunkan was no pretty sight, as any boxing man will understand, when you remember that I had landed a hard, straight, left punch on his nose, as he rushed me; but he was not really damaged; and I set out now to knock some of the steam out of him. I had already sidestepped and slipped him all around a twelve foot circle; and it tickled me a little to see the way the men stood about the decks, almost stiffened with amazement, as they realised that I was not "eaten clean up."

I came in suddenly at the Bully; pushed his right up smartly with my left hand, and landed him a hard, solid punch on the side of the jaw; but not heavy enough to knock him out. He rocked back an instant, with his chin snicked up in the air; and I could see that he was all adrift for the moment. Then he steadied, and rushed me, hitting with right and left.

He was panting badly now, and I slid under his left arm, and hit him a good body thump as I passed him. Then I sprang at him from behind, caught him by his two shoulders, put my knee hard into his back, and brought him down with a deuce of a thud onto his broad back. This shook him badly, and took the evil out of him a lot. When he got up, I hit him a right and left punch over the heart, and as he tried to grab me, I uppercut him under the chin, with a straight-armed, right upward swing.

I guessed now that he'd had a lot of the ugliness dazed out of him, and he would not be able to hurt too much, if I let him hit me. However, I had to take some chances; for it's my experience of life, that gold has to be worked and suffered for! Yet, to make sure he was as weak as possible, I stalled off his next rush, with a heavyish left-hand thump in his great bull neck, and a right-hand punch, pretty hard, in the short ribs. Then I let him hit me; but he was gasping heavily, and rocking a little on his feet as he struck, and the blow I took from him, hardly made my eyes water; yet, I threw out my hands, and sagged, and collapsed backwards on to the hatch, with a thud that shook me up a lot more than his punch. And there I lay, never moving.

"Got yer!" roared Bully Dunkan, with a gasp, and aimed a clumsy kick at me, where I lay; but I had so weakened him, that he staggered over sideways, and sat down heavily beside me on the hatch, and was immediately very sick indeed.

I never moved or opened my eyes, and presently, I heard him bellowing weakly for one of the men to go aft and tell the Steward, who, as you know, was Sandy Meg, to bring the irons.

They handcuffed me first, where I lay, apparently unconscious. I could hear Bully Dunkan, sitting near me on the hatch, groaning a little. After they had handcuffed me, I heard them gather round poor Miles, and then came the chink of the cuffs, and I knew that he too was ironed.

"Take 'em aft, Stooard, an' dump 'em down the lazarette," shouted Dunkan. "You, Lang an' Tarbrey an' Mike, give a hand with the hogs, an' one of you others shove a bucket o' water over that fool Mate o' mine, an' fetch him round…."

He broke off, and groaned a bit; then turned suddenly on my "unconscious" body.

"You—!" he said, vilely, and bashed his sea-booted heel a couple of times into my ribs, where I lay; but he broke nothing; for he was still too shaken to be his true self. Then I was picked up, shoulders and feet, and carried aft. I could hear men's feet stumbling ahead of me, and knew they were carrying Miles first; and behind me, there was the voice of Bully Dunkan, cursing; and then a sound of thrown water, by which I knew they were heaving cold water over the Mate.

"They's washing down th' Hogge!" I heard the man mutter who was carrying my feet…. "Carry 'im easy, mate; I'm 'is friend for life an' hevermore, the way he's outed the First Mate an' pasted the Skipper. Ee's a holy terror!"

I gathered that the latter part of the man's remark applied to me; but I kept my eyes shut.

"Wasn't it just swate the way he played round the Ole Man," said the man at my head. (I could tell it was Mike.) "I'm lackin' to know, bejabers, how he come to get knocked out at all, at all!"

It is unnecessary to say that I did not explain that I was entirely un-knocked-out, if I may so put it. I had a secret plan to carry out, and a ship's fo'cas'le is no place to hold secrets long; so I remained knocked-out and limp, to them and all the world of that moment.

Five minutes later, Miles and I were chained down to the floor of the lazarette; and to make sure that it was done right, Bully Dunkan came groaning and cursing down the steep ladder, and locked and tested the padlocks himself. Then he took the keys of the irons from Sandy Meg, and pocketed them; after which he kicked Miles once, and me twice; and I certainly wished I had hit him about a little more than I had. However, I managed to keep silent, and in a minute he had gone, with the Steward and the men. I heard the heavy trap dropped, and afterwards the sound of a key, locking it.

The first part of my plot was achieved. Miles and I were in the lazarette.

III

Poor Miles lay very quiet, where the men had put him. For my part, I ached considerably, and had something of a fight to check the anger that was boiling up in me for the way Bully Dunkan had kicked the two of us, after we were ironed.

But I reasoned myself out of it. I had arranged the whole thing, with a perfect knowledge of the kind of man the Skipper was; and it was hardly logical, I told myself, to be all of a bubble inside me, because I had received the due portion of Dunkanism which I had earned. It was part of the price we had to pay for the saving of Bully Dunkan's soul; for only by affliction could such a one be saved from his thoroughly earned fate. Incidentally, as I have mentioned before, gold is a painful metal to achieve—either slow or painful; and frequently both.

Thus I shook myself, mentally, and became slowly able to delay the shedding of Bully Dunkan's blood.

I leaned towards poor Miles, in the absolute darkness; but I could not touch him; for the ring-bolts, to which we were chained, were evidently calculated to be just sufficiently far apart to prevent unevenly tempered seamen from mingling their tears.

I saw that it was time I brought into use some of the various little preparations which I had made for our adventure. I reached into my pockets and found, first of all, a box of matches and half a candle.

I lit the candle, and stood it on the deck of the lazarette. Then I took, from a small pocket I had stitched in the waistband of my trousers, a sawn handcuff key, such as is used by those apparently clever jugglers, who make their living by persuading unfortunate and credulous people to lock numberless pairs of handcuffs upon them, immediately afterwards retiring into hiding, while they quickly unlock them with a key like the one I held; after which they return to the audience and exhibit the irons (but not the key) and obtain thereby much applause.

The beauty of this key is at once evident. It is like an ordinary handcuff key, only longer in the barrel and made of steel. It is then sawn lengthways down the barrel, so that it is possible to press it on to the screwed end of the bolt that holds a handcuff shut, and then a mere pull opens the cuff, and the prisoner is free. As a key of this kind will fit almost any standard make of cuff, it is an entirely useful pocket adjunct to adventurers, criminals, conjurers and the like!

With this key, I unlocked the cuff on my right wrist, and let the chain that passed over it, from the ring-bolt in the floor, fall on to my knees. I was free.

I took the candle; put the matches in my pocket, and crept over to Miles. He was lying huddled, where they had dropped him, and I set to and straightened him out. Then I unlocked his cuffs, and began to rub his hands. After a bit, I opened his shirt and rubbed his chest, hard; and presently he moved a little.

"Ssh!" I said; for he had suddenly kicked out. "Keep quiet. You're all right. We're down in the lazarette." But he was not conscious enough yet to comprehend me.

Ten minutes later, he was talking to me, a little stupidly at first; but he improved every half minute.

"Have you got your gun on you?" I asked him, as soon as he was all right.

"Yes," he told me. "In my right sea-boot. And I've those candles in my pockets, you told me to carry around, and two boxes of matches. The auger fixing and the screwdriver are in my left boot; and the long narrow canvas sack you made, is wrapped round my waist, under my shirt."

"That's all right," I said. "I've got my automatic in one sea-boot and the narrow saw and the files in the other; and I've got the keys and a dozen half candles and three boxes of matches and the bottle of dope in my pockets; and a belt-full of cartridges under my shirt. We'll do fine. I've even got a little black beeswax, to hide any bright gaps we may have to make with the files."

"John!" he said, suddenly, heaving himself up into a sitting position. "It's just struck me, they've not taken our sheath-knives or our matches or pipes or tobacco or anything. I've got all mine on me. If they had, they'd have discovered the matches and candles and your bunches of keys. They've forgotten! And that means they'll be coming down, as soon as ever they remember, to search us and take them away. They'll never leave us with our matches and sheath-knives, and I'll bet they'll take our tobacco, so as to stop us having even the comfort of a chew."

"By Jove! I'll bet you're right," I said. "It's a mercy you thought of it. Here, out with everything, automatic, auger, screwdriver, candles, matches, the bag— everything! No, leave one box of matches and your pipe and leave a bit of your plug. That'll make them sure you've not hidden anything; and they'll not maul you as much, searching you—see? I'll do the same. Hurry up, man! They may be down any minute."

I had been emptying my pockets and my boots, while I was speaking, and I even slipped off my hidden belt of cartridge-clips. I took the whole lot of things, and wrapped them in my red cotton handkerchief. Then, taking the lighted candle, I went quietly across the lazarette, and hid the stuff behind the bread barrels.

I came back, and locked Miles up again, and afterwards myself, and blew out and hid the candle.

"When they come, you'd better be sitting up," I told him; "so as to be able to guard your face, if he kicks you."

"Right!" he answered. "Where have you put the key for the cuffs? They mustn't find that on you."

"I've put it behind one of these chocks that keep these sugar-casks from rolling," I told him. "I can just reach it, lying down and stretching."

"Good!" he said; and as he spoke, we heard the key put into the lock of the trap door, somewhere above us in the darkness, over to starboard.

The trap was lifted, and an oblong of shadowy daylight showed in the deck above us.

Then I heard the Skipper's voice; he was cursing Sandy Meg, the Steward. Directly afterwards, his feet came into sight, and his bulk blotted out most of the daylight. He reached the bottom of the ladder, and Sandy Meg came down also, carrying a lantern.

Bully Dunkan walked across to us, with the Steward following and holding the lantern up.

"Well now, I do admire that!" he said, stopping in front of Miles. "So you're sitting up on your little hind legs, Sonny, a-ready. That was a tidy clip I landed you, now; don't ye think so!"

He spoke a bit snuffily, because of the punch I had hit him on the nose, which looked emphatically enlarged, in the lantern-light.

"Now, Steward," he went on, "I'm a-going to take away his little pipe an' matches, *and* his knife…. Lie down, you goat, while I go through you!"

This last was to Miles, and Bully Dunkan gave my friend a push with his foot, that rolled him over onto his side. Then the Skipper went through his pockets, and took away everything he had, including his knife.

When he had done with Miles, he came over to me.

"So *you've* come round too, are you!" he said. "Maybe you thought you could hand it out to me; but you was mistook, dear friend…. You was mistook, I tells you!"

He repeated this in a shout, and then, without another word, as if the memory of the way I'd hammered him, drove him mad, he took a swinging kick at me, and got me in the ribs, with a thud that made me feel sick.

Twice more, he kicked me; then bashed me over onto the deck, with his foot, and went through my pockets. He took all he found, also my sheath-knife.

"Mister Hogge will be coming down in a bit, maybe, to have a little word with you," he said, catching hold of my ears, and twisting them brutally until they bled.

I began to regret that I had locked myself up again. Perhaps it was as well; for if I could have got free that moment, I should certainly have tried to kill him.

However, I managed to keep from making a sound; and then he let go, and stood back a step, staring down at me. I bit my teeth hard together for a moment, so as to steady myself. Then I spoke:—

"How is the Hogge, Cap'n?" I said, and stared up at him, smiling as well as I could. "Tell him, with my compliments, I'll be pleased to hear him grunt a bit, any time he likes."

He never answered a word, for a moment; then burst out into a great laugh.

"I'll hand the Mate that," he said. He roared out again into his brute of a laugh. "Oh, my bonny boy, but ye'll hear him grunt, I'm thinkin'. I'll hand him that, sure I will. It'll rat him rank mad."

He turned away, hove the things he had taken from us, down into an empty box on the floor of the lazarette, out of our reach, and went straight away up the ladder, with the Steward following with the lamp. The trap was slammed, and I heard it locked. Then Miles spoke to me:—

"Did he hurt you much, old man?"

"Not to mention it," I said. "It seemed to tickle him about the Mate. If I understand his kind, right, though; he'll never let the Hogge down here. He'd sooner use us to rag the Hogge with. That's just his way. He's got to be unpleasant to someone, or he couldn't keep well. Did he damage you at all?"

"No," said Miles; "but I wanted badly to plug him."

"Never mind!" I answered. "When this business is through, safely, I'm promising myself the pleasure of cutting loose, properly, just for five heavenly minutes on the Dunk."

IV

Miles and I had talked everything over, a score of times before ever I started the row with the Hogge, which had landed us in our much-desired lazarette.

We knew that the money must be in Bully Dunkan's own cabin; for where else in a windjammer would he be likely to keep it! Also we knew that the trap of the lazarette opened directly under his cabin table; and, finally, I had a bunch of "master" keys, and if these wouldn't do, I could possibly unscrew the lock with the screwdriver.

"We'll tackle the job tonight, Miles," I said, after we had sat in the dark for a couple of minutes, listening. "He'll not keep us down here more than a day or two. It would break his heart to have two or three hundred pounds of sailor-flesh sitting idle. He'll probably give us nothing but water, like Billy Duckworth; more power to Billy for going for him! Then he'll boot us out, as soon as he thinks he's put the fear of God into us sufficiently."

"You mean, if we don't do the job at once, we may be out of here again, before we get the chance," he said.

"Just that," I answered. "Things are ideal for us now in every way. One of the minor reasons why I wanted to be ironed safely down here, was so that he could have no suspicion of either of us; for, I tell you, he'll have the whole ship pretty well capsized, and every man and sea-chest aboard, searched, when he finds the loot is gone, like the little song says, away and away-oh!"

"Um!" said Miles. "I never thought of that. I don't see how you're going to hide the stuff, in that case."

"Think again," I answered. "It all works out perfectly. He has the key of this place in his pocket, and therefore he'll never suppose that the money may be down here."

"Um!" said Miles, again. "And how are we going to get it out of here, without his seeing we're loaded up? Why man! The package they hove into the boat that night, must have weighed getting on for a hundredweight, by the sound it made, and the way they carried it."

"The ventilator," I explained. "It comes down through the poop-deck and the cabin-deck, and opens over that top shelf, just behind you. What do you suppose I made the canvas bag that shape for! We'll put the coin into it, and stand it behind the boxes, right under the ventilator. The ventilator is not in use just now, and the cowl is unshipped, and the sleeve it fits on is covered with a brass cap.

"Well, last night, in the middle watch, it was pretty black as you know; so I took a chance, and crept along to the ventilator, and lifted the cap. It's got a ring inside, for lashing it down by. All I did, was to bend on a chest-lashing to this ring, and let the end come down here. Then I put the lid back in place. It's hanging there now, you'll find; and we've only to make it fast to the neck of the canvas bag, and the job will be done, so far as down here is concerned. The rest we can manage when we get shoved on deck again. It'll be just as simple as the job I had, to fix on the chest-lashing. That all clear, man?"

"Yes," he said. "Very neat plan…. Can't we have a light now, and get out of these irons?"

"Wait a bit," I said. "There's someone at the trap, now."

The trap was opened, and Bully Dunkan and the Steward came down again. The Captain had the lantern, and the Steward carried a bucket of water and a cup. This, he set on the deck of the lazarette, midway between Miles and me, where we could both reach it.

Dunkan kicked us each, and examined our irons; after which he grunted in a satisfied way.

"There's something to get your backs up on, my bonny boys," he said, giving the bucket a push with his foot. "It's all you'll get for forty-eight hours. Don't make hogs of yourselves!"

Then he went, laughing viciously, and ushering Sandy Meg before him up the ladder. The trap shut, and we heard the key turn.

"The—!" said Miles, out of the darkness.

"Couldn't have been better!" I whispered back. "There's grub all round us, there's water in the bucket; what more could a man want! Wait while I find the key."

V

It was some hours later, and we were both out of the irons again, and standing, listening on the ladder that led up to the trap.

Bully Dunkan was in his cabin, and the Hogge was with him, and there was a constant chink of coin, and a low mutter of talk.

"What's that?" I heard the Hogge say; and I sweated a little; for I was trying my bunch of "master" keys on the lock of the trap, and I had made a bit of a rattle, fumbling there in the shadows and swaying candlelight; and the ship rolling more than a trifle.

"It's yon damn Steward," said Bully Dunkan…. "What is it?" he roared out. "What the devil d'yer want?"

"I got the hot water, Sir, for the grog," I heard Sandy Meg's voice say, faintly, because he was evidently the other side of the cabin door.

"Bless his dear heart an' liver!" said Bully Dunkan. Then, in a lower voice:—"Here, shove this chart over the stuff, while I opens the door."

It was plain to both of us, now, beyond all doubt, that the Hogge and the Captain had the dollars nakedly on the table before them, as one might say; and were counting them, with the door locked. I tell you, it made me feel so close to the stuff, that I could have found it in my heart to open the trap there and then, and wade into the two of them, with the aid of our automatics. Only, of course, this would have been clumsy, and might have ended in my having to send the Dunikan (as Miles would insist on calling him) and the Hogge prematurely to an investigation of those high temperatures which they were daily fitting themselves to appreciate.

I heard the cabin door unlocked and opened; and slammed and locked again. Then Bully Dunkan's voice, in a roar:—

"Drop that, you scow-bottomed down-Easter! Haul them dollar gold-pieces out of yer pocket, right this moment!"

"Say!" said the Hogge, "you quit that talk to me, Cap'n, or there'll be trouble. Say!…"

"You make me tired," said Bully Dunkan. "D'yer suppose I didn't see you! Do you suppose, you damn fool, I'm going blind. Ante up them dollars, Sonny dear, or—!"

There was a sudden rustle, as if someone had moved quickly; then the Hogge's voice:—

"All right! *All* right! I was only jokin'. I'll tip the stuff up."

"No, Sonny! Sonny!" came Dunkan's voice. "Quit putting your lily-white hands into yer jacket pockets. Just keep 'em right on the table, plain in sight. They're bonny hands. Deary me, Mr. Mate, I'd no idee you took such keer of yer nails!"

I smiled, where I stood on the ladder; for I could picture the great horny black-rimmed nails of the Hogge. Miles, who was holding the candle, below me, laughed out loud; but checked himself in a moment.

It was plain to us, that the Captain had turned from the door, just in time to catch the Hogge weighting himself down with a spare preliminary handful, or two, of gold, before the division of the dollars had been carried out; and it was plain also, that the Captain had drawn his gun on the Hogge. Altogether, an interesting little situation.

I had just discovered a key on my bunch which turned the lock of the trap; and I thought this might be a suitable moment to make a brief investigation of facts.

"Blow out the light, Miles," I said. Then, very gently, I shot back the lock, and pressed the trap up, half an inch at a time, until I could see along the deck of the cabin.

Close to the edge of the trap, was a liberal pair of feet, in unstinted bluchers. I recognised them as the Hogge's, and wondered what he would think, if he suddenly stuck them out further, and encountered the gaping hole of the little hatchway in which I stood! I hoped sincerely that he would keep still.

A little to my right, and standing about a yard away from the table, were the Bully's boots. My ribs recognised them almost before I did. They were painfully familiar acquaintances. I regarded them a moment, with a sudden pleasurable anticipation of what I should eventually do to their owner.

"People who wear leather sea-boots, ought—"

I had got this far in my voiceless soliloquy, when I saw something else, on the deck, to the left of the Hogge's bluchers, and not a foot away from the edge of the hatch. It was the kettle of hot water for their grog, which the Steward, Sandy Meg, had just handed in.

I had a sudden, and, some might say, an apparently insane longing to possess that kettle. I raised the trap a little higher, and reached out my left hand, slowly, until I could grab the kettle handle; and as I did so, the Bully's voice came, suddenly, and seeming abnormally loud and distinct, owing to the previous moments of silence, and to the fact that now there was no longer the thickness of the trap to deaden the sounds in the cabin.

"Don't move, Sonny!" he said; "not one single little blessed inch, or I'll plug you clean as any whistle you ever blowed."

I stiffened, where I was, and I took very good care not to move, as may be imagined. But I was not idle. I'm not that kind! The hatch cover (or trap) was propped open, resting on my head; my left hand was holding the handle of the kettle, and my right hand was free, and with my right hand, I was deaf-and-dumbing (single-hand-code) to Miles, to pass me up my automatic. Then, I realised that he would not be able to read what I was saying, with the candle out; and I was going to risk what I might call a flying retreat, and chance Dunkan's gun.

But, in the very moment, when I was going to jump and let the hatch fall with a crash, Bully Dunkan spoke again:—

"I'm going to go through your pockets, Sonny son," he said, in his quiet, ugly way. And his feet moved, and went towards the Hogge.

Goodness! But I felt the relief. He had not seen me at all! He was still speaking to the Hogge. With the revulsion of feeling, I described myself briefly and exactly in unspoken phrases as a fool of the completest kind. Then, I lifted the kettle down into the hatchway, and lowered the trap (or hatch-cover) noiselessly shut again.

"Matches, quick, Miles!" I whispered.

"What's the kettle for, John?" he asked me, as the candle-flame rose and brightened. "What were you deaf-and-dumbing?"

"I thought the Dunkan had got me," I whispered. "Quick, the dope! This is the hot water for their grog. I'll make them sleep longer than the seven sleepers. I never knew such luck."

He raced for the bottle of "dope" (sleeping-draught, 'Frisco quality!) and handed it up to me. I poured about half of it into the kettle. I dared not risk more; for I felt that neither of them was ready; that is, not from a Christianlike way of looking at the matter. I told Miles to blow out the candle. Then, very carefully, I lifted the hatch-cover again, and put the kettle back, where I had found it under the table.

Bully Dunkan was standing at the back of the Hogge's chair, evidently going through his pockets, in an unemotional but thorough fashion.

"That's all, dear friend," I heard him say. "I guess I got yer gun; so you'll maybe check yer evil propensities. What say now, to the grog?"

"Don't mind if I do," growled the Hogge.

I shut the hatch just in time, as Bully Dunkan reached under the table for the kettle.

Five minutes later, the Hogge grunted, with more than porcine satisfaction.

"That's good stuff, Cap'n," he said. "You're hell-fire an' you got ugly ways I ain't no use for; but I'll allow as you shore can make a grog-stew."

"I believe you, Sonny," said Bully Dunkan; and he also smacked his lips, in a way that was a good second to the Hogge's.

Down in the lazarette, Miles and I held on to each other, and tried to keep it as silent as we could; but that kind of laugh takes a deal of managing!

VI

During the next half-hour, I stood most of the time on the ladder, close up to the trap, listening.

At first, I could hear the Hogge and Bully Dunkan talking, with the constant accompanying chink, chink of money. Once, the Hogge began to grumble, but in a drowsy undertone, that was pleasantly suggestive to me of good, plain, efficient "dope," or knock-out-mixture—to give it only one or two of its varied names.

Abruptly, there came a dull thud on the deck, close to my head, and the sound of a shower of coins.

"Beas'ly... drunk... 'Ogg!" said Bully Dunkan, in a tone of indescribable senility; and with a long pause between each word.

"The Hogge's gone to sleep on the door, and taken half the gold with him, I should judge by the sounds," I whispered down to Miles.

"How's the Dunikan?" he whispered back.

"Seems to be on his last legs," I said; "that is, by the way he's been trying to reprove the Hogge. He's just told him he's a beas'ly drunk 'Ogg; and it took him nearly half a minute to say it.... Ah! there he goes, too!"

For there had come a second thud on the deck, accompanied by a further cascading of coins.

I waited through a long couple of minutes, during which an absolute silence filled the cabin over my head. Then I lifted the trap slowly, and peeped through. The Hogge lay on his side, within a yard and a half of me. He looked crumpled and inert; but peacefully disposed. Bully Dunkan lay sprawled, at the end of the table, his legs under it, and his head lying on one of the Hogge's sea-boots. He had the same expression of peace.

All around the two of them, lay five-, ten-, and twenty-dollar gold pieces. The two men were literally lying in wealth, if not in the lap of luxury. I never saw quite so much gold on the floor at one time, before or since.

"Come along, Miles," I said. "Bring the bag. They sleep as sleep the Innocent that knows no wrong; nor e'er hath taken aught that did belong, to any…."

I ceased declaiming, and went up through the little hatchway; and in a moment, Miles followed, with the long, strong, bolster-like, canvas bag, which I had made for this moment.

"Behold them, dear man," I said. "It's picturesque to see them lie among the gold."

"Good Lord!" answered Miles; "look at the pile on the table."

"I have," I told him. "And I'm not tired yet. Here you are, hold the bag, while I slide it off into it."

This was a short but pleasant piece of work. Then we set-to and picked up all the gold coins that lay about the deck of the cabin. When we had finished, the bag was simply awesomely full.

"Now, Miles," I said, "there are just one or two things to do, before we go below to our humble abode of darkness. We shall have to sacrifice a handful of gold; but we can spare it."

I took a handful out of the mouth of the long, narrow sack, and stepped across to Bully Dunkan's bunk. I unscrewed and opened the port-light that was in the ship's side, just over his bunk. I took several of the coins and laid them on the rebate of the port-hole, just *outside*. Then I placed a coin or two on the brass rim of the port-hole itself, trusting to luck that they would not slip off, with the rolling of the ship.

After that, I spread three or four coins about, in the sunk recess in the ship's side, which contained the port-light. The rest of the handful of gold, I scattered in a trail across the blankets of Bully Dunkan's bunk, in such a way as to lead the glance at once to the port-hole.

"What's it for, John?" asked Miles.

"Just a little way of easing some of the steam out of the search these two will make, when they wake up and find they're deficient in bullion," I told him. "You see, they'll be stumped. Each will suspect the other, and they'll search the ship, pretty well from truck to keelson. For they'll each argue that the gold *must* be in the ship, as no one would steal it, merely to dump it.

"But, if my little plan works, when they come to look round, and see the gold trail to the port, they'll get a horrid idea that one of them may have put the stuff through into the sea, in the mad, silly sort of way a man will do things when he's drunk.

"Of course, this won't stop them from suspecting each other, and it may not stop them from searching the ship; but, whatever happens, the possibility that one of them may have done this, will be always in the backs of their minds, and it will grow, as they fail to find the gold, until they come to the conclusion that they *must* have dumped the stuff overboard themselves.

"You know what a chap can do, in throwing his cash about, and being generally a fool, when he's boozed…. In rum out rhino! I guess it'll seem the only possible explanation, especially as they know they were safely locked in, when they started drinking.

"There's just one other little thing I've got to do."

I hunted round, until I found the drawer where Bully Dunkan stored his rum. Then I took out a couple of bottles, and knocked off the necks. I reached down a couple of clean glasses from the rack by the door, and poured us each a good tot.

"Here's health, Miles," I said. "We've earned it, working like this for the soul-welfare of the Hogge and his master."

"To you, John," said Miles; and we drank.

"Then I dumped the two glasses out of the port, and took the two bottles of rum, and poured it liberally over the Bully and the Hogge, until they were soaked through, and they smelt to Heaven of the stuff. I took a third bottle, and slopped rum all over the table, and into their empty glasses. Finally, I emptied out what was left of the water and dope, in the kettle, and poured rum into it.

I threw the three empty bottles onto the floor, where I let them roll. I went back to the drawer, and picked up a full bottle. I held this above the others, and let it fall back with a crash. "Drunk men drop bottles, Miles," I observed.

He nodded.

"I guess you don't want them to suspect they were doped," he said. "You're out to make them think they must have gone in for an almightly drunk. That was a cute dodge, putting the rum into the kettle. They'll guess they must have done it, after they got muzzy, and got drinking the stuff neat."

"You've savvied, old friend," I said. "Let's get away below. Phoo! the place smells!"

Miles went down the ladder, half a dozen steps, and I lashed up the neck of the bag of gold with a leather lace out of one of the Captain's drawers. Then I lowered the bag onto Miles' shoulders, and he went slowly down to the bottom of the ladder. There must have been well over a hundred-weight of gold.

I followed Miles, and shut and locked the trap. Miles had already lighted a candle, and we set-to at once, and put the gold behind the row of boxes on the shelf near the deck, right under the place where the cap of the closed ventilator-shaft opened. I had previously fixed two rope grommets in the shoulders of the bag, and to these I attached the hanging end of the chest-lashing, that I had made fast to the ring in the cap of the ventilator-shaft.

"Now, let's store all our tackle away, over behind the bread-casks," I said; "but we'll keep our automatics in our boots, in case the Bully comes down here and cuts loose on us, to ease his feelings. There's no saying what the sweet Dunkan may not be capable of, given a bad head and a sour mouth, an empty gold chest and a full revolver! So we'll keep the little guns handy. Now let us acquire a meal."

Half an hour later, we entered the irons again, and prepared to get some sleep.

"I guess the Bo'sun'll have to keep double watch tonight, John," said Miles, just as I was dozing off.

"Poor beggar!" I answered, and was asleep before he could think of anything else.

VII

I was waked some hours later by a tremendous noise overhead. There were heavy blows on the deck, and Bully Dunkan was shouting, thickly.

"What is it, Miles?" I asked, and sat up in the darkness.

"They're waking up, John," he said.

"They appear to be doing it very thoroughly," I replied. "It sounds as if Dunkan were massaging the Hogge."

"He's bumping his head on the deck," said Miles. "He'll kill him, instead of bringing him round."

"Probably, dear man," I answered; "but I don't think we're out to save the Hogge's bacon! If they finished each other, the world, and the sea especially, would be well shut of them…. Hark to him!"

There was a steady, monotonous bumping now on the deck of the cabin, above. I had no doubt that it was the Mate's head; also, I began to think Miles' prophecy would come right. The bumps were so vigourous, that they made the lazarette resound.

Abruptly, one of the bumps ended, in a curious, breaking sound.

"G'lor'!" said Miles. "Did you hear that? He's broke the Mate's head!"

The heavy blows had ceased, and there was a brief silence.

Suddenly, we both heard the Hogge's voice say, in a dazed tone:—

"Leggo my ears, dam yer! Leggo my ears!"

Miles sighed relief. I could hear him plainly, through the darkness.

"Thought that'd wake yer, my bonnie boy!" said Dunkan's voice. "Where's the gold?"

"Say! What's this blame thing I'm lyin' my 'ead on?" asked the Hogge, still a little dazed-seeming; but palpably returning again to this life.

"Where's the gold?" reiterated Bully Dunkan.

"What's this blame thing I got my 'ead on?" asked the Hogge, again. "It's blame sharp!... Leggo my ears, I tells yer. Leggo!"

There was a short scuffle; then the Hogge's voice again:—

"A broke ceegar-box, you old swine, you! I s'pose you thought it dam funny to bash me down onto that. I'm all cut with the broke wood. Dam your ugly ways!"

"Where's the gold?" asked Bully Dunkan. There was a sharp movement; and then the Hogge's voice, now less dazed than ever:—

"Say! Don't point that blame thing at me. You're too drunk to play with shootin' gear."

"Where's the gold?" asked Bully Dunkan. "I'm goin' to shoot in a minute."

There was a scurrying, lumpish sound, as if the Hogge had sat up suddenly.

"The gold!" he said, in a voice that denoted he was at last awake to the Complete Present. "The gold! Why we was countin' it... on the table. It's there, ain't it? Say! I feel dam bad. How ever much did we put down? I'm all..."

"Where's the gold?" said Bully Dunkan's voice, monotonously.

There were sounds, suggestive of the Hogge's essaying a standing position.

"Say!" he said, after a moment, in a stunned kind of voice, "the dollars is gone! Say...!" He broke off, and I heard his feet go at a clumsy run towards the cabin door. "Say!" he called out, "it's locked! Say, Cap'n! Say! I tell yer the blame door's locked!"

"Where's the gold?" came Bully Dunkan's everlasting reiteration. "You smart Hogge, you! Out with it, or I'll plug yer! Where's the gold?"

There followed a moment's silence.

"No, you blame well don't, Cap'n!" said the Hogge's voice, suddenly full of suspicion. "You don't put that over on *me*, dam yer! You don't foxy *me* that way! No, Siree!"

There was a sudden crash, and a chinkling down on the deck, of broken glass. One of them, probably the Hogge, had evidently thrown one of the empty bottles. There followed the rush of the Hogge's big bluchers, from the direction of the door; and simultaneously, there were two revolver shots, almost together.

Then came the thud of the two men meeting, and through the next five minutes, there was quite high-class trouble up above. Apparently, everything smashable in the cabin got smashed. The thuds, blows, stampings, breathless cussings, and the chorus-crashes of breakages, were impressive and stimulating to listen to.

Finally, it ended.

"That was some row, Miles," I said, through the darkness.

"It was, John," said Miles. "Listen to them now. They're feeling cooler."

The Hogge and Bully Dunkan were apparently collecting themselves. The still uncoordinated fragments refused to attempt clear speech for a time. They wheezed, and achieved odd words and grunts, and displayed a very apparent breathlessness.

Finally, the Hogge amalgamated first.

"Say! You might ha' blame well plugged me, dam your ugly ways!"

"What d'yer want to go slingin' bottles around for, then!" Bully Dunkan managed to articulate, with generous pauses.

They appeared, both of them, to be on the floor; for presently I heard them scrambling and slurring their heavy boots, as they got slowly to their feet.

One of them walked across the cabin, towards the bunk. It was Bully Dunkan; for his voice came the next moment:—

"Look a-here, quick!" he said. "Good Lord! Look a-here!"

The Hogge's bluchers stumbled hastily across the cabin. There was a full quarter minute silence, completely eloquent with horror.

"Say!…" began the Hogge; and was silent again. Then, with simple despair, he said all that he was capable of:— "Say! *All them dollars!*"

Neither man spoke, for maybe a minute after that. They were both acquainted with liquor and its vagaries when imbibed in largish quantity. They both knew that "in liquor," or "full" as they more briefly described it, in the troubled talk that followed, a man will do anything.

"It's worse," said the Hogge, sadly, "than when I got drunk in Val'parazo an' give the bar-man five hundred dollars, all I had. My pay-day for fifteen months. An' next day, he'd not even stand me a drink. Swore I'd not give him a cent. Said he made a point never to take presents."

We heard them moving about.

"I guess this is the kettle, right enough. It's flat; but there's a drop of stuff in it," said Dunkan's voice; and I could hear him tasting something, with a clumsy smacking of his lips.

"It's neat rum," he announced, mournfully. "No wonder we was screwed. I guess we filled the kettle, an' then forgot, an' thought it was water."

"Three empty bottles on the deck," said the Hogge, gloomily, "an' the dee-canter."

There followed a long period of flat silence.

"Guess I'd best go up an' relieve the Bo'sun," said the Hogge, in a sombre voice.

There was no thought of searching the ship. My little plot had worked, just the way I like a plot to work. Bully Dunkan and the Hogge accepted what I might call the Suggestion of the Port Hole, as at once a practicable and a probable solution of the mystery. It tallied both with the teachings of their Experience and the suggestions of their Reason, and I felt that I had done much to help the cause of temperance.

VIII

We were released some hours later, at midday.

That night, during the Hogge's watch, while he was sleeping soundly and illegally on the weather-seat of the cabin-skylight, I crept up onto the poop, lifted the cap of the ventilator, and hauled on the chest-lashing. Half a minute later, I had the long, narrow bag up through the ventilator shaft, and beside me on the deck. I cast off the chest-lashing from the cap of the ventilator, and pressed the cap down into place again.

All this, I had managed, without ever rising to my feet; and the bag had been hard to pull up, in that position. Now, I took a look aft over the skylight. It was a pretty quiet night; but very dark. I could hear the Hogge snoring in a most satisfactory fashion; and the man at the wheel just showed vaguely in the light from the binnacle; so I guessed he could not see me. Then, I gripped the bag in my arms, stood up and walked, barefooted, to the lee stairway, where Miles was waiting for me.

"The bo'sun's locker!" I said; and we carried the bag there. Inside the locker, we fastened the door, and I lighted a candle I had ready in my pocket. Then, among all the mucker of chain, chain-hooks, marlinspikes, serving-mallets, sampson-line, spun-yarn, good Stockholm-tar, and the like, the two of us started to pack the gold into a lot of little canvas bags that Miles and I had made ready for the job. We hurried like mad; for we stood to lose everything, if anyone found us locked in there, at that time of night.

At last, we had all the cash divided up into little bags, about ten or twelve pounds weight each, I should think; and we hid all but four of them at the back of the tar-barrel.

We blew out the candle, unlocked the door, and got out on deck, each of us with a bag in each of the side-pockets of our jackets. We walked forrard into the fo'cas'le, where most of the watch on deck were playing poker, sitting on deck-buckets.

Miles and I opened our sea-chests, and pretended to rummage a bit; and while we were rummaging, we managed to stow away our little bags of gold, without one of the shell-backs seeing us.

We made three more journeys, during the next half hour; and this way, we managed to store the gold away in our sea-chests, without one of all those sinners in that crowded fo'cas'le ever guessing a thing we didn't want guessed! And a good job done, too; when you remember that a fo'cas'le is never empty at sea.

IX

We made a pretty fair passage round; and Miles and I did our best to put up with the Hogge's little ways and Bully Dunkan's, without causing a riot. We each had to stand a kicking or two; and we were each knocked down several times; and we held ourselves back in a way that made me realise what a good Christian must have to go through in this life.

"There's a better time coming," I told Miles. "Keep the lid on until then, old man. We've too much at stake, to risk trouble, till the loot's safe ashore."

The day we reached Boston, Miles and I had a final knocking about from Bully Dunkan and the Hogge, and it took every ounce of our hundred-weight, or so, of hard-earned gold, to enable us to put up with it quietly.

That night, however, we got the stuff safely ashore, and stored it at the house of one of Miles' friends. Then we felt free at last to interview Dunkan and the Hogge, without stint. And my friend Miles was quite as eager as I.

"The Hogge's your mutton," I told him. "The Bully for me! I can still feel where his sea-boot took me in the seat of my pants this morning."

Miles was very well content with the arrangement; and as we both felt we couldn't wait another hour, we decided to go right back to the ship there and then, and see whether Bully Dunkan and the Hogge had got back aboard again.

We met Sandy Meg, returning from the galley to the cabin; and he told us that both of them were in the cabin, and he was just taking their supper aft.

"Sandy Meg," I said, "we're going in to see the Old Man and the Hogge. We're going to tell him we want to be paid off."

"They'll murder you," said Sandy Meg. "The Skipper's rotten to-night. He knocked me flat as soon as the two of 'em come back aboard, just 'cause I'd not got the supper ready. How was I to know they'd be comin' back aboard as soon as this; an' first night ashore, too!"

"Sandy Meg," I said, "you keep out of the cabin for ten minutes. Go up on the poop, and have a free seat in the gallery. You can see what happens, through the skylight. Miles and I are going to paste up those two brutes; and pay them back some of what's coming to them. Don't fret about us. We let them lick us out at sea, for reasons of our own. This is going to be different."

Sandy Meg said never a word; but put his tray down on the main-hatch, silent and grimly joyful, and went up to have his free "gallery seat" through the flap of the open skylight.

Miles and I went in through the door, under the break of the poop, and walked straight into the cabin, where the Dunkan and the Hogge sat, waiting at the table, and looking fretful enough, each of them, to make me think they must have had a poor evening ashore.

"We've come to ask you to pay us off, Cap'n," I said.

They jumped, and then sat silent; neither of them saying a word; being momentarily incapacitated from doing anything else.

"We've come to ask you to pay us off, or else discharge the Hogge, Cap'n," I said.

"We don't like being kicked; but it's not dignified being kicked by a grunter. You'll remember, Cap'n, that I remarked once before that he grunted. I think you agreed with me. It isn't dignified—"

But that was all they allowed me to explain. The Hogge snatched up a plate, and it spoiled the maple-wood bulkshead behind me. Then both he and the Captain came for us, with their fists.

There wasn't much room; but quite sufficient; for I'd not come there to play light. As the Bully rushed me, I propped him off with one clean left hand hit in the neck; and the way his stern met the deck of the cabin, was a thing to remember; at least I can't see him forgetting it.

Miles and the Hogge were having a great time of it, over by the end of the table; and before the Bully had got up and rushed me again, Miles had got that brute of a Hogge up against one of the cabin bulksheads, and was hitting him, quick and monotonous, right and left, right and left, just wherever he pleased. And as he hit, he seemed to be intoning a number of things that the Hogge must have been the better and wiser for hearing.

The Bully was up again by now, and he rushed me, hitting with both hands, like a madman. I slipped clean under his right, and punched him up against the bulkshead, as he tumbled past me.

He came round, like a shot, and took a flying kick at me; but I declined to be at home, and his foot took the edge of the cabin table, instead, and kicked a strip clean off it, fore and aft, about six inches wide.

"Captain, dear," I said, "you'll not have a bit of furniture left; the way you and the Hogge carry on."

He rushed me a third time, putting his head down to butt me in the stomach; but I brought up my knee quickly, and made him straighten wonderfully.

"Now, Bully Dunkan," I said, as he tried twice to hit me with his elbows, "here's what's coming to a brute and a bully and a murderer like you!" And with that, I slipped a left-handed swing of his, and punched him hard on the short ribs with my left hand; then, I crossed in over with my right hand, as his head came forward; and I hit him clean on the side of his chin, close up to the point. I hit with my body and leg to help the blow; and Bully Dunkan went down with a crash, as he had laid many a poor devil of a sailorman out.

Miles had finished now with the Hogge, who lay on the deck, showing no interest in anything; and I decided we had done enough, both for pleasure and for common justice.

"Come along, Miles," I said. "They'll keep in a restful state of mind for a bit, I reckon. Pity we can't lynch them."

Outside on the deck, Sandy Meg nearly hugged us. "My oath!" he said. "My oath; but that did me good to see!"

Miles and I went forrard and rummaged our sea-chests; the chests themselves we decided not to bother with, and presented them to two of the men who were without. Then we said good-bye to the old ship; and went ashore. We had enough to buy new sea-chests, we decided, if ever we were fools enough to need such things again.

The next day, I sent the following letter to Bully Dunkan and the Mate:—

"*Dear Captain and Hogge,*

"Let me commend to your earnest notice the following observations:—

    1.—Handcuffs have keys.

    2.—Lazarette-hatches have the same weakness.

    3.—Dope (especially 'Frisco quality) is most effective, particularly when put into, say, a kettle of hot grog-water, left on the deck near a lazarette hatch.

    4.—Gold, in almost any form; but especially in gold-dollar shape, is a peculiarly useful and likeable metal.

    5.—A punch on the point of the jaw is an instant cure for most evils. N.B. How is your jaw? Hope I didn't hit too hard.

    6.—Hogges grunt. Get rid of the habit or the Hogge.

    7.—There is a little, unknown island, somewhere in the Pacific, known to you and the Hogge. If you will supply us with the latitude and the longitude of same, we shall be pleased to hand the information over to the police, with *all* particulars. Failing which, we must appropriate certain useful metal to our own use.

   "*From an old shipmate.*"

The *Shamraken*
Homeward-Bounder

◆▸◆◂◆

The old *Shamraken*, sailing-ship, had been many days upon the waters. She was old—older than her masters, and that was saying a great deal. She seemed in no hurry, as she lifted her bulging, old, wooden sides through the seas. What need for hurry! She would arrive some time, in some fashion, as had been her habit heretofore.

Two matters were especially noticeable among her crew—who were also her masters—; the first the agedness of each and everyone; the second the *family* sense which appeared to bind them, so that the ship seemed manned by a crew, all of whom were related one to the other; yet it was not so.

A strange company were they, each man bearded, aged and grizzled; yet there was nothing of the inhumanity of old age about them, save it might be in their freedom from grumbling, and the calm content which comes only to those in whom the more violent passions have died.

Had anything to be done, there was nothing of the growling, inseparable from the average run of sailor men. They went aloft to the "job"—whatever it might be—with the wise submission which is brought only by age and experience. Their work was gone through with a certain slow pertinacity—a sort of tired steadfastness, born of the knowledge that such work *had* to be done. Moreover, their hands possessed the ripe skill which comes only from exceeding practice, and which went far to make amends for the feebleness of age. Above all, their movements, slow as they might be, were remorseless in their lack of faltering. They had so often performed the same kind of work, that they had arrived, by the selection of utility, at the shortest and most simple methods of doing it.

They had, as I have said, been many days upon the water, though I am not sure that any man in her knew to a nicety the number of those days. Though Skipper Abe Tombes—addressed usually as Skipper Abe—may have had some notion; for he might be seen at times gravely adjusting a prodigious quadrant, which suggests that he kept some sort of record of time and place.

Of the crew of the *Shamraken*, some half dozen were seated, working placidly at such matters of seamanship as were necessary. Besides these, there were others about the decks. A couple who paced the lee side of the maindeck, smoking, and exchanging an occasional word. One who sat by the side of a worker, and made odd remarks between draws at his pipe. Another, out upon the jibboom, who fished, with a line, hook and white rag, for bonito. This last was Nuzzie, the ship's boy. He was grey-bearded, and his years numbered five and fifty. A boy of fifteen he had been, when he joined the *Shamraken*, and "boy" he was still, though forty years had passed into eternity, since the day of his "signing on"; for the men of the *Shamraken* lived in the past, and thought of him only as the "boy" of that past.

It was Nuzzie's watch below—his time for sleeping. This might have been said also of the other three men who talked and smoked; but for themselves they had scarce a thought of sleep. Healthy age sleeps little, and they were in health, though so ancient.

Presently, one of those who walked the lee side of the main-deck, chancing to cast a glance forrard, observed Nuzzie still to be out upon the jibboom, *jerking* his line so as to delude some foolish bonito into the belief that the white rag was a flying-fish.

The smoker nudged his companion.

"Time thet b'y 'ad 'is sleep."

"i, i, mate," returned the other, withdrawing his pipe, and giving a steadfast look at the figure seated out upon the jibboom.

For the half of a minute they stood there, very effigies of Age's implacable determination to rule rash Youth. Their pipes were held in their hands, and the smoke rose up in little eddies from the smouldering contents of the bowls.

"Thar's no tamin' of thet b'y!" said the first man, looking very stern and determined. Then he remembered his pipe, and took a draw.

"B'ys is tur'ble queer critters," remarked the second man, and remembered his pipe in turn.

"Fishin' w'en 'e orter be sleepin'," snorted the first man.

"B'ys needs a tur'ble lot er sleep," said the second man. "I 'member w'en I wor a b'y. I reckon it's ther growin'."

And all the time poor Nuzzie fished on.

"Guess I'll jest step up an' tell 'im ter come in outer thet," exclaimed the first man, and commenced to walk towards the steps leading up on to the fo'cas'le head.

"B'y!" he shouted, as soon as his head was above the level of the fo'cas'le deck. "B'y!" Nuzzie looked round, at the second call.

"Eh?" he sung out.

"Yew come in outer thet," shouted the older man, in the somewhat shrill tone which age had brought to his voice. "Reckon we'll be 'avin' yer sleepin' at ther wheel ter night."

"'i," joined in the second man, who had followed his companion up onto the fo'cas'le head. "Come in, b'y, an' get ter yer bunk."

"Right," called Nuzzie, and commenced to coil up his line. It was evident that he had no thought of disobeying. He came in off the spar, and went past them without a word, on the way to turn in.

They, on their part, went down slowly off the fo'cas'le head, and resumed their walk fore and aft along the lee side of the maindeck.

II

"I reckon, Zeph," said the man who sat upon the hatch and smoked, "I reckon as Skipper Abe's 'bout right. We've made a trifle o' dollars outer the old 'ooker, an' we don't get no younger."

"Ay, thet's so, right 'nuff," returned the man who sat beside him, working at the stropping of a block.

"An' it's 'bout time's we got inter the use o' bein' ashore," went on the first man, who was named Job.

Zeph gripped the block between his knees, and fumbled in his hip pocket for a plug. He bit off a chew and replaced the plug.

"Seems cur'ous this is ther last trip, w'en yer comes ter think uv it," he remarked, chewing steadily, his chin resting on his hand.

Job took two or three deep draws at his pipe before he spoke.

"Reckon it had ter come sumtime," he said, at length. "I've a purty leetle place in me mind w'er' I'm goin' ter tie up. 'Ave yer thought erbout it, Zeph?"

The man who held the block between his knees, shook his head, and stared away moodily over the sea.

"Dunno, Job, as I know what I'll do w'en thet old 'ooker's sold," he muttered. "Sence M'ria went, I don't seem nohow ter care 'bout bein' 'shore."

"I never 'ad no wife," said Job, pressing down the burning tobacco in the bowl of his pipe. "I reckon seafarin' men don't ought ter have no truck with wives."

"Thet's right 'nuff, Job, fer yew. Each man ter 'is taste. I wer' tur'ble fond uv M'ria—" he broke off short, and continued to stare out over the sea.

"I've allus thought I'd like ter settle down on er farm o' me own. I guess the dollars I've arned 'll do the trick," said Job.

Zeph made no reply, and, for a time, they sat there, neither speaking.

Presently, from the door of the fo'cas'le, on the starboard side, two figures emerged. They were also of the "watch below." If anything, they seemed older than the rest of those about the decks; their beards, white, save for the stain of tobacco juice, came nearly to their waists. For the rest, they had been big vigourous men; but were now sorely bent by the burden of their years. They came aft, walking slowly. As they came opposite to the main hatch, Job looked up and spoke:—

"Say, Nehemiah, thar's Zeph here's been thinkin' 'bout M'ria, an' I ain't bin able ter peek 'im up nohow."

The smaller of the two newcomers shook his head slowly.

"We hev oor trubbles," he said. "We hev oor trubbles. I hed mine w'en I lost my datter's gell. I wor powerful took wi' thet gell, she wor that winsome; but it wor like ter be—it wor like ter be, an' Zeph's hed his trubble sence then."

"M'ria wer a good wife ter me, she wer'," said Zeph, speaking slowly. "An' now th' old 'ooker's goin', I'm feared as I'll find it mighty lonesome ashore yon," and he waved his hand, as though suggesting vaguely that the shore lay anywhere beyond the starboard rail.

"Ay," remarked the second of the newcomers. "It's er weary thing to me as th' old packet's goin'. Six and sixty year hev I sailed in her. Six and sixty year!" He nodded his head, mournfully, and struck a match with shaky hands.

"It's like ter be," said the smaller man. "It's like ter be."

And, with that, he and his companion moved over to the spar that lay along under the starboard bulwarks, and there seated themselves, to smoke and meditate.

III

Skipper Abe, and Josh Matthews, the First Mate, were standing together beside the rail which ran across the break of the poop. Like the rest of the men of the *Shamraken,* their age had come upon them, and the frost of eternity had touched their beards and hair.

Skipper Abe was speaking:—

"It's harder 'n I'd thought," he said, and looked away from the Mate, staring hard along the worn, white-scoured decks.

"Dunno w'at I'll du, Abe, w'en she's gone," returned the old Mate. "She's been a 'ome fer us these sixty years an' more." He knocked out the old tobacco from his pipe, as he spoke, and began to cut a bowl-full of fresh.

"It's them durned freights!" exclaimed the Skipper. "We're jest losin' dollars every trip. It's them steam packets as hes knocked us out."

He sighed wearily, and bit tenderly at his plug.

"She's been a mighty comfortable ship," muttered Josh, in soliloquy. "An' sence thet b'y o' mine went, I sumhow thinks less o' goin' ashore 'n I used ter. I ain't no folk left on all thar 'arth."

He came to an end, and began with his old trembling fingers to fill his pipe.

Skipper Abe said nothing. He appeared to be occupied with his own thoughts. He was leaning over the rail across the break of the poop, and chewing steadily. Presently, he straightened himself up and walked over to leeward. He expectorated, after which he stood there for a few moments, taking a short look round—the result of half a century of habit. Abruptly, he sung out to the Mate....

"W'at d'yer make outer it?" he queried, after they had stood awhile, peering.

"Dunno, Abe, less'n it's some sort o' mist, riz up by ther 'eat."

Skipper Abe shook his head; but having nothing better to suggest, held his peace for awhile.

Presently, Josh spoke again:—

"Mighty cur'us, Abe. These are strange parts."

Skipper Abe nodded his assent, and continued to stare at that which had come into sight upon the lee bow. To them, as they looked, it seemed that a vast wall of rose-coloured mist was rising towards the zenith. It showed nearly ahead, and at first had seemed no more than a bright cloud upon the horizon; but already had reached a great way into the air, and the upper edge had taken on wondrous flame-tints.

"It's powerful nice-lookin'," said Josh. "I've allus 'eard as things was diff'rent out 'n these parts."

Presently, as the *Shamraken* drew near to the mist, it appeared to those aboard that it filled all the sky ahead of them, being spread out now far on either bow. And so in a while they entered into it, and, at once, the aspect of all things was changed.... The mist, in great rosy wreaths, floated all about them, seeming to soften and beautify every rope and spar, so that the old ship had become, as it were, a fairy craft in an unknown world.

"Never seen nothin' like it, Abe—nothin'!" said Josh. "Ey! but it's fine! It's fine! Like 's ef we'd run inter ther sunset."

"I'm mazed, just mazed!" exclaimed Skipper Abe, "but I'm 'gree'ble as it's purty, mighty purty."

For a further while, the two old fellows stood without speech, just gazing and gazing. With their entering into the mist, they had come into a greater quietness than had been theirs out upon the open sea. It was as though the mist muffled and toned down the creak, creak, of the spars and gear; and the big, foamless seas that rolled past them, seemed to have lost something of their harsh whispering roar of greeting.

"Sort o' unarthly, Abe," said Josh, later, and speaking but little above a whisper. "Like as ef yew was in church."

"Ay," replied Skipper Abe. "It don't seem nat'rel."

"Shouldn't think as 'eaven was all thet diff'rent," whispered Josh. And Skipper Abe said nothing in contradiction.

IV

Sometime later, the wind began to fail, and it was decided that, when eight-bells was struck, all hands should set the main t'gallant. Presently, Nuzzie having been called (for he was the only one aboard who had turned in) eight bells went, and all hands put aside their pipes, and prepared to tail on to the ha'lyards; yet no one of them made to go up to loose the sail. That was the b'y's job, and Nuzzie was a little late in coming out on deck. When, in a minute, he appeared, Skipper Abe spoke sternly to him.

"Up now, b'y, an' loose thet sail. D'y think to let er grown man dew suchlike work! Shame on yew!"

And Nuzzie, the grey-bearded "b'y" of five and fifty years, went aloft humbly, as he was bidden.

Five minutes later, he sung out that all was ready for hoisting, and the string of ancient Ones took a strain on the ha'lyards. Then Nehemiah, being the chaunty man, struck up in his shrill quaver:—

"Thar wor an ole farmer in Yorkshire did dwell."

And the shrill piping of the ancient throats took up the refrain:—

"Wi' me ay, ay, blow thar lan' down."

Nehemiah caught up the story:—

" 'e 'ad 'n ole wife, 'n 'e wished 'er in 'ell."

"Give us some time ter blow thar lan' down," came the quavering chorus of old voices.

"O, thar divvel come to 'im one day at thar plough," continued old Nehemiah; and the crowd of ancients followed up with the refrain:— "Wi' me ay, ay, blow thar lan' down."

"I've comed fer th' ole woman, I mun 'ave 'er now," sang Nehemiah. And again the refrain:— "Give us some time ter blow thar lan' down," shrilled out.

And so on to the last couple of stanzas. And all about them, as they chaunteyed, was that extraordinary, rose-tinted mist; which, above, blent into a marvellous radiance of flame-colour, as though, just a little higher than their mastheads, the sky was one red ocean of silent fire.

"Thar wor three leetle divvels chained up ter thar wall," sang Nehemiah, shrilly.

"Wi' me ay, ay, blow thar lan' down," came the piping chorus.

"She tuk off 'er clog, 'n she walloped 'em all," chaunted old Nehemiah, and again followed the wheezy, age-old refrain.

"These three leetle divvels fer marcy did bawl," quavered Nehemiah, cocking one eye upward to see whether the yard was nearly mast-headed.

"Wi' me ay, ay, blow thar lan' down," came the chorus.

"Chuck out this ole hag, or she'll mur—"

"Belay," sung out Josh, cutting across the old sea song, with the sharp command. The chaunty had ceased with the first note of the Mate's voice, and, a couple of minutes later, the ropes were coiled up, and the old fellows back to their occupations.

It is true that eight bells had gone, and that the watch was supposed to be changed; and changed it was, so far as the wheel and look-out were concerned; but otherwise little enough difference did it make to those sleep-proof ancients. The only change visible in the men about the deck, was that those who had previously only smoked, now smoked and worked; while those who had hitherto worked and smoked, now only smoked. Thus matters went on in all amity; while the old *Shamraken* passed onward like a rose-tinted shadow through the shining mist, and only the great, silent, lazy seas that came at her, out from the enshrouding redness, seemed aware that she was anything more than the shadow she appeared.

Presently, Zeph sung out to Nuzzie to get their tea from the galley, and so, in a little, the watch below were making their evening meal. They ate it as they sat upon the hatch or spar, as the chance might be; and, as they ate, they talked with their mates, of the watch on deck, upon the matter of the shining mist into which they had plunged. It was obvious, from their talk, that the extraordinary phenomenon had impressed them vastly, and all the superstition in them seemed to have been waked to fuller life. Zeph, indeed, made no bones of declaring his belief that they were nigh to something more than earthly. He said that he had a feeling that "M'ria" was somewhere near to him.

"Meanin' ter say as we've come purty near ter 'eaven?" said Nehemiah, who was busy thrumming a paunch mat, for chafing gear.

"Dunno," replied Zeph; "but"—making a gesture towards the hidden sky—"yew'll 'low as it's mighty wonnerful, 'n I guess ef 'tis 'eaven, thar's some uv us as is growin' powerful wearied uv 'arth. I guess I'm feelin' peeky fer a sight uv M'ria."

Nehemiah nodded his head slowly, and the nod seemed to run round the group of white-haired ancients.

"Reckon my datter's gell 'll be thar," he said, after a space of pondering. "Be s'prisin' ef she 'n M'ria 'd made et up ter know one anuther."

"M'ria wer' great on makin' friends," remarked Zeph, meditatively, "an' gells wus awful friendly wi' 'er. Seemed as she hed er power thet way."

"I never 'ad no wife," said Job, at this point, somewhat irrelevantly. It was a fact of which he was proud, and he made a frequent boast of it.

"Thet's naught ter cocker thysel on, lad," exclaimed one of the white-beards, who, until this time, had been silent. "Thou'lt find less folk in heaven t' greet thee."

"Thet's trewth, sure 'nuff, Jock," assented Nehemiah, and fixed a stern look on Job; whereat Job retired into silence.

Presently, at three bells, Josh came along and told them to put away their work for the day.

V

The second dog-watch came, and Nehemiah and the rest of his side, made their tea out upon the main hatch, along with their mates. When this was finished, as though by common agreement, they went every one and sat themselves upon the pinrail running along under the t'gallant bulwarks; there, with their elbows upon the rail, they faced outward to gaze their full at the mystery of colour which had wrapped them about. From time to time, a pipe would be removed, and some slowly evolved thought given an utterance.

Eight bells came and went; but, save for the changing of the wheel and look-out, none moved from his place.

Nine o'clock, and the night came down upon the sea; but to those within the mist, the only result was a deepening of the rose colour into an intense red, which seemed to shine with a light of its own creating. Above them, the unseen sky seemed to be one vast blaze of silent, blood-tinted flame.

"Piller uv cloud by day, 'n er piller uv fire by night," muttered Zeph to Nehemiah, who crouched near.

"I reckon 's them's Bible words," said Nehemiah.

"Dunno," replied Zeph; "but them's thar very words as I heerd passon Myles a sayin' w'en thar timber wor afire down our way. 'Twer' mostly smoke 'n daylight; but et tarned ter 'n etarnal fire w'en thar night comed."

At four bells, the wheel and look-out were relieved, and a little later, Josh and Skipper Abe came down on to the maindeck.

"Tur'ble queer," said Skipper Abe, with an affectation of indifference.

"Aye, 'tes, sure," said Nehemiah.

And after that, the two old men sat among the others, and watched.

At five bells, half-past ten, there was a murmur from those who sat nearest to the bows, and a cry from the man on the look out. At that, the attention of all was turned to a point nearly right ahead. At this particular spot, the mist seemed to be glowing with a curious, unearthly red brilliance; and, a minute later, there burst upon their vision a vast arch, formed of blazing red clouds.

At the sight, each and every one cried out their amazement, and immediately began to run towards the fo'cas'le head. Here they congregated in a clump, the Skipper and the Mate among them. The arch appeared now to extend its arc far beyond either bow, so that the ship was heading to pass right beneath it.

"'Tis 'eaven fer sure," murmured Josh to himself; but Zeph heard him.

"Reckon 's them's ther Gates uv Glory thet M'ria wus allus talkin' 'bout," he replied.

"Guess I'll see thet b'y er mine in er little," muttered Josh, and he craned forward, his eyes very bright and eager.

All about the ship was a great quietness. The wind was no more now than a light steady breath upon the port quarter; but from right ahead, as though issuing from the mouth of the radiant arch, the long-backed, foamless seas rolled up, black and oily.

Suddenly, amid the silence, there came a low musical note, rising and falling like the moan of a distant aeolian harp. The sound appeared to come from the direction of the arch, and the surrounding mist seemed to catch it up and send it sobbing and sobbing in low echoes away into the redness far beyond sight.

"They'm singin'," cried Zeph "M'ria wer' allus tur'ble fond uv singin'. Hark ter—"

" 'Sh!" interrupted Josh. "Thet's my b'y!" His shrill old voice had risen almost to a scream.

"It's wunnerful—wunnerful; just mazin'!" exclaimed Skipper Abe.

Zeph had gone a little forrard of the crowd. He was shading his eyes with his hands, and staring intently, his expression denoting the most intense excitement.

"B'lieve I see 'er. B'lieve I see 'er," he was muttering to himself, over and over again.

Behind him, two of the old men were steadying Nehemiah, who felt, as he put it, "a bit mazy at thar thought o' seein' thet gell."

Away aft, Nuzzie, the "b'y," was at the wheel. He had heard the moaning; but, being no more than a boy, it must be supposed that he knew nothing of the *nearness* of the next world, which was so evident to the men, his masters.

A matter of some minutes passed, and Job, who had in mind that farm upon which he had set his heart, ventured to suggest that heaven was less near than his mates supposed; but no one seemed to hear him, and he subsided into silence.

It was the better part of an hour later, and near to midnight, when a murmur among the watchers announced that a fresh matter had come to sight. They were yet a great way off from the arch; but still the thing showed clearly—a prodigious umbel, of a deep, burning red; but the crest of it was black, save for the very apex which shone with an angry red glitter.

"Thar Throne uv God!" cried out Zeph, in a loud voice, and went down upon his knees. The rest of the old men followed his example, and even old Nehemiah made a great effort to get to that position.

"Simly we'm a'most 'n 'eaven," he muttered huskily.

Skipper Abe got to his feet, with an abrupt movement. He had never heard of that extraordinary electrical phenomenon, seen once perhaps in a hundred years—the "Fiery Tempest" which precedes certain great Cyclonic Storms; but his experienced eye had suddenly discovered that the red-shining umbel was truly a low, whirling water-hill, reflecting the red light. He had no theoretical knowledge to tell him that the thing was produced by an enormous air-vortice; but he had often seen a water-spout form. Yet, he was still undecided. It was all so beyond him; though, certainly, that monstrous gyrating hill of water, sending out a reflected glitter of burning red, appealed to him as having no place in his ideas of Heaven. And then, even as he hesitated, came the first, wild-beast bellow of the coming Cyclone. As the sound smote upon their ears, the old men looked at one another with bewildered, frightened eyes.

"Reck'n thet's God speakin'," whispered Zeph. "Guess we're on'y mis'rable sinners."

The next instant, the breath of the Cyclone was in their throats, and the *Shamraken,* homeward-bounder, passed in through the everlasting portals.

Demons of the Sea

❖ • ❖

C ome out on deck and have a look, 'Darky!' " Jepson cried, rushing into
the half-deck. "The Old Man says there's been a submarine earthquake,
and the sea's all bubbling and muddy!"

Obeying the summons of Jepson's excited tone, I followed him out. It was as he
had said; the everlasting blue of the ocean was mottled with splotches of a muddy
hue, and at times a large bubble would appear, to burst with a loud "pop." Aft, the
Skipper and the three Mates could be seen on the poop, peering at the sea through
their glasses. As I gazed out over the gently heaving water, far off to windward
something was hove up into the evening air. It appeared to be a mass of seaweed,
but fell back into the water with a sullen plunge as though it were something more
substantial. Immediately after this strange occurrence, the sun set with tropical
swiftness, and in the brief afterglow things assumed a strange unreality.

The crew were all below, no one but the Mate and the Helmsman remaining on
the poop. Away forward, on the topgallant forecastle head the dim figure of the man
on look-out could be seen, leaning against the forestay. No sound was heard save
the occasional jingle of a chain-sheet, or the flog of the steering gear as a small swell
passed under our counter. Presently the Mate's voice broke the silence, and, looking
up, I saw that the Old Man had come on deck, and was talking with him. From the
few stray words which could be overheard, I knew they were talking of the strange
happenings of the day.

Shortly after sunset, the wind which had been fresh during the day, died down,
and with its passing the air grew excessively hot. Not long after two bells, the Mate
sung out for me, and ordered me to fill a bucket from overside, and bring it to him.

When I had carried out his instructions, he placed a thermometer in the bucket.

"Just as I thought," he muttered, removing the instrument and showing it to the Skipper; "ninety-nine degrees. Why, the sea's hot enough to make tea with!"

"Hope it doesn't get any hotter," growled the latter; "if it does, we shall all be boiled alive."

At a sign from the Mate, I emptied the bucket, and replaced it in the rack, after which I resumed my former position by the rail. The Old Man and the Mate walked the poop side by side. The air grew hotter as the hours passed, and after a long period of silence broken only by the occasional "pop" of a bursting gas bubble, the moon arose. It shed but a feeble light, however, as a heavy mist had arisen from the sea, and through this, the moonbeams struggled weakly. The mist, we decided, was due to the excessive heat of the sea water; it was a very wet mist, and we were soon soaked to the skin. Slowly the interminable night wore on, and the sun arose, looking dim and ghostly through the mist which rolled and billowed about the ship. From time to time we took the temperature of the sea, although we found but a slight increase therein. No work was done, and a feeling as of something impending pervaded the ship.

The fog horn was kept going constantly, as the look-out peered through the wreathing mists. The Captain walked the poop in company with the Mates, and once the Third Mate spoke and pointed out into the clouds of fog. All eyes followed his gesture; we saw what was apparently a black line, which seemed to cut the whiteness of the billows. It reminded us of nothing so much as an enormous cobra standing on its tail. As we looked it vanished. The grouped Mates were evidently puzzled; there seemed to be a difference of opinion among them. Presently as they argued, I heard the Second Mate's voice:

"That's all rot," he said. "I've seen things in fogs before, but they've always turned out to be imaginary."

The Third shook his head and made some reply which I could not overhear, but no further comment was made. Going below that afternoon, I got a short sleep, and on coming on deck at eight bells, I found that the steam still held us; if anything, it seemed to be thicker than ever. Hansard, who had been taking the temperatures during my watch below, informed me that the sea was three degrees hotter, and that the Old Man was getting into a rare old state. At three bells I went forward to have a look over the bows, and a chin with Stevenson, whose look-out it was. On gaining the forecastle head, I went to the side and looked down into the water. Stevenson came over and stood beside me.

"Rum go, this," he grumbled.

He stood by my side for a time in silence; we seemed to be hypnotized by the gleaming surface of the sea. Suddenly out of the depths, right before us, there arose a monstrous black face. It was like a frightful caricature of a human countenance.

For a moment we gazed petrified; my blood seemed to suddenly turn to ice water; I was unable to move. With a mighty effort of will, I regained my self-control and, grasping Stevenson's arm, I found I could do no more than croak, my powers of speech seemed gone. "Look!" I gasped. "Look!"

Stevenson continued to stare into the sea, like a man turned to stone. He seemed to stoop further over, as if to examine the thing more closely. "Lord," he exclaimed, "it must be the devil himself!"

As though the sound of his voice had broken a spell, the thing disappeared. My companion looked at me, while I rubbed my eyes, thinking that I had been asleep, and that the awful vision had been a frightful nightmare. One look at my friend, however, disabused me of any such thought. His face wore a puzzled expression.

"Better go aft and tell the Old Man," he faltered.

I nodded and left the forecastle head, making my way aft like one in a trance. The Skipper and the Mate were standing at the break of the poop, and running up the ladder I told them what we had seen.

"Bosh!" sneered the Old Man. "You've been looking at your own ugly reflection in the water."

Nevertheless, in spite of his ridicule, he questioned me closely. Finally he ordered the Mate forward to see if he could see anything. The latter, however, returned in a few moments, to report that nothing unusual could be seen. Four bells were struck, and we were relieved for tea. Coming on deck afterward, I found the men clustered together forward. The sole topic of conversation with them was the thing which Stevenson and I had seen.

"I suppose, Darky, it couldn't have been a reflection by any chance, could it?" one of the older men asked.

"Ask Stevenson," I replied as I made my way aft.

At eight bells, my watch came on deck again, to find that nothing further had developed. But, about an hour before midnight, the Mate, thinking to have a smoke, sent me to his room for a box of matches with which to light his pipe. It took me no time to clatter down the brass-treaded ladder, and back to the poop, where I handed him the desired article. Taking the box, he removed a match and struck it on the heel of his boot. As he did so, far out in the night a muffled screaming arose. Then came a clamour as of hoarse braying, like an ass, but considerably deeper, and with a horribly suggestive human note running through it.

"Good God! Did you hear that, Darky?" asked the Mate in awed tones.

"Yes, Sir," I replied, listening—and scarcely noticing his question—for a repetition of the strange sounds. Suddenly the frightful bellowing broke out afresh. The Mate's pipe fell to the deck with a clatter.

"Run for'ard!" he cried. "Quick, now, and see if you can see anything."

With my heart in my mouth and pulses pounding madly, I raced forward. The watch were all up on the forecastle head, clustered around the look-out. Each man was talking and gesticulating wildly. They became silent, and turned questioning glances toward me as I shouldered my way among them.

"Have you seen anything?" I cried.

Before I could receive an answer, a repetition of the horrid sounds broke out again, profaning the night with their horror. They seemed to have definite direction now, in spite of the fog which enveloped us. Undoubtedly, too, they were nearer. Pausing a moment to make sure of their bearing, I hastened aft and reported to the Mate. I told him that nothing could be seen, but that the sounds apparently came from right ahead of us. On hearing this, he ordered the man at the wheel to let the ship's head come off a couple of points. A moment later a shrill screaming tore its way through the night, followed by the hoarse braying sounds once more.

"It's close on the starboard bow!" exclaimed the Mate, as he beckoned the Helmsman to let her head come off a little more. Then, singing out for the watch, he ran forward, slacking the lee braces on the way. When he had the yards trimmed to his satisfaction on the new course, he returned to the poop and hung far out over the rail listening intently. Moments passed that seemed like hours, yet the silence remained unbroken. Suddenly the sounds began again, and so close that it seemed as though they must be right aboard us. At this time I noticed a strange booming note that mingled with the brays. And once or twice, there came a sound that can only be described as a sort of "gug, gug." Then would come a wheezy whistling, for all the world like an asthmatic person breathing.

All this while the moon shone wanly through the steam, which seemed to me to be somewhat thinner. Once the Mate gripped me by the shoulder as the noises rose and fell again. They now seemed to be coming from a point broad on our beam. Every eye on the ship was straining into the mist, but with no result. Suddenly one of the men cried out, as something long and black slid past us into the fog astern. From it there rose four indistinct and ghostly towers, which resolved themselves into spars and ropes, and sails.

"A ship! It's a ship!" we cried excitedly. I turned to Mr. Gray; he, too, had seen something, and was staring aft into the wake. So ghostlike, unreal, and fleeting had been our glimpse of the stranger, that we were not sure that we had seen an honest, material ship, but thought that we had been vouchsafed a vision of some phantom vessel like the *Flying Dutchman*. Our sails gave a sudden flap, the clew irons flogging the bulwarks with hollow thumps. The Mate glanced aloft.

"Wind's dropping," he growled savagely. "We shall never get out of this infernal place at this gait!"

Gradually the wind fell until it was a flat calm, no sound broke the deathlike silence save the rapid patter of the reef points, as she gently rose and fell on the light swell. Hours passed, and the watch was relieved and I then went below. At seven bells we were called again, and as I went along the deck to the galley, I noticed that the fog seemed thinner and the air cooler. When eight bells were struck, I relieved Hansard at coiling down the ropes. From him I learned that the steam had begun to clear about four bells, and that the temperature of the sea had fallen ten degrees.

In spite of the thinning mist, it was not until about half an hour later that we were able to get a glimpse of the surrounding sea. It was still mottled with dark patches, but the bubbling and popping had ceased. As much of the surface of the ocean as could be seen had a peculiarly desolate aspect. Occasionally a wisp of steam would float up from the nearer sea, and roll undulatingly across its silent surface, until lost in the vagueness that still held the hidden horizon. Here and there columns of steam rose up in pillars, which gave me the impression that the sea was hot in patches. Crossing to the starboard side and looking over, I found that conditions there were similar to those to port. The desolate aspect of the sea filled me with an idea of chilliness, although the air was quite warm and muggy. From the break of the poop the Mate called to me to get his glasses.

When I had done this, he took them from me and walked to the taffrail. Here he stood for some moments, polishing them with his handkerchief. After a moment he raised them to his eyes and peered long and intently into the mist astern. I stood for some time staring at the point on which the Mate had focused his glasses. Presently, something shadowy grew upon my vision. Steadily watching it, I distinctly saw the outlines of a ship take form in the fog.

"See!" I cried, but even as I spoke, a lifting wraith of mist disclosed to view a great four-masted barque lying becalmed with all sails set, within a few hundred yards of our stern. As though a curtain had been raised, and then allowed to fall, the fog once more settled down, hiding the strange bark from our sight. The Mate was all excitement, striding with quick, jerky steps, up and down the poop, stopping every few moments to peer through his glasses at the point where the four-master had disappeared in the fog. Gradually, as the mists dispersed again, the vessel could be seen more plainly, and it was then that we got an inkling of the cause of the dreadful noises during the night.

For some time the Mate watched her silently, and as he watched the conviction grew upon me that in spite of the mist, I could detect some sort of movement on board of her. After some time had passed, the doubt became a certainty, and I could also see a sort of splashing in the water alongside of her. Suddenly the Mate put his glasses on top of the wheel box and told me to bring him the speaking trumpet. Running to the companionway, I secured the trumpet and was back at his side.

The Mate raised it to his lips, and taking a deep breath, sent a hail across the water that should have awakened the dead. We waited tensely for a reply. A moment later a deep, hollow mutter came from the barque; higher and louder it swelled, until we realized that we were listening to the same sounds we had heard the night before. The Mate stood aghast at this answer to his hail; in a voice barely more than a hushed whisper, he bade me call the Old Man. Attracted by the Mate's hail and its unearthly reply, the watch had all come aft, and were clustered in the mizzen rigging, in order to see better.

After calling the Captain, I returned to the poop, where I found the Second and Third Mates talking with the Chief. All were engaged in trying to pierce the clouds of mist that half hid our strange consort, and to arrive at some explanation of the strange phenomena of the past few hours. A moment later the Captain appeared carrying his telescope. The Mate gave him a brief account of the state of affairs, and handed him the trumpet. Giving me the telescope to hold, the Captain hailed the shadowy barque. Breathlessly we all listened, when again, in answer to the Old Man's hail, the frightful sounds rose on the still morning air. The Skipper lowered the trumpet and stood with an expression of astonished horror on his face.

"Lord!" he exclaimed. "What an ungodly row!"

At this, the Third, who had been gazing through his binoculars, broke the silence.

"Look," he ejaculated. "There's a breeze coming up astern." At his words the Captain looked up quickly, and we all watched the ruffling water.

"That packet yonder is bringing the breeze with her," said the Skipper. "She'll be alongside in half an hour!"

Some moments passed, and the bank of fog had come to within a hundred yards of our taffrail. The strange vessel could be distinctly seen just inside the fringe of the driving mist wreaths. After a short puff, the wind died completely, but we stared with hypnotic fascination, the water astern of the stranger ruffled again with a fresh catspaw. Seemingly with the flapping of her sails, she drew slowly up to us. As the leaden seconds passed, the big four-master approached us steadily. The light air had now reached us and with a lazy lift of our sails, we, too, began to forge slowly through that weird sea. The barque was now within fifty yards of our stern, and she was steadily drawing nearer, seeming to be able to outfoot us with ease. As she came on she luffed sharply, and came up into the wind with her weather leeches shaking.

I looked toward her poop, thinking to discern the figure of the man at the wheel, but the mist coiled around her quarter, and objects on the after end of her became indistinguishable. With a rattle of chain-sheets on her iron yards, she filled away again. We meanwhile had gone ahead, but it was soon evident that she was the better sailor, for she came up to us hand-over-fist. The wind rapidly freshened, and the mist began to drift away before it, so that each moment her spars and cordage became more plainly visible. The Skipper and the Mates were watching her intently, when an almost simultaneous exclamation of fear broke from them.

"My God!"

And well they might show signs of fear, for crawling about the barque's deck were the most horrible creatures I had ever seen. In spite of their unearthly strangeness there was something vaguely familiar about them. Then it came to me that the face that Stevenson and I had seen during the night belonged to one of them. Their bodies had something of the shape of a seal's, but of a dead, unhealthy white. The lower part of the body ended in a sort of double-curved tail on which they appeared to be able to shuffle about. In place of arms they had two long, snaky feelers, at the ends of which were two very humanlike hands, which were equipped with talons instead of nails. Fearsome indeed were these parodies of human beings!

Their faces, which, like their tentacles, were black, were the most grotesquely human things about them, and the upper jaw closed into the lower, after the manner of the jaws of an octopus. I have seen men among certain tribes of natives who had faces uncommonly like theirs, but yet no native I had ever seen could have given me the extraordinary feeling of horror and revulsion which I experienced toward these brutal-looking creatures.

"What devilish beasts!" burst out the Captain in disgust.

With this remark he turned to the Mates and, as he did so, the expressions on their faces told me that they had all realised what the presence of these bestial-looking brutes meant. If, as was doubtless the case, these creatures had boarded the barque and destroyed her crew, what would prevent them from doing the same with us? We were a smaller ship and had a smaller crew, and the more I thought of it the less I liked it.

We could now see the name on the barque's bow with the naked eye. It read: *Scottish Heath*, while on her boats we could see the name bracketted with Glasgow, showing that she hailed from that port. It was a remarkable coincidence that she should have a slant from just the quarter in which yards were trimmed, as before we saw her she must have been drifting around with everything "aback." But now, in this light air, she was able to run along beside us with no one at her helm. But steering herself she was, and although at times she yawed wildly, she never got herself aback. As we gazed at her we noticed a sudden movement on board of her, and several of the creatures slid into the water.

"See! See! They've spotted us. They're coming for us!" cried the Mate wildly.

It was only too true; scores of them were sliding into the sea, letting themselves down by means of their long tentacles. On they came, slipping by scores and hundreds into the water, and swimming toward us in droves. The ship was making about three knots, otherwise they would have caught us in a very few minutes. But they persevered, gaining slowly but surely, and drawing nearer and nearer. The long tentacle-like arms rose out of the sea in hundreds, and the foremost ones were already within a score of yards of the ship, before the Old Man bethought himself to shout to the Mates to fetch up the half-dozen cutlasses that comprised the ship's armoury. Then, turning to me, he ordered me to go down to his cabin and bring up the two revolvers out of the top drawer of the chart table, also a box of cartridges that was there.

When I returned with the weapons, he loaded them and handed one to the Mate. Meanwhile the pursuing creatures were coming steadily nearer, and soon half a dozen of the leaders were directly under our counter. Immediately the Captain leaned over the rail and emptied his pistol into them, but without any apparent effect. He must have realised how puny and ineffectual his efforts were, for he did not reload his weapon.

Some dozens of the brutes had reached us, and as they did so, their tentacles rose into the air and caught our rail. I heard the Third Mate scream suddenly, and turning, I saw him dragged quickly to the rail, with a tentacle wrapped completely around him. Snatching a cutlass, the Second Mate hacked off the tentacle where it joined the body. A gout of blood splashed into the Third Mate's face, and he fell to the deck. A dozen more of those arms rose and wavered in the air, but they now seemed some yards astern of us. A rapidly widening patch of clear water appeared between us and the foremost of our pursuers, and we raised a wild shout of joy. The cause was soon apparent; for a fine, fair wind had sprung up, and with the increase in its force, the *Scottish Heath* had got herself aback, while we were rapidly leaving the monsters behind us. The Third Mate rose to his feet with a dazed look, and as he did so something fell to the deck. I picked it up and found that it was the severed portion of the tentacle of the Third's late adversary. With a grimace of disgust I tossed it into the sea, as I needed no reminder of that awful experience.

Three weeks later we anchored in San Francisco. There the Captain made a full report of the affair to the authorities, with the result that a gunboat was dispatched to investigate. Six weeks later she returned to report that she had been unable to find any signs, either of the ship herself or of the fearful creatures that had attacked her. And since then nothing, as far as I know, has ever been heard of the four-masted barque *Scottish Heath*, last seen by us in the possession of creatures which may rightly be called demons of the sea.

Whether she still floats, occupied by her hellish crew, or whether some storm has sent her to her last resting place beneath the waves, is purely a matter of conjecture. Perchance on some dark, fog-bound night, a ship in that wilderness of waters may hear cries and sounds beyond those of the wailing of the winds. Then let them look to it; for it may be that the demons of the sea are near them.

Out of the Storm

❖◆❖

"Hush!" said my friend the scientist, as I walked into his laboratory. I had opened my lips to speak; but stood silent for a few minutes at his request.

He was sitting at his instrument, and the thing was tapping out a message in a curiously irregular fashion—stopping a few seconds, then going on at a furious pace.

It was during a somewhat longer than usual pause that, growing slightly impatient, I ventured to address him.

"Anything important?" I asked.

"For God's sake, shut up!" he answered back in a high, strained voice.

I stared. I am used to pretty abrupt treatment from him at times when he is much engrossed in some particular experiment; but this was going a little too far, and I said so.

He was writing, and, for reply, he pushed several loosely-written sheets over to me with the one curt word, "Read!"

With a sense half of anger, half of curiosity, I picked up the first and glanced at it. After a few lines, I was gripped and held securely by a morbid interest. I was reading a message from one in the last extremity. I will give it word for word:—

"John, we are sinking! I wonder if you really understand what I feel at the present time—you sitting comfortably in your laboratory, I out here upon the waters, already one among the dead. Yes, we are doomed. There is no such thing as help in our case. We are sinking—steadily, remorselessly. God! I must keep up and be a man! I need not tell you that I am in the operator's room. All the rest are on deck—or dead in the hungry thing which is smashing the ship to pieces.

"I do not know where we are, and there is no one of whom I can ask. The last of the officers was drowned nearly an hour ago, and the vessel is now little more than a sort of breakwater for the giant seas.

"Once, about half an hour ago, I went out on to the deck. My God! the sight was terrible. It is a little after midday; but the sky is the colour of mud—do you understand?—grey mud! Down from it there hang vast lappets of clouds. Not such clouds as I have ever before seen; but monstrous, mildewed-looking hulls. They show solid, save where the frightful wind tears their lower edges into great feelers that swirl savagely above us, like the tentacles of some enormous Horror.

"Such a sight is difficult to describe to the living; though the Dead of the Sea know of it without words of mine. It is such a sight that none is allowed to see and live. It is a picture for the doomed and the dead; one of the sea's hell-orgies—one of the *THING'S* monstrous gloatings over the living—say the alive-in-death, those upon the brink. I have no right to tell of it to you; to speak of it to one of the living is to initiate innocence into one of the infernal mysteries—to talk of foul things to a child. Yet I care not! I will expose, in all its hideous nakedness, the death-side of the sea. The undoomed living shall know some of the things that death has hitherto so well guarded. Death knows not of this little instrument beneath my hands that connects me still with the quick, else would he haste to quiet me.

"Hark you, John! I have learnt undreamt-of things in this little time of waiting. I know now why we are afraid of the dark. I had never imagined such secrets of the sea and the grave (which are one and the same).

"Listen! Ah, but I was forgetting you cannot hear! I can! The Sea is—Hush! the Sea is laughing, as though Hell cackled from the mouth of an ass. It is jeering. I can hear its voice echo like Satanic thunder amid the mud overhead—It is calling to me! call—I must go—The sea calls!

"Oh! God, art Thou indeed God? Canst Thou sit above and watch calmly that which I have just seen? Nay! Thou art no God! Thou art weak and puny beside this foul *THING* which Thou didst create in Thy lusty youth. *It* is *now* God—and I am one of its children.

"Are you there, John? Why don't you answer! Listen! I ignore God; for there is a stronger than He. My God is here, beside me, around me, and will be soon above me. You know what that means. It is merciless. *The sea is now all the God there is!* That is one of the things I have learnt.

"Listen! *IT*, is laughing again. God is *it*, not He.

"It called, and I went out onto the decks. All was terrible. *IT* is in the waist—everywhere. *IT* has swamped the ship. Only the forecastle, bridge and poop stick up out from the bestial, reeking *THING,* like three islands in the midst of shrieking foam. At times gigantic billows assail the ship from both sides. They form momentary arches above the vessel—arches of dull, curved water half a hundred feet towards the hideous sky. Then they descend—roaring. Think of it! You cannot.

"There is an infection of sin in the air: it is the exhalations from the *THING*. Those left upon the drenched islets of shattered wood and iron are doing the most horrible things. The *THING* is teaching them. Later, I felt the vile informing of its breath; but I have fled back here—to pray for death.

"On the forecastle, I saw a mother and her little son clinging to an iron rail. A great billow heaved up above them—descended in a falling mountain of brine. It passed, and they were still there. The *THING* was only toying with them; yet, all the same, it had torn the hands of the child from the rail, and the child was clinging frantically to its Mother's arm. I saw another vast hill hurl up to port and hover above them. Then the Mother stooped and bit like a foul beast at the hands of her wee son. She was afraid that his little additional weight would be more than she could hold. I heard his scream even where I stood—it drove to me upon that wild laughter. It told me again that God is not He, but *IT*. Then the hill thundered down upon those two. It seemed to me that the *THING* gave a bellow as it leapt. It roared about them churning and growling; then surged away, and there was only one—the Mother. There appeared to me to be blood as well as water upon her face, especially about her mouth; but the distance was too great, and I cannot be sure. I looked away. Close to me, I saw something further—a beautiful young girl (her soul hideous with the breath of the *THING*) struggling with her sweetheart for the shelter of the chart-house side. He threw her off; but she came back at him. I saw her hand come from her head, where still clung the wreckage of some form of headgear. She struck at him. He shouted and fell away to leeward, and she—smiled, showing her teeth. So much for that. I turned elsewhere.

"Out upon the *THING*, I saw gleams, horrid and suggestive, below the crests of the waves. I have never seen them until this time. I saw a rough sailorman washed away from the vessel. One of the huge breakers snapped at him! —Those things were teeth. It has teeth. I heard them clash. I heard his yell. It was no more than a mosquito's shrilling amid all that laughter; but it was very terrible. There is worse than death.

"The ship is lurching very queerly with a sort of sickening heave—

"I fancy I have been asleep. No—I remember now. I hit my head when she rolled so strangely. My leg is doubled under me. I think it is broken; but it does not matter—

"I have been praying. I—I—What was it? I feel calmer, more resigned, now. I think I have been mad. What was it that I was saying? I cannot remember. It was something about—about—God. I—I believe I blasphemed. May He forgive me! Thou knowest, God, that I was not in my right mind. Thou knowest that I am very weak. Be with me in the coming time! I have sinned; but Thou art all merciful.

"Are you there, John? It is very near the end now. I had so much to say; but it all slips from me. What was it that I said? I take it all back. I was mad, and—and God knows. He is merciful, and I have very little pain now. I feel a bit drowsy.

"I wonder whether you are there, John. Perhaps, after all, no one has heard the things I have said. It is better so. The Living are not meant—and yet, I do not know. If you are there, John, you will—you will tell *her* how it was; but not—not—Hark! there was such a thunder of water overhead just then. I fancy two vast seas have met in mid-air across the top of the bridge and burst all over the vessel. It must be soon now—and there was such a number of things I had to say! I can hear voices in the wind. They are singing. It is like an enormous dirge—

"I think I have been dozing again. I pray God humbly that it be soon! You will not—not tell *her* anything about, about what I may have said, will you, John? I mean those things which I ought not to have said. What was it I did say? My head is growing strangely confused. I wonder whether you really do hear me. I may be talking only to that vast roar outside. Still, it is some comfort to go on, and I will not believe that you do not hear all I say. Hark again! A mountain of brine must have swept clean over the vessel. She has gone right over on to her side.... She is back again. It will be very soon now—

"Are you there, John? Are you there? It is coming! The Sea has come for me! It is rushing down through the companionway! It—it is like a vast jet! My God! I am dr-own-ing! I—am—dr—"

NIGHT SHADE BOOKS IS AN INDEPENDENT PUBLISHER OF QUALITY SCIENCE-FICTION, FANTASY AND HORROR

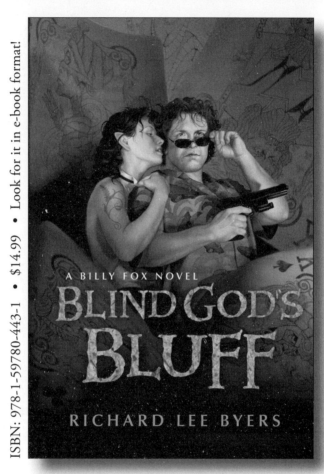

ISBN: 978-1-59780-443-1 • $14.99 • Look for it in e-book format!

A BILLY FOX NOVEL

BLIND GOD'S BLUFF

RICHARD LEE BYERS

Billy Fox, a small-time gambler on a losing streak, has more than enough problems on his hands, owing too much money to some very impatient people. But when he rescues a blinded stranger from a swarm of bloodthirsty fairies, Billy's life gets a lot more complicated. . . .

Seems the stranger is actually a powerful local god who is involved in a high-stakes Florida poker tournament against various supernatural challengers. And with his eyes currently missing, he needs somebody to take his place at the gaming table. Before Billy knows it, he finds himself playing against the likes of an ancient Egyptian mummy, an unbearably seductive succubus, a mechanical man, an insect queen, and a cannibalistic beast-man. And not just cards are in play; magic, bloodshed, and cheating are not only expected, they're encouraged.

Everybody, including a sexy satyr-girl with her own cards up her sleeve, thinks that Billy is in way over his head. But Billy is a born gambler and, when the chips are down, he might just change his luck for good!

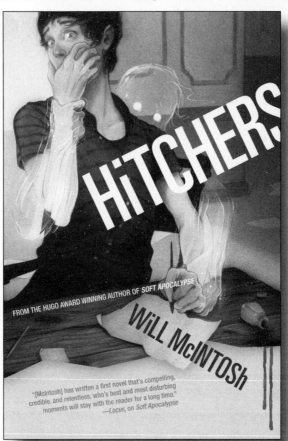

ISBN: 978-1-59780-337-3 • $14.99 • Look for it in e-book format!

FROM THE HUGO AWARD WINNING AUTHOR OF *SOFT APOCALYPSE*

HiTCHERS

WiLL McINTOSh

"[McIntosh] has written a first novel that's compelling, credible, and relentless, who's best and most disturbing moments will stay with the reader for a long time."
—*Locus*, on *Soft Apocalypse*

Two years ago, on the same day but miles apart, Finn Darby lost two of the most important people in his life: his wife Lorena, struck by lightning on the banks of the Chattahoochee River, and his abusive, alcoholic grandfather, Tom Darby, creator of the long-running newspaper comic strip *Toy Shop*.

Against his grandfather's dying wish, Finn has resurrected *Toy Shop*, adding new characters, and the strip is more popular than ever, bringing in fan letters, merchandising deals, and talk of TV specials. Finn has even started dating again.

When a terrorist attack decimates Atlanta, killing half a million souls, Finn begins blurting things in a strange voice beyond his control. The voice says things only his grandfather could know. Countless other residents of Atlanta are suffering a similar bizarre affliction. Is it mass hysteria, or have the dead returned to possess the living?

Finn soon realizes he has a hitcher within his skin… his grandfather. And Grandpa isn't terribly happy about the changes Finn has been making to *Toy Shop*. Together with a pair of possessed friends, an aging rock star and a waitress, Finn races against time to find a way to send the dead back to Deadland… or die trying.

NIGHT SHADE BOOKS IS AN INDEPENDENT PUBLISHER OF QUALITY SCIENCE-FICTION, FANTASY AND HORROR

ISBN: 978-1-59780-394-6 • $14.99 • Look for it in e-book format!

Enormity is the strange tale of an American working in Korea, a lonely young man named Manny Lopes, who is not only physically small (in his own words, he's a 'Creole shrimp'), but his work, his failed marriage, his race, all conspire to make him feel puny and insignificant—the proverbial ninety-eight-pound weakling.

Then one day an accident happens, a quantum explosion, and suddenly Manny awakens to discover that he is big—really big. In fact, Manny is enormous, a mile-high colossus! Now there's no stopping him: he's a one-man weapon of mass destruction. Yet he means well.

Enormity takes some odd turns, featuring characters like surfing gangbangers, elderly terrorists, and a North Korean assassin who thinks she's Dorothy from *The Wizard of Oz*. There's also sex, violence, and action galore, with the army throwing everything it has against the rampaging colossus that is Manny Lopes. But there's only one weapon that has any chance at all of stopping him: his wife.

NIGHT SHADE BOOKS IS AN INDEPENDENT PUBLISHER OF QUALITY SCIENCE-FICTION, FANTASY AND HORROR

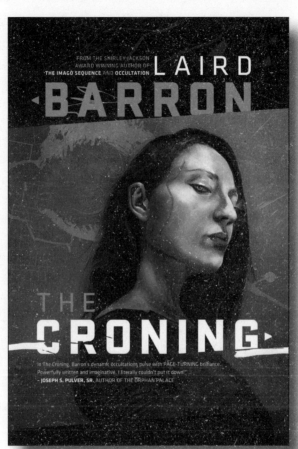

Strange things exist on the periphery of our existence, haunting us from the darkness looming beyond our firelight. Black magic, weird cults and worse things loom in the shadows. The Children of Old Leech have been with us from time immemorial. And they love us…

Donald Miller, geologist and academic, has walked along the edge of a chasm for most of his nearly eighty years, leading a charmed life between endearing absent-mindedness and sanity-shattering realization. Now, all things must converge. Donald will discover the dark secrets along the edges, unearthing savage truths about his wife Michelle, their adult twins, and all he knows and trusts. For Donald is about to stumble on the secret…

…OF THE CRONING.

NIGHT SHADE BOOKS IS AN INDEPENDENT PUBLISHER OF QUALITY SCIENCE-FICTION, FANTASY AND HORROR

ISBN: 978-1-59780-474-5 • $15.99 • Look for it in e-book format!

THE BEST
HORROR
OF THE YEAR

VOLUME FIVE

EDITED BY
ELLEN DATLOW

FEATURING STORIES BY

LAIRD BARRON	JOHN LANGAN
BRIAN HODGE	ALISON J. LITTLEWOOD
STEPHEN KING	LIVIA LLEWELLYN
MARGO LANAGAN	PETER STRAUB
TERRY LAMSLEY	ANNA TABORSKA

AND MANY OTHERS

Fear is the oldest human emotion. The most primal. We like to think we're civilized. We tell ourselves we're not afraid. And every year, we skim our fingers across nightmares, desperately pitting our courage against shivering dread.

What scares you? What frightens you?

Horror wears new faces in these carefully selected stories. The details may change. But the fear remains.

Night Shade Books is proud to present *The Best Horror of the Year: Volume Five*, a new collection of horror brought to you by Ellen Datlow, winner of multiple Hugo, Bram Stoker, and World Fantasy awards.

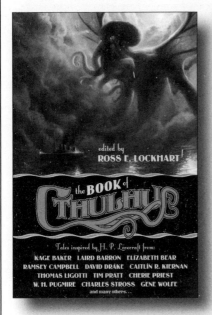

NIGHT SHADE BOOKS IS AN INDEPENDENT PUBLISHER OF QUALITY SCIENCE-FICTION, FANTASY AND HORROR

ISBN:978-1-59780-500-1 • $14.99 • Look for it in e-book format!

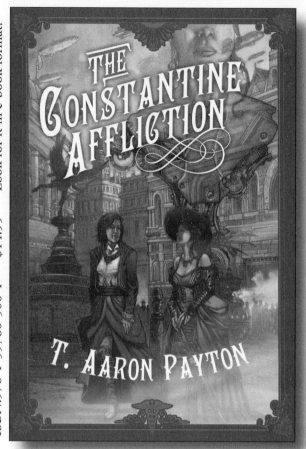

1864. London is a city in transition. The Constantine Affliction—a strange malady that kills some of its victims and physically transforms others into the opposite sex—has spread scandal and upheaval throughout society. Scientific marvels and disasters, such as clockwork courtesans, the alchemical fires of Whitechapel, electric carriages, and acidic monsters lurking in the Thames, have forever altered the face of the city.

Pembroke "Pimm" Halliday is an aristocrat with an interest in criminology, who uses his keen powers of observation to assist the police or private individuals—at least when he's sober enough to do so. Ellie Skyler, who hides her gender behind the byline "E. Skye," is an intrepid journalist driven by both passion and necessity to uncover the truth, no matter where it hides.

When Pimm and Skye stumble onto a dark plot that links the city's most notorious criminal overlord with the Queen's new consort, famed scientist Sir Bertram Oswald, they soon find the forces of both high and low society arrayed against them. Can they save the city from the arcane machinations of one of history's most infamous monsters—and uncover the shocking origin of…The Constantine Afflicion.

NIGHT SHADE BOOKS IS AN INDEPENDENT PUBLISHER OF QUALITY SCIENCE-FICTION, FANTASY AND HORROR

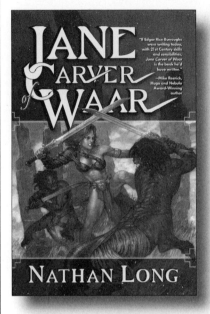 

ISBN: 978-1-59780-396-0
$14.99

ISBN: 978-1-59780-429-5
$14.99

Both available in e-book format!

Watch out, Universe, Jane Carver is back!

Jane Carver, a hell-raising, redheaded biker chick from Coral Gables, Florida, had found a new life and love on Waar, a savage planet of fearsome creatures and swashbuckling warriors. Until the planet's high priests sent her back to Earth against her will.

But nobody keeps Jane from her man, even if he happens to be a purpleskinned alien nobleman.

Against all odds, she returns to Waar, only to find herself accused of kidnaping the Emperor's beautiful daughter. Allying herself with a band of notorious sky-pirates, Jane sets out to clear her name and rescue the princess, but that means uncovering the secret origins of the Gods of Waar —and picking a fight with the Wargod himself.

Good thing Jane is always up for a scrap . . . .

Swords of Waar is the wildly entertaining sequel to *Jane Carver of Waar*, and continues the raucous adventures of science fiction's newest and most ball-busting space heroine.

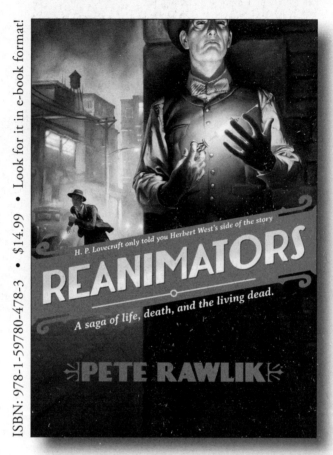

ISBN: 978-1-59780-478-3 • $14.99 • Look for it in e-book format!

Herbert West's crimes against nature are well-known to those familiar with the darkest secrets of science and resurrection. Obsessed with finding a cure for mankind's oldest malady, death itself, he has experimented upon the living and dead, leaving behind a trail of monsters, mayhem, and madness. But the story of his greatest rival has never been told. Until now.

Dr. Stuart Hartwell, a colleague and contemporary of West, sets out to destroy West by uncovering the secrets of his terrible experiments, only to become that which he initially despised: a reanimator of the dead. For more than twenty years, spanning the early decades of the twentieth century, the two scientists race each other to master the mysteries of life… and unlife. From the grisly battlefields of the Great War to the backwoods hills and haunted coasts of Dunwich and Innsmouth, from the halls of fabled Miskatonic University to the sinking of the Titanic, their unholy quests will leave their mark upon the world—and create monsters of them both.

Reanimators is an epic tale of historical horror… in the tradition of *Anno Dracula* and *The League of Extraordinary Gentlemen*.

NIGHT SHADE BOOKS IS AN INDEPENDENT PUBLISHER OF QUALITY SCIENCE-FICTION, FANTASY AND HORROR

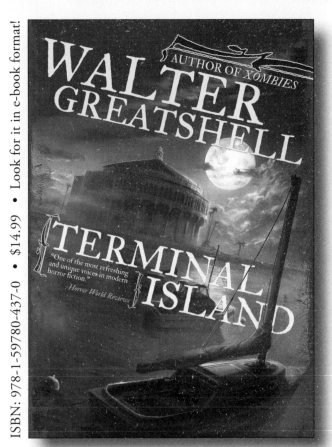

ISBN: 978-1-59780-437-0 • $14.99 • Look for it in e-book format!

Henry Cadmus grew up on Catalina Island, a scenic vacationland off the Southern California coast. But Henry's experiences were far from idyllic. Today, even though Henry has seen firsthand the horrors of war, the ghastly images that haunt his dreams are ones he associates with his childhood… and the island: a snarling pig-man holding a cleaver; a jackal-headed woman on a high balcony, dripping blood; strange occult rituals… and worse. If it was up to Henry, he would avoid the island entirely.

But Henry is returning to Catalina Island. At his wife Ruby's insistence, Henry, Ruby, and their infant daughter are coming to Avalon, so that Henry can face his fears, exorcise his demons, and reconcile with the one he fears most… his mother.

From Walter Greatshell, author of *Xombies* comes *Terminal Island*, a novel of cosmic horror.